ROYALS

Chosen by the Prince

ROYALS
COLLECTION

ROYALS

Chosen by the Prince

Sarah
MORGAN

Rebecca
WINTERS

Cara
COLTER

MILLS
BOON
&

Published in Great Britain 2017
By Mills & Boon, an imprint of HarperCollins*Publishers*
1 London Bridge Street, London, SE1 9GF

ROYALS: CHOSEN BY THE PRINCE © 2017 Harlequin Books S.A.

The Prince's Waitress Wife © 2008 Harlequin Books SA
Special thanks and acknowledgement are given to Sarah Morgan
Becoming the Prince's Wife © 2014 Rebecca Winters
The Dance with a Prince © 2011 Cara Colter

ISBN: 978-0-263-93252-2

09-0418

THE PRINCE'S WAITRESS WIFE

SARAH MORGAN

USA Today bestselling author **Sarah Morgan** writes lively, sexy stories for both the Mills & Boon Modern and Medical Romance lines. As a child, Sarah dreamed of being a writer and, although she took a few interesting detours on the way, she is now living that dream. With her writing career, she has successfully combined business with pleasure and she firmly believes that reading romance is one of the most satisfying and fat-free escapist pleasures available.

CHAPTER ONE

'KEEP your eyes down, serve the food and then leave. No lingering in the President's Suite. No gazing, no engaging the prince in conversation, and no flirting. *Especially* no flirting— Prince Casper has a shocking reputation when it comes to women. Holly, are you listening to me?'

Holly surfaced from a whirlpool of misery long enough to nod. 'Yes,' she croaked. 'I'm listening, Sylvia.'

'Then what did I just say?'

Holly's brain was foggy from lack of sleep and a constant roundabout of harsh self-analysis. 'You said—you told me—' Her voice tailed off. 'I don't know. I'm sorry.'

Sylvia's mouth tightened with disapproval. 'What is the matter with you? Usually you're extremely efficient and reliable, that's why I picked you for this job!'

Efficient and reliable.

Holly flinched at the description.

Another two flaws to add to the growing list of reasons why Eddie had dumped her.

Apparently oblivious to the effect her words were having, Sylvia ploughed on. 'I shouldn't have to remind you that today is the most important day of my career—catering for royalty at Twickenham Stadium. This is the Six Nations championship! The most important and exciting rugby tournament of the year! The eyes of the world are upon us! If we get this right, we're made. And more work for me means more work for you. *But I need you to concentrate!*'

A tall, slim waitress with a defiant expression on her face stalked over to them, carrying a tray of empty champagne glasses. 'Give her a break, will you? Her fiancé broke off their engagement last night. It's a miracle she's here at all. In her position, I wouldn't even have dragged myself out of bed.'

'He broke off the engagement?' Sylvia glanced from one girl to the other. 'Holly, is Nicky telling the truth? Why did he do that?'

Because she was efficient and reliable. Because her hair was the colour of a sunset rather than a sunflower. Because she was prudish and inhibited. Because her bottom was too big…

Contemplating the length of the list, Holly was swamped by a wave of despair. 'Eddie's been promoted to Marketing Director. I don't fit his new image.' So far she hadn't actually cried and she was quite proud of that—proud and a little puzzled. *Why hadn't she cried?* She *loved* Eddie. They'd planned a future together. 'He's expected to entertain clients and journalists and, well, he's driving a Porsche now, and he needs a woman to match.' With a wobbly smile and a shrug, she tried to make light of it. 'I'm more of a small family-hatchback.'

'You are much too good for him, that's what you are.' Nicky scowled and the glasses on the tray jangled dangerously. 'He's a b—'

'Nicky!' Sylvia gave a shocked gasp, interrupting Nicky's insult. 'Please remember that you are the face of my company!'

'In that case you'd better pay for botox before I develop permanent frown-lines from serving a bunch of total losers every day.' Nicky's eyes flashed. 'Holly's ex and his trophy-blonde slut are knocking back the champagne like Eddie is

Marketing Director of some Fortune 100 company, not the local branch of Pet Palace.'

'She's with him?' Holly felt the colour drain from her face. 'Then I can't go up there. Their hospitality box is really close to the President's Suite. It would just be too embarrassing for everyone. All his colleagues staring at me—*her* staring at me—what am I going to do?'

'Replace him with someone else. The great thing about really unsuitable men is that they're not in short supply.' Nicky thrust the tray into the hands of her apoplectic boss and slipped her arm through Holly's. 'Breathe deeply. In and out—that's it—good. Now, here's what you're going to do. You're going to sashay into that royal box and kiss that sexy, wicked prince. If you're going to fall for an unsuitable man, at least make sure he's a rich, powerful one. The king of them all. Or, in this case, the prince. Apparently he's a world-class kisser. Go for it. Tangling tongues at Twickenham. *That* would shock Eddie.'

'It would shock the prince, too.' Giggling despite her misery, Holly withdrew her arm from her friend's. 'I think one major rejection is enough for one week, thanks. If I'm not thin and blonde enough for the Managing Director of Pet Palace, I'm hardly going to be thin and blonde enough to attract a playboy prince. It's not one of your better ideas.'

'What's wrong with it? Straight from one palace to another.' Nicky gave a saucy wink. 'Undo a few buttons, go into the President's Suite and flirt. It's what I'd do.'

'Fortunately she isn't you!' Sylvia's cheeks flushed with outrage as she glared at Nicky. 'And she'll keep her buttons fastened! Quite apart from the fact I don't pay you girls to flirt, Prince Casper's romantic exploits are getting out of hand, and I've had strict instructions from the Palace—no pretty waitresses. No one likely to distract him. *Especially* no blondes. That's why I picked you in the first place, Holly. Red hair and freckles—you're perfect.'

Holly flinched. Perfect? *Perfect for melting into the background.*

She lifted a hand and touched her unruly red hair, dragged into submission with the liberal use of pins. Then she thought of what lay ahead and her battered confidence took another dive. The thought of walking into the President's Suite made her shrink. 'Sylvia—I really don't want to do this. Not today. I just don't feel—I'm having—' What—a bad hair day? A fat day? Frankly it was a battle to decide which of her many deficiencies was the most pronounced. 'They're all going to be thin, blonde, rich and confident.' *All the things she wasn't.* Her hands shaking, Holly removed the tray of empty glasses from her boss's hands. 'I'll take these back to the kitchens. Nicky can serve the royal party. I don't think I can stand them looking at me as if I'm—'

As if I'm nothing.

'If you're doing your job correctly, they shouldn't be looking at you at all.' Unknowingly echoing Holly's own thoughts, Sylvia removed the tray from her hands so violently that the glasses jangled again. Then she thrust the tray back at Nicky. '*You* take these glasses back to the kitchens. Holly, if you want to keep this job, you'll get up to the President's Suite right now. And no funny business. You wouldn't want to attract his attention anyway—a man in his position is only going to be interested in one thing with a girl like you.' Spotting another of the waitresses craning her neck to get a better view of the rugby players warming up on the pitch, Sylvia gave a horrified gasp. 'No, no. You're here to work, not gape at men's legs—' Abandoning Holly and Nicky, she hurried over to the other girl.

'Of course we're here to gape at men's legs,' Nicky

drawled. 'Why does she think we took the job in the first place? I don't know the first thing about scrums and line-outs, but I do know the men are gorgeous. I mean, there are men and there are men. And these are *men*, if you know what I mean.'

Not listening, Holly stared into space, her confidence at an all-time low. 'The wonder is not that Eddie dumped me,' she muttered, 'But that he got involved with me in the first place.'

'Don't talk like that. Don't let him do this to you,' Nicky scolded. 'Please tell me you didn't spend the night crying over him.'

'Funnily enough, I didn't. I've even been wondering about that.' Holly frowned. 'Perhaps I'm too devastated to cry.'

'Did you eat chocolate?'

'Of course. Well—chocolate biscuits. Do they count?'

'Depends on how many. You need a lot of biscuits to get the same chocolate hit.'

'I ate two.'

'Two biscuits?'

Holly blushed. 'Two packets.' She muttered the words under her breath and then gave a guilty moan. 'And I *hated* myself even more afterwards. But at the time I was miserable and *starving*! Eddie took me out to dinner to break off the engagement—I suppose he thought I might not scream at him in a public place. I knew something was wrong when he ordered a starter. He never orders a starter.'

'Well, isn't that typical?' Nicky's mouth tightened in disapproval. 'The night he breaks up with you, he finally allows you to eat.'

'The starter was for him, not me.' Holly shook her head absently. 'I can't eat in front of Eddie anyway. The way he watches me always makes me feel like a pig. He told me it was over in between the grilled fish and dessert. Then he dropped me home, and I kept waiting, but I just couldn't cry.'

'I'm not surprised. You were probably too hungry to summon the energy to cry,' Nicky said dryly. 'But eating chocolate biscuits is good news.'

'Tell that to my skirt. Why does Sylvia insist on this style?' Gloomily, Holly smoothed the tight black skirt over her hips. 'I feel as though I'm wearing a corset, and it's *so* short.'

'You look sexy as sin, as always. And eating chocolate is the first phase in the healing process, so you've passed that stage, which is a good sign. The next stage is to sell his ring.'

'I was going to return it.'

'Return it? Are you mad?' The empty glasses rattled again as Nicky's hands tightened on the tray. 'Sell it. And buy a pair of gorgeous shoes with the proceeds. Then you'll spend the rest of your life walking on his memory. And, next time, settle for sex without emotion.'

Holly smiled awkwardly, too self-conscious to confess that she hadn't actually had sex with Eddie. And that, of course, had been her major drawback as far as he was concerned. He'd accused her of being inhibited.

She bit back a hysterical laugh.

A small family-hatchback with central locking.

Would she be less inhibited if her bottom were smaller?

Possibly, but she wasn't likely to find out. She was always promising herself that she'd diet, but going without food just made her crabby.

Which was why her clothes always felt too tight.

At this rate she was going to die a virgin.

Depressed by that thought, Holly glanced in the direction of the President's Suite. 'I really don't think I can face this.'

'It's worth it just to get a look at the wicked prince in the flesh.'

'He hasn't always been wicked. He was in love once,'

Holly murmured, momentarily distracted from her own problems. 'With that Italian supermodel. I remember reading about them. They were the golden couple. Then she died along with his brother in that avalanche eight years ago. Horribly sad. Apparently he and his brother were really close. He lost the two people he loved most in the world. A family torn apart. I'm not surprised he's gone a bit wild. He must have been devastated. He probably just needs someone to love him.'

Nicky grinned. 'So go up there and love him. And don't forget my favourite saying.'

'What's that?'

'If you can't stand the heat…'

'Get out of the kitchen?' Holly completed the proverb but Nicky gave a saucy wink.

'Remove a layer of clothing.'

Casper strolled down the steps into the royal box, his handsome face expressionless as he stared across the impressive stadium. Eighty-two thousand people were gradually pouring into the stands in preparation for the breathlessly awaited match that was part of the prestigious Six Nations championship.

It was a bitterly cold February day, and his entourage was all muttering and complaining about freezing English weather.

Casper didn't notice.

He was used to being cold.

He'd been cold for eight long years.

Emilio, his Head of Security, leaned forward and offered him a phone. 'Savannah for you, Your Highness.'

Without turning, Casper gave an almost imperceptible shake of his head and Emilio hesitated before switching off the phone.

'Another female heart broken.' The blonde shivering next to him gave a disbelieving laugh. 'You're cold as ice, Cas.

Rich and handsome, admittedly, but very inaccessible emotionally. Why are you ending it? She's crazy about you.'

'That's why I'm ending it.' His voice hard, Casper watched
the players warming up on the pitch, ignoring the woman
gazing longingly at his profile.

'If you're ditching the most beautiful woman in the world,
what hope is there for the rest of us?'

No hope.

No hope for them. No hope for him. The whole thing was
a game, Casper thought blankly. A game he was sick of playing.

Sport was one of the few things that offered distraction. But,
before the rugby started, he had to sit through the hospitality.

Two long hours of hopeful women and polite conversation.

Two long hours of feeling nothing.

His face appeared on the giant screens placed at either end
of the pitch, and he watched himself with detached curiosity,
surprised by how calm he looked. There was a loud female
cheer from those already gathered in the stands, and Casper
delivered the expected smile of acknowledgement, wondering idly whether any of them would like to come and distract
him for a few hours.

Anyone would do. He really didn't care.

As long as she didn't expect anything from him.

He glanced behind him towards the glass windows of the
President's Suite where lunch would be served. An exceptionally pretty waitress was checking the table, her mouth moving
as she recited her checklist to herself.

Casper studied her in silence, his eyes narrowing slightly
as she paused in her work and lifted a hand to her mouth. He
saw the rise and fall of her chest as she took a deep breath—
watched as she tilted her head backwards and stared up at the
ceiling. It was strange body language for someone about to
serve lunch.

And then he realised that she was trying not to cry.

Over the years he'd taught himself to recognise the signs of female distress so that he could time his exit accordingly.

With cold detachment he watched her struggle to hold back the oncoming tide of tears.

She was a fool, he thought grimly, *to let herself feel that deeply about anything*.

And then he gave a smile of self-mockery. Hadn't he done the same at her age—in his early twenties, when life had seemed like an endless opportunity, hadn't he naively allowed his emotions freedom?

And then he'd learned a lesson that had proved more useful than all the hours spent studying constitutional law or international history.

He'd learned that emotions were man's biggest weakness, and that they could destroy as effectively as the assassin's bullet.

And so he'd ruthlessly buried all trace of his, protecting that unwanted human vulnerability under hard layers of bitter life experience. He'd buried his emotions so deep he could no longer find them.

And that was the way he wanted it.

Without looking directly at anyone, Holly carefully placed the champagne-and-raspberry torte in front of the prince. Silver cutlery and crystal glass glinted against the finest linen, but she barely noticed. She'd served the entire meal in a daze, her mind on Eddie, who was currently entertaining her replacement in the premium box along the richly carpeted corridor.

Holly hadn't seen her, but she was sure she was pretty. Blonde, obviously. And not the sort of person whose best friend in a crisis was a packet of chocolate biscuits.

Did she have a degree? Was she clever?

Holly's vision suddenly blurred with tears, and she blinked frantically, moving slowly around the table, barely aware of the conversation going on around her. Oh dear God, she was going to lose it. Here, in the President's Suite, with the prince and his guests as witnesses. It was going to be the most humiliating moment of her life.

Trying to pull herself together, Holly concentrated on the dessert in her hand, but she was teetering on the brink. Nicky was right. She should have stayed in bed and hidden under the duvet until she'd recovered enough to get her emotions back under control. But she needed this job too badly to allow herself the luxury of wallowing.

A burst of laughter from the royal party somehow intensified her feelings of isolation and misery, and she placed the last dessert on the table and backed away, horrified to find that one of the tears had spilled over onto her cheek.

The release of that one tear made all the others rush forward, and suddenly her throat was full and her eyes were stinging.

Oh, please, no. Not here.

Instinct told her to turn around, but protocol forbade her from turning her back on the prince, so she stood helplessly, staring at the dusky pink carpet with its subtly intertwined pattern of roses and rugby balls, comforting herself with the fact that they wouldn't notice her.

People never noticed her, did they? She was the invisible woman. She was the hand that poured the champagne, or the eyes that spotted an empty plate. She was a tidy room or an extra chair. But she wasn't a *person*.

'Here.' A strong, masculine hand passed her a tissue. 'Blow.'

With a gasp of embarrassment, Holly dragged her horrified gaze from those lean bronzed fingers and collided with eyes as dark and brooding as the night sky in the depths of winter.

And something strange happened.

Time froze.

The tears didn't spill and her heart didn't beat.

It was as if her brain and body separated. For a single instant, she forgot that she was about to make a giant fool of herself. She forgot about Eddie and his trophy blonde. She even forgot the royal party.

The only thing in her world was this man.

And then her knees weakened and her mouth dried because he was *insanely* handsome, his lean aristocratic face a breathtaking composition of bold masculine lines and perfect symmetry.

His dark gaze shifted to her mouth, and the impact of that one searing glance scorched her body like the hottest flame. She felt her lips tingle and her heart thumped against her chest.

And that warning beat was the wake-up call she needed.

Oh, God. 'Your Highness.' Was she supposed to curtsy? She'd been so transfixed by how impossibly good-looking he was, she'd forgotten protocol. What was she supposed to do?

The unfairness of it was like a slap across the face. The one time she absolutely did *not* want to be noticed, she'd been noticed.

By Prince Casper of Santallia.

Her horrified gaze slid back to the tissue in his hand. And he *knew* she was upset. There was no hiding.

'Breathe,' he instructed in a soft voice. 'Slowly.'

Only then did she realise that he'd positioned himself right in front of her. His shoulders were wide and powerful, effectively blocking her from view, so that the rest of his party wouldn't see that she was crying.

The problem was, she could no longer remember *why* she'd felt like crying. One sizzling glance from those lazy dark eyes and her mind had been wiped.

Shrinking with embarrassment, but at the same time

relieved to have a moment to compose herself, Holly took the tissue and blew her nose. Despair mixed with fatalistic acceptance as she realised that she'd just given herself a whole new problem.

He was going to complain. And who could blame him? She should have smiled more. She should have paid attention when the bored-looking blonde seated to his right had asked her whether the goat's cheese was organic.

He was going to have her fired.

'Thank you, Your Highness,' she mumbled, pushing the tissue into her pocket. 'I'll be fine. Just don't give me sympathy.'

'There's absolutely no chance of that. Sympathy isn't my thing.' His gorgeous eyes shimmered with sardonic humour. 'Unless it's sympathy sex.'

Too busy holding back tears to be shocked, Holly took another deep breath, but her white shirt couldn't stand the pressure and two of her buttons popped open. With a whimper of disbelief, she froze. As if she hadn't already embarrassed herself enough in front of royalty, she was about to spill out of her lacy bra. Now what? Did she draw attention to herself and do up the buttons, or did she just hope he hadn't noticed...?

'I'm going to have to complain about you.' His tone was gently apologetic and she felt her knees weaken.

'Yes, Your Highness.'

'A sexy waitress in sheer black stockings and lacy underwear is extremely distracting.' His bold, confident gaze dropped to her full cleavage and lingered. 'You make it impossible for me to concentrate on the boring blonde next to me.'

Braced for an entirely different accusation, Holly gave a choked laugh. 'You're joking?'

'I never joke about fantasies,' he drawled. 'Especially sexual ones.'

He thought the blonde was boring?

'You're having sexual fantasies?'

'Do you blame me?' The frank appraisal in his eyes was so at odds with her own plummeting opinion of herself, that for a moment Holly just stared up at him. Then she realised that he *had* to be making fun of her because she knew she wasn't remotely sexy.

'It isn't fair to tease me, Your Highness.'

'You only have to call me Your Highness the first time. After that, it's "sir".' Amused dark eyes slid from her breasts to her mouth. 'And I rather think you're the one teasing *me*.' He was looking at her with the type of unapologetic masculine appreciation that men reserved for exceptionally beautiful women.

And that wasn't her. She knew it wasn't. 'You haven't eaten your dessert, sir.'

He gave a slow, dangerous smile. 'I think I'm looking at it.'

Oh God, he was actually flirting with her.

Holly's legs started to shake because he was so, so attractive, and the way he was looking at her made her feel like a supermodel. Her shrivelled self-esteem bloomed like a parched flower given new life by a shower of rain. This stunningly attractive, handsome guy—this gorgeous, megawealthy prince who could have had any woman in the world—found her so attractive that he wanted to flirt with her.

'Cas.' A spoiled female voice came from behind them. 'Come and sit down.'

But he didn't turn.

The fact that he didn't appear willing or able to drag his gaze from her raised Holly's confidence another few notches. She felt her colour mount under his intense, speculative gaze, and suddenly there was a dangerous shift in the atmosphere. Trying to work out how she'd progressed from tears to tension in such a short space of time, Holly swallowed.

It was *him*, she thought helplessly.

He was just gorgeous.

And way out of her league.

Flirting was one thing, but he had guests hanging on his every word—glamorous women vying for his attention.

Suddenly remembering where she was and who he was, Holly gave him an embarrassed glance. 'They're waiting for you, sir.'

The smooth lift of one eyebrow suggested that he didn't understand why that was a problem, and Holly gave a weak smile. He was the ruling prince. People stood in line. They waited for his whim and his pleasure.

But surely his pleasure was one of those super-groomed, elegant women glaring impatiently at his broad back?

Her cheeks burning, she cleared her throat. 'They'll be wondering what you're doing.'

'And that matters because…?'

Envious of his indifference, she laughed. 'Well—because generally people care what other people think.'

'Do they?'

She gave an awkward laugh. 'Yes.'

'Do *you* care what other people think?'

'I'm a waitress,' Holly said dryly. 'I have to care. If I don't care, I don't get tips—and then I don't eat.'

The prince lifted one broad shoulder in a careless shrug. 'Fine. So let's get rid of them. What they don't see, they can't judge.' Supremely confident, he cast a single glance towards one of the well-built guys standing by the door and that silent command was apparently sufficient to ensure that he was given instant privacy.

His security team sprang into action, and within minutes the rest of his party was leaving the room, knowing looks from the men and sulky glances from the women.

Ridiculously impressed by this discreet display of authority, Holly wondered how it would feel to be so powerful that you could clear a room with nothing more than a look. *And how must it feel to be so secure about yourself that you didn't care what other people thought about your actions?*

Only when the door of the President's Suite closed behind them did she suddenly realise that she was now alone with the prince.

She gave a choked laugh of disbelief.

He'd just dismissed the most glamorous, gorgeous women she'd ever seen in favour of—*her*?

The Prince turned back to her, his eyes glittering dark and dangerous. 'So.' His voice was soft. 'Now we're alone. How do you suggest we pass the time?'

CHAPTER TWO

HOLLY'S stomach curled with wicked excitement and desperate nerves. 'Thank you for rescuing me from an embarrassing moment,' she mumbled breathlessly, desperately racking her brains for something witty to say and failing. She had no idea how to entertain a prince. 'I can't imagine what you must think of me.'

'I don't understand your obsession with everyone else's opinion,' he drawled. 'And at the moment I'm not capable of thinking. I'm a normal healthy guy, and every one of my brain cells is currently focused on your gorgeous body.'

Holly made a sound somewhere between a gasp and a laugh. Disbelieving, self-conscious, but hopelessly flattered, she stroked her hands over her skirt, looked at him and then looked towards the door. '*Those* women are beautiful.'

'Those women spend eight hours a day perfecting their appearance. That's not beauty—it's obsession.' Supremely sure of himself, he took possession of her hand, locking her fingers into his.

Holly's stomach curled with excitement. 'We're not supposed to be doing this. They gave me this job because they thought I wasn't your type.'

'*Major* error on their part.'

'They told me you preferred blondes.'

'I think I've just had a major shift towards redheads.' With a wicked smile, he lifted his other hand and carelessly fingered a strand of her hair. 'Your hair is the colour of a Middle Eastern bazaar—cinnamon and gold. Tell me why you were crying.'

Caught in a spin of electrifying, exhilarating excitement, Holly's brain was in a whirl. For a moment she'd actually forgotten about Eddie. If she told him that her boyfriend had dumped her, would it make her seem less attractive?

'I was—'

'On second thoughts, don't tell me.' Interrupting her, he lifted her hand, checking for a ring. 'Single?'

Detecting something in his tone but too dazed to identify what, Holly nodded. 'Oh yes, completely single,' she murmured hastily, and then immediately wanted to snatch the words back, because she should have played it cool.

But she didn't feel cool. She felt—*relieved that she'd left the engagement ring at home.*

And he was smiling, clearly aware of the effect he was having on her.

Before she could stop him, he pulled the clip out of her hair and slid his fingers through her tumbling, wayward curls. 'That's better.' Very much the one in control, he closed his fingers around her wrists and hooked her arms round his neck. Then he slid his hands down her back and cupped her bottom.

'Oh.' Appalled that he seemed to be focusing on all her worst features, Holly gave a whimper of embarrassment and fought the impulse to wriggle away from him. But it was too late to take avoiding action. The confident exploration of his hands had ensured he was already well acquainted with the contours of her bottom.

'*Dio*, you have the most fantastic body,' he groaned,

moulding her against the hard muscle of his thighs as if she were made of cling film.

He thought she was fantastic?

Brought into close contact with the physical evidence of his arousal, Holly barely had time to register the exhilarating fact that he really did find her attractive before his mouth came down on hers in a hungry, demanding kiss.

It was like being in the path of a lightning strike. Her body jerked with shock. Her head spun, her knees were shaking, and her attempt to catch her breath simply encouraged a still more intimate exploration of her mouth. Never in her life had a simple kiss made her feel like this. Her fingers dug into his shoulders for support and she gasped as she felt his hands slide *under* her skirt. She felt the warmth of his hands against her bare flesh above her stockings, and then he was backing her against the table, the slick, erotic invasion of his tongue in her mouth sending flames leaping around her body and a burning concentration of heat low in her pelvis.

He was kissing her as though this was their last moments on Earth—*as if he couldn't help himself*—and Holly was swept away on the pure adrenaline rush that came with suddenly being made to feel irresistible.

Dimly she thought, *This is fast, too fast*. But, even as part of her analysed her actions with a touch of shocked disapproval, another part of her was responding with wild abandon, her normal insecurities and inhibitions dissolved in a rush of raw sexual chemistry.

Control slipped slowly from her grasp.

When Eddie had kissed her she'd often found her mind wandering—on occasions she'd guiltily caught herself planning meals and making mental shopping lists—but with the prince the only coherent thought in her head was *Please don't let him stop*.

But she *had* to stop, didn't she?

She didn't do things like this.

What if someone walked in?

Struggling to regain some control, Holly gave a low moan and dragged her mouth from his, intending to take a step back and think through her actions. But her good intentions vanished as she gazed up at his lean, bronzed features, her resolve evaporating as she took in the thick, dark eyelashes guarding his impossibly sexy eyes. *Oh, dear God*—how could any woman say no to a man like this? And, if sheer masculine impact wasn't enough, the way he was looking at her was the most outrageous compliment she'd ever received.

'You're staring at me,' she breathed, and he gave a lopsided smile.

'If you don't want men to stare, stay indoors.'

Holly giggled, as much from nerves as humour. 'I am indoors.'

'True.' The prince lifted one broad shoulder in an unmistakeably Latin gesture. 'In which case, I can't see a solution. You'll just have to put up with me staring, *tesoro*.'

'You speak Italian?'

'I speak whichever language is going to get me the result I want,' he purred, and she gave a choked laugh because he was so outrageously confident and he made her feel beautiful.

Basking in warmth of his bold appreciation, she suddenly felt womanly and infinitely desirable. Blinded by the sheer male beauty of his features, and by the fact that this incredible man was looking at *her*, her crushed heart suddenly lifted as though it had been given wings, and her confidence fluttered back to life.

All right, so she wasn't Eddie's type.

But this man—*this incomparably handsome playboy prince who had his pick of the most beautiful women in the world*—found her irresistible.

'You're staring at me too,' he pointed out, his gaze amused as he slid his fingers into her hair with slow deliberation. 'Perhaps it would be better if we both just close our eyes so that we don't get distracted from what we're doing.'

'What *are* we doing?' Weak with desire, Holly could barely form the words, and his smile widened as he gently cupped her face and lowered his mouth slowly towards hers.

'I think it's called living for the moment. And kissing you is the most fantastic moment I've had in a long time,' he said huskily, his mouth a breath away from hers.

She waited in an agony of anticipation, but he didn't seem in a rush to kiss her again, and Holly parted her lips in expectation, hoping that he'd take the hint.

Why on earth had she stopped him?

With a faint whimper of desperation, she looked into his eyes, saw the laughter there and realised that he was teasing her.

'That isn't very kind, Your Highness.' But she found that she was laughing too and her body was on fire.

'I'm not kind.' He murmured the words against her mouth. 'I'm definitely not kind.'

'I couldn't care less—please…' She was breathless and trembling with anticipation. 'Kiss me again.'

Flashing her a megawatt smile of male satisfaction, the prince finally lowered his head and claimed her mouth with his. He kissed her with consummate skill, his touch confident and possessive as he drew every last drop of response from her parted lips.

Her senses were swamped, her pulse accelerating out of control. Holly was aware of nothing except the overwhelming needs of her own body. Her arms tightened around his neck and she felt the sudden change in him. His kiss changed from playful to purposeful, and she realised with a lurch of exhilarating terror that this wasn't a mild flirtation or a game of 'boy kisses girl'. Prince Casper was a sexually experienced man who knew what he wanted and had the confidence to take it.

'Maybe we should slow this down,' she gasped, sinking her fingers into the hard muscle of his shoulders to give extra support to her shaking knees.

'Slow works for me,' he murmured, sliding his hands over the curve of her bottom. 'I'm more than happy to savour every moment of your utterly delectable body, and the game hasn't started yet. Why rush?'

'I didn't exactly mean—oh—' her head fell back as his mouth trailed a hot, sensuous path down her throat 'I can't concentrate on anything when you do that—'

'Concentrate on *me*,' he advised, and then he lifted his head and his stunning dark eyes narrowed. 'You're shivering. Are you nervous?'

Terrified. Desperate. Weak with longing.

'I—I haven't actually done this before.' Her whispered confession caused him to still.

'Exactly what,' he said carefully, 'Haven't you done before?' He released his hold on her bottom and slid his fingers under her chin, forcing her to look at him, his sharply intelligent eyes suddenly searching.

Holly swallowed.

Oh God, he was going to walk away from her. If she told him the truth, this experienced, sophisticated, gorgeous man would let her go and she'd spend the rest of her life regretting it.

Was she really going to let that happen?

No longer questioning herself, she slid her arms back round his neck. She didn't know what was going on here, she had no idea why she was feeling this way, but she knew she didn't want it to stop. 'I meant that I've never done anything like this in such a public place.'

He lifted an eyebrow. 'We're alone.'

'But anyone could walk in.' She wished he'd kiss her again. Would he think she was forward if *she* kissed him? 'What would happen then?'

'They'd be arrested,' he said dryly, 'And carted off to jail.'

'Oh—' Reminded of exactly with whom she was dealing, Holly felt suddenly intimidated. Please, *please,* let him kiss her again. When he'd kissed her she'd forgotten he was a prince. She'd forgotten *everything*. Feeling as though she were standing on the edge of a life-changing moment, Holly gazed up at him and he gave a low laugh.

'You talk too much, do you know that? So—now what? Yes, or no?' He smoothed a rebellious strand of hair away from her flushed cheeks in a slow, sensual movement, and that meaningful touch was enough to raise her temperature several degrees.

He was giving her the choice.

He was telling her that, if he kissed her again, he was going all the way.

'Yes,' she whispered, knowing that there would be a price to pay, but more than willing to pay it. 'Oh, yes.'

If she'd expected her shaky encouragement to be met with a kiss, she was disappointed.

'If you want to slow things down,' he murmured against her throat, 'I suppose I could always eat the dessert that's waiting for me on the table.'

Holly gave a faint whimper of frustration, and then he lifted his head and she saw the wicked gleam in his eyes 'You're teasing me again.'

'You asked me to slow down, *tesoro*.'

She was finding it hard to breathe. 'I've definitely changed my mind about that.'

'Then why don't you tell me what you want?' He gave a sexy, knowing smile that sent her body into meltdown.

'I want you to kiss me again.' *And not to stop*.

'Do you?' His head lowered to hers, thick lashes partially shielding the mockery in his beautiful eyes. 'You're not supposed to give me orders.'

'Are you going to arrest me?'

'Now, there's a thought.' He breathed the words against her mouth. 'I could clap you in handcuffs and chain you to my bed until I'm bored.'

Her last coherent thought was *Please don't let him ever be bored*, and then he lifted her, and the demands of his hands on her thighs made it impossible for her not to wrap her legs around his waist. There was the faint rattle of fine bone-china as he positioned her on the table, and only when she felt the roughness of his zip against the soft flesh of her inner thigh did she realise that he'd somehow manoeuvred her skirt up round her waist.

With a gasp of embarrassment, she grabbed at the skirt, but she felt the hard thrust of his body against hers.

'I *love* the stockings,' he groaned, his dark eyes ablaze with sexual heat as he scanned the lacy suspender-belt transecting her milky-white thighs.

Thighs that definitely weren't skinny.

The fragile shoots of her self-confidence withered and died under his blatant scrutiny, and Holly tugged ineffectually at the hem of her skirt, trying to cover herself. 'Sylvia insists on stockings,' she muttered, and then, 'Do you think you could stop looking at me?'

'No, I definitely couldn't,' he assured her, a laugh in his voice as he released his hold on her bottom, grasped her hands and anchored them firmly around his neck. 'Take a deep breath in for me.'

'Why?'

A wicked smile transformed his face from handsome to

devastating. 'Because I want you to undo a few more buttons without me having to move my hands again. I'm never letting go of your bottom.'

Hyper-sensitive to that particular subject, Holly tensed, only to relax again as she registered the unmistakeable relish with which he was exploring her body. 'You *like* my bottom?'

'I just want to lose myself in you. What's your secret— exercise? Plastic surgery?' He gave another driven groan, captured her hips and drew her hard against his powerful erection. 'What did you *do* to it?'

'I ate too many biscuits,' Holly muttered truthfully, and he gave a laugh.

'I love your sense of humour. And from now on you can expect to receive a box of your favourite kind of biscuits on a daily basis.'

Slightly stunned that he actually seemed to *love* her worst feature, and trying not to be shocked by his unashamed sexuality, Holly was about to speak when his mouth collided with hers again and sparks exploded inside her head. It was like being the centre piece at a fireworks display, and she gave a disbelieving moan that turned to a gasp as her shirt fell open and her bra slid onto her lap.

'Are these also the result of the famous biscuit-diet?' An appreciative gleam in his eyes, he transferred his attention from her bottom to her breasts. '*Dio*, you're so fantastic I'm not even *thinking* about anything else while I'm with you.'

Something about that comment struck a slightly discordant note in her dazzled brain. Before she could dissect his words in more detail, he dragged his fingers across one nipple and shockwaves of pleasure sliced through her body. Then he lowered his dark head and flicked her nipple with his tongue.

Tortured by sensation, Holly's head fell back. Inhibition blown to the wind by his expert touch, driven to the point of explosion by his vastly greater experience, she knew she was completely out of control and didn't even care. She felt like a novice rider clinging to the back of a thoroughbred stallion.

The burning ache in her pelvis grew to unbearable proportions, and she ground herself against him with a whimper of need. Desperate to relieve the almost intolerable heat that threatened to burn her up, she dug her nails into his shoulders.

'Please—oh—please.'

'My pleasure.' His eyes were two narrow slits of fire, his jaw hard, streaks of colour highlighting his cheekbones as he scanned her flushed cheeks and parted lips. Then he flattened her to the table and came down over her, the muscles in his shoulders bunched as he protected her from his weight.

Feeling as though she'd been dropped naked onto a bonfire, Holly gave a low moan that he smothered with a slow, purposefully erotic kiss.

'You are the most delicious thing that has ever been put on my table, my gorgeous waitress,' he murmured, his desperately clever fingers reaching lower. The intimacy of his touch brought another gasp to her lips and the gasp turned to a low moan as he explored her with effortless skill and merciless disregard for modesty.

'Are you protected?' His husky question didn't begin to penetrate her dazed brain, and she made an unintelligible sound, her legs tightening around his back, her body arching off the table in an attempt to ease the fearsome ache he'd created.

His mouth came down on hers again and she felt his strong hands close around her hips. He shifted his position, tilted her slightly, and then surged into her with a decisive thrust that drew a disbelieving groan from him and a shocked gasp from Holly.

An explosion of unbelievable pleasure suddenly splintered into pain, and her sharp cry caused him to still instantly.

Pain and embarrassment mingled in equal measure and for

a moment Holly dug her nails hard into his shoulders, afraid to move in case moving made it worse. And then suddenly the pain was gone and there was only pleasure—dark, forbidden pleasure that beckoned her forwards into a totally new world. She moved her hips restlessly, not sure what she wanted him to do, but needing him to do *something*.

There was the briefest hesitation on his part while he scanned her flushed cheeks, then he surged into her again, but this time more gently, his eyes holding hers the whole time as he introduced her to an intimacy that was new to her. And it was pleasure such as she'd never imagined. *Pleasure that blew her mind.*

She didn't know herself—her body at the mercy of sensual pleasure and the undeniable skill of an experienced male.

Controlled by his driving thrusts, she raced towards a peak and then was flung high into space, stars exploding in her head as he swallowed her cries of pleasure with his mouth, and reached his own peak with a triumphant groan.

Gradually Holly floated back down to earth, aware of the harshness of his breathing and the frantic beating of her own heart. He'd buried his face in her neck, and Holly focused on his glossy dark hair with glazed vision and numb disbelief.

Had that really just happened?

Swamped by an emotion that she couldn't define, she lifted her hand and tentatively touched him, checking that he was real.

She felt an immediate surge of tension through his powerful frame and heard his sharp intake of breath. Then he lifted his head, stared down into her eyes.

To Holly it was the single most intimate moment of her life and when he opened his mouth to speak her heart softened.

'The match has started,' he drawled flatly. 'Thanks to you I've missed kick-off.'

* * *

Keeping his back to the girl, Casper stared blankly through the glass of the President's Suite down into the stadium, struggling to regain some measure of control after what had undoubtedly been the most exciting sexual encounter of his life.

On the pitch below, England had possession of the ball, but for the first time in his life he wasn't in his seat, watching the game.

Which was something else that he didn't understand.

What the hell was going on?

Why wasn't he rushing to watch the game?

And since when had he been driven to have raw, uncontrolled sex on a table with an innocent woman?

Innocent.

Only now was he realising that all the signs had been there. And he'd missed them. *Or had he ignored them?*

Either way, he was fully aware of the irony of the situation.

He'd had relationships with some of the world's most beautiful, experienced and sophisticated women, but none of them had made him feel the way she had.

This was possibly the first time he'd enjoyed uncomplicated, motiveless sex. Sex driven by sheer, animal lust rather than human ambition.

Yes, the girl had known he was a prince.

But he was experienced enough to know that she'd wanted him as a man.

Hearing the faint brush of clothing against flesh, he knew she was dressing. For once he was grateful for the iron self-control and self-discipline that had been drilled into him in his few years in the army, because that was the only thing currently standing between restraint and a repeat performance.

It must have been novelty value, he reflected grimly, his shoulders tensing as he heard her slide her feet into her shoes.

That was the only explanation for the explosive chemistry they shared.

Which left them where, precisely?

He turned to find her watching him, and the confusion in her beautiful green eyes turned to consternation as a discreet tap on the door indicated that his presence was required.

The girl threw an embarrassed glance towards the door and frantically smoothed her skirt over her thighs. It was obvious from the uneven line of buttons on her shirt that she'd dressed in a hurry, with hands that hadn't been quite steady. Her hair was still loose, spilling over her narrow shoulders like a fall of autumn leaves, a beacon of glorious colour that effectively announced their intimacy to everyone who saw her.

Focusing on her soft mouth, Casper felt a sudden urge to power her back against the table and lose himself in her incredible body one more time.

'They'll be waiting for you in the royal box.' Her husky voice cut through his disturbingly explicit thoughts, and she hesitated for a moment and then walked over to him.

'Y-your Highness—are you all right?'

Casper stared down into warm green eyes, saw concern there, and suddenly the urge not to let her go was almost painful. There was something hopeful and optimistic about her, and he sensed she hadn't yet discovered that life was a cold, hard place.

Her smile faltered as she studied the grim set of his features. 'I guess this is what you'd call a bit of an awkward moment. So—well—' she waved a hand '—I have to get back to work and you—well…' Her voice tailed off and her white teeth clamped her lower lip. Then she took a deep breath closed the gap between them, stood on tiptoe and kissed him on the mouth. 'Thank you,' she whispered. 'Thank you for what you've given me.'

Caught by surprise, Casper stood frozen to the spot, enveloped by a warm, soft woman. She tasted of strawberries and summer and an immediate explosion of lust gripped his body.

So he wasn't dead, then, he thought absently, part of him removed from what was happening. *Some things he could still feel.*

And then he heard a massive cheer from the crowd behind him and knew instantly what had happened.

Not so innocent, he thought grimly. Not so innocent that she didn't know how to work the press to her advantage. She was kissing him in the window, in full view of the cameras covering the game and the crowd.

Cameras that were now focusing on them.

She might have been sexually inexperienced, but clearly that hadn't prevented her from having a plan.

Surprised that he was still capable of feeling disillusioned and furious with himself for making such an elemental mistake, Casper locked his fingers round her wrists and withdrew her arms from his neck.

'You can stop now. If you look behind me, I think you'll find that you've achieved your objective.'

Confusion flickered in her eyes and then her attention fixed on something behind him. 'Oh my God.' Her hand covered her mouth. 'H—how did you know?' Her voice was an appalled whisper and she glanced at him in desperate panic. 'They filmed me kissing you. And it's up on the giant screens.' Her voice rose, her cheeks were scarlet, and her reluctant glance towards the stadium ended in a moan of disbelief. 'They're playing it again and again. Oh God, I can't believe this—it looks as though I'm—and my hair is all over the place and my bottom looks *huge*, and—everyone is looking.'

His eyes on the pitch, Casper watched with cool detachment as his friend, the England captain, hit a post with a drop-goal attempt.

'More importantly, you just cost England three points.'

With cold detachment, he realised that he was now going to have to brief his security team to get her out of here, but before he could speak she gave him a reproachful look and sped to the door.

'Do *not* leave this room,' Casper thundered, but she ignored him, tugged open the door, slipped between two of his security guards and sprinted out of sight.

Unaccustomed to having his orders ignored, Casper stood in stunned silence for a few precious seconds and then delivered a single command to his Head of Security 'Find her.'

'Can you give me her name, Your Highness?'

Casper stared through the door. 'No,' he said grimly. 'I can't.'

All he knew was that she clearly wasn't as innocent as he'd first thought.

Feeling nothing except a desperate desire to hide from the world, Holly sprinted out of the room, shrinking as she passed a television screen in time to overhear the commentator say *'Looks like the opening score goes to Prince Casper.'*

Hurtling down the stairs, she ran straight into her boss, who was marching up the stairs towards the President's Suite like a general leading an invading army onto enemy territory.

'Sylvia.' Her breath coming in pants, Holly stared at the other woman in horrified silence, noticing the blaze of fury in her eyes and the tightness of her lips.

'How dare you?' Sylvia's voice shook with anger. 'How dare you humiliate me in this way? I picked you especially because I thought you were sensible and decent. And you have destroyed the reputation of my company!'

'No!' Horribly guilty, overwhelmed by panic and humiliation, Holly shook her head. 'They don't even know who I am, and—'

'The British tabloid press will have your name before you're out of the stadium,' Sylvia spat. 'The entire nation heard the commentator say "That's one girl who isn't lying back thinking of England". If you wanted sleazy notoriety, then you've got it.'

Holly flinched under the verbal blows, feeling as vulnerable as a little rowing boat caught in a heavy storm out at sea. *What had she done?* This wasn't a little transgression that would remain her private secret. This was—this was…

'Prince Casper has kissed lots of women,' she muttered. 'So it won't be much of a story—'

'You're a waitress!' Sylvia was shaking with anger. 'Of course it's a story!'

Holly stared at her in appalled silence, realising that she hadn't once given any thought to the consequences of what they were doing. She hadn't thought at all. It had been impulse, chemistry, intimacy; she bit back a hysterical laugh.

What was intimate about having your love life plastered on sixty-nine-metre screens for the amusement of a crowd of eighty-two thousand people?

She swallowed painfully. 'Sylvia, I—'

'You're fired for misconduct!'

Her world crumbling around her, Holly was about to plead her case when she caught sight of Eddie striding towards them, his face like a storm cloud.

Unable to take any more, Holly gasped another apology and fled towards the kitchens. Heart pounding, cheeks flaming, she grabbed her bag and her coat, changed into her trainers and made for the door.

Nicky intercepted her. 'Where are you going?'

'I don't know.' Feeling dazed, Holly looked at her helplessly. 'Home. Anywhere.'

'You can't go home. It's the first place they'll look.' Brisk and businesslike, Nicky handed her a hat and a set of keys. 'Stick the hat on and hide that gorgeous hair. Then go to my flat.'

'No one knows who I am.'

'By now they'll know more about you than you do. Go to my flat, draw the curtains and don't answer the door to anyone. Have you got the money for a cab?'

'I'll take the bus.' Too shocked to argue, Holly obediently scooped her hair into a bunch and tucked it under the hat.

'No way.' Nicky stuffed a note in her hand. 'Get a taxi—and hope the driver hasn't seen the pictures on the screen. Come to think of it, sit with a hanky over your nose. Pretend you have a cold or something. Go, go, *go!*'

Realising that she'd set into motion a series of events that she couldn't control, Holly started to walk towards the door when Nicky caught her arm.

'Just tell me one thing,' she whispered, a wicked gleam in her eyes. 'The rumours about the prince's talents—are they true?'

Holly blinked. 'I—'

'That good, huh?' Nicky gave a slow, knowing smile. 'I guess that answers my question. Way to go, baby.'

Ruthlessly focusing his mind on the game, Casper watched as the England winger swerved round his opponent and dived for the corner.

The bored blonde gasped in sympathy. 'Oh no, the poor guy's tripped. Right on the line. Why is everyone cheering? That's *so* mean.'

'He didn't trip, he scored a try,' Casper growled, simmering with masculine frustration at her inappropriate comment. 'And they're cheering because that try puts England level.'

'This game is a total mystery to me,' the girl muttered, her eyes wandering to a group of women at the back of the royal box. 'Nice shoes. I wonder where she got them? Are there any decent shops in this area?'

Casper blocked out her comments, watching as the England fly-half prepared to take the kick.

A hush fell over the stadium and Saskia glanced around her in bemusement. 'I don't understand any of this. Why is everyone so quiet? And why does that gorgeous guy keep staring at the ball and then the post? Can't he make up his mind whether to kick it or not?'

'He's about to take a very difficult conversion kick right from the touchline. He's concentrating.' Casper's gaze didn't shift from the pitch. 'And if you open your mouth again I'll have you removed.'

Saskia snapped her mouth shut, the ball snaked through the posts, the crowd roared its approval, and a satisfied Casper turned wearily to the fidgeting blonde next to him. 'All right. *Now* you can ask me whatever you want to know.'

She gave him a hopeful look. 'Is the game nearly over?'

Casper subdued a flash of irritation and resolved never again to invite anyone who didn't share his passion for rugby. 'It's half time.'

'So we have to sit through the whole thing again? Tell me again how you know the captain.'

'We were in the rugby team at school together.'

Clearly determined to engage him in conversation now that there was a pause in the game, Saskia sidled a little closer. 'It was very bad of you to kiss that waitress. You are a very naughty boy, Cas. She'll go to the newspapers, you know. That sort always do.'

Would she?

Casper stared blankly at the crowd, trying to blot out the

scent of her hair and the taste of her mouth—the softness of her deliciously rounded bottom as she'd lifted herself against him.

For a brief moment in time, she'd made him forget. And that was more than anyone else had ever done.

'Why does your popularity never dip?' Clearly determined to ingratiate herself, Saskia kept trying. 'Whatever you do, however scandalous you are, the citizens of Santallia still love you.'

'They love him because he's turned Santallia from a sleepy, crumbling Mediterranean country into a hub of foreign investment and tourism. People are excited about what's happening.' It was one of Casper's friends, Marco, who spoke, a guy in his early thirties who had studied economics with him at university and now ran a successful business. 'Santallia is *the* place to be. The downhill-ski race has brought the tourists to the mountains in the winter, and the yacht race does the same for the coast in the summer. The new rugby stadium is sold out for the entire season, and everyone is talking about the Grand Prix. As a sporting venue, we're second to none.'

Hearing his successes listed should have lifted his mood, but Casper still felt nothing.

He made no effort to take part in the conversation going on around him and was relieved when the second half started because it offered him a brief distraction.

'What Santallia really wants from you is an heir, Cas.' Saskia delivered what she obviously thought was an innocent smile. 'You can't play the field for ever. Sooner or later you're going to have to break your supermodel habit and think about the future of your country. Oh no, fighting has broken out on the pitch. They're all sort of locked together.'

Leaving it to an exasperated Marco to enlighten her, Casper watched as the scrum half put the ball into the scrum. 'That was never straight,' he murmured, a frown on his face as he glanced at the referee, waiting for him to blow the whistle.

'Did you read that survey that put you top of the list of most eligible single men in the world? You can have any woman you want, Cas.' Oblivious to the impact of her presence on their enjoyment, Saskia continued to pepper the entire second half with her inane comments, all of which Casper ignored.

'A minute of play to go,' Marco murmured, and Casper watched as England kept the ball among the forwards until the final whistle shrilled.

The crowd erupted into ecstatic cheers at the decisive England victory, and he rose to his feet, abruptly terminating Saskia's attempts to converse with him.

Responsibility pressing in on him, he strolled over to his Head of Security. 'Anything?'

'No, sir,' Emilio admitted reluctantly. 'She's vanished.'

'You found out her name?'

'Holly, sir. Holly Phillips. She's a waitress with the contract catering company.'

'Address?'

'I already sent a team to her home, sir. She isn't there.'

'But I'm sure the photographers are,' Cas said grimly, and Emilio nodded.

'Two rows of them, waiting to interview her. Prince and waitress—it's going to be tomorrow's headlines. You want her to have protection?'

'A woman who chooses to kiss me in full view of television cameras and paparazzi doesn't need my protection.' Casper spoke in a flat, toneless voice. 'She knew exactly what she was doing. And now she's lying low because being unavailable will make it look as though she has something to hide. And having something to hide will make her story more valuable.'

She'd used him.

Casper gave a twisted smile. *And he'd used her, too, hadn't he?*

Emilio frowned. 'You think she did it to make money, sir?'

'Of course.' She'd actually had the temerity to thank him for what he'd given her! At the time he'd wondered what she meant, but now it was blindingly obvious.

He'd given her media opportunities in abundance.

He searched inside himself for a feeling of disgust or disillusionment. *Surely* he should feel something? Apparently she'd considered the loss of her virginity to be a reasonable price to pay for her moment of fame and fortune and that attitude deserved at least a feeling of mild disappointment on his part

But disillusionment, disgust and disappointment all required expectations and, when it came to women, he had none.

Emilio was watching him. 'You don't want us to find her Your Highness?'

Ruthlessly pushing aside thoughts of her soft mouth and delicious curves, Casper glanced back towards the pitch where the crowd was going wild. 'I think we can be sure that when she's ready she'll turn up. At this precise moment she's lying low, laughing to herself and counting her money.'

CHAPTER THREE

'YOU have *got* to stop crying!' Exasperated and concerned, Nicky put her arms round Holly. 'And—well—it isn't that serious, really.'

'Nicky, *I'm pregnant!* And it's the prince's baby.' Holly turned reddened eyes in her direction. 'How much more serious can it get?'

Nicky winced. 'Isn't it too soon to do a test? It could be wrong.'

'It isn't too soon. It's been over two weeks!' Holly waved a hand towards the bathroom. 'And it isn't wrong. It's probably still on the floor where I dropped it if you want to check, but it doesn't exactly give you a million options. It's either pregnant or not pregnant. And I'm *definitely* pregnant! Oh God, I don't believe it. Once—*once*—I have sex and now I'm pregnant. Some people try for *years*.'

'Yes, well, the prince is obviously super-fertile as well as super-good looking.' Nicky gave a helpless shrug, searching for something to say. 'You always said you couldn't wait to have a baby.'

'But *with* someone! Not on my own. I never, ever, wanted to be a single mother. It was the one thing I promised myself was never going to happen. It *really* matters to me.' Holly pulled another tissue out of the box and blew her nose hard. 'When I dreamed about having a baby, I dreamed about giving it everything I never had.'

'By which I presume you mean a father. God, your dad *really* screwed you up.' With that less than comforting comment, Nicky sank back against the sofa and picked at her nail varnish. 'I mean, how could anyone have a kid like you, so kind and loving, and then basically just, well, walk out? And you were seven—old enough to know you'd been rejected. And not even coming to find you after your mum died. I mean, for goodness' sake!'

Not wanting to be reminded of her barren childhood, Holly burrowed deeper inside the sleeping bag. 'He didn't know she'd died.'

'If he'd stayed in touch he would have known.'

'Do you mind if we don't talk about this?' Her voice high-pitched, Holly rolled onto her back and stared up at the ceiling. 'I have to decide what to do. I've lost my job, and I can't go home because the press are like a pack of wolves outside my flat. And the whole world thinks I'm a giant slut.' Dying of embarrassment, her insides twisting with regret, she buried her face in the pillow.

And she *was* a slut, wasn't she?

She'd had sex with a total stranger.

And not just sex—recklessly abandoned, wild sex. Sex that had taken her breath away and wiped her mind of guilt, worry, *morals*.

Whenever Eddie had touched her, her first thought had always been *I mustn't get pregnant*. When the prince had touched her the only thought in her head had been more, *more*…

What had happened to her?

Yes, she'd been upset and insecure about herself after her break up with Eddie, but that didn't explain or excuse it.

And then she remembered the way the prince had planted

himself protectively in front of her, shielding her from the rest of the group. What other man had ever shown that degree of sensitivity? He'd noticed she was upset, shielded her, and then...

Appalled with herself, she gave another moan of regret, and Nicky yanked the sleeping bag away from her.

'Stop torturing yourself. You're going to be a great mother.'

'How can I be a great mother? I'm going to have to give my baby to someone else to look after while I work! Which basically means that someone else will pick my baby up when it cries.'

'Well, if it's a real bawler that might be an advantage.'

Holly wiped the tears from her face with a mangled damp hanky. 'How can it be an advantage? I want to be there for my baby.'

'Well, perhaps you'll win the lottery.'

'I can't afford to play the lottery. I can't even afford to pay you rent.'

'I don't want rent, and you can sleep on my sofa as long as you need to.' Nicky shrugged. 'You can't exactly go home, can you? The entire British public are gagging for pictures of you. "Where's the waitress?" is today's headline. Yesterday it was "royal's rugby romp". Rumour has it that they're offering a reward to anyone who shops you. Everyone wants to know about that kiss.'

'For crying out loud.' Holly blew her nose hard. 'People in the world are starving and they want to write about the fact that I kissed a prince? Doesn't anyone have any sense of perspective?' *Thank goodness they didn't know the whole story*.

'Well, we all need a little light relief now and then, and people love it when royalty show they're human.' Nicky sprang to her feet. 'I'm hungry and there's no food in this flat.'

'I don't want anything,' Holly said miserably, too embarrassed to admit to her friend that the real reason she was so upset was because the prince hadn't made any attempt to get in touch.

Even though she knew it was ridiculous to expect him to contact her, a small part of her was still desperately hoping that he would. Yes, she was a waitress and he was a prince, but he'd liked her, hadn't he? He'd thrown all the other people out of the room so that he could be with *her*, and he'd said all those nice things about her, and then…

Holly's body burned in a rush of sexual excitement that shocked her. Surely after sex as mind-blowing as that, he might have been tempted to track her down?

But how could he get in touch when the press was staking out her flat? She had a mental image of the prince hiding behind a bush, waiting for the opportunity to bang on her door. 'Do you think he's really annoyed about the headlines?'

'Don't tell me you're worrying about *him*!' Nicky had her hand in a packet of cereal. 'He just pulls up his bloody draw-bridge, leaving the enemy on the outside!'

Holly bit her lip. She was the one who'd kissed him by the window. *She'd had no idea.* 'I feel guilty.'

'Oh, please! This is Prince Casper we're talking about. He doesn't care what the newspapers write about him. *You're* the one who's going to suffer. If you ask me, the least he could have done was give you some security or advice. But he's left you to take the flak!'

Holly's spirits sank further at that depressing analysis. 'He doesn't know where I am.'

'He's a prince,' Nicky said contemptuously, flopping back down on the sofa, her mouth full of cereal. 'He commands a whole army, complete with special forces. He could find you in an instant if he wanted to. MI5, FBI, I don't know—one of that lot. One word from him and there'd be a satellite trained on my flat.'

Shrinking at the thought, Holly slid back into the sleeping bag. 'Close the blinds.' *What had she done?*

'Well, you can go on hiding if that's what you want. Or you could give those sharks outside your flat an interview.'

'Are you mad?'

'No, I'm practical. Thanks to His Royal Highness, you have no job and you're trapped indoors. Sell your story to the highest bidder. "My lunchtime of love" or "sexy Santallian stud"?'

Appalled, Holly shook her head. 'Absolutely not. I couldn't do that.'

'You have a baby to support.'

'And I don't want my child looking back at the year he was conceived and seeing that his life started with me dishing the dirt on his dad in the papers! I just want the whole thing to go away.'

It was ironic, she thought numbly, that she'd fantasised about this exact moment ever since she was a teenager. She'd *longed* to be a mother. Longed to have a child of her own—be able to create the sort of family she'd always wanted.

She'd even lain awake at night, imagining what it must be like to discover that you were pregnant and to share that excitement with a partner. She'd imagined his delight and his pride. She'd imagined him pulling her into a protective hug and fiercely declaring that he would never leave his family.

Not once, ever, had she imagined that she'd be in this position, doing it on her own.

One rash moment, one transgression—*just one*—and her life had been blown apart. Even though she was in a state of shock, the deeper implications weren't lost on her. Her hopes of eventually being able to melt back into her old life unobserved died. She knew that once someone spotted that she was pregnant it wouldn't take long for them to do the maths.

This was Prince Casper of Santallia's child.

Nicky stood up. 'I need to buy some food. Back in a minute.' The front door slammed behind her, and moments later Holly heard the doorbell. Assuming Nicky had forgotten something, she slid off the sofa and padded over to the door.

'So this is where you've been hiding!' Eddie stood in the doorway, holding a huge, ostentatious bunch of dark-red roses wrapped in cheap cellophane.

Holly simply stared, suddenly realising that she'd barely thought about him over the past two weeks.

'I didn't expect to see you here, Eddie.'

He gave a benign smile. 'I expect it seems like a dream.' Sure of himself, Eddie smiled down at her. 'Aren't you going to invite me in?'

'No. You broke off our engagement, Eddie. I was devastated.' Holly frowned to herself. Her devastation hadn't lasted long, though, had it? It had been supplanted by bigger issues—but should that have been possible? Did broken hearts really mend that quickly?

'I can't talk about this on the doorstep.' He pushed his way into the flat and thrust the flowers into her hands. Past their best, a few curling petals floated onto the floor. 'Here. These are for you. To show that I forgive you.'

'Forgive me?' Holly winced as a thorn buried itself into her hand. Gingerly she put the flowers down on the hall table and sucked the blood from her finger. 'What are you forgiving me for?'

'For kissing the prince.' Eddie's face turned the same shade as the roses. 'For making a fool of me in public.'

'Eddie—you were the one partying in that box with your new girlfriend.'

'She was no one special. We both need to stop hurting each other. I admit that I was furious when I saw you kissing the prince, then I realised that it must have been hard on you, watching me get that promotion and then losing me. But it seems to have loosened up something inside you. A whole new you emerged.' He grinned like a schoolboy who had just discovered girls. 'You've always been quite shy and a bit prim. And suddenly you were, well, wild. When I saw you kissing him, I couldn't help thinking it should have been me.'

Looking at him, Holly realised that not once during her entire passionate episode with the prince had she thought 'this should have been Eddie'.

'I know you only did it to bring me to my senses,' Eddie said. 'And it worked. I see now that you are capable of passion. I just need to be more patient with you.'

The prince hadn't been patient, Holly thought absently. He'd been very *impatient*. Rough, demanding, forceful.

'I didn't kiss the prince to make you jealous.' She'd kissed him because she couldn't help herself.

'Never mind that now. Put my ring back on your finger, and we'll go out there and tell the press we'd had a row and you kissed the prince because you were pining for me.'

Life had a strange sense of humour, Holly reflected numbly. Eddie was offering to get back together. But she was already being propelled down a very different path.

'That isn't possible.'

'We're going to make a great couple.' He was smugly confident. 'We'll have the Porsche and the big house. You don't need to be a waitress any more.'

'I like being a waitress,' Holly said absently. 'I like meeting new people and talking to them. People tell you a lot over a cup of coffee.'

'But who wants to be weighed down with someone else's problems when you can stay at home and look after me?'

'It *can't* happen, Eddie—'

'I know it's like a fairy tale, but it *is* happening. By the way, the flowers cost a fortune, so you'd better put them in water. I need the bathroom.'

'Door on the right,' Holly said automatically, and then gave a gasp. 'No, Eddie, you can't go in there.' Oh, dear God, she'd left everything on the floor—he'd see.

Wanting to drag him back but already too late, she stood there, paralysed into inactivity by the sheer horror of the moment. The inevitability was agonising. It was like witnessing a pile-up—watching, powerless, as a car accelerated towards the back of another.

For a moment there was no sound. No movement.

Then Eddie appeared in the door, his face white. 'Well.' His voice sounded tight and very unlike himself. 'That certainly explains why you don't want to get back together again.'

'Eddie—'

'You're holding out for a higher prize.' Looking slightly dazed, he stumbled into the living room of Nicky's flat. Then he looked at her, his mouth twisted with disgust. 'A year we were together! And we never—you made we wait.'

'Because it didn't feel right,' she muttered, mortified by how it must look, and anxious that she'd damaged his ego. That was the one part of this whole situation that she hadn't even been able to explain to herself. Why had she held Eddie at a distance for so long and yet ended up half-naked on the table with Prince Casper within thirty minutes of meeting him? 'Eddie, I really don't—'

'You really don't *what*?' He was shouting now, his features contorted with rage as he paced across Nicky's wooden floor. 'You really don't know why you slept with him? Well I'll tell you, shall I? *You slept with him because he's a bloody prince!*'

'No—'

'And you've really hit the jackpot, haven't you?' He gave a bitter laugh. 'No wonder you weren't excited about my Porsche. I suppose he drives a bloody Ferrari, does he?'

Holly blinked. 'I have no idea what he drives, Eddie, but—'

'But it's enough to know you're getting a prince and a palace!'

'That isn't true. I haven't even decided what to do yet.'

'You mean you haven't decided how to make the most money out of the opportunity.' Eddie strode towards the door of her flat, scooping up the flowers on the way. 'I'm taking these with me. You don't deserve them. And you don't deserve *me*. Good luck in your new life.'

Holly winced as the flowers bashed against the door frame and flinched as he slammed the door.

A horrible silence descended on the flat.

A few forlorn rose petals lingered on the floor like drops of blood, and her finger stung from the sharp thorn.

She felt numb with shock. Awful. And guilty, because it was true that she'd shared something with the prince that she hadn't shared with Eddie.

And she didn't understand that.

She didn't understand any of it.

Two weeks ago she would have relished the idea of getting back together with Eddie.

Now she was just relieved that he'd gone.

Sinking onto Nicky's sofa, she tried to think clearly and logically.

There was no need to panic.

No one would be able to guess she was pregnant for at least four months.

She had time to work out a plan.

Flanked by four bodyguards, gripping a newspaper like a weapon, Casper hammered on the door of the fourth-floor flat.

'You didn't have to come here in person, Your Highness.' Emilio glanced up and down the street. 'We could have had her brought to you.'

'I didn't want to wait that long,' Casper growled. In the past few hours he'd discovered that he was, after all, still capable of emotion. Boiling, seething anger. Anger towards her, but mostly at himself, for allowing himself to be put in this position. What had happened to his skills of risk assessment? Since when had the sight of a delicious female body caused him to abandon caution and reason? Women had been throwing themselves in his path since he'd started shaving, but never before had he acted with such lamentable lack of restraint.

She'd set a trap and he'd walked right into it.

'I *know* she's in there. Get this door open.'

Before his security team could act, the door opened and she stood there, looking at him.

Prepared to let loose the full force of his anger, Casper stilled, diverted from his mission by her captivating green eyes.

Holly.

He knew her name now.

She was dressed in an oversized, pale pink tee-shirt with a large embroidered polar bear on the front. Her hair tumbled loose over her shoulders and her feet were bare. It was obvious that she'd been in bed, and she looked at him with shining eyes, apparently thrilled to see him. 'Your Highness?'

She looked impossibly young, fresh and naïve and Casper wondered again what had possessed him to get involved with someone like her.

She had trouble written across her forehead.

And then she smiled, and for a few seconds he forgot everything except the warmth of that smile. The anger retreated inside him, and the only thing in his head was a clear memory of her long legs wrapped around his waist. Casper gritted his teeth, rejecting the surge of lust, furious with himself, and at the same time slightly perplexed because he'd never in his life felt sexual desire for a woman dressed in what looked like a child's tee-shirt.

This whole scenario was *not* turning out the way he'd expected.

How could he still feel raw lust for someone who'd capsized his life like a boat in a storm? And why was she staring at him as if they were acting out the final scenes of a romantic movie? After the stunt she'd pulled, he'd expected hard-nosed negotiation.

'I see you didn't bother dressing for my visit.' Ignoring the flash of hurt in her eyes, he strode into the tiny flat without invitation, leaving his security team to ensure their privacy.

'Well, obviously I had no idea that you'd be coming.' She tugged self-consciously at the hem of her tee-shirt. 'It's been well over two weeks.'

Casper assessed the apartment in a single glance, taking in the rumpled sleeping bag on the sofa. *So this was where she'd been hiding.* 'I have a degree in maths. I know exactly how long it's been.'

Her eyes widened in admiration. 'You're good at maths? I always envy people who are good with numbers. Maths was never really my thing.' Colour shaded her cheeks. 'But I always had pretty good marks in English. I think I'm more of a creative person.'

At a loss to understand how the conversation had turned to school reports, Casper refocused his mind, the gravity of the situation bearing down on him. 'Do you have any idea what you've done?'

Biting her lip, she looked away for a few seconds, then met his gaze again. 'You're talking about the fact I kissed you in front of the window, aren't you?' Her glance was apologetic.

'It's probably a waste of time saying this, but I really *am* sorry. I honestly had no idea how much trouble that would cause. You have to remember I'm not used to the press. I don't know how they operate.'

'But you're learning fast.' Her attempt at innocence simply fed his irritation. He would have had more respect for her if she'd simply admitted what she'd done.

But no confession was forthcoming. Instead she gave a tentative smile. 'Well, I've been amazed by how persistent they are, if that's what you're saying. That newspaper you're holding—' she glanced at it warily '—is there another story today? I don't know how you stand it. Do you eventually just get used to it?'

Her friendliness was as unexpected as it was inappropriate, and Casper wondered what on earth she thought she was doing. Did she really think she could act the way she had and still enjoy civilised conversation?

The newspaper still in his hand, he strolled to the window of the flat and looked down into the street. How long did they have? By rights the press should already have found them. 'I've had people looking for you.'

'Really?' Her face brightened slightly, as if he'd just delivered good news. 'I sort of assumed— Well, I thought you'd forgotten about me.'

'It would be hard to forget about you,' he bit out, 'Given that your name has been in the press every day for the past fortnight.'

'Oh.' There was a faint colour in her cheeks, and disappointment flickered in her eyes, as if she'd been hoping for a different reason. 'The publicity is awful, isn't it? That's why I'm not at my flat. I didn't *want* them to find me.'

'Of course you didn't. That would have ruined everything, wouldn't it?' He waited for her to crumble and confess, but instead she looked confused.

'You sound *really* angry. I don't really blame you, although to be honest I thought you'd be used to all the attention by now. D-do you want to sit down or something, sir?' Stammering nervously, she swept the sleeping bag from the sofa, along with a jumper, an empty box of tissues and a pair of sheer black stockings that could have come straight from the pages of an erotic magazine. Bending over revealed another few inches of her impossibly long legs, and Casper's body heated to a level entirely inconsistent with a cold February day in London.

'I don't want to sit down,' he said thickly, appalled to discover that despite her sins all he really wanted to do was spread her flat and re-enact their last encounter.

Her gaze clashed with his and everything she was holding tumbled onto the floor. 'C—can I get you a drink? Coffee? It's just instant—nothing fancy—' Her voice was husky and laced with overtones that suggested coffee was the last thing on her mind. Colour darkened her cheeks and she dragged her gaze from his, clearly attempting to deny the chemistry that had shifted the temperature of the room from Siberian to scorching.

'Nothing.'

'No. I don't suppose there's much here that would interest you.' She tugged at the tee-shirt again. 'Sorry—this whole situation is a bit surreal. To be honest, I can't believe you're here. I mean, you're a prince and I'm—'

'Pinching yourself?'

'It is weird,' she confided nervously. 'And a bit awkward, I suppose.'

'Awkward?' Shocked out of his contemplation of her mouth by her inappropriate choice of adjective, Casper turned on her. 'We've gone way beyond *awkward*.' His tone was savage, and he saw her take several steps backwards. 'What were you thinking? What was going on in that manipulative female brain of yours? Was it all about making a quick profit? Or did you have an even more ambitious objective?'

The sudden loss of colour from her face made the delicate freckles on her nose seem more pronounced. 'Sorry?'

Casper slammed the newspaper front-page up onto the coffee table. 'I hope you don't live to regret what you've done.'

He watched as she scanned the headline, her soft, pink lips moving silently as she read: *Prince's Baby Bliss*. Then her eyes flew to his in startled horror. 'Oh, no.'

'Is it true?' The expression on her face killed any hope that the press had been fabricating the story to increase their circulation figures. 'You're pregnant?'

'Oh my God—how can they have found out? How can they possibly know?'

'Is it true?' His thunderous demand made her flinch.

'Yes, it's true!' Covering her face with her hands, she plopped onto the sofa. 'But this isn't how— I mean, I haven't even got my head round it myself.' Her hands dropped. 'How did they find out?'

'They rely on greedy people willing to sell sleaze.' The bite in his tone seemed to penetrate her shock, and she wrapped her arms around her waist in a gesture of self-protection.

'I take it from that remark that you think I told them. And I can see this looks bad, but—' She broke off, her voice hoarse. 'It wasn't me. Honestly. I haven't spoken to the press. Not once.'

'Then how do you explain the fact that the story is plastered over the front pages of every European newspaper? The palace press-office was inundated with calls yesterday from journalists wanting a comment on the happy news that I am at last to be a father.' He frowned slightly, disconcerted by her extreme pallor. 'You're very pale.'

'And that's surprising? Have you *read* that thing?' Her

voice rose. 'It's all right for you. You're used to this. Your face is always on the front of newspapers, but this is all new to me, and I hate it! My life doesn't feel like my own any more. *Everyone* is talking about me.'

'That's the usual consequence of selling your story to a national newspaper.'

But she didn't appear to have heard him. Her eyes were fixed on the newspaper as though he'd introduced a deadly snake into her flat.

'It must have been Eddie,' she whispered, her lips barely moving. 'He knew about the baby. He's the only one who could have done this.'

'You disgust me.' Casper didn't bother softening his tone, and shock flared in her green eyes.

'*I* disgust *you*?' She couldn't have looked more devastated if he'd told her that a much-loved pet had died. 'But you—I mean, we—'

'We had sex.' Casper delivered the words with icy cool, devoid of sympathy as yet another layer of colour fled from her cheeks. 'And you used that to your advantage.'

'Wait a minute—just slow down. How can any of this be to my advantage?' Gingerly she reached for the newspaper and scanned the story. Then she dropped it as though she'd been burned. 'This is *awful*. They know *everything*. Really private stuff, like my dad leaving home when I was seven and the fact I was taken into care, stuff I don't talk about.' Her voice broke. 'My whole life is laid out on the front page for everyone to read. And it's just *horrible*.' Her distress appeared to be genuine and Casper felt a flicker of exasperation.

'What exactly did you think would happen? That they'd only print nice stories about you? Nice stories don't sell newspapers.'

'*I didn't tell them!*' She rose to her feet, her tousled hair spilling over her shoulders. 'It *must* have been Eddie.'

'And what was his excuse? He didn't feel ready for fatherhood? Was he only too eager to shift the responsibility onto some other guy?'

Puzzled, she stared at him for a moment, and then her mouth fell open. 'This isn't Eddie's baby, if that's what you're implying!'

'Really?' Casper raised an eyebrow in sardonic appraisal. 'Then you have been busy. Exactly how many men were you sleeping with a few weeks ago? Or can't you remember?'

Hot colour poured into her cheeks, but this time it was anger, not embarrassment. 'You!' Her voice shook with emotion and her eyes were fierce. 'You're the only man I was sleeping with. The only man I've *ever* slept with. And you know it.'

Casper remembered that shockingly intense and intimate moment when he'd been *sure* she was a virgin. Then he reviewed the facts. 'At the time I really fell for that one. But virgins don't have hot, frantic sex with a guy within moments of meeting him, *tesoro*. Apart from that major miscalculation on your part, you were pretty convincing.'

She lifted her hands to her burning face. 'That was the first time I'd ever—'

'Fleeced a billionaire prince?' Helpfully, Casper finished her sentence, and her eyes widened.

'You think I set some sort of trap for you? You think I *faked* being a virgin? For heaven's sake—what sort of women do you mix with?'

Not wanting to dwell on that subject, Casper watched her with cool disdain. 'I know this isn't my baby,' he said flatly. 'It isn't possible.'

'You mean because it was just the once.' She sank back onto the sofa, stumbling over the words. 'I know it's unlikely, but that's what's happened. And you might be a prince, but that doesn't give you the right to speak to me as though I'm—'

Unsure of herself, her eyes slid to the door, as if she were worried the security guards might arrest her for treason.

'What are you, Holly? What's the correct name for a woman who sleeps with a guy for money?'

Her body was trembling. 'I haven't asked you for money.'

'I'm sure what you earned from the newspapers will keep you and *Eddie* going for a while. What did you have planned—monthly bulletins to keep the income going? *Now* I understand why you thanked me.'

'Th—thanked you?'

'As you kissed me in the window.' His mouth curved into a cynical smile. 'You thanked me for what I'd given you.'

'But that was—' She broke off and gave a little shake of her head. 'I was feeling *really* low that day. The reason you walked over to me in the first place was because I was crying. And I thanked you because you made me feel good about myself. Nothing else. Up to that point in my life, I knew nothing about the way the media worked.'

'You expect me to believe that it's coincidence that you've been in hiding for over two weeks? You were holding out for the big one. The exclusive to end all exclusives.' He saw panic in her eyes and felt a flash of satisfaction. 'I don't think you have any idea what you've done.'

'What *I've* done? You were there, too! You were part of this, and I think you're being *totally* unfair!' Her hands were clasped by her sides, her fingers opening and closing nervously. 'I'm having *your* baby. Frankly, that in itself is enough to make me feel a bit wobbly, without you standing there accusing me of being a—a—' She choked on the word. 'And, as if that isn't bad enough, you're telling me you don't believe it's yours!'

'You want to know what I think?' His tone was the same temperature as his heart—icy cold. 'I think you were already pregnant when you turned on the tears and had sex with me on my table. That's why you were crying. I think you were panicking about how you'd cope with a baby on a waitress's salary. And you saw me as a lucrative solution. All you had to do was pretend to be a virgin, and then I wouldn't argue a paternity claim.'

'That's all rubbish! I had sex with you because—' She broke off and gave a hysterical laugh. 'I don't *know* why I had sex with you! Frankly the whole episode was pretty shocking.'

Their eyes collided, and shared memories of that moment passed between them like a shaft of electricity.

His eyes dropped to her wide, lush mouth and he found himself remembering how she'd tasted and felt. Even though he now realised that she couldn't possibly have been a virgin, he still wanted her with almost indecent desperation.

'*Stop* looking at me like that,' she whispered, and Casper gave a twisted smile, acknowledging the chemistry that held them both fast. Invisible chains, drawing them together like prisoners doomed to the same fate.

'You should be pleased I'm looking at you like that,' he drawled softly, 'Because good sex is probably the only thing we have going for us.'

Even as his mind was withdrawing, his hands wanted to reach out and haul her hard against him. He saw her eyes darken to deep emerald, saw her throat move as she murmured a denial.

'I honestly don't know what's going on here,' she muttered. 'But I think you'd better leave.'

Somehow her continuing claim at innocence made the whole episode all the more distasteful, and the face of another woman flashed into his brain—a woman so captivating that he'd been blind to everything except her extraordinary beauty. 'What sort of heartless bitch would lie about the identity of her baby's father?' Ruthlessly he pushed the memories down, his anger trebling. 'Don't you have a conscience?' His words sucked the last of the colour from her cheeks.

'Get out!' Her voice sounded strange. High pitched. Robotic. 'I don't care if you're a prince, just get out!' Her legs were shaking and her face was as white as an Arctic snow-field. 'I was *so* pleased to see you. That day when you comforted me when I was upset—I thought you were a really nice, decent person. A bit scary, perhaps, but basically nice. When I opened the door and saw you standing there I actually thought you'd come to see if I was OK—can you believe that? And now I feel like a complete fool. Because you weren't thinking about me. You were thinking about yourself. So just go! Go back to your palace, or your castle, or wherever it is you live.' The wave of her hand suggested she didn't care where he lived. 'And do whatever it is you want to do.'

'You've robbed me of that option.'

'Why? Even if the world does think I'm having your baby, *so what*? Don't tell me you're worried about your reputation. You're the playboy prince.' There was hurt in her voice, that same voice that only moments earlier had been soft and gentle. 'Since when has reputation mattered to you? When you have sex with a woman, everyone just smiles and says what a stud you are. I'm sure the fact that you've fathered a child will gain you some major testosterone points. Walk away, Your Highness. Isn't that what you usually do?'

'You just don't get it, do you?' His voice was thickened and raw. 'You have no idea what you've done.'

What exactly *had* she done?

Appalled, Holly stared at him.

The anger in his face was real enough. It was clear that he genuinely believed that he couldn't be the father of her baby. And her only proof was the fact that she'd been a virgin.

But he didn't believe her, did he?

And could she blame him for that? It was true that she hadn't behaved like a virgin. The entire encounter had been one long burst of explosive chemistry. It had been the only time in her life that she'd been out of control.

And that chemistry was back in the room, racking up the tension between them to intolerable levels, the electricity sparking between them like a live cable. His gaze dropped to her lips and she saw in his eyes that his mind was in exactly the same place as hers.

It was like a chain reaction. His glance, her heartbeat, harsh breathing—*her or him?*—and tension—tension like she'd never experienced before.

Streaks of colour accentuated his aristocratic cheekbones and he stepped towards her at exactly the same moment she moved towards him. The attraction was so fierce and frantic that when she heard a ringing sound she actually wondered whether an alarm had gone off.

Then she realised that it was the phone.

Hauling his gaze from hers, Casper inhaled sharply. '*Don't* answer that.'

Still reeling from the explosion of sexual excitement, Holly doubted she'd be capable of answering it even if she'd wanted to. Her legs were trembling and the rhythm of her breathing was all wrong.

She watched dizzily as he crossed the room and lifted a bunch of papers from the printer.

Mouth grim, shoulders tense, he leafed through them and then lifted his gaze to hers. 'What were you doing? Profiling your target?'

Having completely forgotten that she'd actually printed out some of the sheets on him, including a particularly flattering picture, Holly suddenly wished she could sink through the floor. 'I—I was looking you up.' What else could she say? She could hardly deny it, given that he was holding the evidence of her transgression in his hands.

'Of course you were.' He gave a derisive smile. 'I'm sure you wanted to know just how well you'd done. So, now we've cleared that up, let's drop the pretence of innocence, shall we?'

'OK, so I'm human!' Her face scarlet, her knees trembling, Holly ran damp palms over her tee-shirt, wishing she could go and change into something else. He looked like something out of a glossy magazine, and she was dressed in her most comfortable tee-shirt that dated back at least six years. 'I admit that I wanted to find out stuff about you. You were my first lover.'

'So you're sticking to that story.' He dropped the papers back onto the desk and Holly lifted her chin.

'It's *not* a story. It's the truth.'

'I just hope you don't regret what you've done when you have two hundred camera lenses trained on your face and the world's press yelling questions at you.'

She shrank at the thought. 'That isn't going to happen.'

'Let me tell you something about the life you've chosen, Holly.' Tall and powerfully built, he looked as out of place in her flat as a thoroughbred racehorse in a donkey derby. From the stylish trousers and long cashmere coat, to the look of cool confidence on his impossibly handsome face, everything about him shrieked of enormous wealth and privilege. 'Everywhere you go there will be a photographer stalking you, and most of the time you won't even know they're there until you see the picture next day. Everyone is going to want a piece of you, and that means you can no longer have friends, because even friends have their price and you'll never know who you can trust.'

'I don't need to hear this—'

'Yes, you do. You won't be able to smile without someone

demanding to know why you're happy and you won't be able to frown without someone saying that you're suffering from depression and about to be admitted to a clinic.' He hammered home the facts with lethal precision. 'You'll either be too thin or too fat—'

'Too fat, *obviously*.' Heart pounding, Holly sank down onto the sofa. 'Enough. You can stop now. I get the picture.'

'I'm describing your new life, Holly. The life you've chosen.'

There was a tense, electric silence and she licked her lips nervously. 'What are you saying?'

'You have made sure that the whole world believes that this is my baby. And, as a result, the whole world is now waiting for me to take appropriate action.'

Pacing back over to the window, he stared down into the street.

Holly had a sudden sick feeling in her stomach. 'A—appropriate action? What do you mean?'

There was a deathly silence and then he turned, his eyes empty of emotion. 'You're going to marry me, Holly.' The savage bite in his tone was a perfect match for the chill in his eyes. 'And you may think that I've just made your wildest dreams come true, but I can assure you that you're about to embark on your worst nightmare.'

CHAPTER FOUR

'So WHEN do you think he'll be back?' Holly paced across the priceless rug in the Georgian manor house. 'I mean, he's been gone for two weeks, Emilio! I haven't even had a chance to talk to him since that day at the flat.' *The day he'd announced that she was going to marry him.* 'Not that this house isn't fabulous and luxurious and all that—but he virtually kidnapped me!'

'On the contrary, His Highness was merely concerned for your safety,' Emilio said gently. 'The press had discovered where you were and the situation was about to turn extremely ugly. It was imperative that we extracted you from there as fast as possible.'

Remembering the crowd of reporters that had suddenly converged on Nicky's flat, and the slick security operation that had ensured their escape, Holly rubbed her fingers over her forehead. 'Yes, all right, I accept that, but that doesn't explain why he hasn't been in touch. When is he planning to come back? We need to *talk*.'

There was so much she needed to say to him.

When she'd opened the door to the flat and seen the prince standing there, her first reaction had been one of pure joy. For a crazy moment she'd actually thought that he was there because he'd spent the past two weeks thinking about her and decided that he needed to see her again. Her mind had raced forward, imagining all sorts of unrealistic scenarios that she was now too embarrassed to even recall. Her crazy, stupid brain had actually started to believe that extraordinary things *could* happen to someone ordinary like her.

And then he'd strode into her flat like a Roman conqueror neutralising the enemy.

Remembering everything he'd said to her, she felt a rush of misery.

He didn't believe it was his baby and the injustice of that still stung. True, she wasn't exactly proud of the way she'd behaved, but it seemed he'd conveniently forgotten his own role in the affair.

And as for his proposal of marriage—well, that unexpected twist had more than kept her mind occupied over the past two weeks.

Had he meant it? *Was he serious?* And, if he was serious, what was her response going to be?

It was the most difficult decision she'd ever had to make, and the arguments for and against had gone round and round in her head like a fairground carousel. Marrying him meant being with a man who didn't know her or trust her, but *not* marrying him meant denying her baby a father.

And that was the one thing she'd promised herself would never happen to any child of hers.

Reminding herself of that fact, Holly straightened her shoulders and stared across the beautifully landscaped gardens that surrounded the manor.

Their baby was *not* going to grow up thinking that his father had abandoned him. She swallowed down the lump that sprang into her throat. *Their baby was not going to be the only child in school not making a Father's Day card.*

Which meant that her answer had to be yes, regardless of everything else.

What else mattered? Hopefully over time the prince would realise how wrong he had been about her, and once the baby was born it would be a simple matter to prove paternity. Perhaps, then, their relationship could develop.

Realising that Emilio was still watching her, she felt a squeeze of guilt. 'I'm sorry. I'm being really selfish. Is there any news about your little boy? Have you phoned the hospital this morning?'

Remembering just how taciturn and uncommunicative the prince's Head of Security had been when they'd first met, she was relieved that he'd responded to her attempts to be friendly.

'His temperature is down,' he told her. 'And he's responding to the antibiotics, although they're still not sure what it was.'

'Your poor wife must be so tired. And little Tomasso must be missing you. I remember having chicken pox just after—' *Just after her father had left.* The feelings of abandonment were as fresh as ever and Holly walked across to him and touched his arm. 'Go home, Emilio,' she urged. 'Your wife would like the support and your little boy would dearly love to see his daddy.'

'That's out of the question, madam.'

'Why? I'm not going anywhere. I feel really guilty that you're stuck here with me. If it weren't for me, you'd be back home in Santallia.'

Emilio cleared his throat. 'If I may say so, your company has been a pleasure, madam. And you've been a great comfort since Tomasso was ill. I'll never forget your kindness that first night when he was first taken into hospital and you stayed up and kept me company.'

'I've never been thrashed so many times at poker in my life. It's a good job I don't have any money to lose,' Holly said lightly. 'The moment the prince turns up, you're going home.'

But what if he didn't turn up?

Perhaps he didn't want to marry her any more.

Perhaps he'd changed his mind.

Or perhaps he'd just imprisoned her here, away from the press, until the story died down? After all, he believed that she'd talked to the press. Was he keeping her here just to ensure her silence?

Her thoughts in turmoil, Holly spent the rest of the morning on the computer in the wood-panelled study that overlooked the ornamental lake. Resisting the temptation to do another trawl of the Internet for mentions of Prince Casper, she concentrated on what she was doing and then wandered down to the kitchen to eat lunch with the head chef and other members of the prince's household staff.

'Something smells delicious, Pietro.' Loving the cosy atmosphere of the kitchen, she warmed her hands on the Aga. Naturally chatty by nature, and delighted to find herself suddenly part of this close community, Holly had lost no time in getting to know everyone living and working in the historic manor house.

'It's a pleasure to cook for someone who enjoys her food, madam,' the chef said, smiling warmly as he gestured towards some pastries cooling on a wire rack. 'Try one and give me your verdict. You're eating for two, remember.'

'Well, I'd rather not be the size of two. I'm not sure I'm meant to be developing cravings this early, but already I don't think I can live without your *pollo alla limone*.' Holly still felt slightly self-conscious that everyone clearly felt so possessive about her baby. She bit into a pastry and moaned with genuine appreciation. 'Oh, please—this is *sublime*. Truly, Pietro. I've never tasted anything this good in my life before. What is it?'

Pietro blossomed. 'Goat's cheese, with a secret combination of herbs—' He broke off as Emilio entered the room and Holly smiled.

'Emilio, thank goodness.' She took another nibble of pastry. 'You're just in time to stop me eating the lot by myself.'

'Miss Phillips.' The bodyguard's eyes were misted, and Holly dropped the pastry, alarmed to see this controlled man so close to the edge.

'What? What? Has something happened? Did the hospital ring?'

'How can I ever thank you? You are—' Emilio's voice was gruff and he cleared his throat. 'A very special person. My wife called—she just received a delivery of beautiful toys. How you managed to arrange that so quickly I have no idea. Tomasso is thrilled.'

'He liked his parcel?' Relieved that nothing awful had happened, Holly retrieved the pastry and threw Pietro an apologetic glance. 'Sorry. Slight overreaction there on my part. Just in case you can't tell, I briefly considered drama as a career. So he liked the toys? I couldn't decide between the fire engine and the police car.'

'So you bought both.' Emilio shook his head. 'It was unbelievably generous of you, madam.'

'It was the least I could do given I'm the reason you're not with him.' Holly frowned and glanced towards the window. 'What's that noise? Are we being invaded?'

Still clutching the spoon, Pietro peered over her shoulder. 'It's a helicopter, madam.' His cheerful smile faded and he straightened his chef's whites and looked nervously at Emilio. 'His Royal Highness has returned.'

Chilled by the wind, and battling with a simmering frustration that two weeks of self-imposed absence hadn't cured, Casper sprang from the helicopter and strode towards the house.

Although he'd managed to put several countries and a stretch of water between them, he'd failed to wipe Holly from his thoughts. Even the combined demands of complex state business and the successful conclusion to negotiations guaranteeing billions of dollars of foreign investment hadn't succeeded in pressing the stop button on the non-stop erotic fantasy that had dominated his mind since that day at the rugby.

Even while part of him was angry with her for her ruthless manipulation, another part of his mind was thinking about her incredible legs. He knew she was a liar, but what really stayed in his head was her enticing smile and the taste of her mouth.

And that was fine. Because her manipulation had given him a solution to his problem.

As he approached the house, two uniformed soldiers that he didn't recognise opened the doors for him, backs ramrod straight, eyes forward.

Casper stopped. '*Where* is Emilio?'

One of them cleared his throat. 'I believe he is in the kitchen, Your Highness.'

'The *kitchen*?' Casper approached a nervous footman. 'Since when did my kitchen represent a major security risk?'

'I believe he is with Miss Phillips and the rest of the staff, sir.'

Having personally delivered the order that Emilio should watch her, Casper relaxed a fraction. Contemplating the difficult two weeks Holly must have had with his battle-hardened security chief, he almost smiled. Emilio had been known to drive soldiers to tears, but he felt no sympathy for her. After all, *she* was the one who had decided to name him as the father of her unborn baby. She deserved everything she had coming to her.

Striding towards the kitchen with that thought uppermost in his mind, he pushed open the door, astonished to hear the rare sound of Emilio's laughter, and even more surprised to see his usually reserved Head of Security straighten a clasp in Holly's vibrant curls in an unmistakeably affectionate manner.

Holly was smiling gratefully and Casper felt like an interloper, intruding on a private moment. Experiencing a wild surge of quite inexplicable anger, he stood in the doorway.

The rest of the staff were eating and chatting, and Emilio was the first to notice him. 'Your Highness.' Evidently shocked at seeing the prince in the kitchen, he stiffened respectfully. 'I was just about to come upstairs and meet you.'

'But you had other things to distract you,' Casper observed tightly, strolling into the kitchen and taking in the empty plates and the smell of baking in a single, sweeping glance.

Without waiting for him to issue the order, the various members of his household staff rose to their feet and hastily left the room.

Pietro hesitated and then he, too, melted away without being asked.

Only Emilio didn't move.

Casper slowly undid the buttons on his long coat. 'I'm sure you have many demands on your time, Emilio,' he said softly, but the bodyguard stood still.

'My priority is protecting Miss Phillips, sir.'

'That's true.' Casper removed his coat and dropped it over the back of the nearest chair. 'But not,' he said gently, 'From me.'

Emilio hesitated and glanced at Holly. 'You have the alarm I gave you, madam, should you need me for anything.'

There was no missing the affection in Holly's smile. 'I'll be fine, Emilio, but thank you.'

Watching this interchange with speechless incredulity, Casper was engulfed by a wave of anger so violent that it shook him.

Against his will he was transported back eight years, and suddenly he was seeing another woman smiling at another man.

Pain cut through the red mist of his anger, and he glanced down at his hand and realised that he was gripping the back of the chair so tightly his knuckles were white.

'Your Highness?' Holly's voice penetrated his brain. 'Are you all right?'

Locking down his thoughts with ruthless focus, Casper transferred his gaze to Holly, but the bitter taste of betrayal remained. 'Emilio is a married man. *Do you have no sense of decency?*'

'I—I'm sorry?'

'I've no doubt his wife and child will be sorry, too.'

Her expression changed from concern to anger. 'How dare you? How dare you turn everything beautiful into something sordid. Emilio and I are friends—nothing more.' She lifted a hand to her head. 'Oh God, I can't believe you'd even think— *what is the matter with you?* It's almost as if you believe the worst of people so that you can't be disappointed.'

Was that what he did? Stunned by that accusation, Casper felt as cold as marble. 'Despite a short acquaintance, Emilio would clearly die for you.'

'We've been living in each other's pockets for two weeks— what did you expect? On second thoughts, don't answer that.' She took a deep breath. 'Look, maybe you don't know me well enough to know *I* wouldn't do that, but you know Emilio. He was telling me that he's been with you for twenty years! How could you think that of someone so close to you?'

Because he knew only too well that it was the people closest to you who were capable of the greatest betrayal. And causing the greatest pain.

Casper released his grip on the chair and flexed his bloodless fingers.

'Whatever the nature of your relationship, Emilio is in charge of my security. He can't perform his duties effectively if he's flirting in the kitchen.'

'Nor can he perform his duties on an empty stomach. We were eating lunch, not flirting. Or aren't your staff allowed to eat lunch?'

'You're not a member of my staff.' Casper glanced round the homely kitchen. 'And there is a formal dining-room upstairs for your use.'

'It's as big as a barn, and I don't want to eat on my own. Where's the fun in that?' Her expression made it clear that she thought it should have been obvious that eating alone was a stupid idea. 'Sorry, but sitting alone at one end of a vast table is a bit sad. I prefer the company of real people, not paintings.'

'So you've been distracting Emilio.'

'Actually, yes. I've been trying to take his mind off his worries.' Her shoulders stiffened defensively. 'Did *you* know that his little boy has been taken into hospital? And he's been stuck here with me, fretting himself to death while—'

The anger drained from Casper. 'His son is ill?'

'Yes, and he—'

'What is wrong with the child?'

'Well, it started with a very high temperature. I don't think his wife was too worried at that point, so she gave him the usual stuff but nothing seemed to bring his temperature down. Then she was putting him to bed when—'

'*What is wrong with the child?*' Impatient for the facts, Casper sliced through her chatter, and she gave him a hurt look.

'I'm *trying* to tell you! You're the one who keeps interrupting.'

Attempting to control his temper, Casper inhaled deeply. 'Summarise.'

'I *was* summarising.' Affronted, she glared at him. 'So, his temperature went up and up and then he had a fit, which apparently can be normal for a toddler because they're hopeless at controlling their temperature, and so they took him in and did some tests and—'

'That isn't a summary, it's a three-act play!' Exasperated, Casper strode across to her and placed a finger over her mouth. 'Stop talking for one minute and answer my question in no more than three words—*what is wrong with Emilio's son?*'

Her lips were soft against his finger and he felt the warmth of her breath as she parted her lips to respond.

'Virus,' she muttered, and Casper withdrew his hand as if he'd been scalded, taken aback by the rush of sexual heat that engulfed him. The urge to take possession of her luscious mouth was so strong that he took a step backwards.

'And is his condition improving?'

'Yes, but—'

'That's all I need to know.' Needing space, Casper turned and strode purposefully towards the door, but she hurtled after him and caught his arm.

'No! No, it isn't all you need to know! "Virus" and "improving" doesn't give you a clue about what it's been like for poor Emilio! Those are just facts, but it's the feelings that matter.' She waved an arm. 'He was stuck here with me while they were doing all these tests, and he was worried sick and—' She broke off, clearly unsettled by his silence. 'Don't you *care*? You're *so* cold! Y-you just stand there looking at me, not saying anything. What do you think it's been like for Emilio being stuck here with me while his little boy is ill?'

Casper scanned her flushed cheeks and lifted an eyebrow in sardonic mockery. 'Noisy?'

Her hand fell from his arm. 'I'm only talking too much because you make me nervous.'

Only both of them knew that there was more than nerves shimmering between them.

It was there in her eyes—awareness, excitement, longing.

Distancing himself, Casper yanked open the door. 'Then I'll give you a moment to collect yourself.' He left the room, issued a set of instructions to a waiting security-guard, and then returned to the kitchen to find Holly pacing the room in agitation.

She threw him a reproachful look. 'All right, maybe I do talk a lot, but that's just the way I am, and nobody's perfect. And you're the one who left me here without even telling me when you'd be back!' Her chin lifted. 'Did you think I'd sit in silence for two weeks?'

Casper strode over to the large table and poured himself a glass of water from the jug on the table. 'It was fairly obvious to me from our last meeting that you and silence have never been intimately acquainted.'

'Well, I don't expect you to understand, because you're obviously the strong silent type who uses words like each one costs a fortune, but I like people. I like talking to them.'

And they liked talking to her, if the buzz of conversation around the kitchen table had been anything to go by.

And she knew about Emilio's son.

Casper tried to remember a time when people had been that open with him, and realised that they never had been.

Even before tragedy had befallen the royal family of Santallia, he'd lived a life of privileged isolation. Because of his position, people were rarely open and honest.

And he'd learned the hard way that trust was one gift he couldn't afford to bestow.

Because of his error of judgement, his country had suffered.

And now he had the chance to make amends. *To give the people what they wanted.*

And as for the rest of it—physically the chemistry between them was explosive, and that was all he required.

He drank deeply and then put the glass down, his eyes locking with hers.

Immediately engulfed by a dangerous tension, Casper tried to analyse what it was about her that he found so irresistibly sexy.

Not her dress sense, that was for sure. Her ancient jeans had a rip in the knees, her pale-pink jumper was obviously an old favourite, and the colour in her cheeks had more to do with the heat coming from the Aga than artful use of make-up.

Accustomed to women who groomed themselves to within an inch of their lives, he found her lack of artifice oddly refreshing.

Her beauty wasn't the result of expensive cosmetics or the hand of a skilled surgeon. Holly was vibrant, passionate and desperately sexy, and all he wanted to do was flatten her to the table and re-enact every sizzling moment of their first meeting.

Exasperated and baffled by the strength of that inappropriate urge, Casper dragged his eyes back to her face. 'Emilio failed to pass on the message that you were to buy a new wardrobe.'

'No. He told me.' She hooked her thumbs into the waistband of her jeans and the movement revealed a tantalising glimpse of smooth, flat stomach. 'I just didn't need anything. What do I need a new wardrobe for? I've spent the mornings helping Ivy and the afternoons helping Jim prune the trees in the orchard.'

'*Who* is Ivy?'

'Your housekeeper. She lost her husband eight months ago and she's been very down, but she has started joining us for lunch, and she's been talking about— Sorry.' She raised a hand in wary apology. 'I forgot you just want facts. OK, facts. I can do that. Ivy. Housekeeper. Depressed. Improving.' She ticked them off her fingers. 'How's that? You're smiling, so I must have done OK.'

Surprised to discover that he was indeed smiling, Casper shook his head slowly. 'Your gift for conversation has clearly given you a great deal of information about my staff.'

'It's important to understand people you work with.'

'When I left you here, my intention was not for you to work alongside the staff.'

'I had to do something with my day. You gave orders that I couldn't leave the premises. I was trapped here.'

'You were brought here for your own safety.'

'Was I?' Her brilliant green eyes glowed bright with scepticism. 'Or was I brought here for *your* safety, so that I couldn't talk to the press?'

'That particular boat has already sailed,' Casper said tightly, his temper flaring at her untimely reminder of just how effectively she'd manipulated the media. 'You're here for your protection.'

'Do you have any idea how weird that sounds?' Holly glanced pointedly at the rip in her jeans. 'I mean, one minute I'm a waitress who no one notices unless they want to complain about their food, and the next I'm someone who needs twenty-four-hour protection.'

'You're carrying the heir to the throne.'

'And that's all that matters?' She tilted her head to one side, studying his expression. 'You'll put aside your personal feelings for me because of the baby?'

What personal feelings?

Emotion had no place in his life.

On one previous occasion he'd allowed himself to be ruled by emotion and the consequences had been devastating.

As far as he was concerned, his relationship with Holly was a business transaction, nothing more.

Casper stared into her anxious green eyes, wondering why she didn't look more triumphant.

She'd successfully secured a future for herself and her child.

Or was she suddenly realising just how high a price she'd paid for that particular social leap?

'I don't want to discuss this again.' Crushing any future urge on her part to dwell on the unfortunate circumstances of their wedding, Casper strolled forward, realising that he hadn't yet revealed the reason for his return.

'Y—you're a bit crabby. Perhaps you need to eat,' she said helpfully, scooping up a plate from the table. 'Try one of Pietro's pastries. It's a new recipe and they're really delicious.'

'I'm not hungry.' His intention had just been to deliver his orders and then spend the afternoon catching up on official papers. He hadn't expected to be drawn into a discussion.

Nor had he expected an ongoing battle with his libido.

'Just taste them.' Apparently unaware of his reluctance, she broke off a piece of the pastry and lifted it to his lips. 'They're fresh out of the oven. Try.'

Drowning in her subtle floral scent and her smile, Casper's senses reeled and he grasped for control. 'I have things to tell you.'

'Eat first.'

Casper ate the pastry and wished he hadn't, because as his lips touched her fingers again he was immediately plunged into an erotic, sensual world that featured Holly as the leading lady in a scene dominated by scented oils and silk sheets.

She withdrew her hand slowly, her eyes darkening as they both silently acknowledged the dangerous sexual charge that suffused every communication they shared.

'What is it you need to tell me, Your Highness?'

'Casper.'

For the space of a heartbeat, she looked at him and then she gave a twisted smile. 'I don't think so. I'm not comfortable enough with you. Maybe it's just because you've had a long journey, but you're very cold. Intimidating. I feel as though you're going to say "off with her head" any minute.'

'You can't call me Your Highness in the wedding ceremony.'

Shock flared in her eyes. 'I sort of assumed the wedding was off. You haven't *once* phoned me whilst you've been away.'

Casper thought of the number of times he'd reached for the phone before he'd realised what he was doing. 'I had nothing to say.'

Holly lifted her hands and made a sound that was somewhere between a sob and laughter. 'Well, if you had nothing to say to me in two weeks, it doesn't bode well for a lifetime together, does it? But I do have things I want to say to you.' She drew in a breath. 'Starting with your offer of marriage. I've given it a lot of thought.'

'That doesn't surprise me. I expect it's been two weeks of non-stop self-congratulation while you enjoy your new life and reflect on the future.' His cynical observation was met with appalled silence and she stared at him for a moment, her delicate features suddenly pinched and white.

Then the plate slipped from her hands and smashed on the kitchen floor, scattering china and pastry everywhere.

'How *dare* you say that? You have a real gift for saying really horrible things.' Her small hands curled into fists by her sides. *'Have you any idea how hard all of this is for me?* Well, let me tell you what my life has been like since you walked into it!

'First there is that huge picture of me on the screen so the whole world can see the size of my bottom, then the press crawl all over my life, exposing things about me that I haven't even told my closest friends and making me out to be some psycho nutcase. *Then* I discover I'm pregnant, and I was really happy about that until you showed up and told me that you didn't believe it was yours. So basically since I've met you I've been portrayed publicly as a fat, abandoned slut with no morals! How's my new life sounding so far, Your Highness? Not good—so don't *talk* to me about how I must be congratulating myself because, believe me, my confidence is at an all-time low.' Her breathing rapid, she sucked in several breaths and Casper, who detested emotional scenes, erected barriers faster than a bank being robbed.

'I warned you that—'

'I haven't finished!' She glared at him. 'You think this is an easy decision for me, but it isn't! This is our baby's future we're talking about! And, whatever you may think, I didn't plan this. Which is why I've done nothing but agonise over what to do for the past two weeks. *Obviously* I don't want to be married to a man who can't stand the sight of me, but neither do I want my baby to be without a father. It's been a horrible, *horrible* choice, and frankly I wouldn't wish it on anyone! And if you need that summarised in two words I'd pick "scary" and "sacrifice".'

In the process of formulating an exit strategy, Casper looked at her with raw incredulity. '*Sacrifice*?'

'Yes. Because, although I'm sure having a father is right for our baby, I'm *not* sure that being married to you is right for me. And there's no need to use that tone. I don't care about the prince bit, nor do I care about your castle or your bank account.' Her voice was hoarse. 'But I won't have our child growing up thinking that his father abandoned him. And that's why I'll marry you. By the time he's old enough to understand what is going on, you will have realised how wrong you are about me and given me a big, fat apology. But don't think this is easy for me. I have no wish to marry a man who can't talk about his feelings and doesn't show affection.'

Casper responded to this last declaration with genuine astonishment. 'Affection?' How could she possibly think he'd feel affection for a woman who had good as slapped him with a paternity suit?

She rolled her eyes. 'You see? Even the word makes you nervous, and that says everything, doesn't it? You were quite happy to have hot sex with me, but anything else is completely alien to you.' She covered her face with her hands, and her voice choked. 'Oh, what am I doing? How can we even *think* about getting married when there's nothing between us?'

'We share a very powerful sexual chemistry, or we wouldn't be in this position right now,' Casper responded instantly, and her hands dropped and she gave a disbelieving laugh.

'Well, that's romantic. There's no mistaking your priorities. Summarised in three words, it would be sex, sex, sex.'

'Don't underestimate the importance of sex,' Casper breathed, watching as her lips parted slightly. 'If we're going to be sharing a bed night after night, it helps that I find you attractive.' Surprisingly, his statement appeared to finally silence her.

She stared at him, her eyes wide, her lips slightly parted. Then she rubbed her hands over her jeans in a self-conscious gesture. 'You find me—attractive? Really?'

'*Obviously* your dress sense needs considerable work,' he said silkily. 'And generally speaking I'm not wild about jeans, although I have to confess that you manage to look good in them. Apart from that, and as long as you don't *ever* wear anything featuring a cartoon once you're officially sleeping in my bed, yes, I'll find you attractive.'

A laugh burst from her throat. 'I can't believe you're telling me how to dress—or that I'm listening.'

'I'm not telling you how to dress. I'm telling you how to keep me interested. It's up to you whether you follow the advice or not.'

'And that's supposed to be enough? A marriage based on sex?' She shook her head slowly. 'It doesn't make sense. I still don't understand why, if you genuinely don't believe this is your baby, you'd be willing to marry me. Instead of facts, why don't you give me feelings?'

He didn't have feelings.

He hadn't allowed himself feelings for eight years.

'Given all the research you did on the royal house of Santallia, I would think you'd be aware of the reasons. I'm the last of the line. I'm expected to produce an heir. To the outside world, it appears that I've done that.'

'You're giving me facts again,' she said softly. 'How do you *feel*, Your Highness?'

Ignoring her question, Casper paced over to the window, his tension levels soaring. 'The people of Santallia are currently in a state of celebration. The moment the story broke on the news, they were making plans for the royal wedding. There will be fireworks and state banquets. Apparently my popularity rating has soared. School children have already been queuing outside the palace with home-made cards and teddies for the baby—little girls with stars in their eyes.' He turned, looking for signs of remorse. 'Are you feeling guilty yet, Holly? Is your conscience pricking you?'

'Teddies?' Instead of retreating in the face of his harsh words, she appeared visibly moved by the picture he'd painted. Her hand slid to her stomach in an instinctively protective gesture, and he saw tears of emotion glisten in her eyes. 'They're that pleased? It *is* wonderful that everyone is longing for you to get married and have a baby. You must be very touched that they care so much.'

'It's because they care so much that we're standing here now.'

Her gaze held his. 'So, if they wanted you to have a baby so badly, and you're so keen to please them, why haven't you done it before? Why haven't you married and given them an heir?' She broke off abruptly and he knew from the guilty flush on her cheeks that her research had included details about his past relationships.

He could almost see her mind working, thinking that she knew what was going on in his.

Fortunately, she didn't have a clue.

No one did. He'd made sure of that.

The truth was safely buried where it could do no harm. *And it was going to stay buried.*

Observing his lack of response, she sighed. 'What's going on in your head? I don't understand you!'

'I don't require you to understand me,' Casper said in a cool tone. 'I just require you to play the part you auditioned for. From now on, you'll just do as you're told. You'll smile when I tell you to smile and you'll walk where I tell you to walk. In return, you'll have more money than you know how to spend, and a lifestyle that most of the world will envy.'

She opened her mouth and closed it again, her face a mask of indecision. 'I don't know. I really don't know.' She stooped and started picking up pieces of broken china, as if she needed to do something with her hands. 'I thought I'd made up my mind, but now I'm not sure. How can I accept your proposal when you *scare* me? You use three words, I use thirty. I've never met anyone so emotionally detached. I—I'm just not comfortable with you.' She put the china carefully on the table.

'Comfortable?'

She rubbed her fingers over her forehead, as if her brain was aching and she wanted to soothe it. 'We'll hardly be great parents if I'm bracing myself for conflict every time you enter a room. And then there's the fact that I don't exactly fit the profile of perfect princess.'

'The only thing that matters is that the world thinks you're carrying my child. As far as the people of Santallia are concerned, that makes you the perfect princess.'

'But not *your* perfect princess. You don't seem to care who you marry. Did you love her very much?' She blurted out the question as though she couldn't stop herself, and then gave an apologetic sigh. 'I'm sorry. Perhaps I shouldn't. But you lost your fiancée, Antonia, and it's stupid to pretend that I don't know about it, because everyone knew—'

No one knew.

'Enough!' Stunned that she would dare tread on such dangerous territory, Casper sent her a warning glance, and in that single unsettling moment he had the feeling that she was looking deep inside him.

'I *am* sorry,' she said quietly. 'Because I certainly don't want to hurt you. But I don't see how we're going to have any sort of marriage when you won't let another human being get close. You create this barrier around you. Frankly, how I ever felt relaxed enough with you to have sex, I have no idea. At the moment my insides feel as though I swallowed a knotted rope.' But even as she said the words the tension in the air crackled and snapped and he saw her chest rise and fall as her breathing quickened.

The sexual chemistry was more powerful than both of them, and Casper wasn't even aware that he'd moved until his hands slid into her hair and he felt her lips parting in response to the explicit demands of his mouth.

Enforced abstinence and sexual denial had simply increased the feverish craving, and he hauled her hard against him, driven by a sensual urgency previously unknown to him.

Her lips were soft and sweet, and the scent and taste of her closed over him, drowning his senses until every rational thought was blown from his brain by a powerful rush of erotic pleasure.

She moaned with desperation, her arms winding round his neck, her body trembling against his as she arched in sensua

invitation, her abandoned response a blatant invitation to
further intimacy.

In the grip of an almost agonising arousal, Casper closed
possessive hands over her hips and lifted her onto the kitchen
table. She was pliant and shivering against him, the sensuous
movements of her body shamelessly urging him on.

And then the gentle hiss of water boiling on the Aga penetrated the red fog in his mind and he froze, his seeking hands
suddenly still as he realised what he was doing.

And where he was doing it.

Another time, another table.

Deploring the lack of control that gripped him whenever
he was with this woman, he dragged his mouth from hers
with a huge effort of will, and stared down into her dazed,
shocked eyes. Her mouth was damp and swollen from his
kiss, and she was shaking with the same wild excitement that
was driving him.

His usual self-restraint severely challenged by her addictive sexuality, Casper released his grip on her hips and
stepped backwards.

'Hopefully that should have satisfied any worries you
might have about whether or not you'll be able to relax with
me when the time comes.'

She slid off the table, her fingers fastened tightly round the
edge for support. 'Your Highness.' Her voice was smoky with
passion. 'Casper—'

'We're short on time.' Ruthlessly withdrawing from the
softness he saw in her eyes, he glanced at his watch. 'I've
flown in a team of people to help you prepare.'

'Prepare for what?' Her eyes dropped to his mouth, and it
was obvious that she wasn't really listening to what he was
saying—*that her body was still struggling with the electricity that sparked between them.*

'The wedding. We fly to Santallia tonight. We're getting married tomorrow.' He paused, allowing time for his words to sink in. 'And that's not a proposal, Holly. It's an order.'

CHAPTER FIVE

THE roar of the crowd reached deafening proportions, and the long avenue leading from the cathedral to the palace was a sea of smiling faces and waving flags.

'I can't believe the number of people,' Holly said faintly as she settled herself in the golden carriage. The rings on the third finger of her left hand felt heavy and unfamiliar, and she glanced down in disbelief. 'And I can't believe we're married. You certainly don't hang around, do you? You could have given me a little more warning.'

'Why?'

Why? Only Casper could ask that question, she thought wryly. Fiddling nervously with the enormous diamond ring, she wondered whether there was something wrong with her. Here she was, living a life straight out of the pages of a child's fairy tale, and she would have swapped the lot for some kind words from the man next to her.

Her life was moving ahead too fast for comfort.

Having spent the previous afternoon with a top dress designer who had apparently cleared her schedule to accommodate the prince's request to dress his bride, she'd been transferred by helicopter to the royal flight and then arrived in the Mediterranean principality of Santallia as the sun was setting.

'I loved The Dowager Cottage, by the way.'

'It was built for my great-great grandmother so that she could escape occasionally from the formality of life in the palace. I'm pleased you were comfortable.'

Physically, yes, but mentally...

Unable to sleep, Holly had spent most of the night sitting on the balcony that looked over the sea, thinking about what was to come.

Thinking about Casper.

Hoping she was doing the right thing.

Exhausted from thinking and worrying, she'd eventually sprawled on the bed, only to be woken by an army of dress designers, hairdressers and make-up artists prepared to turn her from gauche waitress into princess. And then she'd been driven through this same cheering crowd to the cathedral that dominated the main square of Santallia Town.

She remembered very little of the actual service—very little except the memory of Casper standing powerful and confident by her side as they exchanged vows. And at that moment she'd been filled with a conviction that she was doing the right thing.

She was giving her baby a father. A stability that she'd never had. *Roots and a family.*

How could that be a mistake?

As the carriage began to move forward down the tree-lined avenue, she glanced at the prince, only to find him studying her intently.

Startlingly handsome in his military uniform, Casper lifted her hand to his lips in an old-fashioned gesture that was greeted with cheers of approval from the crowd. 'The dress is a great improvement on ripped jeans,' he drawled, and she glanced down at herself, fingering the embroidered silk with reverential fingers.

'It's impressive what a top designer can do when required,

although I was terrified of tripping over on those steps.' She couldn't take her eyes from the cheering crowd. Everywhere she looked there were smiling faces and waving flags. 'They *really* love you.'

'They're here to see you, not me,' he said dryly, but she remembered what she'd read about him on the Internet—about his devotion to his country—and knew it wasn't true.

Although he'd never expected to rule, Prince Casper had stepped into the role, burying his own personal grief in order to bring stability to a country in turmoil.

And they loved him for it.

'Do you ever wish you weren't the prince?' The question left her lips before she could stop it and he gave a faint smile.

'You have a real gift for voicing questions that other people keep as thoughts.' He relaxed in the seat, undaunted by the crowds of well-wishers. 'And the answer is no, I don't wish it. I love my country.'

He loved his country so much that he'd marry a woman he didn't love because the people expected it.

Holly glanced at the sun-baked pavements and then at the perfect blue sky. 'It's beautiful here,' she agreed. 'When I looked out of the window this morning, the first thing I saw was the sea. It felt like being on holiday.'

'You looked very pale during the service.' His eyes lingered on her face. 'You were on your feet for a long time. I was worried that you might keel over.'

'And presumably a prostrate bride wouldn't have done anything for your public image,' she said lightly. 'I was fine.'

'I'm reliably informed that the early weeks of pregnancy are often the most exhausting.'

He'd talked to someone about her pregnancy? Her heart lurched, and it suddenly occurred to her just how little she knew about his life here. Had he been talking to a woman?

She was aware that his name had been linked with a number of European beauties. Was he…?

'No,' he drawled. 'I wasn't.'

Her eyes widened. 'I didn't say anything—'

'But you were thinking it,' he said dryly. 'And the answer is no, my conversation wasn't with a lover. It was with a doctor.'

'Oh.' She blushed scarlet, mortified that her thoughts had been so transparent, but filled with unimaginable relief that he hadn't asked another woman. 'When did you speak to a doctor?'

'While you were at Foxcourt Manor, I interviewed a handful of the top European obstetricians. It's important that you feel comfortable with your doctor. After all, you're not good with detached and cold, are you?' He gave a faint smile as he alluded to their previous conversation, and Holly was so touched that for a moment she forgot the presence of the cheering, waving crowd.

'You did that for me?'

'I don't want you upset.'

'That was incredibly thoughtful.' She wanted to ask whether he'd really done it for her or the baby, but decided that it didn't matter. The fact that he'd noticed that much about her personality was encouraging.

'You're stunning,' he murmured, his gaze lingering on her glossy mouth and dropping to the demure neckline of her dress. 'The perfect bride. And you've coped with the crowd really well. I'm proud of you.'

'Really?' Deciding not to mention the fact that she found *him* far more intimidating than any crowd, Holly relaxed for the first time in what felt like an eternity. She felt drugged by happiness and weak with relief at the change in him.

He was unusually attentive and much more approachable.

Perhaps, she mused silently, he'd finally deduced that the baby must be his.

What other explanation was there for his sudden change of attitude?

'And now you need to fulfil your first duty as royal princess.' He smiled down at her. 'Smile and wave at the crowd. They're expecting it.'

Finding it hard to believe that anyone would care whether she waved at them or not, Holly tentatively raised her hand, and the immediate roar of approval from the crowd made her blink in amazement. 'But I'm just someone ordinary,' she muttered, and the prince's eyes gleamed with wry amusement.

'That's why they love you. You're living proof that fairy-tale endings can happen to ordinary people.'

The last of her insecurities faded and Holly gave a bubble of laughter, her mood lifting still further as she saw the smiles of genuine delight on the faces of the people pressing against the barriers.

Flanked by mounted guards, the carriage moved slowly down the tree-lined avenue, and ahead of her she was surprised to see Emilio's bulky frame.

'But you sent Emilio home.' Puzzled, she glanced at the prince. 'He came to say goodbye to me yesterday, and told me that you'd been brilliant.'

'He insisted on returning this morning.' Casper gave a faint smile. 'On such a huge public occasion he refused to entrust your security to anyone else.'

'Oh, that's so kind.' Incredibly touched, Holly gave Emilio a wave. 'There do seem to be millions of people. What's this street like on a normal day?'

Casper settled back against the seat. 'The road leads directly to the palace. It's a favourite tourist route. Turn to the right at the bottom, and you reach the sea.'

Holly was still smiling at the crowd when she saw a toddler stumble and fall to the ground, his little body trapped against the metal barriers by the sheer pressure of the crowd. 'Oh no!

Stop the coach!' Before Casper could respond, Holly opened the door of the carriage, hitched her white silk dress up round her middle and jumped down into the road.

Oblivious to the havoc she was creating in the security operation, she hurried across to the bawling toddler and the panicking mum. 'Is he all right? Oh my goodness—can everyone move back a bit, please?' Raising her voice and gesturing at the crowd, she breathed a sigh of relief as everyone shifted slightly and she saw the mother safely lift the sobbing child. 'Phew. It's a bit crowded, isn't it? Is he all right? There—don't cry, sweetheart. Have you got a smile for me?' She reached out to the child who immediately stopped crying and stared at her in wonder.

'It's your tiara, Your Royal Highness, it's all sparkly, and he loves everything sparkly.' The woman flushed scarlet. 'We all wanted to get a good view of you, madam.'

Holly noticed a trickle of blood on the child's forehead. 'He's cut his head on the barrier. Does someone have a plaster?'

'Holly.'

Hearing her name, she looked over her shoulder and saw Casper striding towards her, a strange expression on his face. 'Holly, you're giving the security team heart-failure.'

'I'm sorry about that, but do you have a handkerchief or something?' She glanced anxiously back at the toddler who now had his thumb in his mouth.

Casper hesitated and then produced a handkerchief from the pocket of his uniform.

Holly took it and leaned over the barrier to press it gently against the toddler's forehead. 'There. It doesn't look too bad when you look at it closely.' One of the security team produced a plaster and vaulted the barrier to deal with the child, and Holly suddenly realised that the crowd was cheering for Casper.

The prince delivered a charismatic smile and slipped his arm round his bride. 'Next time, don't leave the coach. It isn't safe.'

'It isn't safe for that toddler, either. People are crushing too close to the barriers. What was I supposed to do?' She knew it was foolish to read too much into his comment, but she couldn't help it. Would he warn her not to leave the coach if he didn't care about her?

The cheering intensified, and then there was a yell from the crowd that turned into a chant.

'Kiss her, Prince Casper! *Kiss, kiss, kiss...!*'

Holly blushed scarlet but Casper, clearly as experienced at seducing a crowd as he was women, pulled her gently into his arms and lowered his mouth to hers with his usual cool confidence. Stunned by the unexpected gentleness of that kiss, Holly melted against him, stars exploding in her head and her heart.

Would he kiss her like that if he didn't care?

Surely it was another sign that he finally believed that she must be telling the truth? *That he'd been wrong about her.*

The crowd gave a collective sigh of approval, and when Casper finally lifted his head there was another enormous roar of approval.

'Now you've charmed the crowd, we need to go back to the coach.' Amusement in his eyes, he tucked her hand into his arm. 'And you need to stop jumping out of carriages and behave with some decorum. Not only are you now a princess, but you're a pregnant princess.'

'I know, but—' She glanced towards the crowd. 'Some of these people have been standing outside all night, even the children—do we have to go in the carriage? Couldn't we just walk? We could chat to people along the way.'

Casper's dark brows locked in a disapproving frown. 'It would be a major security risk.'

'I *know* you don't care about that. When you're in public you always walk. I read that you have a constant argument with your bodyguards and the security services.' She bit her lip, suddenly wishing she hadn't reminded him of her Internet moment, but he simply smiled and took her hand firmly in his.

'In this instance I was thinking of *your* safety. Don't you find the crowds daunting?'

'I think it's lovely that they've made the effort to come and see me get married,' Holly confessed. Spying two small girls holding a bunch of flowers that they obviously picked themselves, she pushed her elaborate bouquet towards an astonished Casper and hurried across. 'Are those for me? They're so pretty. Are they from your garden?' She talked to the girls, then to their mother, shook what felt like a million hands, and slowly and gradually made her way along the avenue towards the palace. But it took a long time because everyone had something to say to her and she had plenty to say in return.

Several people pushed teddies into her arms for the baby, and eventually she needed help to carry everything.

After an hour of chatting to a stunned and delighted crowd, Holly finally allowed herself to be urged back into the carriage.

'Clearly I misjudged you.' Casper settled himself beside her, indicating with his head that the procession should move on.

Holly's heart soared. 'Y-you did?'

'Yes. I thought you'd find the whole day impossibly daunting. But you're a natural.' He gave a wry smile. 'I've never seen anyone so skilled at talking about nothing with such enthusiasm and for such a long time.'

Holly digested this statement, decided that it was a compliment of sorts, and tried not to be disappointed that he'd been referring to the way she'd handled herself in public, rather than his opinion of her pregnancy.

Reminding herself that she had to be patient, she smiled. 'How can it be daunting when everyone is so nice?' Holly waved again and spied another group of children in the crowd. She opened her mouth to ask if they could stop, but Casper met her questioning glance with a slow shake of his head.

'No. Absolutely not. Delighted though I am that you've managed to please the crowd, we have about two-hundred foreign dignitaries and heads of state currently waiting for us at the palace and we're already late. I'd rather not cause a diplomatic incident if we can avoid it.' But his tone was in direct contrast to the warmth in his eyes. 'You've done well, *tesoro.*'

His praise made her glow inside and out, and she felt so ridiculously happy that she couldn't stop smiling. All right, so they'd had a shaky start to their relationship, but one of the advantages of that was that it could only improve.

Feeling optimistic about the future, Holly smiled all the way through the formal banquet, all the way through the dancing and all the way up to the moment when she was finally escorted to the prince's private quarters in a wing of the palace suspended above the sea.

It was only as the door closed behind them, leaving the guests and the guards on the outside, that reality hit her.

They were alone.

And this was their wedding night.

Gripped by a sudden attack of nerves, Holly gave a faltering smile, instinctively breaking the throbbing, tense silence that had descended on them. 'So this is where you actually live. It's beautiful—so much light and space, and—'

'*Stop* talking.' Casper reached for her clenched hands, gently prised them apart and then slid them round his waist and backed her against the door with an unmistakeable sense of purpose.

Trapped between solid oak and six foot two of raw male

virility, Holly found she could barely breathe, let alone talk. Dry mouthed, knees shaking, she was aware only of the simmering undercurrents of sexuality that emanated from his powerful frame as he took her face in strong, determined hands, his mouth on a direct collision course with hers.

Holly closed her eyes in willing surrender, senses singing, nerves on fire. When the kiss didn't come, she whimpered a faint protest. 'Casper?'

His mouth hovered a breath from hers. 'Open your eyes.'

Her eyes opened obediently and she stared up at him, her heart skipping several beats as she scanned the aristocratic lines of his masculine features. 'Please—kiss me.'

'I intend to do a great deal more than that, *angelo mio...*'

Held captive by his lazy, confident gaze her heart started to pound, and searing heat pooled low in her pelvis. She probably should have played it cool, but Holly was too aroused to remember the meaning of cool.

Her body was in the grip of a strong, explosive excitement that simply intensified as his mouth finally glided onto hers with effortless skill.

His tongue probed the interior of her mouth with erotic expertise, and Holly just melted, moaning low in her throat as his strong hands brought her writhing hips into contact with his potent masculine arousal.

'Not here.' His voice thickened, he pulled away from her and scooped her easily into his arms. 'This time, *tesoro*, we'll make it to the bed. And we're taking our time over it.' He strode through several rooms and then up a winding staircase that led to a bedroom in a turret.

Trembling, *mortified* by how much she wanted him, Holly clutched at his shoulders as he set her down on the floor, barely conscious of the beautiful circular room, the high arched windows or the vaulted ceiling. Her body was on fire with anticipation, and her entire focus was on the man now undressing her with deft, experienced fingers.

As tens of thousands of pounds worth of designer silk slithered unrestrained to the floor, her old insecurities resurfaced, and Holly was grateful for the relative protection of moonlight and underwear. But Casper showed merciless disregard for her inhibitions, peeling off her panties in a slick, decisive movement and tumbling her trembling, naked body onto the enormous four-poster bed.

'Don't move. I like looking at you.' Having positioned her to his satisfaction, Casper sprang to his feet and removed his own clothing with impatient fingers, his eyes scanning her squirming body and flushed cheeks as he undressed with unself-conscious grace and fluidity. 'You are *so* beautiful.'

As his carelessly discarded clothes hit the floor, Holly quickly discovered that there was more than enough light for her to make out bronzed skin and bold male arousal. Dizzy from that brief glimpse of raw masculinity, she drew in a sharp breath as he came down on top of her.

Shocked by the sudden contact with his lean, powerful frame, Holly's pulse rate shot into overdrive and she slid her hands over his shoulders, her back arching as his clever mouth fastened over her nipple, and he plundered her sensitive flesh with sure, skilled flicks of his tongue.

Lightning bursts of sensation exploded through her body, and as his seeking fingers traced a path to that place where the ache had become almost intolerable Holly shifted restlessly against the silk sheets, the wanton movement giving him the access he needed.

With slow, sensitive strokes, he explored the most intimate part of her until Holly was sobbing his name, begging him for more, in the grip of such a terrifying craving that she knew if he stopped now she'd die.

Casper shifted her hips and his own position, giving her just time to register the silken throb of his arousal before he plunged deep into her moist, aching interior, and her world exploded.

Rocketing from earth to ecstasy, Holly shot straight into a shattering climax, only dimly registering Casper's disbelieving curse and the sudden faltering of his rhythm as his own control was threatened by her body's violent response. Sobbing his name, Holly dug her fingers into the slick flesh of his shoulders, so out of her mind with excitement that she was incapable of doing anything except hold on as each driving thrust drove her back towards paradise.

Her body splintered into pieces again, and this time she felt him reach his own release, and she hugged him tightly, overwhelmed by what had to be the most incredible experience of her life.

'You're a miracle in bed,' Casper said huskily, rolling onto his back and taking her with him.

Stunned by the whole experience, and prepared to snuggle against his chest, Holly gave a whimper of shock as he closed his hands over her hips and lifted her so that she straddled him.

'Casper, we can't!'

But they did.

Again and again, until Holly couldn't think or move.

Finally she lay there, sated and exhausted, one arm draped over his powerful chest, her cheek against the warmth of his bronzed shoulder.

She could hear the sounds of the sea through one of the open windows and she closed her eyes, feeling a rush of happiness.

She no longer had any doubts that she'd done the right thing.

They'd been married for less than a day and already his attitude to her was softening. Yes, he found it hard to talk about his emotions, but he didn't have trouble showing them, did he?

He'd been tender, passionate, demanding, skilled, thoughtful.

Just thinking about it made her body burn again, and she slid her fingers through the dark hairs that hazed his chest, fascinated by the contrast between his body and hers.

'I had no idea it was possible to feel like that.' She spoke softly and gently, and pressed an affectionate kiss against his warm flesh, hugging him tightly. 'You're fantastic—' She broke off as he withdrew from her and sprang from the bed.

Without uttering a single word in response to her unguarded declaration, he strode through a door and slammed it behind him.

Holly flinched at the finality of that sound, and her head filled with a totally unreasonable panic.

He'd left. He'd just walked out without saying anything. Desperate to stop him leaving, she kicked back the tangle of silken covers and sprinted towards the door.

And then she heard the sounds of a shower running and realised that the door led to a bathroom.

A tidal wave of relief surged over her and she stopped. Her limbs suddenly drained of strength, she plopped back onto the bed.

He hadn't walked out.

He wasn't her father.

This was different.

Or was it?

Feeling unsettled, confused and desperately hurt, she lay on her back, staring up at the canopy of the four-poster bed.

Rejection wasn't new to her, was it?

So why did it hurt so badly?

Eventually the noise of the shower stopped and moments later Casper strolled back into the bedroom. He'd pulled on a black robe and his hair was still damp from the shower.

Without looking at her, he walked into what she presumed was a dressing room and emerged wearing a pair of trousers, a fresh shirt in his hand.

'Aren't you coming back to bed? Did I say something?' Feeling intensely vulnerable, Holly sat up in the bed and twisted the ends of her hair with nervous fingers. 'One minute we were lying there having a cuddle and the next you sprang out of bed and stalked off. I feel as though you're upset, but I don't know why.'

'Go to sleep.' He shrugged his shoulders into the shirt and fastened the buttons with strong, sure fingers. *Those same fingers that had driven her wild.*

'How can I possibly sleep? *Talk* to me!' Suddenly it felt wrong to be naked, and she reached for the silk nightdress that someone had laid next to her pillow and pulled it over her head. 'What's wrong? Is it the whole wedding thing?' She wanted to ask whether he was thinking about the fiancée he should have married, Antonia, but she didn't want to risk making the situation worse.

'Go back to bed, Holly.'

'How can I possibly do that? Don't shut me out, Casper.' Her voice cracked and she slid out of bed and walked over to him. 'I'm your *wife*.'

'Precisely.' He looked at her then, and his eyes were cold as ice. 'I have already fulfilled my side of the deal by marrying you.'

Holly froze with shock. 'Deal?'

'You wanted a father for your baby. I needed an heir.'

Her legs buckled and she sank down onto the edge of the bed. 'You make it sound as though I picked you at random.'

'Not at random. I think you targeted me very carefully.'

'You still believe this isn't your baby. Oh God. I really thought you'd changed your mind about that—you seemed different today—and when we—' She glanced at the rumpled sheets on the bed, her eyes glistening with tears. 'You made love to me and it felt—'

'We had sex, Holly.' His voice was devoid of emotion. 'Love didn't come into it, and it never will, make no mistake about that. Don't do that female thing of turning a physical act into something emotional.'

Her hopes exploded like a balloon landing on nails.

'It wasn't just the sex,' she whispered. 'You've been different today. Caring. Ever since the moment I arrived at the cathedral.' Her voice cracked. 'You've been smiling at me, you had your arm around me. *You kissed me.*'

'We're supposed to look as though we're in love.' Apparently unaffected by her mounting distress, he strode over to an antique table next to the window. 'Do you want a drink?'

'No. I don't want a drink!' Her heart was suddenly bumping hard and she felt physically sick. 'Are you saying that everything that happened today was for the benefit of the crowd?'

He poured himself a whisky but didn't touch it. Instead he stared out of the window, his knuckles white on the glass, his handsome face revealing nothing of his thoughts. No emotion. 'They wanted the fairy tale. We gave it to them. That's what we royals have to do. We give the people what they want. In this case, a love match, a wedding and an heir.'

She blinked rapidly, determined to hold back the tears. 'So why did you marry *me*?'

He lifted the glass to his lips. 'Why not?'

'Because you could have married someone you loved.'

He lowered the glass without drinking. 'I don't want love.'

Because he'd had it once and now it was gone?

Holly's throat closed. 'That's a terrible thing to say and a terrible way to feel,' she whispered. 'I know you lost and I know you must have suffered, but—'

'You don't know anything.'

'Then tell me!' She was crying openly now, tears flooding her cheeks. 'I'm devastated that the whole of today was a sham. I know it's difficult for you to talk about Antonia, and frankly it isn't that easy to hear it, either. But I know we're not going to have any sort of marriage unless we're honest with each other.'

Please don't let him walk out on me. Please don't let that happen.

'Honest?' He slammed the glass down onto the table and turned to look at her. 'You lie about your baby, you lie all the way to the altar wearing your symbolic white dress, and then you suggest we're *honest*? It's a little late for that, don't you think?'

'*It's your baby*,' Holly said hoarsely. Her insides were twisted in pain as she felt her new life crumbling around her. 'And I don't know how you can believe otherwise.'

'Don't you? Then let me tell you.' He strolled towards her, his eyes glittering dark and deadly. 'It can't be my baby, Holly, because I can't have children. I don't know whose baby you're carrying, my sweet wife, but I know for sure it isn't mine. I'm infertile.'

CHAPTER SIX

'NO.' HOLLY sat down hard on the nearest chair, her heart pounding. 'That isn't possible,' she said hoarsely. 'I am living proof that it isn't possible. Why would you even think that?'

'Eight years ago I had an accident.'

The accident that had killed his brother and Antonia. 'I know about the accident.'

'You know only what I chose to reveal.' He paced across the room and stared out over the ocean. 'Everyone knew that Santallia lost the heir to the throne. Everyone knew my fiancée died. No one knew that the accident crushed my pelvis so badly that my chances of ever fathering a child were nil.'

Holly's mind was in turmoil. 'Casper—'

'We had a crisis on our hands.' He thrust his hands into his pockets, the movement emphasising the hard masculine lines of his body. 'My brother was dead. I was suddenly the ruling prince and I was in intensive care, hitched up to a ventilator. When I recovered, everyone was celebrating. It was the wrong time to break the news to the people that their prince couldn't give them what they wanted.'

Holly sank her hands into her hair, struggling to take in what he was saying. 'Who told you?'

'The doctor who treated me.'

'Well, the doctor was wrong.' Her hands fell to her sides and she walked across to him, her tone urgent. 'Look at me, Casper. *Listen* to me. Whatever you may have been told—whatever you think—you are not infertile. I *am* having your baby.'

'Don't do this, Holly.' He drew away from her. 'I've accepted your child as mine, and that's all that matters. You've given me my heir. The public think you're a genius.' He stared into his drink. 'At some point, I'll have to tell the people the truth. Let them decide about the succession.'

As the implications of his words sank in, Holly shook her head, horrified by what that would mean. 'No. You mustn't do that.'

'Because your newfound popularity would take a nosedive?' He gave a cynical smile. 'You think Santallia might rather not know that its new innocent princess has rather more sexual experience than they'd like?'

'Casper, my sexual experience encompasses you and only you.' Frustrated that she couldn't get through to him, Holly turned away and walked over to the window. Dawn was breaking and the rising sun sent pink shadows over the sea, but she saw nothing except her child's future crumbling before her. 'You should see a doctor again. You should have more tests. They made a mistake.'

'The subject is closed.'

'Fine. Don't have tests, then.' Anger and frustration rose out of her misery. 'But don't you *dare* announce to the world that this isn't your baby!' Her eyes suddenly fierce, she turned on him. 'I do *not* want our child having that sort of scar on his background. And once you've said something like that, you can never take it back.'

'They have a right to know about the baby's paternity.'

Holly straightened her shoulders. 'Once the baby is born, I'll prove our baby's paternity. Until then, you say nothing.'

'If you're so confident about paternity, then why wait? There are tests that can be done now. Or are you buying yourself more time?'

She lifted her hands to her cheeks, so stressed that she could hardly breathe. 'Tests now would put the baby at risk and I won't do that. But don't you dare tell anyone this isn't your baby. *Promise me, Casper.*'

'All right.'

Celebrating that minor victory, Holly sank onto the curved window seat and stared down at the sea lapping at the white sand below. 'Why didn't you tell me this when we were in London?'

'Because you didn't need to know.'

'How can you say that?'

'You wanted a father for your baby and I needed an heir. The details were irrelevant and they still are. You have a prince, a palace and a fortune. This drama is unnecessary.'

'I wanted our baby to know its father,' Holly whispered softly, her hand covering her abdomen in an instinctive gesture of protection. 'I thought marrying you *was* the right thing to do.'

'If it's any consolation, I wouldn't have let you make any other decision. And I don't want to talk about this again, Holly. You'll have everything you need and so will the baby.'

No. No, she wouldn't.

Holly closed her eyes, trying to ignore the raw wound caused by his admission that the whole day had been a lie.

She'd felt lonely before, but nothing had come close to the feeling of isolation that engulfed her following Casper's rejection.

She desperately wanted to talk to someone—to confide.

But there was no one.

She was alone.

Except that she wasn't really alone, was she? She had their baby to think about—to protect.

Once he or she was born, she'd be able to prove that Casper was the father. And until then she just had to try and keep their hopelessly unstable little family unit together.

That was all that mattered.

Starved of affection from Casper and desperately worried about the future, Holly threw herself into palace life and her royal duties.

She spent hours pouring over a map until she was familiar with every part of Santallia. Determined to develop the knowledge of a local, she persuaded Emilio to drive her round. The result was that she shocked and delighted the public by her frequent impromptu appearances. Oblivious to security or protocol, she talked to everyone, finding out what they liked and how they felt.

And one thing that always came across was how much they loved Casper.

'You're just what he needs,' one old lady said as Holly sat by her bed in the hospital, keeping her company for half an hour after an exhausting morning of official visits. 'After the accident we thought he wouldn't recover, you know.'

Holly reached forward to adjust the old lady's pillows. 'You mean because he was so badly injured?'

'No. Because he lost so much. But now he has you to love.'

But he didn't want love, did he?

Holly managed a smile. 'I need to go. Tonight it's dinner with a president and his wife, no less. Do you want more tea before I go?'

'I want you to tell me about the state visit. What will you be wearing?'

'Actually, I'm not sure.' Holly thought about her extensive wardrobe. No one could accuse Casper of being stingy, she thought ruefully. The trouble was, she now had such a variety of gorgeous designer clothes that choosing had become impossible, but even that wasn't a problem, because she now had someone to do it for her. When she'd first realised that a member of staff had been employed purely to keep her wardrobe in order and help her select outfits, she'd gaped at Casper.

'You mean it's someone's whole job just to tell me how to dress?'

He'd dismissed her amazement with a frown. 'How else will you know what to wear for the various occasions? Her job is to research every engagement in advance and make the appropriate choice of outfit. It will stop you making an embarrassing mistake.'

The news that he found her potentially embarrassing had done nothing for Holly's fragile confidence, and she'd humbly accepted the woman's help.

Thinking of it, Holly smiled at the old lady. 'I think I'm wearing a blue dress. With silver straps. A bit Hollywood, but apparently the president loves glamour.'

'You're so beautiful, he'll be charmed. And blue is a good colour for you. I've been admiring your bracelet—I had one almost exactly like that when I was your age.' The woman's eyes misted. 'My husband gave it to me because he said it was the same colour as my eyes. I lost it years ago. Not that it matters. The trouble with getting old is you don't have the same opportunities to dress up.'

'You don't need an occasion,' Holly said blithely, slipping the bracelet off and sliding it onto the old lady's bony wrist. 'There. It looks gorgeous.'

'You can't give me that.'

'Why not? It looks pretty on you. I must go or they'll start moaning at me. Try not to seduce any of the doctors.' Holly rose to her feet, silently acknowledging that part of her was reluctant to return to the palace. She loved visiting everyone and chatting. When she was out and about and talking to people, it was easier to pretend that she wasn't desperately lonely.

That her marriage wasn't empty.

Casper seemed to think that presents were a reasonable substitute for his company.

It had taken only a couple of days for her to discover that he set himself a punishing work schedule, spending much of the day involved in state business or royal engagements.

Since their wedding they'd spent virtually no daylight hours alone together. Every evening there seemed to be yet another formal banquet, foreign dignitaries to be entertained, another evening of smiles and polite conversation.

And the fact that he never saw her was presumably intentional, she thought miserably as she said her farewells to all the ladies on the ward and allowed Emilio to guide her back to the car.

Casper didn't want to spend time with her, did he?

All he wanted from the relationship was a hostess and someone with whom to enjoy a few exhausting hours of turbo-powered, high-octane sex every night.

He wasn't interested in anything else. Not conversation. Not even a hug. *Certainly* not a hug.

Holly slid into the back of the car, waving to the crowd who had gathered. *What would they say,* she wondered, *if they knew their handsome prince had never spent a whole night with her?*

He just took her to bed, had sex and then disappeared somewhere, as if he was afraid that lingering might encourage her to say something that he didn't want to hear.

Did he have another woman? Was that where he went when he left their bed?

To someone else?

Casper had a seemingly inexhaustible sex drive, and

Holly was well aware that there had been another woman in his life when he'd first met her in England. One of the papers had mentioned some European princess, and another a supermodel.

Were they still on the scene?

Feeling mentally and physically exhausted, Holly rested her head on the back seat of the limousine and promptly fell asleep.

She woke at Emlio's gentle insistence, walked into her beautiful bedroom with the view to die for and flopped down on her huge, fabulous bed.

Just five minutes, she promised herself.

Five minutes, then she'd have a shower and get ready for the evening.

Simmering with impatience after a long and incredibly frustrating day of talks with the president and the foreign minister, Casper strode through to the private wing of the palace.

In his pocket was an extravagant diamond necklace, designed for him by the world's most exclusive jeweller who had assured him that any woman presented with such an exquisite piece would know she was loved.

Casper had frowned at that, because love played no part in the relationship he had with Holly. But she was doing an excellent job fulfilling her role as princess. She deserved to be appreciated.

And this was why she'd married him, wasn't it?

For the benefits that he could offer her.

Contemplating her reaction to such a generous gift, a faint smile touched his mouth, and he mentally prepared himself for a stimulating evening.

Lost in a private fantasy which involved Holly, the diamonds and very little else, Casper strolled into his private sanctuary.

The first thing that hit him was the unusual silence.

Silence, he reflected with a degree of wry humour, had become something of a scarcity since he'd married Holly.

First there was the singing. She sang to herself as they were getting ready for the evening. She sang in the shower, she sang as she dressed, she even sang as she did her make-up. And if she wasn't singing she was talking, apparently determined to fill every moment of the limited time they had alone together with details about her day. Who she'd spoken to, what they'd said in return—she was endlessly fascinated by every small detail about the people she'd met.

In fact silence was such an alien thing since Holly had entered his life, that he noticed the absence of sound like others would notice the presence of a large elephant in the room.

Slightly irritated that she obviously hadn't yet returned from her afternoon of visits, Casper removed his tie with a few deft flicks of his fingers while swiftly scanning his private mail.

Finding it strangely hard to concentrate without background noise, he had to force himself to focus while he scribbled instructions for his private secretary. Intending to take a quick shower while waiting for Holly to return, he took the stairs up to the bedroom suite.

Holly lay still on the bed, fully clothed, as if she'd fallen there and not moved since. Her glorious hair tumbled unrestricted around her narrow shoulders and her eyes were closed, her dark lashes serving to accentuate the extreme pallor of her cheeks.

In the process of unbuttoning his shirt, Casper stilled.

His first reaction was one of surprise, because she was blessed with boundless energy and enthusiasm and he'd never before seen her sleeping during the day.

His second reaction was concern.

Knowing that she was an extremely light sleeper, he waited for her to sense his presence and stir. Contemplating the feminine curve of her hip, he felt an immediate surge of arousal, and decided that the best course of action would be to join her on the bed and wake her personally.

Glancing at his watch, he calculated that if they limited the foreplay they would still make dinner with the president.

He dispensed with his shirt, his eyes fixed on the creamy skin visible at the neckline of her flowery dress. *Stunning*, he thought to himself, and settled himself on the edge of the bed, ready to dedicate the next half hour to making her *extremely* happy.

But she didn't stir.

Disconcerted by her lack of response, Casper reached out a hand and touched her throat, feeling a rush of relief as he felt warm flesh and a steady pulse under his fingertips.

What had he expected?

Unsettled by the sudden absence of logic that had driven him to take the pulse of a sleeping woman, he withdrew his hand and rose to his feet, struggling against an irrational desire to pick up the phone and demand the immediate presence of a skilled medical team.

She was just tired, he assured himself, casting another long look in her direction. Acting on impulse, he reached down and gently removed her shoes. Then he stared at her dress and tried to work out whether it was likely to impede her rest in any way. For the first time in his life, a decision eluded him. Did he remove it and risk waking her, or leave it and risk her being uncomfortable?

A stranger to prevarication, Casper stood in a turmoil of indecision, his hand hovering over her for several long minutes. In the end he compromised by pulling the silk cover over her body.

Then he backed away from the bed, relieved that at least there had been no one present to witness such embarrassing vacillation on his part.

He made thousands of decisions on a daily basis, some of them involving millions of pounds, some of them involving millions of people.

It was incomprehensible that he couldn't make one small decision that affected his wife's comfort.

Holly awoke to darkness. With a rush of inexplicable panic, she sat up and only then did she notice Casper seated by the window.

'What time is it?' Disorientated and fuzzy headed, she reached across to flick on the lamp by the bed. 'It must be really late. And I need to change for dinner.'

'It's one in the morning. You've missed dinner.'

The lamp sent a shaft of light across the room, and she saw that his white dress-shirt was unbuttoned at the throat and that his dinner jacket was slung carelessly over the back of the chair.

'I missed it?' Holly slid her hand through her hair, trying to clear her head. 'How could I have missed it?'

'You were asleep.'

'Then you should have woken me.' Mortified, she pushed down the luxurious silk bed cover and realised that she was still wearing the clothes she'd had on when she'd done her day of royal visits. 'I only wanted a short nap.'

'Holly, you slept as though you were dead.' His dark eyes glittered in the subtle light. 'I decided that it was better to make your excuses to the president than produce a wife in a coma.'

Holly pulled a face. 'What must he have thought?'

'He thought you were pregnant,' Casper drawled, a faint smile touching his mouth. 'He and his wife have four children, and he spent the entire evening lecturing me on how a pregnant woman often feels most tired during the first few months and how rest is important.'

'God, how awful for you,' Holly mumbled, forcing herself

to get out of bed even though every part of herself was dying to lie down and sleep for the rest of the night. 'I feel really bad, because I know how important this dinner was to you. Your private secretary told me that you wanted to talk about all that trade stuff and about carbon emissions or something. Some forestry scheme?'

A strange expression flickered across his face. 'You frequently talk to my private secretary?'

'Of course.' Holly tried unsuccessfully to suppress a yawn as she padded over to him in bare feet. 'Carlos and I often talk. How else am I going to know what the point of the evening is? I mean, you don't see these people because you like their company, do you?' Feeling decidedly wobbly, she sank down on the window seat next to him. 'I'm sorry I slept.'

'Don't be. Though I must admit you had me worried for a while. It wasn't until I was greeted with silence that I realised how accustomed I am to hearing you singing into a hairbrush.'

Holly turned scarlet at the thought that he'd witnessed that. 'You hear me singing?'

'The whole of the palace hears you singing.'

Horrified by that disclosure, Holly shrank back on the seat. 'I didn't know anyone could hear me,' she muttered. 'Singing always cheers me up.'

His eyes lingered thoughtfully on her face. 'Do you need cheering up?'

How was she supposed to answer that? Holly hesitated, knowing that if she told him that she felt lonely, *that she missed him*, he'd withdraw in the same way he always did when she made a move towards him. He'd remind her that his company wasn't part of their 'deal'.

'I just like singing,' she said lamely. 'But next time I'll make sure no one is listening.'

'That would be a pity, especially given that several of the staff have told me what a beautiful voice you have.' He reached into his pocket and withdrew a slim box. 'I bought you a present.'

'Oh.' She tried to look pleased. After all, he was trying, wasn't he? It wouldn't be fair to point out that her wardrobes were bulging with clothes and that she only had one pair of feet on which to wear shoes, and that what she *really* wanted was a few hours in his company when they weren't having sex. 'Thank you.'

'I hope you like it.' His confident smile suggested that he wasn't in any doubt about that, and Holly flipped open the lid of the dark-blue velvet box and was dazzled by the sparkle and gleam of diamonds.

'My goodness.'

'They're pink diamonds. I know you like pink. Apparently they're very rare.'

When had he even noticed that she liked pink?

He was such a contradiction, she thought numbly, lifting the necklace from the box and instantly falling in love with it. He spent hardly any time alone with her, but he seemed to be trying to please her.

And he'd noticed that she liked pink.

'It's beautiful,' she said honestly, fastening the necklace round her neck and walking across the room to admire herself in the mirror. 'Is it very valuable?'

'Would knowing how much it cost make it a more welcome gift?' There was an edge to his tone that she didn't understand.

'No, of course not.' She touched the sparkling diamonds nervously. 'I'm just wondering whether I dare wear it out of the bedroom.'

He relaxed slightly. 'It's yours to lose, keep or trade,' he drawled softly, and Holly frowned, puzzled by his comment but too tired to search for a hidden meaning.

'You do say the weirdest things.' Suppressing a yawn, she

walked back to the window seat, feeling the weight of the diamonds against her throat. 'I've never worn diamonds before. And I never imagined wearing them in bed.'

'I intended them to go with your dress this evening.' His gaze was fixed on her face. 'You're extremely tired.'

'Long day.'

'Too long. The official visits have to stop, Holly.'

'What? *Why?*' Hurt and upset by the apparent criticism, Holly sat up straighter in her seat. 'What am I doing wrong? I've worked so hard.'

'Precisely. You're working too hard.'

For a moment Holly just gaped at him in disbelief. 'That's the most unfair criticism I've ever heard. How can I be working *too* hard?'

'If you're so exhausted you're falling asleep, then you're working too hard.'

'That's nothing to do with the official visits. I'm falling asleep because you keep me awake half the night!' She looked at him in exasperation, her temper mounting. 'Oh, that's it, isn't it? You don't like me working hard because you're afraid I'm going to be too tired to perform in the bedroom! Is that all you care about, Casper? Whether I have the energy for sex?'

'You're doing that uniquely female thing of twisting words for the purpose of starting a row.' Ice cool, he watched her with masculine detachment and Holly felt a flash of frustration.

'No, I'm not. I *hate* rows. I would never, ever choose to row with anyone. I *hate* conflict.' The ironic gleam in his eyes somehow served to make her even more infuriated. 'And you'd know I hate conflict if you'd bothered to spend a few hours alone in my company! But you don't, do you? Do you realise we've never even been on a proper date? You are so, so selfish! You just come to bed and do your whole virile, macho-stud thing, and then you swan off, leaving me.'

One dark brow lifted in cool appraisal. 'Leaving you?'

'Exhausted,' she muttered, and a sardonic smile touched his mouth.

'So I leave you to sleep. By my definition, that makes me unselfish, not selfish. And it brings me back to my earlier point, which is that you're working too hard.'

'You always have to win, don't you?' Holly sank back down onto the window seat, the bout of anger having sapped the last of her energy. It just wasn't worth arguing with him.

'It isn't about winning. Believe it or not, I do have your welfare at heart. After I left you this afternoon, I asked a few questions. Questions I should have asked a long time ago it seems.' There was a frown in his eyes. 'It's no wonder you're so tired. Apparently you've been working flat out since the day after our wedding. You've been doing ten to fifteen visits a day! And you spend ages with everyone. From what I've been told, you don't even give yourself a lunch break.'

'Well, there's a lot to fit in.' Holly defended herself. 'Have you any idea how many requests the palace receives? People send letters, sometimes official and sometimes handwritten. Stacks and stacks of them. There have already been requests for me to go and visit schools and hospitals, open this or that, make an official visit, cut ribbons, smash bottles of champagne—I judged a dog show last week and I don't know *anything* about dogs. And then there are the individuals, people who are ill and can't get out—'

'Holly.' His tone was a mixture of amusement and disbelief. 'You're not supposed to say yes to all of them. The idea is that you pick and choose.'

'Well if I say yes to one and not another then I'm going to offend someone!' Holly glared at him and then subsided. 'And anyway, I'm enjoying myself. I like seeing people. For some reason that I absolutely don't understand, it cheers them up to see me. And I won't give it up!'

People liked her. People approved of her.

She felt as though she was making a difference, and it felt good.

'You're working yourself to the bone. From now on I'm giving instructions that you're to do no more than two engagements a day,' he instructed. 'On a maximum of five days a week.'

'No!' Horrified by that prospect, Holly pushed her hair out of her eyes. 'What am I going to do the rest of the time? You obviously don't want to see me during the hours of daylight, you're—you're like a vampire or something! You just turn up at night.'

Thick dark lashes concealed his expression. 'You have unlimited funds and virtually unlimited opportunities for entertainment.' His soft drawl connected straight with her nerve endings, and Holly felt everything weaken.

'Well there's no point in doing stuff if you don't have anyone to share it with. I'm lonely. And that's the other thing you don't seem to understand about me. I'm a people person. So don't tell me I have to stop doing my own engagements.'

'Holly, you're exhausted.'

'I'm pregnant,' she said flatly, pulling her legs under her and trying hard to hide another yawn. 'All the books say that in another couple of weeks I'll be bounding with energy.'

'And what are you going to do then?' His tone was dry. 'Work nights?'

Her eyes collided with his and Holly sucked in some air, horrified to discover that the mere mention of the word 'night' was sufficient to trigger a reaction in her body. Her nipples tightened, her pelvis ached and she suddenly felt as though she'd downed an entire bottle of champagne in one gulp.

Clearly tracking the direction of her thoughts, he gave a slow, confident smile and suddenly she wanted to thump him because he was unreasonably, unfairly gorgeous, and he knew it.

As his gaze welded to her mouth, Holly acknowledged the overwhelming surge of excitement with something close to despair. '*Don't* look at me like that. You're doing it again— all you think about is sex.'

'And what are you thinking about right now, *tesoro*? The share price?' His tone was mocking as he pulled her gently but firmly to her feet. 'A new handbag?'

A moan of disbelief escaped her parted lips as he brought his mouth down on hers and backed her purposefully towards the bed.

This was Casper at his most dominant and she really, *really* wanted to be able tell him that she was too tired, or just not interested.

'I can't believe you make me feel this way.' Her body exploded under the hard, virile pressure of his and she tumbled back onto the mattress, forced to admit that she was a lost cause when it came to resisting him.

She wanted him *so* much.

And if this was all their relationship was…

He came over her with the fluid assurance of a male who has never known rejection, arousal glittering in his beautiful eyes. 'Exactly how tired are you?'

Trying to look nonchalant, she shrugged. 'Why do you ask?'

He lowered his arrogant, dark head, his mouth curving into a sardonic smile as it hovered close to hers. 'Because I'm about to do my virile, macho-stud thing,' he mocked gently, and Holly felt her stomach flip with desperate excitement.

Weak with desire, *hating* herself for being so feeble where he was concerned, she gasped as his hand slid under the silk of her nightdress. 'Casper.'

His hand stilled and there was a wicked gleam in his eyes. 'Unless you're too tired?'

Driven by the desperate urgency of her body, Holly swallowed her pride. 'I'm not *that* tired…'

'You have time to shower while I make some calls.' Freshly shaved, his hair still damp, Casper straightened his silk tie and reached for his jacket. 'I'll join you for breakfast.'

Elated that he'd spent the entire night with her for the first time, and reluctant to risk disturbing the fragile shoots of their relationship, Holly decided not to confess that mornings weren't her best time and that she couldn't touch breakfast.

Waiting until he'd left the room, she slid cautiously out of bed, felt her stomach heave alarmingly and just made it to the bathroom in time.

'*Dio,* what is the matter?' Casper's voice came from right behind her. 'Are you ill? Is it something you ate?'

'Don't you knock? I thought I locked the door.' Mortified that he should witness her at her lowest, Holly leaned her head against the cool tiles, willing her stomach to settle. 'Please, Casper, show a little sensitivity and go away.'

'First you accuse me of not spending time with you, then you want me to go away.' Casper lifted his hands in a gesture of frustrated incredulity. 'Make up your mind!'

'Well, *obviously* I don't want you around while I'm being sick!'

'You're incredibly pale.' Looking enviably fit and impossibly handsome, he frowned down at her. 'I'm calling a doctor.'

'Casper.' She gritted her teeth, terrified that she'd be ill in front of him. 'It's fine. It happens all the time. It will fade in a minute.'

'*What* happens all the time?' His dark gaze was fixed on her face, the tension visible in his powerful shoulders. 'I've never seen you like this before.'

'That's because you're never here in the morning,' she muttered, wondering what cruel twist of fate had made him decide to pick this particular morning to linger in her company. 'You go to bed with me, but you choose to wake up somewhere else.' *With someone else.* The words were left unsaid, but a gleam of sardonic humour flickered in his very sexy dark eyes.

'You think I spend half the night making love with you and then move on to the next woman? A sort of sexual conveyor-belt, perhaps?'

'I honestly don't want to know where you go at three in the morning.' She gave a moan as another wave of nausea washed over her. 'Oh, go away, please. I don't even care at the moment—I can't *believe* you're seeing me like this. You're never going to find me sexy again.'

'There is not the slightest chance of that happening.' After a moment's hesitation he dropped to his haunches and stroked her hair away from her face with a surprisingly gentle hand. 'I am sorry you feel ill. Wash your face. It will make you feel better.' He stood up, dampened a towel and wiped it gently over her face.

'I already feel better. It passes.' She sat back on her heels and gave him a wobbly smile. 'I bet you're regretting all those times you could have stayed the whole night and had breakfast with me. I'm thrilling company in the morning, don't you think?'

With a wry smile, he lifted her easily to her feet. 'Does food help? If I suggested something to eat would you hit me?'

'I've never been an advocate of violence.' It felt weird, having a conversation with him that wasn't based on conflict. And frustrating that they were having it when she was still in her nightdress.

But at least she was wearing diamonds, she thought wryly. Conscious of his sleek good looks and her own undressed state, Holly glanced towards the shower. 'I think I'd like a shower. Do I still have time?'

'Yes. But don't lock the door.' His tone was gruff. 'I don't want you collapsing.'

'I'm fine.' This new level of attentiveness was unsettling. There was a shift in their relationship that she didn't understand.

But she knew better than to read anything into it.

She showered quickly, selected a cream skirt from her wardrobe and added a tailored jacket that allowed a peep of her pretty camisole. She scooped her hair up and then had a moment of agonising indecision as she remembered that he seemed to prefer her hair down. Up or down? Removing the clips, her hair tumbled around her shoulders in a mass of soft curls.

Deciding that she should have left it up, she started to twist it again and then caught herself.

What was she doing? For crying out loud, she was going to eat breakfast with the man, that was all. It wasn't a formal dinner or a state occasion. Just breakfast.

Pathetic, she told her reflection. Absolutely pathetic.

It was just for the baby. For the baby's sake she wanted them to have a happy, successful marriage.

Afraid to examine that theory too closely in case it fell apart, she walked onto the terrace to join him for breakfast. Casper was talking on the phone, looking lean and sleek, his hips resting casually against the balustrade that circled the pretty balcony. Behind him stretched the ocean, the early-morning sunlight catching the surface in a thousand dazzling lights.

The billionaire prince, she thought weakly, envious of his confidence and the ease with which he handled his high profile existence. She'd watched him in action at state occasions and been impossibly awed by the deft way in which he handled every situation and solved every problem. She

realised now that she'd had no idea of the weight of responsibility that rested on him, and yet he apparently coped easily,
with no outward evidence of stress or self-doubt.

As he continued his conversation, his eyes slid to hers and
held. Electricity jolted her and Holly's heart bumped hard
against her ribs.

Wondering how he could have this effect on her when
she'd just spent most of the night in bed with him, she plopped
down onto the nearest chair.

She felt light-headed and dizzy and wasn't sure whether
to blame pregnancy, lack of food or the shattering impact of
the extremely sexy man who was currently watching her with
disturbing intensity, apparently paying no attention what-
soever to the person on the other end of the phone.

Cheeks pink, trying to distract herself, Holly cautiously
examined the food that had been laid out on the table.

Terminating the call, Casper dropped his phone into his
pocket and strolled across to her. 'I've talked to the doctor.'

'You have?'

'He suggests that you eat dry toast now. And tomorrow
you're to eat a dry biscuit before you move from the bed.'

'That sounds exciting. And guaranteed to put on extra
pounds just when I don't need them.'

Casper gave a predatory smile. 'Since we've already estab-
lished the positive impact of biscuits on a certain part of your
anatomy, I think we can safely assume that I'm not going to
find you sexually repulsive any time soon.'

'I didn't say you were.'

'But you were thinking it.' He sat down opposite her and
helped himself to fresh fruit. 'Eventually I'm hoping you'll
realise that you have a fabulous body. Then we can make love
with the lights on. Or even during daylight.'

She blushed, as self-conscious about his suggestion that

they make love in daylight as she was flattered by his comments about her body. 'You're not around during the day.'

'The promise of you naked would be sufficient incentive to persuade me to ditch my responsibilities.'

'All you think about is sex. I don't know whether to be flattered or exasperated.'

'You should be flattered. I'm a man. I'm programmed to think about nothing but sex.' Apparently seeing nothing wrong in that admission, he reached across and lifted the coffee pot. 'More?'

Holly pulled a face and shook her head. 'I've gone off it. Don't ask me why. Something to do with being pregnant, I think.'

Without arguing, he poured her a fresh orange-juice instead. 'And now I want to know why you assumed I was spending part of the night with another woman.'

Her insides tumbled. 'Well—it just seemed like the obvious answer.'

'To what question?'

'To where you go at three in the morning. Up until today, you've never woken up next to me. We have sex. You leave. That's the routine.'

'That doesn't explain why you'd believe I was seeing another woman.'

'You're a man.' She mimicked his tone, hoping that her attempt at humour would conceal the fact that she was absolutely terrified of his answer. 'And that's what men are programmed to do.'

'I get up at three in the morning because I'm aware that you need some sleep,' he said softly. 'And if I'm in bed with you I don't seem to have any self-control.'

Stunned by that unexpected confession, Holly felt her insides flip. 'But by the time you leave the bed we've already—' Her cheeks heated. 'I mean surely even you couldn't?'

'I definitely could,' he assured her silkily. 'It seems where you're concerned, I have a limitless appetite. So you see, *tesoro*, you don't have to worry about the effects of daylight, biscuits, or anything else for that matter. I'm so addicted to your body I even find you sexy in a cartoon tee-shirt—not that I'd ever allow you to wear one of those again,' he went on, clearly concerned she might decide to put that claim to the test.

Basking in the novel experience of being considered irresistible, Holly sipped her orange juice. He didn't reveal anything about his own emotions and they didn't talk about their problems, but they seemed to have reached some sort of truce. 'So where *do* you go when you leave our bed?'

'I work. Usually in the study.'

Holly gave a disbelieving laugh because that altogether more simple explanation hadn't occurred to her. 'I just assumed—The thing is, I've been so worried.' Weak with relief, she confessed, 'I mean, I know you had loads of relationships before me.'

'I sense this is turning into one of those female questions where every answer is always going to be the wrong one,' he drawled and she bit her lip.

'But—were you with someone when we met at the rugby?'

'Technically, no.'

'What's that supposed to mean? I read about a super-model—'

'You don't want to believe everything you read.'

'But —'

His tone was impatient. 'What can you possibly gain from this line of questioning?'

Reassurance? She gave a painful laugh as she realised the foolishness of that. Reassurance about what—that he loved her? He didn't. She knew he didn't. 'I was just—interested.'

'You were just being a woman. Forget it.' He rose to his feet. 'Remember that the past is always behind you. Are you ready?'

'For what?' She decided that this wasn't the right time to

point out that the past wasn't behind him, even if he believed that it was. It was obvious to her that it was with him every agonising minute of the day. 'Where are we going?'

His gaze lingered on her face. 'To spend some time together. Isn't that what you wanted? You said that I don't spend any time with you during the day,' he reminded her softly. 'And that we've never actually been on a date. So we're going to rectify that.'

'We're going on a date?' Holly couldn't stop the smile. 'Where?'

'The most romantic city in the world. Rome.'

CHAPTER SEVEN

'THIS is your idea of a date? When you said we were visiting romantic Rome, I imagined wandering hand in hand to the Spanish Steps and the Colosseum. Not sitting in a rugby stadium,' Holly muttered, taking her seat and waving enthusiastically to the very vocal crowd.

Casper gave her a rare smile. 'You wanted to be alone with me. We're alone.'

'This is your idea of alone?' Holly glanced at the security team surrounding them, and then at the enormous crowd who were cheering as the players jogged onto the pitch. 'Are you delusional?'

'Stadio Flaminio is a small stadium—intimate.'

Holly started to laugh. 'I suppose everything is relative. It's small compared with Twickenham. This time we're only in the company of thirty thousand people. But is this really your idea of romantic? A rugby match?'

'We met during a rugby match,' Casper reminded her, and their eyes clashed as both of them remembered the sheer breathless intensity of that meeting. 'I am mixing my two passions. Rugby and you.'

He didn't actually mean *her,* did he? He meant her body.

'I—I've never actually watched a game before,' Holly confessed shakily, dragging her eyes from his and wondering what it was about him that reduced her to jelly. 'I was always working. I don't even know the rules.'

'One team has to score more points than the other,' Casper said dryly, leaning forward as the game started, his gaze intent on the pitch.

'By all piling on top of each other?' Holly winced as she watched the players throw themselves into the game with no apparent care for their own safety. 'It's all very macho, isn't it? Lots of mud, blood and muscle.'

'They're following strict rules. Watch. You might find it exciting.'

And she did.

At first she sat in silence, determined not to ruin his enjoyment by asking inane questions, and equally determined to try and understand what he loved about the game. But, far from ignoring her, he seemed keen to involve her in everything that was going on.

There was a sudden roar from the crowd as a man powered down the field with the ball.

'He's fast,' Holly breathed, and Casper's shoulders tensed and then he punched the air.

'He's scored the opening try.'

'That's when he puts the ball down on the line—and that's five points, right?'

Casper was absorbed in the game, but not too absorbed to make the occasional observation for her benefit. Gradually he explained the rules, until the game no longer looked like a playground fight fuelled by testosterone, and instead became an extremely exciting sporting challenge.

Towards the second half of the match Holly discovered that she was leaning forward too, her eyes on the pitch, equally absorbed by what was happening. 'That was a brilliant run through the Italian defence.' Turning to find Casper watching her, she blushed. 'What? Did I say something stupid?'

'No.' His voice was husky and there was a strange light in his eyes. 'You are quite right. It *was* a brilliant run by England. You are enjoying yourself?'

'Very much.' She gave a tentative smile, and turned back to the pitch. 'That tackle was by the Italian hooker, is that right?' Suddenly aware that the sun was shining down on them, and she was far too hot, she released a few buttons on her jacket. 'I can't believe they named a rugby position after a prostitute.'

'They are called hookers because they use their feet to hook the ball in the scrum. They're a key…' His voice tailed off in the middle of the sentence, and all his attention was suddenly focused on the delicate lace of her camisole. 'Sorry, what was the question?' He dragged his gaze up to hers, his eyes suddenly blank, and she gave a feminine smile.

'You were teaching me about rugby.'

'If you really want to learn,' he breathed, leaning closer to her, 'Don't start undressing in the middle of my answer.'

'I was hot.'

He gave a wry smile. 'So am I.'

Delighted by the effect she was having on him, her eyes sparkled. 'Where were we? Oh yes—you were telling me about the hooker.'

He stroked a finger over her cheek. 'Unless you want to find yourself participating in an indecent act in a public place,' he purred, 'I suggest you stop teasing. And the hooker is a key position in attacking and defensive play.'

Suddenly she wished they were somewhere more private. 'So you played rugby at school and university, is that right?' Swiftly she changed the subject. 'That's how you know the England captain?'

'He has been a close friend of mine for years.'

And watching rugby was probably one of the few occasions when he could switch off and forget he was a prince, Holly thought to herself as they both settled down to watch the game again.

The match ended with an England victory, and Casper and Holly joined the players at the post-match reception.

Casper was guest of honour and gave a short, humorous speech that had everyone laughing. Watching him mingle with the players and guests afterwards, Holly was fascinated by the change in him. As he smoothly and skilfully dealt with all the people who wanted to speak to him, there was no sign of the icily reserved man she'd been living with, and in his place was the confident, charismatic prince who had seduced her.

But this was his public persona, she reminded herself.

He switched on the charm and gave them what they expected.

But at what personal sacrifice?

He'd buried his own needs for those of other people.

And now he was laughing with the England captain, his old friend, and Holly pushed aside darker thoughts as he introduced her.

'You look different without the mud,' she confessed naïvely, and the man lifted her hand to his lips with laughter in his eyes.

'So you're the woman who distracted me at Twickenham. There I was, focusing on the ball, trying to block out the world around me, and suddenly Royal Boy here is kissing this stunning woman.'

Holly blushed. 'You've known each other a long time.'

'I know all his secrets, but I wouldn't dare tell.' The man grinned. 'He's bigger and tougher than me.'

Holly's eyes slid to Casper's broad shoulders and she reflected on the fact that his physique was every bit as impressive as this man who was a sporting hero to millions. Her stomach squirmed with longing and she felt herself blushing as her eyes met his questioning gaze.

'I really enjoyed the game,' she said hastily. 'Thanks for taking me.'

The England captain punched Casper on the arm. 'I can understand why you married her. Any woman who thanks you for taking them to a game of rugby has got to be worth hanging onto.' He winked. 'And it helps that she looks gorgeous.'

'All right, enough.' Casper curved an arm around Holly's shoulders in an unmistakeably possessive gesture. 'Time for you to go and charm someone else.'

Finally they were escorted to the waiting limousine, and Holly slid inside. 'I really envy the fact that when you speak all the words come out in the right order.'

Casper's glance was amused. 'And that's surprising?'

'Well, I'm all right with words generally, but in a tricky situation they never come out the way I want them too. I always think of the right thing to say about four days after the opportunity to say it has passed. And I'm *hopeless* at standing up for myself because I hate conflict. The moment anyone glares at me I just want them to stop being angry, and the words tie themselves in knots in my mouth.'

'You stood up to me that day in your friend's flat.'

'That was an exception,' she muttered. 'You were saying awful things to me, none of them true. Generally if someone yells at me I turn into a mute.' The car sped through the centre of Rome, negotiating the clog of traffic and tourists.

'No matter how hard I try, I can't imagine you as a mute,' Casper said dryly, and Holly shrugged.

'I envy your confidence. I've never had much of that.' She studied his profile. 'You must miss the days when you could just go to rugby matches and spend time with your friends.

Was it hard for you—becoming the ruling prince? I mean, it wasn't what you expected, was it?'

For a moment he didn't answer, then his mouth tightened slightly. 'The circumstances were hard.'

Had he just shut it away? she wondered. For eight years? If so, no wonder he seemed so cold and detached with her. He'd never given himself a chance to heal.

'Have you *ever* talked about it?' Concern for him made her bold. 'Sorry, but bottling it up for ever can't be a good thing.'

'Holly—'

'Sorry, sorry; OK, I won't ask again,' she said hastily. 'But do you think you could at least give me some detail about how your work evolved? It's just a bit embarrassing when people who have lived here all their lives say things to me and I have to look as though I know what they're talking about, while I really don't have a clue. Someone was praising you for your vision and courage—something to do with the way you transformed the way Santallia did things. I tried to look as though I knew what he was talking about, but obviously I didn't. I just thought it might help if you told me a bit about—things. I don't want to look thick.' Retreating slightly in her seat as she saw Casper lift long bronzed fingers to his forehead, she braced herself for the explosion of Mediterranean volatility that was inevitably going to follow a gesture of frank exasperation.

Surprisingly, when he looked at her there was laughter in his eyes. 'Has anyone ever told you you'd make an excellent torture weapon? You go on and on until a guy is ready to surrender.'

'It's just jolly hard to talk to people if you don't have all the information, and I don't happen to think silence is healthy,' Holly mumbled, and Casper gave a shake of his head.

'Fine. Tonight over dinner, I will outline the highlights of my life so far. And it's only fair to warn you that you'll be bored out of your mind.'

'We're having dinner? Don't tell me, there will be seven hundred other people there.'

'Just the two of us.'

'Just us?' A dark, dangerous thrill cramped her stomach. Perhaps finally, they'd have the opportunity to deepen their relationship. And she knew she wouldn't be bored hearing about his past. She was fast discovering that nothing about him bored her.

'Just us, Holly.' His voice was soft and his eyes lingered on her mouth. 'Late dinner. After our trip to the opera.'

'You're taking me to the opera? Seriously?'

'Given that you sing all the time, I thought you might enjoy it.'

In the darkened auditorium, Casper found himself focusing on Holly's face rather than the opera.

He could see the glisten of tears in her eyes as she responded to the emotional story being played out on the stage in front of them, and marvelled at how open she was with her feelings.

Since the curtain had risen, she'd appeared to have forgotten his existence, so lost was she in Mozart's score and the beauty of the singing.

Casper's eyes rested on the seductive curve of her shoulders, bared by the exquisite sequinned dress that appeared to be superglued to her exotic curves. Around the slender column of her neck were the pink diamonds, glittering against her smooth, pale skin.

From the tip of her simple satin shoes to the elegant coil of her newly straightened hair, she'd slipped into the role of princess with astonishing ease.

Their trip had somehow become public knowledge and, when their limousine had pulled up outside the opera house, a crowd had gathered hoping to see them.

But far from being daunted, or even disappointed that their 'private' evening had become public, she'd spent several minutes chatting, smiling and charming both the crowd and the photographers, until Casper had pointed out that they were going to miss the opera.

And when they'd walked into their box there had been no privacy because every head in the opera house had turned to gaze. Even now he was sure that half the audience were straining to catch a glimpse of his wife, rather than the soprano currently giving her all on the stage.

But Holly wasn't bothered.

He'd misjudged her, he admitted to himself, studying her profile in the darkness.

He'd thought that she would struggle with her new life.

But her only complaint was that he didn't spend enough time with her.

In the grip of a sudden surge of lust, Casper contemplated suggesting that they cut out during the interval, but he couldn't bring himself to do that because she was so obviously enjoying herself.

She was so enthusiastic about everything—meeting people, opera—even rugby.

Casper frowned slightly, admitting to himself that she'd surprised him. Over and over again. He'd expected her to struggle with the crowds and the attention but she'd responded like a professional. He'd thought she'd be tongue tied at official functions, but she was so warm and friendly that everyone was keen to engage her in conversation. He'd expected her to snap at him for dragging her to the rugby, but after the initial humour she'd shown as much interest and energy in that as she did with everything.

He remembered her comment about being lonely and his mind wandered back to the newspaper article that had revealed her pregnancy. At the time he'd been so angry, he hadn't paid attention.

But hadn't there been some revelation about her father?

'So this *palazzo* is owned by one of your friends?' Holly wandered onto the roof terrace, which felt like a slice of paradise in the centre of such a busy city. A profusion of exotic plants and flowers twisted around the ornate iron balustrade, and in the distance she could see the floodlit Colosseum. 'You certainly have influential friends.'

'It is more private than staying in a hotel, or as the guest of the President.'

For once they were guaranteed complete privacy, and that fact alone somehow increased the feeling of intimacy.

She'd wanted to be alone, but now that they were, she felt ridiculously self-conscious.

'I love the diamonds.' She touched her necklace and he smiled.

'They look good on you. I'm glad you didn't change.'

Aware that Casper had watched her more than the opera, Holly had opted to wear the same dress for dinner. The fact that he hadn't been able to take his eyes off her had been a heady experience.

'You like my dress?' Smoothing her hands over her hips in a typically feminine gesture, she glanced down at herself. 'It's not too clingy?'

'It's you I like,' he murmured, 'not the dress.' He stroked a hand over her shoulder and Holly decided that she might wear the dress for ever.

'All right, now this feels like being on a date,' she said, laughing nervously as she took the glass of champagne he was offering her. 'The weather is gorgeous. It's really warm, considering it's only March.'

'You finally have me alone, and our topic of conversation is going to be the weather?' Casper trailed appreciative dark eyes down her body. 'Has today tired you out?'

'No.' Her nerves on fire, she walked to the edge of the balcony and stared at the ruins of the Colosseum, reminding herself to be careful what she said. 'It's been fun. Thank you.'

'It's probably less tiring than the visits you've been doing. You're in the early stages of pregnancy. Your doctor told me that it can be an exhausting time. Most women in your position would have been lying in the sun with a book.'

'If I wasn't married to you, I'd be waiting tables, pregnant or not,' Holly said dryly, glancing at her luxurious, privileged surroundings with something close to disbelief. 'Being married to you isn't exactly tiring. Someone else makes all the arrangements and tells me where I need to be and when. I even have someone who suggests what I wear. Someone does my hair and make-up. I just turn up and chat to people.'

'And chatting is your favourite occupation. Are you hungry?' Amusement shimmered in his eyes as he steered her towards the table. Silver glinted and candles flickered, and the air was filled with the scent of flowers. 'I must admit I hadn't expected you to cope so well with all the attention. When I first met you, you seemed very insecure. I hadn't factored in how warm and friendly you are. You have a real talent with people.'

'I do?' Warmed by his unexpectedly generous praise, Holly glowed, smiling her thanks at a member of staff who discreetly placed a napkin on her lap. 'That's a nice thing to say.'

'Why were you a waitress?'

'What's wrong with being a waitress?'

'Don't be defensive.' He waited while a team of staff served their food and then dismissed them with a discreet glance towards the door. 'There's nothing wrong with being a waitress, but you could have done a great deal more. You're obviously very bright—even if maths isn't "your thing".'

'I've never been very ambitious.' Holly sipped her drink, wondering if honesty would destroy the atmosphere. 'I know it isn't trendy or politically correct to admit to it, but all I really wanted was to have a baby. When other girls wanted to be doctors or lawyers, I just wanted to be a mum. Not just any mum, but a brilliant mum. And before you say anything, yes, I suppose a psychologist would have a field day with that and say I wanted to make up for my parents' deficient parenting—but actually I don't think that had anything to do with it. I think I just have a very strong maternal instinct.'

'You're right, it isn't politically correct to admit that.' His eyes held hers. 'Most of the women I know think babies are something to be postponed until they've done all the other things in life.'

Not wanting to think about the women he knew, Holly looked away. 'I always saw children as a beginning, not as an end.' She glanced towards the open glass doors and saw several members of staff hovering. 'Do you think—could they just put the dishes on the table and leave us alone?'

She didn't even see him gesture and yet the staff melted away and the doors were closed, leaving them alone.

'I love it when you do that.' Holly grinned and picked up her fork. 'Do the whole powerful prince thing: "you are dismissed". Do you ever eat in restaurants?'

'Occasionally, but it usually causes too much of a security headache for all concerned. You enjoyed the opera, didn't you?'

'It was fantastic. The costumes, the music.' She sighed. 'Can we go again some time?'

'You've never been before? But you were living in London—a mecca for culture.'

'If you have money. And, even then, London can be a pretty lonely place,' Holly said lightly. 'Loads of people all going about their business, heads down, not looking left or right. I hated the anonymity of it—the fact that no one cared about anyone else. I always thought it would be great to live in a small village where everyone knows everyone, but I needed the work, and there's always work in a city.'

'You don't like being on your own, do you?'

Holly played with her fork. 'No. I suppose I was on my own a lot as a child and I hated it. After my dad left, my mum had to go out to work, and she couldn't afford childcare so she pretty much left me to my own devices. Then she died, and—' She poked at the food on her plate. 'Let's just say I don't associate being on my own with happy feelings. Screwed-up Holly.'

'You seem remarkably balanced to me, considering the state of the world around us.' He gave a faint smile. 'A little dreamy and naïve perhaps. Did you read fairy tales as a child?'

'What's that supposed to mean? I don't believe in fairies, if that's what you're asking me.'

'But you believe in love,' he drawled, curling his long fingers around the slender stem of his glass.

'Love isn't a fairy tale.'

'Isn't it?' The flickering candles illuminated the hard planes of his handsome face and the cynical glitter of his eyes.

'Do you realise how weird this is? I mean—you're the prince with the palace and you're telling me you don't believe in fairy tales. Bizarre.' Holly laughed. 'And, if you were already living out the fairy story, what did your nannies read you? Something about normal people?'

'I was swamped by literature drumming in the importance of responsibility and duty.'

Pondering that revealing statement, Holly studied him thoughtfully. 'So it was all about what your country needed.

Not about you as a person. What was your childhood like? Did it feel weird being a prince?'

'I've never been anything else, so I have no idea. But my childhood was pretty normal.' He leaned forward and topped up her glass. 'I was educated at home, and then went to boarding school in England, university in the States and then returned here to work on the tourist development programme.'

'Everyone says you did a brilliant job. Do you miss it?'

'I still keep my eye on all the projects. I'm probably more involved than I should be.' He was unusually communicative, and if Holly was only too aware that they weren't talking about any of the difficult stuff, well, she decided it didn't matter. At least they were talking about *something*. And at least they were alone together instead of surrounded by a crowd of dignitaries.

'I wish we could do this more often,' she said impulsively and then blushed as he rose from the table, a purposeful gleam in his eyes.

'We will. And now that's enough talking.' He pulled her gently to her feet and she stood, heart thumping, and he slid his hands around her face and gave an unexpected smile.

'For the rest of the evening,' he murmured softly, 'It's actions, not words. How does this spectacular dress come off?'

'Zip at the back,' Holly murmured, offering no resistance as he lowered his head to hers.

As always the skilled touch of his mouth sent her head into a spin, and she gave a moan of pleasure as his arms slid round her and he pulled her hard against his powerful frame.

'I want you.' He murmured the words against her lips, his mouth hot and demanding. 'I want you naked, right now.'

Her tummy tumbling, Holly gasped as he lifted her easily and carried her through to the gorgeous bedroom. The French doors remained open and she could hear the faint rush of the sea as he laid her down on the four-poster bed.

Would he notice that her boobs had grown and that her stomach was now slightly rounded? Holly squirmed slightly against the sheets and he kissed her again, using his skill and experience to drive away her inhibitions.

When he slid a hand over her stomach she tensed, and when his mouth trailed down her body she moaned and arched against him, unable to resist what he did to her.

And he did it over and over again, until she finally floated back down to earth, stunned and disconnected and with no clue as to how much time had passed.

Casper shifted above her, fire and heat flickering in his molten dark eyes as his satisfied gaze swept her flushed cheeks. 'I've *never* wanted a woman as much as I want you.'

Heart thudding, Holly gazed up at him. 'I love you.' The confession was torn from her in that moment of vulnerability, and she wrapped her arms round him and buried her face in his neck, breathing in the scent of virile male. 'I love you, Cas. I love you.'

And it was true, she realised helplessly. She did love him.

He was complicated, and he'd hurt her, but somewhere along the way she'd stopped trying to make their relationship work for the sake of the baby, and had started to fall in love.

Or perhaps it had always been there. From that first moment they'd met at the rugby match. Certainly there'd been *something*. How else could you explain the fact that she'd shared an intimacy with him she'd never shared with any other man?

Shocked by her own revelation, it took her a moment to realise that Casper had made no response.

He hadn't spoken and he hadn't moved.

It was as if her words had turned him to stone.

And then he rolled out of the affectionate circle of her arms and onto his back.

The honesty of her confession somehow made his sudden withdrawal all the more shocking. Wracked by a sense of isolation and rejection, Holly instinctively snuggled against him, but his tension was unmistakeable.

'Don't ever say that to me, Holly. Don't ever confuse great sex with love.'

'I'm not confused. I know what I feel. And I don't expect you to say it back, but that doesn't mean I can't say it to you.' Tentatively, she slid her arm over the flat, muscular plains of his stomach. 'I love you. And you don't have to be afraid of that.'

He muttered something under his breath and then shook her off and sprang off of bed. '"I love you" has to be the most overused phrase in the English language. So overused that it's lost its meaning.'

Holly crumpled as she watched her gift devalued in a single stroke. 'It hasn't lost its meaning to me.'

'No?' His eyes hard, he thrust his arms into a robe. 'Usually when people say "I love you" they mean something else. They mean, "you're great in bed", or perhaps, "I love the fact that you're rich and you can show me a good time". For you it's probably, "I love the fact that you were prepared to take on my baby".'

Holly flinched as though he'd slapped her. 'How can you say that?' Her voice cracked. 'Even after this time we've spent together, you still don't know me, do you? I'm trying to do what's best for our child, and you're being needlessly cruel—'

'Honest.'

'I've never said those words to anyone in my life before, and you just threw them back in my face.' The breath trapped in her throat, she watched him. 'Just so that there is no mis-understanding, let me tell you what "I love you" means to me. It means that I care more about your happiness than my own. And I care *all the time*, not just when we're having great sex. "I love you" means ignoring the pain you inflict every time you accuse me of lying, because I *know* you've been hurt yourself even though you won't talk to me about it. It means being patient and trying to accept that you find it hard to share your thoughts and feelings with me. And it's because I love you that I'm still standing here, swallowing my pride and trying to make this work, even when you hurt me on purpose.'

There was a long, deathly silence and then he lifted his hands, pressed his fingers to his temples and inhaled deeply. 'If that's really what you feel, then I'm sorry,' he said hoarsely, and his voice was strangely thickened. 'I can't give you anything back. I don't have that capacity any more.'

Without waiting for her response, he strode out of the bedroom, leaving her alone.

CHAPTER EIGHT

As the door slammed shut between them, Holly flopped back onto the pillows, emotionally shattered.

How had such a perfect evening ended so badly?

Why should her simple declaration of love have had such a dramatic effect on his mood?

She thought back to his dismissive comments about fairy stories, love and happy endings.

Yes, he'd lost his fiancée, but even extreme grief shouldn't lead to that degree of cynicism should it?

And what had he meant when he said he *couldn't* love?

Was he saying that he believed a person could only love once in their lives?

Was that what was going on in his head?

Or was he saying that he couldn't love *her?*

Frustrated and desperately upset, Holly slipped out of bed, slipped her arms into a silk robe and walked across the bedroom. She stood for a moment with her hand on the door, wanting to follow him and yet afraid of further rejection.

Her hand dropped to her side and she stared at the door, her head a whirlpool of indecision.

She wanted him to talk, and yet she was afraid of hearing what he had to say.

She didn't want to hear that loving and losing another woman had prevented him ever loving again.

Because that would mean that there was no hope for them.

And yet not talking about it wasn't going to change things, was it?

Hoping she was doing the right thing, Holly slowly opened the door, realising that she had no idea where he'd gone.

What if he'd left the *palazzo*?

And then she saw a chink of light under the door to the library that they'd been shown when they'd arrived earlier.

Taking a deep breath, she tapped lightly on the door and opened it.

Casper stood with his back to her, staring out of the window.

Holly closed the door carefully. 'Please don't walk away from me,' she said quietly. 'If we need to have a difficult conversation, then let's have it. But don't avoid it. We don't stand any chance if you don't talk to me.' She knew from the sudden tension in his shoulders that he'd heard her, but it seemed like ages before he responded.

'I can't give you what you want, Holly. Love wasn't part of our deal.'

'Stop talking about it as a deal!' She stared at his back helplessly. 'Could you *please* at least look at me? This is hard enough without being able to see your face.'

He turned and she froze in shock, because his handsome face looked as though it had been chiselled from white marble. His eyes were blank of expression and yet the depth of his pain was evident in the very stillness of his body.

'Talk to me, Cas.' Forgetting her own misery, she walked across to him. 'Why can't you love? Is it because you lost Antonia? Is that it? Is this still about your grief?' And then she saw something in his face—a hardness—and everything fell into place. His comments. His beliefs. His *cynicism*.

Suddenly she just *knew*. 'Oh God—she did something dreadful to you, didn't she?'

'Holly—'

Ignoring his warning tone, she slid her hand into his larger one. 'All this time I've been assuming you were madly in love with her, and perhaps you were once.' Her eyes were on his rigid profile. 'But she let you down, didn't she? That's the reason you were so cynical about my motives. That's the reason you say you can't love. You don't *want* to let yourself love. Because you loved once before and she hurt you so badly. She did something, I know she did. *Tell* me about it.'

'Holly.' His voice thickened, and he turned on her. 'Just leave it.'

'No, I won't leave it.' She tightened her grip on his hand, refusing to let him withdraw. 'I want to know. I *deserve* to know.' Tears clogged her throat. *'What did she do?'*

A muscle worked in his lean jaw, and he stared at her, his eyes empty of emotion. 'She was sleeping with my brother.'

His revelation was so unexpected that Holly just stared at him. 'Oh, dear God.'

He gave a twisted smile and looked at her, his eyes strangely blank of emotion. 'Shall I tell you what Antonia meant when she said "I love you"? She meant that she loved the glitter and glamour of royal life. All the high-profile stuff. Only in those days I was working flat out in a commercial role. I didn't do many public engagements. I never expected to be the ruling prince. I didn't even want it. But Antonia did. For her, "I love you" meant "I love what you can do for my lifestyle", and once she found someone who could do more for her she transferred her "love" to them. The life my brother offered her was just too tempting.'

'I'm so sorry.'

'Don't be. I was naïve.' He removed his hand from hers. 'I was young enough and arrogant enough not to question her notion of love. I thought she cared about me and that what we shared was real.'

'The accident.'

Casper drew in a breath. 'We were on a skiing trip, Antonia and I. My brother joined us unexpectedly, and that was when I realised what was going on. Stupidly I confronted both of them, right there, at the top of the mountain where the helicopter had dropped us. My brother skied off and she followed.' He was silent for a moment. 'I went after them but I was quite a way behind. They caught the full force of the avalanche. There was nothing I could do. I was swept into a tree and knocked unconscious.'

'Did you tell anyone?' Her voice was soft. 'When you recovered, did you tell anyone the truth?'

'The country was in a state of crisis—defiling my brother's memory would have achieved nothing.'

'Forget about your country—what about *you*?'

'I couldn't forget about my country. I had a responsibility to the people.'

Holly swallowed down the lump in her throat. 'So you just buried it inside and carried on.'

'Of course.'

'And the only way to cope with so much emotion was to block it out.' Impulsively she slid her arms around his waist. 'Now I understand why you don't believe in love. But that wasn't love, Cas. She didn't love you.'

He closed his hands over her shoulders and gently but firmly prised her away from him. 'Close your book of fairy tales, Holly.' His voice was rough. 'The fact that you know the truth doesn't change anything.'

'It changes it for me.'

'Then you're deluding yourself.' His tone was harsh. 'Inside that dreamy head of yours, you're telling yourself that I'll fall in love with you. And that is never going to happen.'

She ignored the shaft of pain. 'Because you're afraid of being hurt again?'

'After the accident I switched off my emotions because that was the only way of getting through each day. I didn't want to feel. I couldn't afford to feel. How could I fulfil my responsibilities if I was wallowing in my personal grief?'

'So you shut it down, but that doesn't mean—'

'Don't do this!' With a soft curse, he lifted her face to his and forced her to meet his gaze. 'I'm not capable of feeling. And I'm not capable of love. I don't want love to be part of my life. We share great sex. Be grateful for that.'

That bleak confession made her heart stumble, and her voice was barely a whisper in the dimly lit room as she voiced the question that had been worrying her since the day she'd discovered she was pregnant. 'If you really can't love me, then I'll try and accept that. But I have to ask you one thing, Casper.' She was so terrified of the answer that she almost couldn't bear to ask the question. But she *had* to ask it. 'Do you think you can love our baby?'

His gaze held hers for a long moment and then his hands dropped to his side. 'I don't know,' he said hoarsely. 'I honestly don't know.'

Her hopes crashed into a million pieces.

'Don't say that to me, Cas.'

'You wanted the truth. I'm giving you the truth.'

And this time it was Holly who walked out of the room and closed the door between them.

'I'm worried about her, Your Highness. She isn't eating properly and she cancelled an engagement this afternoon.'

Emilio's normally impassive features were creased with worry. 'That isn't like her. I thought you ought to know.'

Casper glanced up from the pile of official papers on his desk. 'I expect she's tired.' Holly had been asleep when he'd finally joined her in the bed the previous night. *Or had she been pretending?* He frowned, wondering why that thought hadn't occurred to him before. 'And pregnant women are often faddy in their eating.'

'The princess isn't faddy, sir.' Emilio acted as though his feet had been welded to the spot. 'She loves her food. Even hot-tempered Pietro didn't have a single tantrum when he was cooking for her. Since you came back from Rome two weeks ago, she has eaten next to nothing. And she's stopped singing.'

Casper slowly and carefully put down the draft proposal he was reading.

She'd also stopped smiling, talking and cuddling him.

Since that night in Rome, Holly had behaved with a polite formality that was totally at odds with her outgoing personality. She answered his questions, but she asked none of her own, and she was invariably in bed asleep by the time he joined her.

She was dragging herself around like a wounded animal trying to find a place to die, and Casper gritted his teeth.

He had no reason to feel guilty.

And it should be a matter of indifference to him that his Head of Security clearly suspected that he had something to do with Holly's current level of distress. 'You are responsible for her physical well-being, not her emotional health.' His tone cool, Casper closed the file on his desk. 'It isn't your concern.'

'The princess was extremely kind to me when Tomasso was ill.' Emilio stood there, looking as though a hurricane wouldn't dislodge him. 'I want to make sure nothing is wrong. Two days ago when she opened the new primary school she just picked at her food, and yesterday when lunch was sent up to the apartment it came back untouched. Shall I ask her staff to call the doctor?'

'She doesn't need the doctor.' Casper pushed back his chair violently and stood up. 'I'll talk to her.'

'I think she needs a doctor.' In response to the sardonic lift of Casper's eyebrows, Emilio coloured. 'It's just that, if there is something upsetting her, she might need to talk to someone.'

'*Talk* to someone?' Casper looked at him with naked incredulity. 'Emilio, since when did a hardened ex-special forces soldier advocate talking therapy?'

Emilio didn't back down. 'Holly likes to talk, Your Highness.'

'I had noticed.'

But he wasn't talking to her, was he? Casper lifted a hand and rubbed his fingers over his forehead. 'I'll talk to her, Emilio. Thank you for bringing it to my attention.'

Still Emilio didn't move. 'She might prefer to talk to someone outside. Someone who isn't close to her.'

'You think she won't want to talk to me?'

'You can be intimidating, sir. And you're very—blunt. Holly is very optimistic and romantic.'

Not any more. *He was fairly sure he'd killed both those traits*.

Reflecting on that fact, Casper sucked in a breath. 'I can't promise romantic, but I will make sure I'm approachable.'

'May I say one more thing, sir?'

'Can I stop you?'

Ignoring the irony in the prince's tone, Emilio ploughed on. 'I have been by your side since you were thirteen years old. Holly—Her Royal Highness,' he corrected himself hastily, 'Isn't like any of the women you've been with before. She's genuine.'

Genuine? Casper shook his head, not sure whether to be relieved that she'd done such a good PR job on his staff, or exasperated that everyone just took her at face value. They saw nothing beyond the pretty smile and the chatty personality. Apparently it hadn't occurred to a single other person that this baby might not be his. That genuine, kind Holly Phillips might have another side to her.

That people and relationships were not always the way they appeared.

He wondered whether his loyal Head of Security had known Antonia had been sleeping with his brother.

'Thank you, Emilio. I'll deal with it.'

'Will you still be attending the fundraising dinner, sir?'

Casper frowned. 'Yes, of course.'

'The car will be ready at seven-thirty, sir.'

'One question, Emilio.' Casper lifted a hand and the bodyguard stopped. 'Which engagement did she cancel?'

Emilio met his gaze. 'The opening of a new family centre for children from split families, sir. It was an initiative designed to give lone parents support and children the opportunity to spend time with male role-models.' He hesitated and then bowed. 'I'll arrange the car for later.'

Casper stood still for a moment.

Then he cursed long and fluently, cast a frustrated glance at the volume of work on his desk, and turned his back on it and strode through the private apartments looking for Holly.

Holly lay on the bed with her head under the pillow.

She had to get up.

She had things to do. Responsibilities.

But her mind was so exhausted with thinking and worrying that she couldn't move.

'Holly.'

The sound of Casper's voice made her curl the pillow over her head. She didn't want him to see that she'd been crying.

She didn't want to see him at all. 'Go away. I'm tired. I'm having a sleep.'

'We have to talk.'

She curled up like a foetus. 'I'm still trying to get over the last talk we had.'

She heard the strong tread of his footsteps, and then the pillow was firmly prised from the tight ball of her fists. 'You're going to suffocate yourself.'

Holly kept her face turned away from him. 'I think better under the pillow.'

The pillow landed on the floor with a soft thud, and then she felt his hands curve around her and he lifted her into a sitting position. 'I want to look at you when I talk to you.' His fingers lifted her chin and his eyes narrowed. '*Dio*, have you been crying?'

'No, my face always looks like a tomato.' Mortified, she jerked her chin away from his fingers. 'Just go away, Casper.'

But he didn't move.

'The staff tell me you're not eating. They're worried about you.'

'That's kind of them.' Holly rubbed her hands over her arms. 'But I don't fancy anything to eat.'

'You cancelled your engagement this afternoon.'

'I really am sorry about that.' She wished he wouldn't sit so close to her. *She couldn't concentrate when he was this close*. 'But the subject was a bit—painful. I just couldn't face it. I will go, I promise. The visit is going to be rearranged. Just not this week.' Why was it that she just wanted to fling her arms around his neck and sob?

Terrified that she'd give in to the impulse, she wriggled off the bed and walked over to the glass doors that were open onto the balcony.

A breeze played with the filmy curtains, and beyond the

profusion of plants she could see sunlight glistening on the surface of a perfect blue sea.

Although it was only early April, it promised to be a warm day.

And she'd never felt more miserable in her life.

'Forget the visit.' Casper gave a soft curse and strode across to her, pulling her into his arms. 'Enough, Holly.' His voice was rough. 'This is about Rome, isn't it? We've been dancing round the issue for two weeks. Perhaps I was a little too blunt.'

'You were honest.' She stood rigid in his arms, trying to ignore the excitement that fluttered to life in her tummy.

She didn't want to respond.

'You're making yourself ill.'

'It's just hard, that's all.' Holly tried to pull away from him but he held her firmly. 'Normally when I have a problem I talk it through and that's how I deal with things.'

He cupped her face, his eyes holding hers. 'Then talk it through.'

'You make it sound so simple. But who am I supposed to talk to, Casper?' Her voice was a whisper. 'It's all private stuff, isn't it? I can just imagine what some of the more unscrupulous staff would do with a story like that.'

His eyes narrowed. 'You're learning about the media.'

'Yes, well, I've had some experience now.' She was desperately aware of him—of the hardness of his thighs pressing against hers, of the strength of his arms as he held her firmly.

'This is your chance to get your revenge.'

'You really ought to get to know me, instead of just turning me into some stereotypical gold digger. I don't want revenge, Casper. I don't want to hurt you. I just want you to love our baby.' And her. She wanted him to love her. 'And the fact that you can't…' The dilemma started to swirl in her head again. 'I don't know what to do.'

'You've lost weight.' His hands slid slowly down her arms and his mouth tightened. 'You can start by eating.'

'I'm not hungry.'

'Then you should be thinking about the baby.'

It was like pulling the pin out of a hand grenade.

Erupting with a violence that was new to her, Holly lifted a hand and slapped him hard. 'How *dare* you tell me I should be thinking about the baby? I think of nothing else!' Sobbing with fury and outrage, she backed away from him, his stunned expression blurring as tears pricked her eyes. 'From the moment I discovered I was pregnant the baby is the *only* thing I've been thinking of. When you turned up at the flat, that day you were *horrid* to me, I spent two weeks going round and round in circles trying to work out what to do for the best, but I decided that, as this is your baby, marrying you was the right thing to do. Even when you told me that you believe you're infertile I didn't panic, because I know it isn't true and sooner or later you're going to know that too. Then you told me that you couldn't ever love me and that *hurt*—' Her voice cracked. 'Yes, it hurt, but I made myself accept it because I kept reminding myself that it isn't me that matters. But when you said you didn't know if you could love our baby—'

'Holly.' His voice was tight. 'You have to calm down—'

'*Don't tell me to calm down!* Antonia did a dreadful thing to you. Really dreadful. But that isn't our baby's fault. And now I don't know what to do.' She paced the floor, so agitated that she couldn't keep still. 'What sort of a mother would I be if I stayed with a man who can't love his own child? I always thought that the only thing that mattered was to have a father. But is it worse to grow up with a father who doesn't love you? I don't know, and maybe I've done the wrong thing by marrying you, maybe I am a bad mother, but don't *ever* accuse me of not thinking about our baby!'

Casper muttered something in Italian and ran a hand over the back of his neck, tension visible in every angle of his powerful frame. 'I did *not* say that you were a bad mother.'

'But you implied it.'

'Enough!' It was a command, and Holly stilled, her legs trembling so much that she was almost relieved when he strode towards her and scooped her into his arms.

'I hate you,' she whispered, and then she burst into tears and buried her face in his shoulder.

'*Dio,* you have to stop this, you're making yourself ill. Ssh.' He laid her gently on the bed and then lay down next to her and pulled her into his arms, ignoring her attempts to resist. 'Calm down.' He stroked her hair away from her face but Holly couldn't stop crying.

'I'm sorry I hit you. I'm sorry.' Her breath was coming in jerks. 'I've never hit anyone in my life before. It's just that I so badly want you to love the baby. I *need* you to love it, Cas.' She covered her face with her hands. 'You don't know what it's like to have a father that doesn't care. It makes you feel worthless. If your own father doesn't love you, why should anyone else?'

He gave a soft curse, rolled her onto her back and lowered his body onto hers.

Then he gently removed her hands and wiped her face with the edge of the sheet.

'Hush.'

Still crying, she pushed at his powerful chest. 'Cas, don't—' But her protest was cut off by the demands of his mouth, and within seconds she could no longer remember why she hadn't wanted him to kiss her.

The explosion of sexual excitement anaesthetised the turmoil in her brain and she kissed him back, her body responding to his.

Only when she was soft and compliant did Casper finally lift his head.

'Don't use sex like this,' she moaned, and he gave a grim smile.

'I was trying to stop you crying. Now it is my turn to talk,' he said softly. 'And you're not going to interrupt.' He wiped her damp cheeks with a sweep of his thumb. 'I won't make you false promises of love. I can't do that, and it wouldn't be fair to you because I will not lie. But I do promise you this.' His dark eyes locked with hers, demanding her attention. 'I promise that I will be a good father to the baby. I promise that I will not walk off and leave the child, as your father did to you. I promise that I will do everything in my power to make sure that the child grows up feeling secure and valued. I accepted responsibility for the child and I intend to fulfil that responsibility to the best of my ability.'

Numb, sodden with misery, Holly stared up at him. It wasn't what she wanted, but it was a start. And, if he was prepared to do that for a child that he didn't believe was his, perhaps once he discovered that he was the baby's father then…

He'd coped with hurt by turning off his emotions. Maybe nothing could switch them back on again.

Her natural optimism flickered to life.

But she could hope.

'Your favourite lunch, Your Highness. *Pollo alla limone.*'

'Yum.' Holly put down the letter she was writing. 'Pietro, you have no idea how grateful I am that you decided to leave England and work here for a while. The whole of the palace must be rejoicing. Not that the other chefs weren't brilliant, of course,' she said hastily, and Pietro smiled as he placed a simple green salad next to the chicken.

'I'm not cooking for the rest of the palace, madam. Just for you. Those were the prince's orders.'

'Really? I didn't know that.' Thinking of all the other thoughtful gestures the prince had made since that terrible afternoon when she'd hit him, something softened inside her. 'He brought you all the way over here, for *me?*'

'His Royal Highness is most concerned about your comfort and happiness. But so are we all. You and the *bambino*. You say jump, we say "off which cliff?"' Pietro beamed as he lifted a jug. 'Sicilian lemonade?'

'Don't even bother asking. You know I'm addicted.' Smiling, Holly held out her glass to be filled. 'So, are you happy here?'

'*Si,* because to see you blooming with health gives me satisfaction. And when the baby comes no one will prepare his food except me! I have talked to the gardeners, and we are designing a special vegetable patch—all organic and grown in the Santallia sunshine.'

'Puréed Santallian carrot—' Taking a mouthful of chicken, Holly almost choked as she noticed Casper standing in the doorway.

Sunlight glinted off his dark hair, and he looked so outrageously handsome that her heart dropped.

Why did she have to feel like this?

It was no wonder she struggled to keep a degree of emotional distance when he had such a powerful effect on her.

Right from that very first day at the rugby, she'd failed to hold herself back.

Even now, when she knew he had the ability to hurt her and her child, she was willing to risk it all.

She swallowed the lump of food in her mouth and put down her fork. 'I—I didn't know you were joining me for lunch. Here—' she pushed her plate towards him '—Pietro always cooks for the five thousand—we can share.'

'No, madam!' Appalled, Pietro clasped his hands in front of him and then remembered himself and bowed stiffly. 'I can bring more from the kitchen.'

'*Grazie.*' Casper gave Pietro a rare smile and sat down opposite Holly, his eyes on the pile of envelopes. 'You've been busy.'

'I'm replying to all these children who are sending me pictures and letters. There are hundreds. And look, Cas.' Relieved for an excuse to focus on something other than the way he made her feel, Holly put down her fork and reached for a pink envelope. 'A little girl sent me this soft toy she made. Isn't it sweet?'

Casper's brows rose as he stared at the object. 'What is it supposed to be?'

'Well, it's…' Holly studied the pink fluffy wedge closely and then frowned. 'I thought it might be a pig, or possibly a sheep. I'm not absolutely sure,' she conceded, 'But I love it. She's only six. Don't you think it's brilliant?'

'So you are writing to thank her for sending you a something?' Casper stretched his legs out, his eyes amused. 'That is one letter I would like to read.'

'I'll think of something to say.' Holly put the fluffy object away carefully. 'People are so kind. And talking of kind…' She bit her lip and looked up at him. 'Thank you for arranging for Pietro to come here. And for flying Nicky out for a week. That was so thoughtful.'

'I thought you needed someone to talk to. And she was very loyal to you when you were in trouble.'

'Is that why you gave her that beautiful bracelet? She loved it. And we had such a good time at the beach. Thank you.'

He seemed about to say something in response, but at that moment several staff appeared with lunch.

Pietro served the prince with a flourish. 'If there is anything else, please call,' he murmured and then retreated, leaving them alone.

Casper glanced at Holly. 'Eat,' he drawled, 'Or Pietro will resign.'

Holly smiled, very conscious of his eyes on her. 'I'd be the size of a small-tower block if I ate everything Pietro gave me.'

'Does that explain why the palace cats are putting on weight?'

Holly picked up her fork again. 'I *am* eating.'

'I know. The doctor is very happy with your health, including your weight gain.'

Her heart fluttered. 'You asked him?'

Their eyes clashed. 'I care, Holly.'

She believed him. He'd demonstrated that over and over again. But it was impossible to forget the words he'd spoken in Rome. And she couldn't stop asking herself whether caring was going to be enough. 'The nursery is finished.' Pushing the thought away, she gave a bright smile. 'The designer you suggested is brilliant. It looks gorgeous.'

'Good. I bought you a present.' He handed her a box. 'I hope you like it.'

Holly's hand shook as she took it from him. 'I don't need anything.'

'A present shouldn't be something you need. It should be wantonly extravagant.'

Holly flipped open the box and gasped. 'Well, it's certainly that!' Carefully she lifted the diamond bracelet from its velvet nest. 'It matches my necklace.'

He was trying to compensate for the fact that he didn't love her.

The thought almost choked her.

'*Now* what's wrong?' His voice rough, he laid his fork down.

'Nothing.' She fastened the bracelet around her wrist and gave him a brilliant smile. 'What could possibly be wrong?'

'You're holding back. For once there is plenty going on in your head that isn't coming out of your mouth, and that makes me uneasy.' After a moment's hesitation, he reached across the table to take her hand. 'You're still not yourself, Holly. I feel as though I can never quite reach you.'

'We're together every night.'

'Physically, yes. We have incredible sex and then you turn your back on me and say good night.'

Colour flaming in her cheeks, Holly studied the remains of the chicken on her plate.

She could feel the hot sunshine on the back of her neck, the whisper of a breeze playing with her hair and the blaze of heat in his eyes as he watched her.

'I'm trying to—we're different.' Staring miserably at the glittering diamonds, she wondered absently whether the extravagance of the gift was inversely related to his feelings for her. *The emptier his heart, the bigger the diamonds?* 'I'm very demonstrative by nature, and you're—not. All the worst moments in our relationship have been when I've shown my feelings. You back off. You shut down like a nuclear reactor detecting a leak. Nothing must escape.'

Casper frowned and his grip tightened on her hand. 'So you're protecting me?'

'No.' Finally she lifted her eyes and looked at him. 'I'm protecting myself.'

CHAPTER NINE

DETERMINED to keep busy, Holly threw herself into her public engagements and wrote as many personal replies as she could to the many letters and cards she received. She discovered that if she kept herself busy she didn't think so much and that was a good thing because her thoughts frightened her.

She didn't want to think what might happen if Casper didn't love their baby.

And, since that couldn't immediately be resolved, she pushed the thought away.

When the baby was born, she'd worry. Until then, she'd hope.

And in the meantime she fussed in the nursery, as if being born into perfect surroundings might somehow compensate for deficiencies in other areas of the baby's life.

She was sitting in the hand-carved rocking chair, reading a book about childbirth one morning, when one of the palace staff told her she had a personal visitor.

Not expecting anyone, Holly put the book down and walked through to the beautiful living-room with the windows overlooking the sparkling Mediterranean.

Eddie stood there, looking awkward and out of place.

'Eddie?' Shocked to see him, Holly walked quickly across the room. 'What are you doing here?'

'What sort of a question is that? We were friends once.'
He gave a twisted smile. 'Or can't you have friends now
you're a royal?'

'Of course I can have friends.' Holly blushed, feeling really
awkward and uncomfortable and not sure why. 'But obviously
I wasn't expecting to see you and—how are you?'

'OK. Doing well, actually. The job's turning out well.'

'Good. I'm pleased for you.' And she was, she realised,
picking over her feelings carefully. She wasn't angry with
him. If anything, she was grateful. If he hadn't broken their
engagement, she might well have married him, and that would
have been the biggest mistake of her life—because she knew
now that she didn't love him and she never had.

Loving Casper had taught her what love was, and it wasn't
what she'd felt for Eddie.

'I was owed some holiday.' Thrusting his hands into his
pockets, he walked over to the windows. 'I'm spending a
week in the Italian lakes, but I thought I'd call in here on the
way. Booked myself a room at the posh hotel on the beach.
Stunning view. Can't imagine Lake Como being any prettier
than this.' He took a deep breath, rubbed a hand over the back
of his neck and turned to face her. 'I came here to apologise,
actually. For going to the press. I— It was a rotten thing to do.'

'It's OK. You were upset.' Touched that he'd bothered to
apologise, Holly smiled. 'People do funny things when
they're upset.'

'I didn't mean to make things difficult for you.' Eddie
shrugged sheepishly. 'Well, I suppose I did. I was angry and
jealous and—' he cleared his throat '—I wasn't sure if you'd
want to see me to be honest. But I needed to say sorry. I've
been feeling guilty.'

'Please don't give it another thought.'

Eddie seemed relieved. 'It was jolly hard getting in to see

you. Layers and layers of security. It was that big fellow who fixed it for me.'

'Emilio?'

'That's him. The prince's henchman. Not that the prince needs him. From what I can gather, he can fire his own gun if the need arises. Is he treating you well?'

Holly thought about the diamonds and the long nights spent in sexual ecstasy. And she thought about the fact he didn't love her.

'He's treating me well.'

'Just thought I'd check.' Eddie gave a lopsided smile. 'In case you'd changed you mind and wanted to escape.' He waved a hand around their luxurious surroundings. 'I might not be able to offer you a palace, but—'

'I never wanted a palace, Eddie,' Holly said softly, resting a hand protectively over the baby. 'Family, being loved— those are the things that are important to me.'

'I was going to say I think I was a bit too ambitious for you, but then I realised how bloody stupid that sounds now that you're living with a prince in a palace!' He pulled a face. 'We weren't absolutely right together, were we?'

'No, we weren't,' Holly said honestly. 'And ambition has nothing to do with the reason I'm living here. Cas is my baby's father, Eddie. That's why I'm here.'

'To begin with I was so angry with you. I thought you'd tried to make a fool out of me—'

Holly frowned. 'I'm not like that.'

'I know you're not,' Eddie said, a bit too hastily. 'I hope the prince knows how lucky he is. Anyway, I ought to be going.'

'Already? Don't you want coffee or something?' Holly walked across to him and held out a hand in a gesture of conciliation. 'It was sweet of you to come and see me. I appreciate it. And sweet of you to apologise.'

He hesitated and then took her hand. 'I just wanted to check you're OK. If you ever need anything…'

'She has everything she needs.' A harsh voice came from behind them, and Holly turned to see Casper standing in the doorway, his eyes glittering like shards of ice.

Visibly nervous, Eddie gave a slight bow. 'Your Highness. I— Well, I just wanted to see Holly—say hello—you know how it is. I was just leaving.'

Casper's threatening gaze didn't shift from his face. 'I'll show you out.'

Shocked and more than a little embarrassed by Casper's rudeness, Holly gave Eddie a hug to make up for it. 'Thank you for looking me up.'

Eddie hugged her back awkwardly, one eye on the prince. 'Good to see you looking so well. Bye, Holly.' He left the living room, and moments later Casper strode back into the room, his eyes simmering black with anger.

'I allow you a great deal of freedom,' he said savagely, 'But I do not expect you to entertain your lover in our living room.'

'That's ridiculous.' Holly watched him unravel with appalled disbelief. 'He is *not* my lover. And I don't understand why you're being possessive.'

He didn't care about her, did he?

He didn't want her love.

'But he *was* your lover!' A thunderous expression on his face, Casper prowled across the living room, tension emanating from every bit of his powerful frame. 'And yes, I'm possessive! When I find the father of your baby in my living room, holding your hand, I'm possessive!'

Something snapped inside Holly.

'I never had sex with Eddie! I have never slept with anyone except you!' Consumed by an anger she didn't know she could feel, Holly threw the words at him. 'All you ever say is

your baby, but it's *our* baby, Casper. *This is your baby too.*
And I'm sick of tiptoeing round the issue.'

His voice strangely thickened, Casper faced her down.
'Don't ever, *ever* touch another man!'

'Why? I *like* hugging, and you don't want me hugging you!'
Flinging the words at him like bricks, Holly took a step backwards, a hand over her stomach. 'I can't live like this any more.
I can't live in this—this—emotional desert! I'm afraid to touch
you in case you back away, and I'm afraid to speak in case I
say the wrong thing. I've tried *so hard* to do everything right.
I know this marriage wasn't what you wanted, but I've done
my best. I've worked and worked, and I've been *loyal.* I haven't
once talked about you to anyone, not even when you pushed
me away and I was so lonely I wanted to die! But not once, in
all that time, have I ever given you reason not to trust me.'

A muscle flickered in his jaw. 'It isn't a question of trust.'

'Of course it is!' Her voice was high-pitched and unlike her
usual tone. 'I forgave you for what you thought about me at the
beginning of our relationship because I was honest enough to
admit that I didn't exactly behave like a virgin, even though
that's what I was. I've made allowances for the fact that Antonia
hurt you so badly, and I've made allowances for the fact that your
position as ruling prince meant you weren't allowed to grieve.
But when have you *ever* made allowances for me? Never. Not
once have you given me the benefit of the doubt. *Not once.*' Her
heart was racing and she felt suddenly light-headed.

Casper inhaled sharply. 'Holly—'

'*Don't look at me as if I've lost it!* I am *not* hysterical. In
fact, this is probably the sanest moment I've had since I've
met you. I've always assumed that you act the way you do
because of Antonia, but I'm starting to think it has more to
do with your bloody ego!'

'I've never heard you swear before.'

'Yes, well, our relationship has been full of firsts. First sex, first swearing, first slap around the face—' Feeling the baby kick, Holly placed a hand on her bump and rubbed gently. 'You know what I think, Cas? I don't think this has anything to do with Antonia. I think it's more to do with your macho, alpha, king of the world, dominant—' she waved a hand, searching for more adjectives '—*man* thing. You couldn't bear the thought that I'd slept with another man, and the really ridiculous, crazy thing is *I haven't*!'

'You were engaged to him.'

'But I didn't have sex with him! That's the main reason he dumped me, because I was too shy to take my clothes off!' She glared at him, silencing his next remark with a warning glance. 'And *don't* ask me what happened when I met you, because I still haven't worked that one out. You have a way of undressing a woman that James Bond would envy.'

'You were devastated when you broke up with him.'

'Obviously not *that* devastated or I wouldn't have been having crazy, abandoned sex on a table with you the next day.' A hysterical laugh escaped from her throat. 'Just because you're incapable of indulging in a relationship that doesn't include sex, it doesn't mean I'm the same. Now get out, and stay away from me until you've learned how to be human.'

In the grip of a savage rage, Casper strode through his private rooms and slammed the door of his study.

He'd lost his temper with a pregnant woman.

What had he been thinking?

But he knew the answer to that. He hadn't been thinking at all.

From the moment he'd walked into the living room and seen Eddie standing there holding Holly's hand, his brain had been engulfed in a fiery fog of red-hot jealousy.

Never before had he felt the overwhelming urge to wipe another person from the face of the earth, but he had today.

The thought that Eddie had been near her.

He felt physically sick, his forehead damp and his palms sweating.

He needed to apologise to Holly, but first he needed to make sure that Eddie didn't set foot in her life again.

Not pausing to question the sense of his actions, he ordered his driver to take him to the hotel where Eddie was staying. Ignoring the amazed looks of the hotel reception-staff as they gave him the room number he wanted, Casper dismissed his security guards and then took the stairs two at a time.

Outside the room, he took a deep breath.

He was *not* going to kill him.

Having forced that thought into his head, he hammered on the door.

Eddie pulled it open and the colour drained from his face. 'Your Highness—this is—'

'Why did you break the engagement?' Casper slammed the door shut behind him, guaranteeing their privacy.

Eddie's mouth worked like a fish, and then he gave a slight smile and a shrug, his ego reasserting itself. 'Man to man? Actually I met a stunning blonde. She had amazing—you know.' He gestured with his hands and Casper gritted his teeth and forced himself to ask the question he'd come to ask.

'Did you sleep with Holly?' His voice was thickened, and Eddie gave a confident smile and a knowing wink.

'God, yes—she was bloody insatiable.'

Forgetting his promise to himself, Casper punched the other man hard in the jaw and Eddie staggered backwards, clutching his face.

'God, you've broken my jaw—I'll have you for this!'

'Go ahead.' Casper hauled the man to his feet by the front

of his shirt, ignoring the tearing sound as the fabric gave way. 'So you had sex with Holly, and then you dumped her. Is that what you expect me to believe?'

Eddie touched his jaw gingerly. 'Some girls you have sex with, some girls you marry, you know what I mean?' Fear flickered in his eyes as he registered Casper's expression. 'Still, money changes a person. I'm sure she's changed since she's married you, Your Highness.'

'Are you? I think Holly is the same girl she's always been.' His tone flat, Casper released the other man, shaking him off like a bug from a leaf.

Eddie spluttered with relief and backed away, his hand on his jaw, and then his chest. 'You ripped my shirt.'

'You're lucky I stopped at your shirt.'

'Do you know how much I'm going to get for this story?' Eddie's face was scarlet with rage and Casper shot him a contemptuous glance.

'So it *was* you who sold the story to the paper the first time.'

'Is that what Holly told you?'

'*Don't* call her Holly. To you, it's Her Royal Highness.' Casper flexed his long fingers and had the satisfaction of seeing Eddie take another step backwards. 'And if you *ever* mention the princess's name again, the next thing I rip will be your throat.'

'I thought princes were supposed to be civilised,' Eddie squeaked from his position of safety, and Casper gave a slow, dangerous smile as he strode towards the door.

'I never did believe in fairy stories.'

'I'll be fine, Emilio, honestly. I just feel like some sea air, and The Dowager Cottage is so pretty, right on the sand. It reminds me of the night before my wedding.' *When she'd still been full of hope.*

Holly's face ached from the effort of smiling, and she stuffed a few items into a large canvas bag, as if a day on the beach was just what she wanted, but Emilio didn't look convinced.

'I will call His Highness and—'

'No, don't do that.' Holly interrupted him quickly, wincing as the baby kicked her hard. 'I just want to be on my own for a bit.'

And she didn't want to be in the palace when Casper eventually returned from wherever it was he'd stalked off to.

She just couldn't stand yet another confrontation.

And she had no idea what they were going to do about their marriage. Could they really limp along like this with just her love and hot sex to hold them together?

Was it enough?

Her head started to throb again and she made a conscious effort to switch off her thoughts for the baby's sake, wondering whether the tension was the reason he was kicking so violently.

For the baby's sake, she needed to try and relax.

Without further question, Emilio summoned her driver, and once she arrived at The Dowager Cottage Holly kicked off her shoes and made a conscious effort to unwind. 'I'm just going to sit on the beach for a bit.' She smiled at the man who had become a friend. 'Thanks, Emilio.'

'Pietro made you this, madam.' He handed her a small bag. 'Just a few of your favourite snacks.'

'He is such a sweetie.' Choked by the warmth that they'd showed her, she suddenly rose on tiptoe to kiss Emilio. 'And so are you,' she said huskily, her lips brushing his cheek. 'You've been *so* kind to me all the way through this. Thank you.'

Emilio cleared his throat. 'You are a very special person, madam.'

'I'm a waitress,' Holly reminded him with a dry tone, but Emilio shook his head.

'No.' His voice was soft. 'You're a princess. In every sense that matters.'

Holly blinked several times and suddenly found that she had a lump in her throat. She was so touched by his words that for a moment she couldn't reply.

She *could* be happy with her life, she told herself. She had friends.

'Well, let's hope that's one kiss that the paparazzi didn't manage to catch on camera.' Lightening the atmosphere with a cheeky wink, she walked onto the sand.

'I'll be right here, madam,' Emilio called after her, adjusting the tiny radio he wore in his ear. 'You know how to call me.'

'Thanks. But no one has access to this beach. I'll be fine. Go inside and relax. It's too hot to stand out here.'

Her pale-blue sun dress swinging around her bare calves, Holly walked to the furthest end of the beautiful curving beach and plopped herself down on the sand.

For a while she just stared out to sea. Then she opened the bag Pietro had sent, but discovered she wasn't hungry.

Finally she opened her book.

'You're holding that book upside down. And you should be wearing a hat.' Casper stood there, tall and powerful, the width of his shoulders shading her from the sun. 'You'll burn.'

Holly dropped the book onto the sand. 'Please go away. I want to be alone.' *What she didn't want was to feel this immediate rush of pleasure that always filled her whenever he was near.*

'You *hate* being on your own,' he responded instantly. 'You are the most sociable person I have ever met.'

Holly brushed the sand from the book, her fingers shaking. 'That depends on the company.'

His arrogant, dark head jerked back as though she'd hit him

again, but instead of retaliating he settled himself on the sand next to her, the unusual tension in his shoulders suggesting that he was less than sure of his welcome.

'You're *extremely* angry with me, and I can't blame you for that.' He studied her for a moment and then reached gently for her hand and curled her slender fingers into a fist. 'You can hit me again if you like.'

'It didn't make me feel any better.' She pulled her hand away from his, hating herself for feeling a thrill of excitement instead of indifference. 'And I'd be grateful if you'd stop looking at me like that.'

'How am I looking at you?'

'You're sizing up the situation so that you can decide which of your slick diplomatic skills are required to talk me round.'

'I wish it were that easy.' Casper lifted one broad shoulder in a resigned gesture. 'Unfortunately for me, I have no previous experience of handling a situation like this.'

'Which is?'

'Grovelling.' A gleam of self-mockery glinting in his sexy eyes, he reached for her hand again, this time locking it firmly in his. 'I was wrong about you. The baby is mine. I know that now.'

Holly closed her eyes tightly, swamped by a rush of emotions so powerful that she couldn't breathe.

He believed her. He trusted her.

Finally, he trusted her.

And then she realised that something wasn't quite right about his sudden confession and her eyes flew open. 'Wait a minute.' She snatched her hand away from his because she couldn't keep her mind focused when he was touching her. 'The last time I saw you, you were accusing me of having an affair with Eddie—when did you suddenly become rational?'

Dark streaks of colour highlighted his aristocratic bone

structure, and Casper spread his hands in a gesture of concilia-tion. 'I believe you, Holly. That's all that matters.'

'No.' Holly scrambled to her feet, knowing that she only stood a chance of thinking clearly if he wasn't within touching distance. 'No, it isn't. You went to the doctor, didn't you?'

A muscle flickered in his bronzed cheek. 'Yes.'

Holly wrapped her arms around her waist and gave a painful laugh. 'So you placed your trust in medical science, not me.'

'Holly…'

'So they've told you that you're capable of fathering a child. That's good. But it still doesn't tell you that this child is yours, does it?'

His stunning dark eyes narrowed warily, as if he sensed a trick question. 'I have no doubt that the baby is mine.' He drew in a long breath, his shimmering gaze fixed on her face, as-sessing her reaction. 'I have no doubt that you have been telling me the truth all along.'

'Really? What makes you so confident that I didn't have sex with the whole rugby team once I'd finished with you?' Her voice rising, Holly winced as the baby planted another kick against her ribs, and glared as Casper lifted a hand in what was obviously intended to be a conciliatory gesture.

'You're overreacting because you're pregnant. You're very hormonal and—'

'Hormonal? Don't patronise me! And anyway, if I'm hormonal, what's *your* excuse? You overreact all the time! You accuse me of having sex with just about everyone, even though it should have been perfectly obvious to you that I'd never been with a man before. You thought I was some scheming hussy doing some sort of—of—' she searched for an analogy '—paternity lottery. Trying to win first prize of a prince in the "most eligible daddy" contest.'

Casper rose to his feet, a tall, powerful figure, as imposing in casual clothes as he was in a dinner jacket. His mouth tightened and his lean, strong face was suddenly watchful. 'You have to agree I had reason to feel like that.'

'To begin with, maybe. But *not* once you knew me.' Dragging her eyes away from the hint of bronzed male skin at the neck of his shirt, Holly stooped and stuffed her few items back into her bag. She wasn't going to look at him. So, he was devastatingly handsome. So what? 'I loved you, Casper, and you threw it back at me because you're afraid.'

He inhaled sharply. 'I am not afraid. And you're stuffing sand in your bag along with the books.'

'I don't care about the sand! And you *are* afraid—you're so afraid you've shut yourself down so that you can't ever be hurt again.' Frustrated and upset, she emptied her bag and started again, this time shaking the sand onto the beach.

Casper stepped towards her, dark eyes glittering. 'I came here to apologise.'

Holly stared at him, wishing he wasn't so indecently handsome. *Wishing that she didn't still ache for him to touch her.* 'Then you definitely need more practice, because where I come from apologies usually contain the word sorry at least once.' With a violent movement, she hooked the bag onto her shoulder and reached for her hat, but he caught her arm and held her firmly.

'You are *not* walking away from me.'

'Watch me.' With her free hand, she jammed the hat onto her head and then gasped as he swung her into his arms. 'Put me down *right now*.'

'No.' Ignoring her protest and her wriggling, Casper walked purposefully to the end of the beach, took a narrow path without breaking stride and then lowered her onto soft white sand.

'You've probably put your back out,' Holly muttered, her

fingers curling over his warm, bronzed shoulders to steady herself. 'And it serves you right.'

'You don't weigh anything.'

Noticing their surroundings for the first time, Holly gave a soft gasp of shock, because she'd never seen anywhere quite as beautiful.

'I had no idea there was another beach here. It's stunning.'

'When we were children, my brother and I called it the secret beach.' His tone gruff, Casper spread the rug on the sand and gently eased the bag from her shoulders. 'We used to play here, knowing that no one could see us. It was probably the only real privacy we had in our childhood. We made camps, dens, we were pirates and smugglers, and—'

'All right—enough.' Emotion welling up inside her, Holly held up a hand, and Casper looked at her with exasperation.

'I thought talking was good.'

'*Not* when I'm angry with you.' Holly flopped onto the rug and shot him a despairing look. 'I'm so, *so* angry with you, and when you start talking like that I find it really hard to stay angry.'

Evidently clocking that up as a point in his favour, Casper joined her on the rug, his usual confidence apparently fully restored by her reluctant confession. 'You find it hard to be angry with me?' Gently, he pushed her onto her back and supported himself on one elbow as he looked down at her. 'You have forgiven me?'

'No.' She closed her eyes tightly so that she couldn't see his thick dark lashes and impossibly sexy eyes. But she could feel him looking at her. 'You've hurt me *really* badly.'

'*Sì*, I have. But now I am saying sorry. Open your eyes.'

'No. I don't want to look at you.'

'Open your eyes, *tesoro*.' His voice was so gentle that her eyes fluttered open, and she tumbled instantly into the depths of his dark eyes.

'Nothing you say is going to make any difference,' she muttered, and he gave a slow smile.

'I know that isn't true. You're always telling me that I should know who you are by now, and I think I do.' He lifted his hand and stroked her cheek gently. 'I know you are a very forgiving person.'

'Not that forgiving.' Her heart was pounding against her chest, but she refused to make it easy for him.

Lowering his head, Casper brought his mouth down on hers in a devastatingly gentle kiss that blew her mind. 'I am sorry, *angelo mio*. I am sorry for not believing that the baby was mine—for implying that you targeted me.'

Holly lay still, waiting, hoping, praying, *dying a little*— knowing that he was never going to say what she wanted to hear.

His eyes quizzical, Casper gently turned her face towards him. 'I'm apologising.'

'I know.'

He frowned. 'I'm saying sorry.'

'Yes.' His apparent conviction that he'd done what needed to be done made her want to hit him again and he gave an impatient sigh.

'Clearly I'm saying the wrong things, because you're lying there like a martyr burning at the stake. *Dio*, what is it that you want from me?' Without waiting for her answer, he lowered his mouth to hers and kissed her with devastating expertise.

Holly was immediately plunged into an erotic, sensual world that sucked her downwards. Struggling back to the surface, she gasped, 'I don't want to do this, Casper—'

'Yes, you do—this side of our relationship has always been good.' He eased his lean, powerful frame over hers, careful to support most of his weight on his elbows. 'Am I hurting the baby?'

'No, but I don't want you to—' She broke off as she saw his expression change. 'What? What's the matter?'

'The baby kicked me.' There was a strange note to his voice, and Holly felt her heart flip because she'd never seen Casper less than fully in control of every situation. He pulled away slightly and slid a bold but curious hand over the smooth curve of her abdomen. 'He kicked me really hard.'

'Good. Because quite frankly, if you weren't pinning me to the sand at this precise moment, I'd kick you myself for being so arrogant!' Holly glared at him but his face broke into a slow, sure smile of masculine superiority as he transferred his hand to the top of her thigh.

'No, you wouldn't. You're non-violent.'

'Funnily enough, *not* since I met you,' Holly gritted, and he gave a possessive smile.

'I bring out your passionate side, I know. And I love the way you're prepared to fight for my baby.'

'*Your* baby? So now you think you produced it all by yourself? Just because you've finally decided to acknowledge the truth—' Holly gasped as Casper shifted purposefully above her, amusement shimmering in his gorgeous dark eyes as his mouth hovered tantalisingly close to hers.

Tiny sparks of fire heated her pelvis, and her whole body was consumed by an overpowering hunger for this man.

Her mouth was dry, her heart was thundering in her chest, and she couldn't drag her eyes away from his beautiful mouth and the dangerous glitter in his eyes. 'Cas—you're squashing the baby!'

'I'm putting no weight on you at all,' he breathed, one sure, confident hand sliding under her summer dress and easing her thighs apart.

And then, with a slow smile that said everything about his intentions, he lowered his head. His mouth captured hers in a raw, demanding kiss just as his skilled fingers gently explored the moist warmth of their target, and Holly exploded with a hot, electrifying excitement that eradicated everything from her brain except pure wicked pleasure.

She ached, she throbbed, she was *desperate*, and when he slid a hand beneath her hips and lifted her she wound her legs around him in instinctive invitation, urging him on.

She'd become accustomed to the wild, uninhibited nature of their love-making. Right from the start the sexual chemistry had been so explosive that there had been times when it was hard to know which of them was the most out of control.

But this time felt different.

Casper surged into her quivering, receptive body and then paused, his breathing ragged as he scanned her flushed cheeks. 'Am I hurting you?'

'No.' Not in the way he meant.

Holly closed her eyes tightly, moaning as he eased himself deeper, every thought driven from her head by the silken strength of him inside her.

She'd never known him so careful, and yet there was something about the slow, deliberate thrusts that were shockingly erotic.

She was no longer aware of the warmth of the sun or the sounds of the sea, because everything she felt was controlled by this man.

Her body spun higher and higher, her excitement out of control, until she gave a sharp cry and tumbled off the edge into a climax so intense that her mind blanked. She dug her nails hard into the hard muscle of his sleek, bronzed shoulders as her world shattered around her and her body tightened around his.

'I can feel that,' he groaned, and then he surged into her for a final time, his climax driving her straight back into another orgasm.

When the stars finally stopped exploding in her head, she opened her eyes and pressed her lips against his satin-smooth skin, desperately conscious that she'd succumbed to him yet again.

'That,' Casper murmured huskily, 'Was amazing.' Clearly in no hurry to move, he stroked her hair away from her face and stared into her eyes with a warmth that she hadn't seen before. 'Now, where were we in our conversation? I've lost track.'

Appalled at her own weakness, Holly closed her eyes. 'I was about to kick you but the baby did it for me.'

'You were about to forgive me,' Casper said confidently, and she opened her eyes and looked up at him.

'So is that what it was all about this time? Apology sex?'

Casper didn't answer for a moment, his hand unsteady as he stroked her hair away from her face. 'It was love sex, *tesoro*,' he said huskily, and Holly stilled.

It was like seeing a shimmer of water in the desert.

Real or a mirage?

'Love sex?' She was almost afraid to say the words. 'What do you mean, "love sex"?'

'I mean that I love you.'

Her heart was thudding. 'You told me that you weren't capable of love.'

'I was wrong. And I was trying to show you I was wrong. I think I express myself better physically than verbally.' His eyes gleamed with self-mockery. 'I was always better at maths than English. I'm the cold, analytical type, remember?'

A warm feeling spread through Holly's limbs and she started to tremble. 'Actually, that isn't true,' she said gently. 'You're very good with words.'

'But hopeless at matching them to the right emotion, if my lack of success at an apology is anything to go by.' Gently, he stroked a hand over her cheek. 'I love you, Holly. I think I loved you from the first moment I saw you. You were warm, gorgeous, sexy.' His eyes flickered to her mouth. 'You were *so* sexy I couldn't keep my hands off you.'

'And the moment we'd had sex, you wanted me to leave. Stop dressing it up, Casper. I'm not stupid.'

'I am the one who has been stupid,' he confessed in a raw tone. 'Stupid for not seeing what was under my nose. When we had sex the day of the rugby, I didn't know what had happened. I was living this crazy, cold, empty existence, and suddenly there you were. I was shocked by how I felt about you. I actually did think that you were different—and then you kissed me in the window.'

'You thought I'd done it for a photo opportunity.'

'Yes.' He didn't shrink from the truth. 'That is what I thought. And everything that happened after that seemed to back up my suspicions. You hid from the world and then announced that you were pregnant. It seemed to me that you were trying to make maximum impact from the story.'

'From your description, I should obviously be considering a career in public relations.'

'You have to understand that, when you're in the public eye, these things happen. You grow to expect them.' Casper drew away from her and sat up, his gaze thoughtful. 'Women have always wanted me for what I can give them. Even Antonia, who I thought loved me.'

Holly pulled a face. 'Yes, well, I can see why your experience with her made you very suspicious of women. I'm not stupid.'

'No, you're certainly not. And I'm not blaming Antonia. The blame lies entirely with myself.' Casper's admission was delivered with uncharacteristic self-deprecation. 'I allowed myself to see only bad in women, I expected only bad from women. And the chances of you having become pregnant on that one single occasion when I'd been told I was infertile—to have believed your story would have required a better man than me.'

'You're obviously super-fertile.'

He gave an aggressively masculine smile. 'So it would seem. And now I need to ask you something.' The smile faded and there was an unusual vulnerability in his dark eyes. 'Do you still love me? *Can* you still love me? You haven't said those words for a long time.'

Holly swallowed, her heart thudding hard. 'You didn't want to hear them,' she whispered. 'When I said them, or when I showed affection, you backed off. I didn't want to scare you away.'

'I taught myself to block out emotion because it was the only way I could survive,' Casper said roughly, leaning forwards and cupping her face in his hands. 'And I'm still waiting for you to answer my question.'

'I'm scared even to say the words,' she admitted with a strangled laugh. 'In case the whole bubble pops.'

'Say you can still love me, Holly. I need to hear you say it.'

'I never stopped loving you,' she said softly. 'I just stopped saying it because it upset you. That's another thing that "I love you" means to me. It means for ever. True love isn't something you can switch on and off, Casper. It's always there, sometimes when you'd rather it wasn't.'

Casper's breathing fractured, and he hauled her into his arms and held her tightly. 'Don't say that, because it reminds me how much I hurt you, and you have no idea how guilty I feel. You must have felt so alone, but I swear to you that you will never feel alone again.'

'I don't want you to feel guilty. I love you so much.'

'I don't deserve you.'

'You might well be saying that to yourself when I'm singing in the shower,' Holly joked feebly, and his grip tightened.

'After the way I behaved, most women would have walked away. I was so afraid you would do the same.'

'I would never do that.'

'No.' He withdrew slightly and stroked her cheek gently. 'You have an exceptionally lovely nature. You are kind, tolerant and forgiving. You have tremendous strength, and I truly admire your single-minded determination to do the very best for our baby. And our baby is so lucky to have you as a mother,' he murmured, pulling her against him again with firm, possessive hands.

Holly buried her face in his shoulder. 'I was terrified that you wouldn't love the baby.'

'And I was terrified to open up enough to love anything, because I saw love as a source of pain.'

'I know.' Holly touched his face. 'You were so wounded. I always knew that, and when we got together I told myself that, as long as I was patient, you would heal. I was so sure that everything would turn out all right, but I couldn't get through to you. I couldn't find the answer.'

'You were the answer.' Casper lifted her chin and silenced her fears with a possessive kiss. 'There will be no more problems between us. Ever.'

'Are you kidding?' Half laughing, half crying, Holly shook her head. 'You are stubborn, arrogant and used to getting your own way. How can we not have problems?'

'Because you are kind, tolerant and you adore me.' Casper, looking too gorgeous for his own good with roughened dark hair and the beginnings of stubble grazing his jaw, snuggled her against him again. 'And you have reminded me what true love really is.' His hand rested protectively on her rounded abdomen and his voice was suddenly husky. 'I never thought I believed in fairy tales, but this baby has changed my mind. I have great wealth and privilege, but the one thing I never thought I'd have is a family. You've given me that.'

Holly glanced up at him and then towards the fairy tale turrets of Santallia Palace in the distance. 'A family.' She savoured the word, and then smiled up at him, everything she felt shining in her eyes. 'That sounds like a very happy ending to me.'

* * * * *

BECOMING THE PRINCE'S WIFE

REBECCA WINTERS

*To my four wonderful, outstanding children
Bill, John, Dominique and Max. They've had to
put up with a mother whose mind is constantly
dreaming up new fairy tales like the one I've
just written. Their unqualified love and constant
support has been the greatest blessing in my life.*

Rebecca Winters lives in Salt Lake City, Utah. With canyons and high alpine meadows full of wildflowers, she never runs out of places to explore. They, plus her favourite holiday spots in Europe often end up as backgrounds for her romance novels, because writing is her passion, along with her family and church. Rebecca loves to hear from readers. If you wish to email her, please visit her website at cleanromances.com.

CHAPTER ONE

As CAROLENA BARETTI stepped out of the limousine, she could see her best friend, Abby, climbing the stairs of the royal jet. At the top she turned. "Oh, good! You're here!" she called to her, but was struggling to keep her baby from squirming out of her arms.

At eight months of age, little black-haired Prince Maximilliano, the image of his father, Crown Prince Vincenzo Di Laurentis of Arancia, was becoming big Max, fascinated by sights and sounds. Since he was teething, Carolena had brought him various colored toys in the shape of donuts to bite on. She'd give them to him after they'd boarded the jet for the flight to Gemelli.

The steward brought Carolena's suitcase on board while she entered the creamy interior of the jet. The baby's carryall was strapped to one of the luxury leather chairs along the side. Max fought at leaving his mother's arms, but she finally prevailed in getting him fastened down.

Carolena pulled a blue donut from the sack in her large straw purse. "Maybe this will help." She leaned over the baby and handed it to him. "What do you think, sweetheart?"

Max grabbed for it immediately and put it in his mouth to test it, causing both women to laugh. Abby gave her a hug. "Thank you for the gift. Any distraction is a blessing! The only time he doesn't move is when he's asleep."

Carolena chuckled.

"So you won't get too bored, I brought a movie for you to watch while we fly down. Remember I told you how much I loved the French actor Louis Jourdan when I was growing up?"

"He was in *Gigi,* right?"

"Yes, well, I found a movie of his in my mother's collection. You know me and my love for old films. This one is called *Bird of Paradise.* Since we'll be passing Mount Etna, I think you'll love it."

"I've never heard of that movie, but thank you for being so thoughtful. I'm sure I'll enjoy it."

"Carolena—I know this is a hard time for you, but I'm so glad you decided to come. Vincenzo and Valentino need to discuss business on this short trip. It will give you and me some time to do whatever we want while Queen Bianca dotes on her grandson."

"When Max smiles, I see traces of Michelina. That must delight her."

"I know it does. These days it's hard to believe Bianca was ever upset over the pregnancy. She's much warmer to me now."

"Thank heaven for that, Abby."

"You'll never know."

No, Carolena supposed she wouldn't. Not really. Abby Loretto had offered to be a surrogate mother to carry Their Highnesses' baby, but they'd both been through a trial by fire when Michelina was suddenly killed.

Carolena was thrilled for the two of them who, since that time, had fallen deeply in love and weathered the storm before marrying. Now they had a beautiful baby boy to raise and she was glad to have been invited to join them for their brief holiday.

Today was June fourth, a date she'd dreaded every June for the past seven years. It marked the death of her fiancé, Berto, and brought back horrendous guilt. She and Berto had shared a great love, but it had come to a tragic end too soon. All because of Carolena.

She'd been too adventurous for her own good, as her own wonderful, deceased grandmother had always told her. *You go where angels fear to tread without thinking of anyone but yourself. It's probably because you lost your parents too soon and I've failed you. One day there'll be a price to pay for being so headstrong.*

Tears stung her eyelids. How true were those words.

Berto's death had brought about a permanent change in Carolena. Outside of her professional work as an attorney, she never wanted to be responsible for another human life again. Though she'd dated a lot of men, her relationships were of short duration and superficial. After seven years, her pattern of noncommitment had become her way of life. No one depended on her. Her actions could affect no one or hurt anyone. That was the way she liked it.

Dear sweet Abby had known the date was coming up. Out of the goodness of her heart she'd insisted Carolena come with them on this trip so she wouldn't brood. Carolena loved her blonde friend for so many reasons, especially her thoughtfulness because she knew this time was always difficult for her.

As she strapped herself in, several bodyguards entered the body of the jet followed by black-haired Vincenzo. He stopped to give his wife and son a kiss before hugging Carolena. "It's good to see you. Gemelli is a beautiful country. You're going to love it."

"I'm sure I will. Thank you for inviting me, Vincenzo."

"Our pleasure, believe me. If you're ready, then we'll take off. I told Valentino we'd be there midafternoon."

Once he'd fastened himself in and turned to Abby with an eagerness Carolena could see and feel, the jet taxied to the runway. When it took off into a blue sky, it left the Principality of Arancia behind, a country nestled along the Riviera between France and Italy.

Before heading south, she could see the coastal waters of the Mediterranean receding, but it was obvious Abby and Vincenzo only had eyes for each other. Theirs was a true love story. Watching them was painful. There were moments like now when twenty-seven-year-old Carolena felt old before her time.

Thank goodness she had a movie to watch that she hadn't seen before. The minute it started she blinked at the sight of how young Louis Jourdan was. The story turned out to be about a Frenchman who traveled to Polynesia and fell in love with a native girl.

Carolena found herself riveted when the volcano erupts on the island and the native girl has to be sacrificed to appease the gods by jumping into it. The credits said the film had been made on location in Hawaii and used the Kilauea volcano for the scenes.

As the royal jet started to make its descent to Gemelli, she saw smoke coming out of Mount Etna, one of Italy's volcanoes. After watching this film, the thought of it erupting made her shiver.

The helicopter flew away from the new hot fumarole in the western pit of the Bocca Nuova of Mount Etna. The fumarole was a hole that let out gas and steam. After the scientific team had observed an increased bluish degassing from a vent in the saddle, they sent back video and seismic records before heading to the National Center of Geophysics and Volcanology lab in Catania on the eastern coast of Sicily.

En route to the lab the three men heard deep-seated explosions coming from inside the northeast crater, but there was no cause for public alarm in terms of evacuation alerts.

Once the center's helicopter touched ground, Crown Prince Valentino waved off his two colleagues and hurried to the royal helicopter for the short flight to Gemelli in the Ionian Sea. Their team had gotten back late, but they'd needed to do an in-depth study before transmitting vital data and photos.

Valentino's brother-in-law, Crown Prince Vincenzo Di Laurentis, along with his new wife, Abby, and son, Max, would already have been at the palace several hours. They'd come for a visit from Arancia and would be staying a few days. Valentino was eager to see them.

He and Vincenzo, distant cousins, had done shipping business together for many years but had grown closer with Vincenzo's first marriage to Michelina, who'd been Valentino's only sister. Her death February before last had left a hole in his heart. He'd always been very attached to his sibling and they'd confided in each other.

With his younger brother Vitale, nicknamed Vito, away in the military, Valentino had needed an outlet since her death. Lately, after a long day's work, he'd spent time quietly partying with a few good friends and his most recent girlfriend, while his mother, Bianca, the ruling Queen of Gemelli, occupied herself with their country's business.

As for tonight, he was looking forward to seeing Vincenzo as his helicopter ferried him to the grounds, where it landed at the rear of the sixteenth-century baroque palace. He jumped out and hurried past the gardens and tennis courts, taking a shortcut near the swimming pool to reach his apartment in the east wing.

But suddenly he saw something out of the corner of his eye that stopped him dead in his tracks. Standing on the end of the diving board ready to dive was a gorgeous, voluptuous woman in a knockout, fashionable one-piece purple swimsuit with a plunging neckline.

It was just a moment before she disappeared under the water, but long enough for him to forget the fiery fumarole on Mount Etna and follow those long legs to the end of the pool. When she emerged at the deep end with a sable-colored braid over one shoulder, he hunkered down to meet her. With eyes as sparkling green as lime zest, and a mouth with a passionate flare, she was even more breathtaking up close.

"Oh— Your Highness! I didn't think anyone was here!"

He couldn't have met her before or he would have remembered, because she would be impossible to forget. There was no ring on her finger. "You have me at a disadvantage, *signorina.*"

She hugged her body close to the edge of the tiled pool. He got the impression she was trying to prevent him from getting the full view of her. That small show of modesty intrigued him.

"I'm Carolena Baretti, Abby Loretto's friend."

This woman was Abby's best friend? He'd heard Abby mention her, but Vincenzo had never said anything. Valentino knew his brother-in-law wasn't blind… Though they hadn't told him they were bringing someone else with them, he didn't mind. Not at all.

"How long have you been here?"

"We flew in at two o'clock. Right now the queen is playing with Max while Abby and Valentino take a nap." A nap, was it? He smiled inwardly. "So I decided to come out here for a swim. The air is like velvet."

He agreed. "My work took longer than I thought, making it impossible for me to be here when you arrived. I've planned a supper for us in the private dining room tonight. Shall we say half an hour? One of the staff will show you the way."

"That's very gracious of you, but I don't want to intrude on your time with them. I had a light meal before I came out to swim and I'll just go on enjoying myself here."

He got the sense she meant it. The fact that she wasn't being coy like so many females he'd met in his life aroused his interest. "You're their friend, so it goes without saying you're invited." His lips broke into a smile. "And even if you weren't with them, I *like* an intrusion as pleasant as this one. I insist you join us."

"Thank you," she said quietly, but he had an idea she was debating whether or not to accept his invitation, mystifying him further. "Before you go, may I say how sorry I am about the loss of Princess Michelina. I can see the resemblance to your sister in you and the baby. I know it's been devastating for your family, especially the queen. But if anyone can instill some joy into all of you, it's your adorable nephew, Max."

The surprises just kept coming. Valentino was taken aback. The fact that she'd been in Abby's confidence for a number of years had lent a sincere ring to this woman's remarks, already putting them on a more intimate footing. "I've been eager to see him again. He's probably grown a foot since last time."

An engaging smile appeared. "Maybe not quite another foot yet, but considering he's Prince Vincenzo's son, I would imagine he'll be tall one day."

"That wouldn't surprise me. *A presto,* Signorina Baretti."

Carolena watched *his* tall physique stride to the patio and disappear inside a set of glass doors. Long after he'd left, she was still trying to catch her breath. When she'd broken the surface of the water at the other end of the rectangular pool, she'd recognized the striking thirty-two-year-old crown prince right away.

Her knowledge of him came from newspapers and television that covered the funeral of his sister, Princess Michelina. He'd ridden in the black-and-gold carriage with his brother and their mother, Queen Bianca, the three of them grave and in deep grief.

In a recent poll he'd been touted the world's most sought-after royal bachelor. Most of the tabloids revealed he went through women like water. She could believe it. Just now his eyes had mirrored his masculine admiration of her. Everywhere they roved, she'd felt heat trail over her skin. By that invisible process called osmosis, his charm and sophistication had managed to seep into her body.

But even up close no camera could catch the startling midnight blue of his dark-lashed eyes. The dying rays of the evening sun gilded the tips of his medium cut dark blond hair and brought out his hard-boned facial features, reminiscent of his Sicilian ancestry. He was a fabulous-looking man.

Right then he'd been wearing jeans that molded his powerful thighs, and a white shirt with the sleeves shoved up to the elbows to reveal hard-muscled forearms. No sign of a uniform this evening.

Whatever kind of work he did, he'd gotten dirty. She wondered where he'd been. There were black marks on his clothes and arms, even on his face, bronzed from being outdoors. If anything, the signs of the working man intensified his potent male charisma. He wasn't just a handsome prince without substance.

Carolena was stunned by her reaction to him. There'd been many different types of men who'd come into her life because of her work as an attorney; businessmen, manufacturers, technology wizards, mining engineers, entrepreneurs. But she had to admit she'd never had this kind of visceral response to a man on a first meeting, not even with Berto, who'd been her childhood friend before they'd fallen in love.

The prince had said half an hour. Carolena hadn't intended to join the three of them this evening, but since he'd used the word *insist,* she decided she'd better go so as not to offend him. Unfortunately it was growing late. She needed to hurry inside and get ready, but she wouldn't have time to wash her hair.

She climbed out of the pool and retraced her steps to the other wing of the palace. After a quick shower, she unbraided her hair and swept it back with an amber comb. Once she'd applied her makeup, she donned a small leopard-print wrap dress with ruched elbow-length sleeves. The tiny amber stones of her chandelier earrings matched the ones in her small gold chain necklace. On her feet she wore designer wedges in brown and amber.

The law firm in Arancia where she worked demanded their attorneys wear designer clothes since they dealt with an upper-class clientele. Abby had worked there with her until her fifth month of pregnancy when she'd been forced to quit. After being employed there twenty months and paid a generous salary, Carolena had accumulated a wonderful wardrobe and didn't need to worry she wouldn't have something appropriate to wear to this evening's dinner.

A knock at the door meant a maid was ready to take her to the dining room. But when she opened it, she received another shock to discover the prince at the threshold wearing a silky charcoal-brown sport shirt and beige trousers.

He must not have trusted her to come on her own. She didn't know whether to be flattered or worried she'd made some kind of faux pas when she'd declined his invitation at first. Their eyes traveled over each other. A shower had gotten rid of the black marks. He smelled wonderful, no doubt from the soap he used. Her heart did a tiny thump before she got hold of herself.

"Your Highness— This is the second time you've surprised me this evening."

He flashed her a white smile. "Unexpected surprises make life more interesting, don't you think?"

"I do actually, depending on the kind."

"This was the kind I couldn't resist."

Obviously she *had* irritated him. Still, she couldn't believe he'd come to fetch her. "I'm honored to be personally escorted by none other than the prince himself."

"That wasn't so hard to say, was it?" His question brought a smile to her lips. "Since I'm hungry, I thought I'd accompany you to the dining room myself to hurry things up, and I must admit I'm glad you're ready."

"Then let's not waste any more time."

"Vincenzo and Abby are already there, but they didn't even notice me when I passed by the doors. I've heard of a honeymoon lasting a week or two, even longer. But eight months?"

Carolena chuckled. "I know what you mean. While we were flying out, they were so caught up in each other, I don't think they said more than two words to me."

"Love should be like that, but it's rare."

"I know," she murmured. Vincenzo and Michelina hadn't enjoyed a marriage like that. It was no news to Carolena or Valentino, so they left the subject alone.

She followed him down several corridors lined with tapestries and paintings to a set of doors guarded by a staff member. They opened onto the grounds. "We'll cut across here past the gardens to the other wing of the palace. It's faster."

There was nothing stiff or arrogant about Prince Valentino. He had the rare gift of being able to put her at ease and make her feel comfortable.

She looked around her. "The gardens are glorious. You have grown a fabulous collection of palms and exotic plants. Everything thrives here. And I've never seen baroque architecture this flamboyant."

He nodded. "My brother, Vito, and I have always called it the Putti Palace because of all the winged boy cherubs supporting the dozens of balconies. To my mother's chagrin, we used to draw mustaches on them. For our penance, we had to wash them off."

Laughter rippled out of her. "I'm afraid to tell Abby what you said for fear she'll have nightmares over Max getting into mischief."

"Except that won't be for a while yet." His dark blue

eyes danced. No doubt this prince had been a handful to his parents. Somehow the thought made him even more approachable.

"With all these wrought-iron balustrades and rustication, the palace really is beautiful."

"Along with the two-toned lava masonry, the place is definitely unique," he commented before ushering her through another pair of doors, where a staff member was on duty. Their arms brushed in the process, sending little trickles of delight through her body. Her reaction was ridiculous. It had to be because she'd never been this close to a prince before. Except for Vincenzo, of course, but he didn't count. Not in the same way.

They walked down one more hall to the entrance of the dining room where Abby and Vincenzo sat at the candlelit table with their heads together talking quietly and kissing. Gilt-framed rococo mirrors made the room seem larger, projecting their image.

Valentino cleared his throat. "Should we come back?" He'd already helped Carolena to be seated. The teasing sound in his voice amused her, but his question caused the other two to break apart. While Abby's face flushed, Vincenzo got to his feet and came around to give Valentino a hug.

"It's good to see you."

"Likewise. I'm sorry I took so long. It's my fault for leaving work late today, but it couldn't be helped."

"No one understands that better than I do. We took the liberty of bringing Carolena with us. Allow me to introduce you."

Valentino shot her a penetrating glance. "We already met at the swimming pool."

Carolena felt feverish as she and Abby exchanged a silent glance before he walked around to hug her friend. Then he took his place next to Carolena, who still hadn't recovered from her initial reaction to his masculine appeal.

In a moment, dinner was served, starting with deep-fried risotto croquettes stuffed with pistachio pesto called arancini because they were the shape and size of an orange. Pasta with clams followed called spaghetti alle vongole. Then came the main course of crab and an aubergine side dish. Valentino told them the white wine came from their own palace vineyard.

"The food is out of this world, but I'll have to pass on the cannoli dessert," Carolena exclaimed a little while later. "If I lived here very long I'd look like one of those fat Sicilian rock partridges unable to move around."

Both men burst into laughter before Valentino devoured his dessert.

Carolena looked at Abby. "What did I say?"

Vincenzo grinned. "You and my wife have the same thought processes. She was afraid pregnancy would make her look like a beached whale."

"We women have our fears," Abby defended.

"We certainly do!"

Valentino darted Carolena another glance. "In that purple swimsuit you were wearing earlier, I can guarantee you'll never have that problem."

She'd walked into that one and felt the blood rush to her cheeks. That suit was a frivolous purchase she wouldn't have worn around other people, but since she'd been alone… Or so she'd thought. "I hope you're right, Your Highness."

His eyes smiled. "Call me Val."

Val? Who in the world called him that?

He must have been able to read her mind because his next comment answered her question. "My brother and I didn't like our long names, so we gave ourselves nicknames. He's Vito and I'm Val."

"V and V," she said playfully. "I'm surprised you didn't have to wash your initials off some of those putti."

Another burst of rich laughter escaped his throat. When it subsided, he explained their little joke to Vincenzo and Abby.

Carolena smiled at Abby. "I'd caution you never to tell that story to Max, or when he's more grown up he might take it into his head to copy his uncles."

"Fortunately we don't have putti," Vincenzo quipped.

"True," Abby chimed in, "but we do have busts that can be knocked over by a soccer ball."

Amidst the laughter, a maid appeared in the doorway. "Forgive the intrusion, Your Highness, but the queen says it seems the young prince has started to cry and is running a temperature."

In an instant both parents jumped to their feet bringing an end to the frivolity.

Wanting to say something to assure them, Carolena said, "He's probably caught a little cold."

Abby nodded. "I'm sure you're right, but he's still not as used to the queen yet and is in a strange place. I'll go to him." She put a hand on Vincenzo's arm. "You stay here and enjoy your visit, darling."

At this point, Valentino stood up. "We'll have all day tomorrow. Right now your boy needs both of you."

"Thank you," they murmured. Abby came around to give Carolena a hug. "See you in the morning."

"Of course. If you need me for anything, just phone me."

"I will."

When they disappeared out the doors, Carolena got to her feet. "I'll say good-night, too. Thank you for a wonderful dinner, Your Highness."

He frowned. "The name's Val. I want to hear you say it."

She took a deep breath. "Thank you…Val."

"That's better." His gaze swept over her. "Where's the fire?"

"I'm tired." Carolena said the first thing that came into her head. "I was up early to finish some work at the firm before the limo arrived to drive me to the airport. Bed sounds good to me."

"Then I'll walk you back."

"That won't be necessary."

He cocked his dark blond head. "Do I frighten you?"

Your appeal frightens me. "If anything, I'm afraid of disturbing your routine."

"I don't have one tonight. Forget I'm the prince."

It wasn't the prince part that worried her. He'd made her aware of him as a man. This hadn't happened since she'd fallen in love with Berto and it was very disturbing to her.

"To be honest, when you showed up at the swimming pool earlier, you looked tired after a hard day's work. Since it's late, I'm sure you'd like a good sleep before you spend the day with Vincenzo tomorrow."

"I'm not too tired to see you back to your room safely."

"Your Highness?" The same maid came to the entrance once more. "The queen would like to see you in her apartment."

"I'll go to her. Thank you."

He cupped Carolena's elbow to walk her out of the dining room. She didn't want him touching her. The contact made her senses come alive. When they passed the guard and reached the grounds, she eased away from him.

"After getting to know Vincenzo, I realize how busy you are and the huge amount of calls on your time. Your mother is waiting for you."

"I always say good-night to my mother before retiring. If our dinner had lasted a longer time, she would have had a longer wait."

There was no talking him out of letting her get back to her room by herself. "What kind of work were you doing today?" She had to admit to a deep curiosity.

He grinned. "I always come home looking dirty and need to wash off the grime."

She shook her head. "I didn't say that."

"You didn't have to. Volcanoes are a dirty business."

Carolena came to a standstill before lifting her head to look at him. "You were up on Mount Etna?"

"That's right."

His answer perplexed her. "Why?"

"I'm a volcanologist with the National Center of Geophysics and Volcanology lab in Catania."

"You're kidding—" After that movie she'd watched on the plane, she couldn't believe what he'd just told her.

One corner of his compelling mouth lifted. "Even a prince can't afford to be an empty suit. Etna has been my backyard since I was born. From the first moment I saw it smoking, I knew I had to go up there and get a good look. Once that happened, I was hooked."

With his adventurous spirit, she wasn't surprised but knew there was a lot more to his decision than that. "I confess it would be fantastic to see it up close the way you do. Have you been to other volcanoes?"

"Many of them."

"You lucky man! On the way down here I watched a Hollywood movie with Louis Jourdan about a volcano erupting in Polynesia."

"You must mean *Bird of Paradise*."

"Yes. It was really something. Your line of work has to be very dangerous."

For a second she thought she saw a flicker of some emotion in his eyes, but it passed. "Not so much nowadays. The main goal is to learn how to predict trouble so that timely warnings can be issued for cautioning and evacuating people in the area. We've devised many safe ways to spy on active volcanoes over the decades."

"How did your parents feel about you becoming a volcanologist?"

A smile broke the corner of his mouth, as if her question had amused him. "When I explained the reasons for my interest, they approved."

That was too pat an answer. He sounded as if he wanted to get off the subject, but she couldn't let it go. "What argument did you give them?"

His brows lifted. "Did you think I needed one?"

She took a quick breath. "If they were anything like my grandmother, who was the soul of caution, then yes!"

He stopped outside the entrance to her wing of the palace. Moonlight bathed his striking male features, making them stand out like those of the Roman-god statues supporting the fountain in the distance. His sudden serious demeanor gave her more insight into his complex personality.

"A king's first allegiance is to the welfare of his people. I explained to my parents that when Etna erupts again, and she will, I don't want to see a repeat of what happened in 1669."

Carolena was transfixed. "What *did* happen?"

"That eruption turned into a disaster that killed over twenty-nine thousand people."

She shuddered, remembering the film. "I can't even imagine it."

He wore a grim expression. "Though it couldn't happen today, considering the sophisticated warning systems in place, people still need to be educated about the necessity of listening and heeding those warnings of evacuation."

"In the film, there'd been no warning."

"Certainly not a hundred years ago. That's been my

greatest concern. Gemelli has a population of two hundred thousand, so it can't absorb everyone fleeing the mainland around Catania, but I want us to be prepared as much as possible."

"How do you get your people prepared?"

"I've been working with our government to do mock drills to accommodate refugees from the mainland, should a disaster occur. Every ship, boat, barge, fishing boat would have to be available, not to mention housing and food and airlifts to other islands."

"That would be an enormous undertaking."

"You're right. For protection against volcanic ash and toxic gas, I've ordered every family outfitted with lightweight, disposable, filtering face-piece mask/respirators. This year's sightings have convinced me I've only scratched the surface of what's needed to be done to feel at all ready."

"Your country is very fortunate to have you for the watchman."

"The watchman? That makes me sound like an old sage."

"You're hardly old yet," she quipped.

"I'm glad you noticed." His remark caused her heart to thud for no good reason.

"I'm very impressed over what you do."

"It's only part of what I do."

"Oh, I know what a prince does." She half laughed. "Abby once read me Vincenzo's itinerary for the day and I almost passed out. But she never told me about *your* scientific background."

"It isn't something I talk about."

"Well, I think it's fascinating! You're likean astronaut or a test pilot, but the general population doesn't know what you go through or how you put your life on the line."

"That's a big exaggeration."

"Not at all," she argued. "It's almost as if you're leading a double life. What a mystery you are!"

She wouldn't have put it past Abby to have chosen that particular film because she knew about Valentino's profession and figured Carolena would get a kick out of it once she learned about his secret profession.

After a low chuckle, he opened the doors so they could walk down the hallway and around the corner to her room. She opened her door. Though she was dying to ask him a lot more questions about his work in volcanology, she didn't want him to think she expected his company any longer. She was also aware the queen was waiting for him.

"It's been a lovely evening. Thank you for everything."

His eyes gleamed in the semidarkness. "What else do you do besides give unsuspecting males a heart attack while you're diving?"

Heat scorched her cheeks. "I thought I was alone."

"Because I was late getting back, I cut through that part of the grounds and happened to see you. It looks like I'm going to have to do it more often."

He was a huge flirt. The tabloids hadn't been wrong about him. "I won't be here long enough to get caught again. I have a law practice waiting for me back in Arancia."

He studied her for a moment. "I heard you're in the same firm with Abby."

"We were until her marriage. Now she's a full-time mother to your nephew."

A heart-stopping smile appeared. "It must be tough on your male colleagues working around so much beauty and brains."

"They're all married."

"That makes it so much worse."

She laughed. "You're outrageous."

"Then we understand each other. Tomorrow we'll be eating breakfast on the terrace off the morning room. I'll send a maid for you at eight-thirty. *Buona notte,* Carolena."

"Buona notte."

"Val," he said again.

"Val," she whispered before shutting the door. She lay against it, surprised he was so insistent on her using his nickname, surprised he'd made such an impact on her.

After their delicious meal, she wasn't ready for bed yet. Once she'd slipped on her small garden-print capri pajamas, she set up her laptop on the table and started to look up Mount Etna. The amount of information she found staggered her. There were dozens of videos and video clips she watched until after one in the morning.

But by the time she'd seen a video about six volcanologists killed on the Galeras volcano in the Colombian Andes in 1993, she turned off her computer. The scientists had been standing on the ground when it began to heave and then there was a deafening roar. The volcano exploded, throwing boulders and ash miles high and they'd lost their lives.

The idea of that happening to the prince made her ill. She knew he took precautions, but as he'd pointed out, there was always a certain amount of risk. The desire to see a vent up close would be hard to resist. That's what he did in his work. He crept up close to view the activity and send back information. But there might come a day when he'd be caught. She couldn't bear the thought of it, but she admired him terribly.

The playboy prince who'd had dozens of girlfriends didn't mesh with the volcanologist whose name was Val. She didn't want to care about either image of the sensational-looking flesh-and-blood man. When Carolena finally pulled the covers over her, she fell asleep wishing she'd never met him. He was too intriguing for words.

At seven-thirty the next morning her cell phone rang, causing her to wonder if it was the prince. She got a fluttery feeling in her chest as she raised up on one elbow to reach for it. To her surprise it was Abby and she clicked on. "Abby? Are you all right? How's Max?"

"He's still running a temperature and fussing. I think he's cutting another tooth. The reason I'm calling is because I'm going to miss breakfast with you and stay in the apartment with him. It will give Vincenzo and Valentino time to get some work done this morning."

"Understood. I'm so sorry Max is sick."

"It'll pass, but under the circumstances, why don't you order breakfast in your room or out by the pool. I'll get in touch with you later in the day. If you want a limo, just dial zero and ask for one to drive you into town, and do a little shopping or something."

"Don't worry about me. I'll love relaxing by the pool. This is heaven after the hectic schedule at the law firm."

"Okay, then. Talk to you soon."

This was a good turn of events. The less she saw of Valentino, the better.

CHAPTER TWO

By TEN-THIRTY A.M., Valentino could see that Vincenzo wasn't able to concentrate. "Let's call it a day. I can see you want to be with Abby and Max. When I've finished with some other business, we'll meet for dinner."

Vincenzo nodded. "Sorry, Valentino."

"You can't help this. Family has to come first." He walked his brother-in-law out of his suite where they'd had breakfast while they talked. When they'd said good-bye, he closed the door, realizing he had a free day on his hands if he wanted it.

In truth, he'd never wanted anything more and walked over to the house phone to call Carolena Baretti's room, but there was no answer. He buzzed his assistant. "Paolo? Did Signorina Baretti go into town?"

"No. She had breakfast at the pool and is still there."

"I see. Thank you."

Within minutes he'd changed into trunks and made his way to the pool with a beach towel and his phone. He spotted her sitting alone reading a book under the shade of the table's umbrella. She'd put her hair in a braid and was wearing a lacy cover-up, but he could see a spring-green bikini beneath it.

"I guess it was too much to hope you were wearing that purple swimsuit I found you in last evening."

She looked up. Maybe it was a trick of light, but he thought she looked nervous to see him. Why?

Carolena put her book down. "You've finished your work with Vincenzo already?"

He tossed the towel on one of the other chairs. "Between you and me, I think he wanted to take a nap with his wife."

A smile appeared. "They deserve some vacation time away from deadlines."

"Amen. We'll do more work tomorrow when Max is feeling better. Come swim with me."

She shook her head. "I've already been in."

"There's no law that says you can't swim again, is there?" He put his phone on the table.

"No. Please—just forget I'm here."

"I'm afraid that would be impossible," he said over his shoulder before plunging in at the deep end to do some laps. When he eventually lifted his head, he was shocked to discover she'd left the patio and was walking back to her wing of the palace on those long shapely legs.

Nothing like this had ever happened to him before. Propelled into action, he grabbed his things and caught up to her as she was entering the door of her apartment. Valentino stood in the aperture so she couldn't close it on him.

"Did you go away because I'd disturbed you with

my presence? Or was it because you have an aversion to me, *signorina?*"

Color swept into her cheeks. "Neither one."

His adrenaline surged. "Why didn't you tell me you preferred to be alone?"

"I'm just a guest. You're the prince doing your own thing. This is your home. But I had no intention of offending you by leaving the pool."

He frowned. "Yesterday I asked if you were afraid of me. You said no, but I think you are and I want to know why. It's true that though I've been betrothed to Princess Alexandra for years, I've had a love life of sorts. In that way I'm no different than Vincenzo before he married Michelina. But I've the feeling Abby has painted me as such a bad boy to you, you're half terrified to be alone with me."

"Nothing of the sort, Your Highness!" She'd backed away from him. "Don't ever blame her for anything. She thinks the world of you!"

That sounded heartfelt. "Then invite me in so we can talk without the staff hearing every word of our conversation."

She bit her lip before standing aside so he could enter. "I'll get you a dry towel so you can sit down." He closed the door and watched her race through the suite. She soon came hurrying back with a towel and folded it on one of the chairs placed around the coffee table.

"Thank you," he said as she took a seat at the end of the couch.

He sat down with his hands clasped between his legs and stared at her. "What's wrong with you? Though

I've told you I find you attractive, it doesn't mean I'm ready to pounce on you." She averted her eyes. "Don't tell me you don't know what I'm talking about."

"I wasn't going to, and I didn't mean to be rude. You have to believe me."

She sounded sincere enough, but Valentino wasn't about to let her off the hook. "What else am I to think? Last night I thought we were enjoying each other's company while we talked, but today you act like a frightened schoolgirl. Has some man attacked you before? Is that the reason you like to be alone and ran the minute I dived into the water?"

Her head lifted. "No! You don't understand."

"Since you're a special guest, help me so I don't feel like some pariah."

"Forgive me if I made you feel that way." Her green orbs pleaded with him. "This has to do with me, not you."

"Are you this way on principle with every man you meet? Or am I the only one to receive that honor?"

She stood up. "I—I'm going through a difficult time right now." Her voice faltered. "It's something I really can't talk about. Could we start over again, as if this never happened?"

Much as he'd like to explore her problem further, he decided to let it rest for now. "That all depends." On impulse he said, "Do you like to ride horses?"

"I love it. I used to ride all the time on my grand-parents' farm."

Good. "Then I'll have lunch sent to your room, and I'll collect you in an hour. We'll ride around the grounds. It's someplace safe and close to Abby, who's hoping you're having a good time. But if you're afraid of what happened to my sister while she was riding, we could play tennis."

"I'm not afraid, but to go riding must be a painful reminder to you."

"I've worked my way through it. Accidents can happen anytime. To worry about it unnecessarily takes away from the quality of life. Don't you think?"

Her eyes suddenly glistened. "Yes," she whispered with such deep emotion he was more curious than ever to know what was going on inside her, and found himself wanting to comfort her. Instead he had to tear himself away.

"I'll be back in an hour." Reaching for his towel and phone, he left the apartment and hurried through the palace to his suite. Maybe by the end of their ride today, he'd have answers…

Carolena stood in the living room surprised and touched by his decency. He'd thought she'd been assaulted by a man and wanted to show her she didn't need to be afraid of him while he entertained her. No doubt he felt an obligation to her with Vincenzo and Abby indisposed.

He was sensitive, too. How many men would have worried she might be afraid to ride after what had happened to his sister? She'd gotten killed out riding, but he didn't let that stop him from living his normal life. His concern for Carolena's feelings increased her admiration for him.

So far she'd been a perfectly horrid guest, while he

was going out of his way to make this trip eventful for her when he didn't have to. This wasn't the behavior of a playboy. The crown prince was proving to be the perfect host, increasing her guilt for having offended him.

Within the hour he came for her in a limo and they drove to the stables across the vast estate. Once he'd picked the right mare for her, they headed out to enjoy the scenery. In time, he led them through a heavily wooded area to a lake. They dismounted and walked down to the water's edge.

"What a beautiful setting."

"We open it to the public on certain days of the month."

"Abby used to tell me she felt like a princess in a fairy tale growing up on the palace grounds in Arancia. If I lived here, I'd feel exactly the same way. You and your siblings must have spent hours here when you were young." On impulse she asked, "Were they interested in volcanology, too?"

His eyes swerved to hers. She had the feeling she'd surprised him by her question. "Quite the opposite."

That sounded cryptic. "What's the real reason you developed such a keen interest? It isn't just because Etna is there."

"It's a long story." There was that nuance of sadness in his voice again.

"We've got the rest of the afternoon." She sank onto her knees in the lush grass facing the water where an abundance of waterfowl bobbed around. "Humor me. Last night I was up until one o'clock looking at video clips of Etna and other volcanoes. They were incredible. I really want to know what drove you to become so interested."

He got down on the grass next to her. "My father had a sibling, my uncle Stefano. He was the elder son and the crown prince, but he never wanted to be king. He fought with my grandfather who was then King of Gemelli.

"Uncle Stefano hated the idea of being betrothed and having to marry a woman picked out for him. Our country has never had a sovereign who wasn't married by the time he ascended the throne. It's the law. But Stefano didn't ever want to be king and left home at eighteen to travel the world. I knew he had various girlfriends, so he didn't lead a celibate life, but he never married.

"In time, volcanoes fascinated him and he decided he wanted to study them. To appease my grandparents, he came home occasionally to touch base. I was young and loved him because he was so intelligent and a wonderful teacher. He used to take me up on Etna.

"The day came when I decided I wanted to follow in his footsteps and announced I was going to attend the university to become a geologist. My parents could see my mind was made up.

"While I was at school, the family got word he'd been killed on the Galeras volcano in the Colombian Andes."

"*Valentino—*" she gasped. "I read about it on the website last night. One of the people killed was your uncle?"

Pain marred his striking male features. "He got too close. The ash and gas overpowered him and he died."

She shuddered. "That's horrible. I should have thought

it would have put you off wanting anything more to do with your studies."

"You might think it, but I loved what I was doing. Statistics prove that on average only one volcanologist dies on the job each year or so."

"That's one too many!"

"For our family it was traumatic because of the consequences that followed. His body was shipped home for the funeral. A few weeks later my grandfather suffered a fatal heart attack, no doubt from the shock. His death meant my father took over as king with my mother at his side.

"While we were still grieving, they called me into their bedroom and told me they were all right with my desire to be a volcanologist. But they prayed I wouldn't disappoint them the way my uncle had disappointed my grandfather. They said my uncle Stefano had disgraced the family by not taking up his royal duties and marrying.

"I was torn apart because I'd loved him and knew he'd suffered because he'd turned his back on his royal heritage. But when I heard my parents' sorrow, I promised I would fulfill my princely obligation to the crown and marry when the time was right. They wouldn't have to worry about me. Michelina and I made a pact that we'd always do our duty."

"You mean that if she'd wanted to marry someone else other than Vincenzo, she would still have done her duty."

He nodded. "I asked her about that, knowing Vincenzo didn't love her in the way she loved him. She said it didn't matter. She was committed and was hoping he'd fall in love with her one day."

"Did you resent him for not being able to love your sister?"

"How could I do that when I don't love Alexandra? When I saw how hard he tried to make Michelina happy by agreeing to go through the surrogacy process, my affection for him grew. He was willing to do anything to make their marriage better. Vincenzo is one of the finest men I've ever known. When he ended up marrying Abby, I was happy for him."

"You're a remarkable person. So was your sister."

"I loved her. She could have told our parents she refused to enter into a loveless marriage, but she didn't. Uncle Stefano's death had affected all of us, including our brother, Vito. One day after his military service is over, he, too, will have to marry royalty because he's second in line to the throne."

"The public has no idea of the anguish that goes on behind locked royal doors."

"We're just people who've been born to a strange destiny. I didn't want to disappoint my parents or be haunted with regrets like my uncle. Fortunately, Mother is still capable of ruling, and my time to fulfill my obligation hasn't come yet."

"But it will one day."

"Yes."

"It's hard to comprehend a life like yours. May I be blunt and ask you if you have a girlfriend right now?"

"I've been seeing someone in town."

She had to suppress a moan. *Did you hear that, Carolena?* "And she's all right with the situation?"

"Probably not, but from the beginning she's known we couldn't possibly have a future. In case you're wondering, I haven't slept with her."

Carolena shook her head. "You don't owe me any explanation."

"Nevertheless, I can see the next question in your eyes and so I'll answer it. Contrary to what the media says about me, there have been only a few women with whom I've had an intimate relationship, but they live outside the country."

"Yet knowing you are betrothed has never stopped any of them from wanting to spend time with you?"

"No. The women I've known haven't been looking for permanency, either." He smiled. "We're like those ships passing in the night."

It sounded awful. Yet, since Berto, she hadn't been looking for permanency, either, and could relate more than he knew.

"I've warned my latest girlfriend our relationship could end at any time. You're within your rights to condemn me, Carolena."

"I could never condemn you," she whispered, too consumed by guilt over how she'd accidentally brought out Berto's death to find fault with anyone. "You've had every right to live your life like any ordinary man. But like your uncle, it must have been brutal for you to have grown up knowing your bride was already chosen for you."

"I've tried not to think about it."

Her mind reeled from the revelations. "Does your betrothed know and understand?"

"I'm quite sure Princess Alexandra has had relationships, too. It's possible she's involved with someone she cares about right now. Her parents' expectations for her haven't spared her anguish, either."

"No," she murmured, but it was hard to understand. How could any man measure up to Valentino? If Princess Alexandra was like his sister, she'd been in love with Valentino for years. "Does she support your work as a volcanologist?"

"I haven't asked her."

"Why not?"

"Up to now we've been living our own lives apart as much as possible."

"But this is an integral part of your life!"

He sat up, chewing on the end of a blade of grass. "Our two families have spent occasional time together over the years. But the last time my brother was home on leave and went to Cyprus with me and my mother, he told me that Alexandra admitted she never liked the idea that I was a volcanologist."

"And that doesn't worry you?"

He studied her for a long moment. "It's an issue we'll have to deal with one day after we're married."

"By then it will be too late to work things out between you," she cried. "How often do you fly to Catania?"

"Four times a week."

"She's not going to like that, not if she hates the idea of it."

He gave her a compassionate smile. "Our marriage won't be taking place for a long time, so I choose not to worry about it."

"I don't see how you can stand it."

"You learn to stand it when you've been born into a royal family. Why fate put me in line for the throne instead of you, for example, I don't know."

"You mean a woman can rule?"

"If there are no other males. Under those circumstances, she must marry another royal so she can reign. But my grandparents didn't have a daughter. Uncle Stefano should have been king, but he rebelled, so it fell to my father to rule."

Tears trickled down her cheeks. "How sad for your uncle."

"A double sadness, because though he'd abdicated in order to choose his own life, he was burdened with the pain of disappointing his parents."

"There's been so much pain for all of you. And now your own sister and father have passed on."

He nodded. "It's life."

"But it's so much to handle." Her voice trembled. Carolena wanted to comfort him but realized no one could erase all that sadness. She wiped the moisture off her cheeks. "You didn't have to tell me anything. I feel honored that you did."

His gaze roved over her. "Your flattering interest in what I do prompted me to talk about something I've kept to myself for a long time. It felt good to talk about it. Why don't you try it out on me by telling me what's bothering you."

Her eyes closed tightly for a moment. "Let's just say someone that I loved died and it was my fault. Unlike you, I can't seem to move on from the past."

"Maybe you haven't had enough time to grieve."

Carolena could tell him seven years had been more than enough time to grieve. At this point, grief wasn't her problem. Guilt was the culprit. But all she said to him was, "Maybe."

"It might be therapeutic to confide in someone. Even me."

His sincerity warmed her heart, but confiding in him would be the worst thing she could do. To remain objective around him, she needed to keep some barriers between them. "You have enough problems."

"None right this minute."

He stared hard at her. "Was his death intentional?"

"No."

"I didn't think it was. Have you gone for counseling?"

"No. It wouldn't help."

"You don't know that."

"Yes, I do." In a panic, she started to get up. He helped her the rest of the way. "Thank you for being willing to listen." It was time to change the subject. "Your uncle would be so happy to see how he guided you on your particular path, and more especially on how you're putting that knowledge to exceptional use. If I'd had such an uncle, I would have made him take me with him, too. What you do can be dangerous, but it *is* thrilling."

"You're right about that," he said, still eyeing her

speculatively. "Shall we head out? By the time we reach the palace, hopefully Vincenzo will have good news for us about Max and we can all eat dinner together."

"I hope so."

They mounted their horses and took a different route to the stable. A limo was waiting to take them back to her wing of the palace. When they arrived, she opened the car door before he could. "You don't need to see me inside. Thank you for a wonderful day."

He studied her through veiled eyes. "It was my pleasure. I'll call you when I've spoken with Vincenzo."

She nodded before getting out of the limo. After hurrying inside, she took a quick shower, applied her makeup and arranged her hair in a loose knot on top of her head. For the first time in years her thoughts hadn't been on Berto. They'd been full of the prince, who'd brought her alive from the moment he'd appeared at the side of the pool.

No matter that he had a girlfriend at the moment, it was hard to breathe every time Carolena thought of the way he'd looked at her. She could understand why any woman lucky enough to catch his eye would be willing to stay in a relationship as long as possible to be with him. There was no one like him.

Needing to do something with all this energy he'd generated through no fault of his own, she got dressed, deciding to wear a short-sleeved crocheted lace top in the same egg shell color as her linen pants. The outfit was light and airy. She toned it with beige ankle-strap crisscross espadrilles.

While she was waiting for a phone call, she heard

a knock on the door and wondered if it might be the prince. With a pounding heart she reached for her straw bag and opened it, but it was the maid, and Carolena was furious at herself for being disappointed.

"*Signorina?* His Highness has asked me to accompany you to dinner. He's waiting on the terrace."

What about Abby and Vincenzo? "Thank you for coming to get me."

No shortcuts through the grounds this time, but it gave Carolena the opportunity to see more of the ornate palace. By the time she arrived at the terrace, Vincenzo had already joined the prince, but there was no sign of Abby or Max. The two men stood together chatting quietly.

She had the impression this terrace was a recent addition. It was a masterpiece of black-and-white marble checkerboard flooring, Moorish elements and cream-colored lattice furniture in Italian provincial. A collection of exotic trees and flowering plants gave the impression they were in a garden.

Valentino's dark blue gaze saw her first. He broke from Vincenzo and moved toward her wearing jeans and a sand-colored polo shirt. "*Buonasera,* Carolena. You look beautiful."

Don't say that. "Thank you."

His quick smile was a killer. "I hope you're hungry. I told the kitchen to prepare chicken the way Abby tells me you like it."

"You're very kind." Too kind. She flashed him a smile as he helped her get seated. Valentino had no equal as a host. She decided he had no equal, period.

Vincenzo walked over and kissed her cheek before sitting down at the round table opposite her. A sumptuous-looking meal had been laid out for them. A maid came out on the terrace just then and told Valentino his mother wanted to speak to him when he had a minute. He nodded before she left.

"Where's Abby, Vincenzo?"

"Max fussed all day and is still feverish, so we're taking turns."

"The poor little thing. Do you think it's serious?"

"We don't know. Our doctor said it could be a virus, but Max isn't holding down his food. That has me worried."

"I don't blame you. Is there something I can do to help?"

"Yes," Valentino inserted. "If Max is still sick tomorrow, you can keep me company, since Vincenzo will be tied up taking care of his family."

He actually sounded happy about it, but the news filled Carolena with consternation. She'd been with him too much already and her attraction to him was growing. She flicked him a glance. "You don't have to worry about entertaining me. I brought my laptop and always have work to do."

"Not while you're here." Valentino's underlying tone of authority quieted any more of her excuses. "No doubt you and Abby had intended to visit some of the shops and museums in Gemelli while on holiday, but I can think of something more exciting for tomorrow *if* you're up to it."

Vincenzo shot her a glance she couldn't decipher. "Be careful."

She chuckled. "Is that a warning?"

After finishing his coffee, a glimmer of a smile appeared. "On my first business visit here years ago, Valentino dangled the same option in front of me."

"What happened?"

He studied her for a moment. "That's for you to find out."

"Now you've made me nervous."

"Maybe you should be." She couldn't tell if Vincenzo's cryptic response was made in jest or not.

"You've frightened her," Valentino muttered. Again, Carolena was confused by the more serious undertone of their conversation.

"Then I'm sorry and I apologize." Vincenzo put down his napkin and got to his feet. "Enjoy your evening. We'll talk again in the morning. Please don't get up."

"Kiss that baby for me and give Abby my love."

"I will."

She'd never seen Vincenzo so preoccupied. Being a new father wasn't easy, but she sensed something else was on his mind, as well.

"What went on just now?" she asked as soon as he left the terrace.

Valentino had been watching her through narrowed eyes. "I'm afraid he thinks my idea of a good time could backfire." Carolena believed there was more to it than that, but she let it go for now.

"You mean it might be one of those surprises that's the wrong kind for me?"

"Possibly."

"Well, if you don't tell me pretty soon, I might expire on the spot from curiosity."

She thought he'd laugh, but for once he didn't. "I'd like to take you sailing to Taormina. It's an island Goethe called 'a part of paradise.' The medieval streets have tiny passages with secrets I can guarantee you'll love."

"It sounds wonderful, but that wasn't the place you had in mind when you were talking with Vincenzo."

"I've had time to think the better of it."

A rare flare of temper brought blood to her cheeks. "Vincenzo is Abby's husband, not mine."

"And he enjoys her confidence."

"In other words, he's trying to protect me from something he thinks wouldn't be good for me."

"Maybe."

Carolena's grandmother used to try to protect her the same way. But if she got into it with the prince, she'd be acting like the willful child her grandparent used to accuse her of being. Averting her eyes, she forced herself to calm down and said, "It's possible Max will be better, but in case he isn't, I'd love a chance to go sailing. It's very kind of you."

She heard his sharp intake of breath. "Now you're patronizing me."

"What do you expect me to do? Have a tantrum?" The question was out of her mouth before she could stop it. She was mortified to realize she was out of control. Something had gotten into her. She didn't feel at all herself.

"At least it would be better than your pretense to mollify me," came the benign response.

What? "If you weren't the prince—"

"I asked you to forget my title."

"That's kind of hard to do."

"Why don't you finish what you were about to say. If I weren't the prince…"

"Bene." She sucked in her breath. "If neither of you were princes, I'd tell you I've been taking care of myself for twenty-seven years and don't need a couple of guys I hardly know to decide what's best for me. If that sounds ungracious, I didn't mean for it to offend you, but you did ask."

A look of satisfaction entered his eyes. "I was hoping you would say that. How would you like to fly up on Etna with me in a helicopter? We'll put down in one spot and I'll show you some sights no visitor gets to see otherwise."

Gulp. She clung to the edge of the table from sheer unadulterated excitement. Valentino intended to show her that ten-thousand-foot volcano up close? After seeing that movie, what person in the world wouldn't want the opportunity? She couldn't understand why Vincenzo thought it might not be a good experience for her.

"You love your work so much you'd go up there on your day off?"

"You can ask that after what I revealed to you today? Didn't you tell me you thought it sounded thrilling?"

"Yes." She stood up and gazed into those intelligent,

dark blue eyes. Ignoring the warning flags telling her to be prudent, she said, "I'd absolutely love it."

A stillness surrounded them. "Never let it be said I didn't give you an out."

"I don't want one, even if Vincenzo thought I did."

A tiny nerve throbbed at the side of his hard jaw. "If Max is still sick in the morning, we'll leave around eight-thirty. You'll need to wear jeans and a T-shirt if you brought one. If not, you can wear one of mine."

"I have one."

"Good, but you can't go in sandals."

"I brought my walking boots."

"Perfect."

"I'll see you in the morning then."

As she started to leave, he said, "Don't go yet."

Valentino—I can't spend any more time with you to-night. I just can't! "Your mother is waiting for you and I have things to do. I know the way back to my room."

"Carolena?"

With a pounding heart, she paused at the entrance. "Yes?"

"I enjoyed today more than you know."

Oh, but I do, her heart cried.

"The horseback ride was wonderful. Thank you again." In the next breath she took off for the other wing of the palace. Her efforts to stay away from him weren't working. To see where he spent his time and share it with him was too great a temptation to turn down, but she recognized that the thing she'd prayed would never happen was happening!

She was starting to care about him, way too much.

Forget the guilt over Berto's death that had prevented her from getting close to another man. Her feelings were way too strong for Valentino. Already she was terrified at the thought of handling another loss when she had to fly back to Arancia with Abby and Vincenzo.

But if she said she wasn't feeling well now and begged off going with him tomorrow, he'd never believe her. Though she knew she was walking into emotional danger by getting more involved, she didn't have the strength to say no to him. *Help*.

CHAPTER THREE

LETTING CAROLENA GO when it was the last thing he wanted, Valentino walked through the palace to his mother's suite. The second he entered her sitting room he was met with the news he'd been dreading all his adult life.

While he'd been riding horses with Carolena, his mother had worked out the details of his coming marriage to Princess Alexandra of Cyprus. Both royal families had wanted a June wedding, but he'd asked for more time, hoping for another year of freedom. Unfortunately they'd forced him to settle on August tenth and now there was no possibility of him changing his mind.

Tonight his mother had pinned him down, gaining his promise there'd be no more women. By giving his word, it was as good as writing it in cement.

Ages ago he and Michelina had talked about their arranged marriages. Valentino had intended to be true to Alexandra once their marriage date was set, but he'd told Michelina he planned to live a full life with other women until his time came.

She, on the other hand, never did have the same problem because she'd fallen in love with Vincenzo long before they were married and would never have been unfaithful to him. Vincenzo was a good man who'd kept his marriage vows despite the fact that he didn't feel the same way about her. Valentino admired him more than any man he knew for being the best husband he could under the circumstances.

But after seeing Abby and Vincenzo together while they'd been here, he longed for that kind of love. A huge change had come over Vincenzo once he and Abby had fallen for each other. He was no longer the same man. Valentino could see the passion that leaped between them. Last night he'd witnessed it and knew such a deep envy, he could hardly bear it.

After eight months of marriage their love had grown stronger and deeper. Everyone could see it, his mother most of all. Both she and Valentino had suffered for Michelina. She'd had the misfortune of loving Vincenzo who couldn't love her back in the same way. It would have been better if she hadn't fallen for him, but he couldn't handle thinking about that right now.

The only thing to do where Alexandra was concerned was try to get pregnant soon and build a family the way his own parents had done. Even if the most important element was missing, children would fill a big hole. That's what Michelina had tried to do by going ahead with the surrogacy procedure.

Unfortunately, he hadn't counted on the existence of Carolena Baretti. Her unexpected arrival in Gemelli had knocked him sideways for reasons he hadn't been able to identify yet. Instead of imagining his future life, his thoughts kept running to the gorgeous brunette who was a guest in the other wing of the palace.

Something had happened to him since he'd come upon Abby's friend in the swimming pool that first evening. He'd promised his mother no more women and he'd meant it. But like a lodestone he'd once found on an ancient volcano crater attracting his tools, her unique personality and stunning physical traits had drawn him in.

He'd met many beautiful women in his life, but never one like her. For one thing, she hadn't thrown herself at him. Quite the opposite. That in itself was so rare he found himself attracted on several levels.

Because she was Abby's best friend, she was already in the untouchable category, even if he hadn't promised his mother. Yet this evening, the last thing he'd wanted to do was say good-night to her.

They'd shared a lot today. Intimate things. Her concern for him, the tears she'd shed for his uncle, touched him on a profound level. He'd never met a woman so completely genuine. To his chagrin she made him feel close to her. To his further disgust, he couldn't think beyond having breakfast with her in the morning.

With his blood effectively chilled now that the conversation with his mother was over, he excused himself and called for his car to come around to his private entrance. He told his driver to head for Tancredi's Restaurant on the east end of the island, a twenty-minute drive.

Once on his way, he phoned his best friend from his university days to alert him he was coming. Matteo owned the place since his father had died. He would be partying in the bar with a few of their mutual friends now that there were no more customers.

After the limo turned down the alley behind the restaurant, Matteo emerged from the backdoor and climbed inside.

"Ehi, Valentino—"

"Sorry I'm late, but tonight certain things were unavoidable."

"Non c'è problema! It's still early for us. Come on. We've been waiting for you."

"I'm afraid I can't."

"Ooh. Adriana's not going to like hearing that."

"She's the reason I asked you to come out to the limo. Can I depend on you to put it to her gently that I won't be seeing her again?"

He frowned. "Why not?"

They stared at each other before Matteo let out an epithet. "Does this mean you're finally getting married?" He knew the union had been arranged years ago.

Valentino grimaced. "Afraid so." Once he'd gone to his mother's apartment, she'd forced him to come to a final decision after talking with his betrothed's parents. "They're insisting on an August wedding and coronation. The president of the parliament will announce our formal engagement next week."

He realized it was long past time to end his brief, shallow relationship with Adriana. For her best interest he should have done it a month ago. Instinct told him she would be a willing mistress after his marriage, but Valentino didn't feel that way about her or any woman. In any case, he would never go down that path.

Matteo's features hardened. "I can't believe this day has finally come. It's like a bad dream."

A groan escaped Valentino's throat. "But one I'm committed to. I've told you before, but I'll say it again. You've been a great friend, Matteo. I'll never forget."

"Are you saying goodbye to me, too?" he asked quietly.

His friend's question hurt him. "How can you even ask me that?"

"I don't know." Matteo drove his fist into his other palm. "I knew one day there was going to be a wedding and coronation and I know of your loyalty. Now everything's going to change."

"Not my friendship with you."

"I hope not. It's meant everything to me."

"My father told me a king has no friends, but I'm not the king yet. Even when I am, you'll always be my friend. I'll call you soon." He clapped him on the shoulder before Matteo got out of the limo. Once he'd disappeared inside the restaurant, Valentino told his driver to head back to the palace. But his mood was black.

After a sleepless night he learned that Max wasn't any better, so he followed through on his plans to pick up Carolena at her apartment. He found her outside her door waiting for him. The sight of her in jeans and a T-shirt caused another adrenaline rush.

Her eyes lifted to his. "Is there anything else you can think of I might need before we leave?"

He'd already taken inventory of her gorgeous figure and still hadn't recovered. "We'll be flying to the center in my helicopter. Whatever is missing we will find there."

"Then I'm ready." Carolena shut the suite and followed him down the hallway and out the doors. They crossed the grounds to the pad where his helicopter was waiting. "I hope this isn't a dream and I'm going to wake up in a few minutes. To see where you spend your time kept me awake all night."

Nothing could have pleased Valentino more than to know she was an adventurous woman who'd taken an interest in his research. But he knew in his gut her interest in him went deeper than that. "Perhaps now you'll understand that after a day's work on the volcano, I have trouble getting to sleep, too."

Besides his family and bodyguards, plus close friends like Matteo, he rarely shared his love for his work with anyone outside of his colleagues at the center. For his own protection, the women he'd had relationships with knew nothing about his life.

He'd called ahead to one of the center's pilots who would be taking them up. The helicopter was waiting for them when they touched down.

"Dante Serrano, meet Signorina Carolena Baretti from Arancia. She's the best friend of my brother-in-law's wife. They're staying at the palace with me for a few days. I thought she might like to see Etna at closer range."

The pilot's eyes flared in male admiration and surprise before he shook Carolena's hand and welcomed her aboard. This was a first for Valentino, let alone for Dante, who'd never known Valentino to fly a female with him unless she happened to be a geologist doing work.

He helped her into the seat behind the pilot, then took the copilot's seat. While the rotors whined, he turned to her. "Your first volcano experience should be from the air."

"I'm so excited to be seeing this up close, I can hardly stand it." Her enthusiasm was contagious. "Why does it constantly smoke?"

"That's because it's continually being reshaped by seismic activity. There are four distinct craters at the summit and more than three hundred vents on the flanks. Some are small holes, others are large craters. You'll see things that are invisible or look completely different from the surface."

"You're so right!" she cried after they took off. Once they left Catania, they passed over the fertile hillsides and lush pines. "The vistas are breathtaking, Val. With the Mediterranean for a background, these snow-topped mountains are fabulous. I didn't expect to see so much green and blue."

Her reaction, on top of her beautiful face, made it impossible for Valentino to look anywhere else. "It's a universe all its own."

'I can't believe what I'm seeing."

The landscape changed as they flew higher and higher. "We're coming up on some black lava deserts. Take a good look. Mount Etna is spitting lava more violently than it has in years, baffling us. Not only is it unpredictable, the volcano is raging, erupting in rapid succession."

He loved her awestruck squeals of delight. "I suppose you've walked across those deserts."

"I've climbed all over this volcano with Uncle Stefano."

"No wonder you love your work so much! I would, too!"

"The range of ash fall is much wider than usual. That's why I always come home dirty."

"Now I understand. Come to think of it, you did look like you'd been putting out a fire."

Dante shared a grin with Valentino. "Signorina Baretti," He spoke over his shoulder. "Even in ancient times, the locals marveled at the forces capable of shooting fountains of lava into the sky. In Greek and Roman mythology, the volcano is represented by a limping blacksmith swinging his hammer as sparks fly.

"Legend has it that the natural philosopher Empedocles jumped into the crater two thousand five hundred years ago. What he found there remained his secret because he never returned. All that remained of him were his iron shoes, which the mountain later spat out."

"That's a wonderful story, if not frightening."

All three of them laughed.

"The really fascinating part is coming up. We're headed for the Bove Valley, Etna's huge caldera. You're going to get a bird's-eye view of the eastern slope." They flew on with Dante giving her the full treatment of the famous volcano that produced more stunned cries from Carolena.

"How big is it?"

"Seven kilometers from east to west, six kilometers from north to south."

She was glued to the window, mesmerized. Valentino knew how she felt. He signaled Dante to fly them to Bocca Nuova.

"When we set down on the side of the pit, you'll see a new fumarole in the saddle between the old and new southeast crater. I want you to stay by me. This is where I was working the other day. You won't need a gas mask at this distance, but you can understand why I want every citizen of Gemelli to be equipped with one."

"After seeing this and hearing about your uncle Stefano, I understand your concern, believe me."

Before long, he helped her out and they walked fifty yards to a vantage point. "This is a place no one is allowed except our teams. The organized tours of the thousands of people who came to Etna are much farther below."

Soon they saw the vent releasing the same bluish gas and ash he'd recorded the other day.

"This fumarole was formed by that long fissure you can see."

While they stood there gazing, the noise of explosions coming from deep within the volcano shook the ground. When she cried out, he automatically put his arm around her shoulders and pulled her tight against his side. He liked the feel of her womanly body this close.

"Don't be alarmed," he murmured into her fragrant hair. "We're safe or I wouldn't have brought you up here."

She clung to him. "I know that, but I have to tell you a secret. I never felt insignificant until now." Those were his very thoughts the first time he'd come up on Etna. After a long silence, she lifted her eyes to him. In them he saw a longing for him that she couldn't hide when she said, "It's awesome and mind blowing all at the same time."

Those dazzling, dark-fringed green eyes blew him away, but not for the reasons she'd been alluding to. He was terrified over the feelings he'd developed for her. "You've taken the words right out of my mouth."

The desire to kiss her was so powerful, it took all the self-control he possessed not to crush her against him. He was in serious trouble and knew it.

Fighting his desire, he said, "I think you've seen enough for today. We've been gone a long time and need to eat. Another day and I'll take you on a hike through some lava fields and tunnels you'll find captivating." *Almost as captivating as I'm finding you.*

"I doubt I'll ever be in Gemelli again, but if I am, I'll certainly take you up on your offer. Thank you for a day I'll never *ever* forget." He felt her tremulous voice shake his insides.

"Nor will I." The fact that she was off-limits had no meaning to him right now.

On their way back to the center, he checked his phone messages. One from Vincenzo and two from his mother. He checked Vincenzo's first.

I'm just giving you a heads-up. Max isn't doing well, so we're flying back to Arancia at nine in the morning. Sorry about this, but the doctor thinks he may have gas-

troenteritis and wants to check him out at the hospital.
Give me a call when you're available.

Valentino's lips thinned. He was sorry about the
baby, but it meant Carolena would be leaving in the
morning.

The queen's first message told him she was upset
they were going to have to leave with her grandson.
She was crazy about Max and her reaction was understandable. Her second message had to do with wedding
preparations. Since he couldn't do anything about either situation at the moment, he decided to concentrate
on Carolena, who would be slipping away from his life
much sooner than he'd anticipated.

Once they touched down at the center and had
thanked Dante for the wonderful trip, they climbed on
board Valentino's helicopter. But instead of flying back
to the palace where his mother expected him to join her
the second he got back, he instructed his pilot to land
on the royal yacht anchored in the bay. They could have
dinner on board away from the public eye.

Carolena was a very special VIP and the crew would
think nothing of his entertaining the close friend of his
new sister-in-law who was here with the prince of Arancia visiting the queen.

He called ahead to arrange for their meal to be served
on deck. After they arrived on board and freshened
up, they sat down to dinner accompanied by soft rock
music as the sun disappeared below the horizon. Both
of them had developed an appetite. Valentino loved it
that she ate with enjoyment.

"Try the Insolia wine. It has a slightly nutty flavor

with a finish that is a combination of sweet fruit and sour citrus. I think it goes well with swordfish."

"It definitely does, and the steak is out of this world, Val. Everything here in Gemelli is out of this world."

From the deck they could see Etna smoking in the far distance. She kept looking at it. "To think I flew over that volcano today and saw a fumarole up close." Her gaze swerved to his. "Nothing I'll ever do in life will match the wonder of this day, and it's all because of you."

He sipped his wine. "So the surprise didn't turn out to be so bad, after all."

"You know it didn't." Her voice throbbed, revealing her emotion. "I can't think why Vincenzo warned me against it. Unless—"

When she didn't finish, he said, "Unless what?"

"Maybe watching Michelina when she had her riding accident has made him more cautious than usual over the people he loves and cares about. Last night I could tell how worried he was about Max."

Valentino hadn't thought of that, but he couldn't rule it out as a possibility, though he didn't think it was Vincenzo's major concern. Now that they were talking about it, his conversation at dinner with Vincenzo in front of her came back to haunt him.

He'd been warning Valentino, but maybe not about the volcano. Unfortunately, Vincenzo had always been a quick study. Possibly he'd picked up on Valentino's interest in Carolena. Whatever had gone on in Vincenzo's mind, now was the time to tell her about the change in their plans to fly back to Arancia.

"I checked my voice mail on the way to the yacht. You can listen." He pulled his cell phone from his pocket and let her hear Vincenzo's message.

In an instant everything changed, as he knew it would. "The poor darling. It's a good thing we're going home in the morning. I'm sure Max will be all right, but after no sleep, all three of them have to be absolutely miserable."

Make that an even four.

The idea of Carolena leaving Gemelli filled him with a sense of loss he'd never experienced before. The deaths of his father and sister were different. It didn't matter that he'd only known her twenty-four hours. To never be with her again was anathema to him.

He could have predicted what she'd say next. "We'd better get back to the palace. I need to pack."

"Let's have our dessert first. You have to try *cassata alla sicilana*." Anything to prolong their time together.

"Isn't that a form of cheesecake?"

"Cake like you've never tasted anywhere else."

An impish smile broke one corner of her voluptuous mouth. "Something tells me you're a man who loves his sweets."

"Why do you think that?"

"I don't know. Maybe it's because of the way you embrace life to the fullest and enjoy its richness while at the same time reverencing it. When the gods handed out gifts, you received more than your fair share."

He frowned. "What do you mean?"

"There aren't many men who could measure up to

you. Your sister used to sing your praises to Abby, who said she worshipped you."

"The feeling was mutual, believe me."

"According to Abby, Michelina admitted that the only man who came close to you was Prince Vincenzo. That's high praise indeed. Luckily for your country, you're going to be in charge one day."

One day? That day was almost upon him!

For the wedding date to have been fixed at the same time he'd met Signorina Baretti, the pit in Valentino's stomach had already grown into a caldera bigger than the one he'd shown her today.

He'd spun out every bit of time with her he could squeeze and had no legitimate choice but to take her back to the palace.

"It's getting late. I'm sure Vincenzo will want to talk to you tonight."

Valentino shook his head. "With the baby sick, that won't be happening." In truth, he wasn't up to conversation with Vincenzo or his mother. For the first time in his life he had the wicked instinct to do what he wanted and kidnap this woman who'd beguiled him.

"I have a better idea. It's been a long day. We'll stay on the yacht and fly you back on time in the morning. I'll instruct the maid to pack your things. As for tonight, anything you need we have on board."

Carolena's breath caught. "What about your girlfriend? Won't she be expecting you?"

His dark blue eyes narrowed on her face. "Not when I'm entertaining family and friends. As for the other question you don't dare ask, I've never brought a woman on board the yacht or taken one up on the volcano."

He'd been so frank and honest with her today, she believed him now. His admission shook her to her core. "If I didn't know better, I would think you were propositioning me," she teased to cover her chaotic emotions. There she went again. Saying something she shouldn't have allowed to escape her lips.

His jaw hardened. "I'm a man before being a prince and I *am* propositioning you, but I can see I've shocked you as much as myself."

She could swear that was truth she'd heard come out of him. Carolena was Abby's friend, yet that hadn't stopped him, and obviously that fact wasn't stopping her. It was as if they were both caught in a snare of such intense attraction, they knew no boundaries.

"Do you want to know something else?" he murmured. "I can see in those glorious green eyes of yours that you'd like to stay on board with me tonight. True desire is something you can't hide. We've both felt it since we met, so there's no use denying it."

"I'm not," she confessed in a tremulous voice. Carolena could feel her defenses crumbling and started to tremble. Never had she been around a man who'd made her feel so completely alive.

"My kingdom for an honest woman, and here you are."

"Only you and Vincenzo could say such a thing and get away with it."

Her humor didn't seem to touch him. "Tell me about

the man who died. You *were* speaking about a man. Are you still terribly in love with him?"

His question reached the core of her being. "I'll always love him," she answered honestly.

He reached across the table and grasped her hand. "How long has he been gone?"

She couldn't lie to him. "Seven years."

After a moment of quiet, he said, "That's a long time to be in love with a memory. How did he die?"

"It doesn't matter. I don't want to talk about it."

Those all-seeing eyes of his gazed through to her soul. "Yet somehow you still feel responsible for his death?"

"Yes."

"Has it prevented you from getting close to another man?"

"I've been with other men since he died, if that's what you mean."

"Carolena—tell me the truth. Is there one man who's vitally important to you now?"

Yes. But he's not in Arancia.

"No one man more than another," she dissembled.

She heard his sharp intake of breath. "Then do you dare stay with me the way you dared to get close to Etna's furnace today? I'm curious to see how brave a woman you really are."

His thumb massaged her palm, sending warmth through her sensitized body until her toes curled. "You already know the answer to that."

"Dance with me, *bellissima,*" he begged in a husky

whisper. "I don't give a damn that the crew can see us. You've entranced me and I need to feel you in my arms."

It was what she wanted, too. When she'd heard Vincenzo say that they were leaving in the morning, she'd wanted to cry out in protest that she'd only gotten here. She hadn't had enough time with Valentino. *Not nearly enough.*

He got up from the table and drew her into his arms. She went into them eagerly, aching for this since the time he'd put his arm around her up on the volcano. It felt as if their bodies were meant for each other. She slid her arms around his neck until there was no air between them. They clung out of need in the balmy night air that enveloped them like velvet.

His hands roved over her back and hips as they got a new sense of each other only touch could satisfy. They slow danced until she lost track of time. To hold and be held by this amazing man was a kind of heaven.

She knew he was unattainable. Abby had told her he'd been betrothed to Princess Alexandra in his teens, just like Vincenzo's betrothal to Princess Michelina. One day Valentino would have to marry. He'd explained all that yesterday.

Carolena understood that. It didn't bother her since she shunned the idea of commitment that would lead to her own marriage. Marriage meant being responsible for another person's happiness. She couldn't handle that, but selfishly she did desire this one night with Valentino before she flew back to Arancia and never saw him again.

Tonight he'd made her thankful she'd been born a

woman. Knowing he wanted her as much as she wanted him brought indescribable joy. One night with him would have to be enough, except that he still hadn't kissed her yet and she was dying for it. When he suddenly stopped moving, she moaned in disappointment.

His hands squeezed her upper arms. "The steward will show you downstairs to your cabin," he whispered before pulling the phone from his pocket. "I'll join you shortly."

Carolena was so far gone she'd forgotten about the prying eyes of the crew, but Valentino was used to the whole world watching him and did what was necessary to keep gossip to a minimum. Without words she eased away from him and walked over to the table for her purse before following the steward across the deck to the stairs.

The luxury yacht was a marvel, but Carolena was too filled with desire for Valentino to notice much of anything. Once she reached the cabin and the steward left, she took a quick shower and slipped into one of the white toweling bathrobes hanging on a hook. The dressing room provided every cosmetic and convenience a man or woman could need.

She sat in front of the mirror and brushed her hair. *Entranced* was the right word. Though she knew she'd remain single all her life, she felt as if this was her wedding night while she waited for him to come. The second he entered the room he would hear the fierce pounding of her heart.

Soon she heard his rap on the door. "Come in," she called quietly. He walked in and shut the door behind him, still dressed in the clothes he'd worn during their trip.

Without saying anything, he reached for her hand and drew her over to the bed where he sat down and pulled her between his legs. His gaze glowed like hot blue embers. Everywhere it touched, she was set on fire. Her ears picked up the ragged sound of his breathing.

"You look like a bride."

But, of course, she wasn't a bride, and she sensed something was wrong. She could feel it. "Is that good or bad?"

He ran his hands up and down her arms beneath the loose sleeves of her robe as if even his fingers were hungry for her. "Carolena—" There was an unmistakable plea for understanding in his tone.

"Yes?" Whatever was coming, she knew she wasn't going to like it.

"I talked frankly with you yesterday about my personal life. But what you couldn't know was that last night after you went back to your room, I met with my mother." His chest rose and fell visibly. "While you and I were out riding, my wedding date to Princess Alexandra was finally set in stone. We're being married on August tenth, the day of my coronation."

Carolena stood stock-still while the news sank in. That was only two months from now...

"Though I made the promise to my mother that I'd be faithful to Alexandra from here on out, I really made it to myself and have already gotten word to my latest girlfriend that it's over for good."

She could hardly credit what she was hearing.

"But little did I know I was already being tested by none other than Abby's best friend."

A small cry escaped her throat. "I shouldn't have come, but Abby kept insisting." She shivered. "This is all my fault, Val."

"There you go again, taking on blame for something that's no one's fault. If we were to follow that line of thinking, shall I blame myself for inviting Vincenzo to come on this trip? Shall we blame him for bringing his wife and her best friend?"

His logic made Carolena feel like a fool. "Of course not."

"At least you admit that much. In my whole life I've never wanted a woman more than I've wanted you, since the moment we met at the swimming pool. But it's more than that now. Much more."

"I know. I feel it, too." But she remained dry eyed and smiled at him. "The gods are jealous of you. They're waiting for you to make a mistake. Didn't you know that?"

He squeezed her hands gently. "When I dared you to stay with me tonight, I crossed a line I swore I would never do."

"I believe you. But the fact is, it takes two, Val. I didn't know your wedding date had been set, of course. Yet even knowing you were betrothed, I crossed it, too, because I've never known desire like this before, either. I've never had an affair before."

"Carolena..."

He said her name with such longing, she couldn't stand it. "Let's not make this situation any more impossible. Go back to the palace tonight knowing you've passed your test."

"And leave you like this?" he cried urgently, pulling her closer to him. "You don't really mean that!"

"Yes. I do. You have Vincenzo to think about, and a mother who's waiting for your return. Your wedding's going to take place soon. You need to concentrate on Alexandra now."

But she knew he wasn't listening. He got to his feet, cupping her face in his hands. "I don't want to leave you." He sounded as if he was in agony. "Say the word and I won't."

Abby could hear her grandmother's voice. *You go where angels fear to tread without worrying about anyone else but yourself.*

Not this time, *nonnina.*

"Thank you for your honesty. It's one of your most sterling qualities. You truly are the honorable man your sister idolized. But I have enough sins on my conscience without helping you add one to yours."

His brows formed a bar above his eyes. "You told me you caused the death of the man you loved, but you also said it wasn't intentional."

She averted her eyes. "It wasn't."

"Then no sin has been committed."

"Not if we part now. I don't want you going through life despising yourself for breaking the rule you've set. Believe it or not, I *want* you to go, Val," she told him. "After the promise you made to your parents when your uncle died, I couldn't handle it otherwise."

"Handle what? You're still holding back on me. Tell me what it is."

"It's no longer of any importance."

"Carolena—"

He was willing to break his vow for her because he wanted her that much. Just knowing that helped her to stay strong. But he didn't realize all this had to do with her self-preservation.

"Val, if it's all right with you, I'd like to remain on board until tomorrow morning and then fly back to the palace. But please know that when I leave Gemelli, I'll take home the memory of a man who for a moment out of time made me feel immortal. I'll treasure the memory of you all my life."

She pulled away from him and walked over to the door to open it. *"Addio,* sweet prince."

CHAPTER FOUR

THE MOMENT VALENTINO walked into the palace at eleven that night, he texted Vincenzo, who was still up. They met in Valentino's suite.

"How did your day go?" his brother-in-law asked after he'd walked into the sitting room.

Valentino was still on fire for the woman who'd looked like a vision when he'd walked into her cabin.

"After we left Etna, I thought Carolena would like dinner on the yacht where there's a wonderful view of the island. She's staying there overnight. My pilot will fly her back in the morning. You should have seen her when we got out of the helicopter and walked over to view one of the fumaroles. She was one person who really appreciated the experience."

"Michelina would never step foot on Etna and was always afraid for you. Sorry about this morning. I guess I thought it might frighten Carolena."

Valentino had forgotten about his sister's fear. It showed how totally concentrated he'd been on Carolena. "If she was, she hid it well. Now I want to hear about Max. How is he?"

"For the moment both he and Abby are asleep. It'll be a relief to get him home. After the doctor tells us what's wrong and we can relax, I'd like it if you could arrange to fly to Arancia so we can talk business."

He nodded. "I'm as anxious as you to get started on the idea we've discussed. I'll clear my calendar." It would mean seeing Carolena again. He was going to get the truth out of her one way or another.

"Abby thinks Carolena would be a good person to consult over the legalities of the plans we have in mind. Did I mention her expertise is patent law? It's exactly what we need."

She was a patent attorney? Valentino's heart leaped to think he didn't need to find an excuse to see her again when he had a legitimate reason to be with her before long. On his way to the palace, he'd come close to telling the pilot he'd changed his mind and wanted to go back to the yacht.

"Valentino? Did you hear what I said?"

"Sorry. The news about her work in patent law took me by surprise. Abby and Carolena are both intelligent women. With them being such close friends and attorneys, it will be a pleasure to have them consult with us. I've worried about finding someone we could really trust."

"Amen to that. We don't want anyone else to get wind of this until it's a fait accompli," Vincenzo muttered. "Abby asked me to thank you for taking such good care of Carolena today."

If he only knew how dangerously close Valentino had come to making love to her. Once that happened, there'd be no going back because he knew in his gut he'd want her over and over again. That would jeopardize both their lives and put them in a different kind of hell.

"It's always a rush to go up on Etna with someone who finds it as fascinating as I do."

"She really liked it?"

"I wish I had a recording while we were in the air."

Vincenzo smiled. "That'll make Abby happy. She brought Carolena along because seven years ago yesterday her fiancé was killed days before she became a bride. Apparently this date in June is always hard for her. They were very much in love."

Fiancé?

Valentino's gut twisted in deepest turmoil when he remembered telling her she looked like a bride. More than ever he was determined to find out what kind of guilt she'd been carrying around all this time.

"Abby says she dates one man after another, but it's only once or twice, never really getting to know anyone well. She believes she's depressed and is pretty worried about her. Abby was hoping this trip would help her get out of herself. Sounds like your day on the volcano may have done just that."

The revelations coming one after the other hit Valentino like a volcanic bomb during an eruption.

"I hope so."

"I'd better get back to our suite. It'll be my turn to walk the floor with Max when he wakes up again. My poor wife is worn out."

"From the looks of it, so are you." He patted Vincenzo on the shoulder before walking him to the door.

"I'll have breakfast sent to your suite at eight. Carolena will be waiting for you on the helicopter."

"Thanks for everything, Valentino."

"The queen says this will pass. She ought to know after raising me and my siblings. See you in the morning."

After his brother-in-law left, Valentino raced out of the palace to the swimming pool. He did laps until he was so exhausted he figured he might be able to sleep for what was left of the rest of the night. But that turned out to be a joke. There were certain fires you couldn't put out.

The next morning when he walked out to the landing pad with Vincenzo and his family, Carolena was still strapped in her seat. One of his security men put the luggage from her room on board as he climbed in.

Other than a smile and another thank-you for the tour of the volcano, she displayed no evidence of having missed Valentino or passing a tormented night. They were both accomplished actors playing roles with such expertise they might even have deceived each other. Except for the slight break he heard in her voice that caused his heart to skip several beats.

Four days later Carolena had just finished taking a deposition in her office and had said goodbye to her client when her new secretary, Tomaso, told her Abby was on the line. She hoped it was good news about the baby and picked up.

"Abby? How are you? How's Max?"

"He's doing great. The gastroenteritis is finally gone."

"Thank heaven!"

"I feel so terrible about what happened on our trip."

"Why do you say that? I was sorry for you, of course, but I had a wonderful time!"

"You're always such a good sport. I know it made Valentino's day for someone to be excited about his work."

"He's an incredible man, Abby." Carolena tried to keep the tremor out of her voice.

"He was impressed with you, too. That's one of the reasons I'm calling. He flew into Arancia this morning so he and Vincenzo can talk business."

She almost had heart failure. It was a good thing she was sitting down. Valentino was here?

"Since you're a patent law attorney, both men want you to meet with them. They need your legal counsel along with mine."

Her pulse raced off the chart. "Why?" She'd thought she'd never see him again and had been in such a depression, she'd decided that if she didn't get over it, she would have to go for professional help.

"They're putting together a monumental idea to benefit both our countries. I'll tell you all about it when you get here. Can you come to the palace after work? The four of us will talk and have dinner together."

Carolena jumped up from her leather chair. No, no, no. She didn't dare put herself into a position like that again. Legitimate or not, Valentino had to know how hard this was going to be for her. She didn't have his self-control.

If for any reason she happened to end up alone with him tonight, she might beg him to let her spend the night because she couldn't help herself. How wicked would that be? She'd spend the rest of her life mourning another loss because there could never be another time with him. This was one time Carolena couldn't do what Abby was asking.

"I'm afraid I can't."

"Why not?"

"I have a date for the symphony."

"Then cancel it. I just found out this morning that Valentino is rushed for time. Did I tell you his wedding and coronation are coming up in August?"

She bit her lip. "No. I don't believe you mentioned it."

"He'd hoped to get this business settled before flying back to Gemelli tomorrow."

Here today, gone tomorrow? She couldn't bear it. This request had put her in an untenable position. What to do so she wouldn't offend her friend? After racking her brain, she came up with one solution that might work. It would *have* to work since Carolena didn't dare make a wrong move now.

She gripped the phone tighter. "I have an idea that won't waste Valentino's time. Would it be possible if you three came to the office this afternoon?" Neutral ground rather than the palace was the only way for her to stay out of temptation's way.

"I'm afraid not. It would require too much security for the two of them to meet anywhere else. The security risk is higher than usual with Valentino's coronation coming up soon. How would it be if you cleared your slate for this afternoon and came to the palace? Say two o'clock?"

By now Carolena was trembling.

"We'll talk and eat out by the pool. If you leave the palace by six-thirty, you'll be in time for your date."

Carolena panicked. "I'd have to juggle some appointments." That was another lie. "I don't know if Signor Faustino will let me. I'm working on a big case."

"Bigger than the one for the princes of two countries?" Abby teased.

Her friend had put her on the royal spot. The writing was on the wall. "I—I'll arrange it." Her voice faltered.

"Perfect. The limo will pick you up at the office at one forty-five. Come right out to the terrace by the pool after you arrive."

"All right," she whispered before hanging up.

In an hour and a half Carolena would be seeing Valentino again. Already she had this suffocating feeling in her chest. It was a good thing she had another client to take up her time before the limo came for her. When she left the office she'd tell Tomaso she was going out for a business lunch with a client, which was only the truth.

Luckily she'd worn her sleeveless black designer shift dress with the crew neck and black belt to work. She'd matched the outfit with black heels. There was no need to do anything about her hair. All she had to do was touch up her makeup. When she showed up at the palace, it would carry out the lie that she'd be going to the symphony later.

Valentino had just finished some laps in the pool when he saw Carolena walk past the garden toward them in a stunning, formfitting black dress. Only a woman with her figure could wear it. Abby had told him she was going to the symphony later with a man.

She'd parted her hair in the middle above her forehead and had swept a small braid from each side around to the back, leaving her dark hair long. Two-tiered silvery earrings dangled between the strands. He did a somersault off the wall of the pool to smother his gasp.

If he'd hoped that she wouldn't look as good to him after four days, he could forget that! The trick would be to keep his eyes off her while they tried to do business. While Abby laid out their lunch beneath the overhang, Vincenzo sat at one of the tables working on his laptop. Both of them wore beach robes over their swimsuits. Max was down for a nap in the nursery.

She headed for Abby. A low whistle came out of Vincenzo and he got up to greet her. "I've never seen you looking lovelier, Carolena."

"Thank you," she said as the two women hugged.

Valentino climbed out of the shallow end of the pool and threw on a beach cover-up. "We're grateful you could come this afternoon."

Carolena shot him a brief glance. "It's very nice to see you again, Val. Signor Faustino was thrilled when he found out where I was going. Needless to say, he considers it the coup of the century that I've been summoned to help the princes of Gemelli and Arancia with a legal problem."

Abby was all smiles. "Knowing him, he'll probably make you senior partner at their next meeting."

"Don't wish that on me!" That sounded final.

Valentino moved closer. "You mean, it isn't your dream?"

"Definitely not." She seemed so composed, but it was deceiving, because he saw a nerve throbbing frantically at the base of her throat where he longed to kiss her.

He smiled. "Our conversation on the deck of the yacht was cut short and didn't give us time to cover your dreams before I had to leave."

Being out of the sun, she couldn't blame it for the rose blush that crept into her face. "As I recall, we were discussing *your* dreams for Gemelli, Val."

Touché. But his unrealized personal dream that had lain dormant deep in his soul since his cognizance of life was another matter altogether.

"In truth, I hope to make enough money from the law practice that one day in the future I can buy back my grandparents' small farm and work it." Her green eyes clouded for a moment. "I'm a farmer's daughter at heart."

"I understand your parents are not alive."

"No, nor are my grandparents. Their farm was sold. There have been Barettis in Arancia for almost a hundred years. I'm the only Baretti left and want to keep up the tradition by buying the place back."

Had her fiancé been a farmer, too? Valentino knew a moment of jealousy that she'd loved someone else enough to create such a powerful emotion in her.

"I had no idea," he murmured, "but since it's in your blood, that makes you doubly valuable for the task at hand." His mind was teeming with new ideas to keep her close to him.

"Abby said you and Vincenzo were planning something monumental for both your countries. I confess I'm intrigued."

"Hey, you two," Abby called to them. "Come and help yourselves to lunch first, then we'll get down to business."

He followed Carolena to the serving table. After they'd filled their plates, they sat down at one of the round tables where the maid poured them iced tea. Once they'd started eating, he said, "Vincenzo? Why don't you lay the groundwork for the women and we'll go from there."

"Our two countries have a growing problem because of the way they are situated on coastal waters. We all know the land around the Mediterranean is one of the most coveted terrains on earth. Over the years, our prime properties of orange and lemon groves that have sustained our economies for centuries have been shrinking due to man's progress. Our farmers are being inundated with huge sums of money to sell their land so it can be developed for commercial tourism."

"I know that's true," Carolena commented. "My grandfather was approached many times to sell, but he wouldn't do it."

Vincenzo nodded. "He's the type of traditional farmer fighting a battle to hold on to his heritage. Farmers are losing their workers, who want to go to the city. In the process, we're losing a vital and precious resource that has caused Valentino and me to lose sleep. Something has to be done to stop the trend and rebuild the greatness of what we've always stood for. We've come up with an idea to help our farmers by giving them a new incentive. You tell them, Valentino."

Carolena's gaze swerved to him. He could tell Vincenzo had grabbed the women's attention.

"We need to compete with other countries to increase our exports to fill the needs of a growing world market and build our economies here at home. The lemons of Arancia are highly valued because of their low acidity and delicate flavor.

"Likewise the blood oranges of Gemelli are sought after for their red flesh and deep red juice. The juice is exceptionally healthy, being rich in antioxidants. What we're proposing is to patent our fruit in a joint venture so we can grow an enviable exporting business.

"With a unique logo and marketing strategy, we can put our citrus fruits front and center in the world market. When the buyer sees it, they'll know they're getting authentic fruit from our regions alone and clamor for it."

"That's a wonderful idea," Carolena exclaimed. "You would need to be filed as a Consortium for the Promotion of the Arancian Lemon and the Gemellian Blood Orange. The IGP logo will be the official acknowledgment that the lemons and oranges were grown in your territories according to the traditional rules."

Vincenzo leaned forward. "That's exactly what we're striving for. With the right marketing techniques, the citrus business should start to flourish again. We'll come up with a name for the logo."

"That's easy," Abby volunteered. "AG. Two tiny letters stamped on each fruit. You'll have to make a video that could be distributed to every country where you want to introduce your brand."

Bless you, Abby. She was reading Valentino's mind. He needed more time alone with Carolena to talk about their lives. Abby had just given him the perfect excuse. He exchanged glances with Vincenzo before he looked at Carolena.

"The right video would sell the idea quickly, but we need a spokesperson doing the video to put it across. You'd be the perfect person for several reasons, Carolena."

"Oh, no." He saw the fear in her eyes and knew exactly what put it there, but he couldn't help himself. What he felt for Carolena was stronger than anything he'd ever known.

"You have the looks and education to sell our idea," Valentino persisted. "We'll start in Gemelli with you traveling around to some of the orange groves. With a farming background that dates back close to a century, you'll be the perfect person to talk to the owners."

Valentino could tell by the way Vincenzo smiled at Carolena that he loved the idea. His friend said, "After you've finished there, we'll have you do the same thing here in Arancia with our lemon farmers. We'll put the video on television in both countries. People will say, 'That's the beautiful Signorina Baretti advertising the AG logo.' You'll be famous."

She shook her head. "I don't want to be famous."

"You get used to it," Valentino quipped. "While you're in Gemelli, you'll stay at the palace and have full security when you travel around with the film crew.

I'll clear my calendar while you're there so I can be on hand. The sooner we get started, the better. How long will it take you to put your affairs in order and fly down?"

"But—"

"It'll be fun," Abby spoke up with enthusiasm. "I can't think of another person who could do this."

"Naturally you'll be compensated, Carolena," Vincenzo added. "After coming to the aid of our two countries, you'll make enough money to buy back your grandparents' farm, if that's what you want."

She got up from the chair on the pretense of getting herself another helping of food. "You're all very flattering and generous, but I need time to think about it."

Valentino stared up at her. "Do that while you're at the symphony tonight with your date, and we'll contact you in the morning for your answer." He could swear she didn't really have plans. She proved it when she looked away from him.

Forcing himself to calm down, he checked his watch. "Since we have several hours before you have to leave in the limo, I suggest we get to work on a script. Perhaps the video could start with you showing us your old farm. It will capture everyone's interest immediately. We'll shoot that segment later."

"It's a beautiful place!" Abby cried. "You'll do it, right?" she pleaded with her friend. "You've worked nonstop since law school. It's time you had some fun along with your work. Your boss, Signor Faustino, will get down on his knees to you."

Vincenzo joined in. "I'll have you flown down on the jet."

Valentino found himself holding his breath.

You go where angels fear to tread, Carolena.

The words pummeled her as the royal jet started its descent to Gemelli's airport. As she saw the smoke of Etna out of the window, memories of that glorious day and evening with Valentino clutched at her heart.

She'd be seeing him in a few minutes. If this offer to do the video had been Valentino's wish alone, she would have turned him down. But the excitement and pleading coming from both Abby and Vincenzo two days ago had caused her to cave. Deep down she knew a great deal was riding on this project for their two countries.

After another sleepless night because of Valentino, she'd phoned Abby the next morning to tell her she'd do it. But her friend had no idea of her fatal attraction to him.

It *was* fatal and Valentino knew it. But he was bound by a code of honor and so was she. If she worked hard, the taping could be done in a couple of days and she could go back to Arancia for good.

One of Valentino's staff greeted the plane and walked her to her old room, where she was once again installed. He lowered her suitcase to the parquet floor. "In forty-five minutes His Highness will be outside in the limo waiting to take you for a tour of some orange groves. In the meantime, a lunch tray has been provided for you."

"Thank you."

After quickly getting settled, she ate and changed

into jeans and a blouson, the kind of outfit she used to wear on her grandparents' farm. Earlier that morning she'd put her hair in a braid to keep it out of her way. On her feet she wore sensible walking boots. Inside her tote bag she carried a copy of the script, which she'd read over many times.

Before walking out the door, she reached for it and for her grandmother's broad-brimmed straw hat she'd always worn to keep out the sun. Armed with what she'd need, she left the room for the limo waiting out at the side entrance of the palace.

When she walked through the doors, Valentino broke away from the driver he'd been talking to and helped her into the limo. The sun shone from a blue sky. It was an incredible summer day. Once inside, he shut the door and sat across from her wearing a navy polo shirt and jeans. He looked and smelled too marvelous for words.

Within a minute they left the palace grounds and headed for the outskirts of the city. "I've been living for you to arrive," he confessed in his deep voice. "How was the symphony?"

His unexpected question threw her. "Wonderful."

"That's interesting. I found out it wasn't playing that night, nor did you go to dinner with your boyfriend. In case you were wondering, the limo driver informed Vincenzo you told him to take you back to your apartment. Why manufacture an excuse?"

Heat rushed to her face. "I'm sure you know the reason."

"You mean that you were afraid you might end up alone with me that evening?"

"I thought it could be a possibility and decided to err on the side of caution."

"Once I overheard Vincenzo tell Abby about your fictional evening out, you don't know how close I came to showing up at your apartment that night."

This wasn't going to work. The longing for him made her physically weak. "Does your mother know you flew me up on Etna?" she blurted.

"She has her spies. It's part of the game. That's why I didn't attack you on the deck of the yacht."

"But we danced for a long time."

He leaned forward. "Dancing is one thing, but the steward would have told her I didn't spend the night with you. In fact, I wasn't in your room more than a few minutes."

"She's no one's fool, Val."

"What can I say?" He flashed her a brief smile. "She's my mother. When she thought you'd gone out of my life by flying back to Arancia with Abby and Vincenzo, no doubt she was relieved. But now that you're here again so soon, she knows my interest in you goes deeper than mere physical attraction."

"With your marriage looming on the horizon, she has every right to be upset."

"That's a mother's prerogative. For that, I apologize."

Valentino's life truly wasn't his own. Every move he made was monitored. Only now was she beginning to appreciate how difficult it must have been for him growing up, but she couldn't worry about that right now. She had a job to do. The sooner she got to it, the sooner she could fly back to Arancia. *Away from him.*

The surrounding countryside basked under a heavenly sun. They came to the first grove where the trees were planted in rows, making up football-pitch-length orchards. She watched men and women in blue overalls go from tree to tree, quickly working their way up and down ladders to fill plastic crates with the brightly colored produce. It brought back memories from her past.

The limo pulled to a stop. "We'll get out and walk from here."

He opened the door to help her. With a shaky hand she reached for her hat. The moment she climbed out, the citrus smell from the many hectares of orange groves filled her senses.

Valentino's dark blue eyes played over her face and figure with a hunger that brought the blood to her cheeks. When she put the hat on her head, he felt the rim of it. "I like that touch of authenticity."

"It was my grandmother's. I thought I'd wear it to bring me luck." Maybe it would help her to keep her wits. But already she was suffering from euphoria she shouldn't be feeling. It was because they were together again. For a while, happiness drove away her fears as they began walking toward the *masseria,* the typical farmhouse in the area.

"As you can see, the groves here have a unique microclimate provided by the brooding volcano of Etna. Warm days and cool nights allow us to produce what we feel are the best blood oranges in the world."

"You ought to be the one on the video, Val. I can hear your love of this island in your voice."

"Yet anyone will tell you a beautiful woman is much more exciting to look at."

Not from her vantage point. Valentino was drop-dead gorgeous. Abby had said as much about Michelina's older brother before Carolena had ever even seen a picture of him.

Several of the security men went on ahead to bring the grove owner to her and Valentino. The man and his son were delighted to be interviewed and would have talked for hours. No problem for them to be part of the video.

After saying goodbye, they drove on to the next orange grove, then the next, stopping for a midafternoon lunch brought from the palace kitchen. Six stops later they'd reached the eastern end of the island. Already it was evening. They'd been so busy, she hadn't realized how much time had passed.

Carolena gave him a covert glance. "There wasn't one farmer who didn't want to be a part of your plan to keep people on the farms and grow more profits."

He sat back in the seat looking relaxed, with his arms stretched out on either side of him. "You charmed everyone. Being a farmer's daughter and granddaughter got them to open right up and express their concerns. I marveled at the way you were able to answer their questions and give them the vision of what we're trying to do."

"I had a script. You didn't. Give yourself the credit you deserve, Val. They fell over themselves with joy to think their prince cares enough about the farmers to honor them with a personal visit. Securing their future secures the entire country and they know it."

"I believe Vincenzo and I are onto something, Carolena, and you're going to be the person who puts this marketing strategy over. After a hard day's work, this calls for a relaxing dinner. I've told the driver to take us to a restaurant here on the water where we can be private and enjoy ourselves. I called ahead to place our order."

This was the part she was worried about. "I think we should go back to the palace."

"You're worrying about my mother, but since she's been worrying about me since I turned sixteen, it's nothing new. I hope you're hungry. We're going to a spot where the *tunnacchiu 'nfurnatu* is out of this world. The tuna will have been caught within the last hour."

It was impossible to have a serious talk with Valentino right now. After they'd eaten, then she'd speak her mind.

The limo pulled down a narrow alley that led to the back entrance of the restaurant he'd been talking about. Valentino got out first and reached for her hand. He squeezed it and didn't let go as he led them to a door one of the security men opened for them.

Cupping her elbow, he walked her down a hallway to another door that opened on to a small terrace with round candlelit tables for two overlooking the water. But they were the only occupants. She shouldn't have come to this romantic place with him, but what could she do?

The air felt like velvet, bringing back memories of their night on the yacht. A profusion of yellow-and-orange bougainvillea provided an overhang Carolena found utterly enchanting.

He helped her to be seated, then caressed her shoulders. She gasped as his touch sent a white-hot message through her. "I've been wanting to feel you all day." Between the heat from his body, plus the twinkling lights on the water from the other boats, she sensed the fire building inside her.

"Benvenuto, Valentino!" An unfamiliar male voice broke the silence, surprising Carolena.

Valentino seemed reluctant to remove his hands. "Matteo Tancredi, meet my sister-in-law's best friend, Carolena Baretti. Carolena, Matteo is one of my best friends and the owner of this establishment."

"How do you do, *signor.*" She extended her hand, hoping his friend with the broad smile and overly long brown hair didn't notice the blush on her face.

"I'm doing very well now that Valentino is here. He told me he was coming with the new star of a video that is going to make Gemelli famous."

She shook her head. "Hardly, but we're all hoping this venture will be a success."

"Anything Valentino puts his mind to is certain to produce excellent results." She heard a nuance of deeper emotion in his response. Still staring at her, he said, "I'll bring some white wine that is perfect with the fish. Anything you want, just ask."

"Thank you."

The two men exchanged a private glance before Matteo disappeared from the terrace. Valentino sat down opposite her. A slight breeze caused the candle to flicker, drawing her attention to his striking features. She averted her eyes to stop making a feast of him.

"Where did you meet Matteo?"

"At the college in Catania."

"Is he married?"

"Not yet. He was studying geology when his father took ill and died. The family needed Matteo to keep this place running, so he had to leave school."

"Wasn't there anyone else to help?"

"His mother and his siblings, but his father always relied on Matteo and didn't like the idea of him going to college."

"Matteo's the eldest?"

"Yes."

"Like the way your father relied on you rather than your younger brother?"

He stared at her through shuttered eyes. "Yes, when you put it that way."

"I can see why. After watching you as you talked with the farmers today, I think you should be the one featured on the film, Val. You're a natural leader."

Before she could hear his response, Matteo brought them their dinner and poured the wine. "Enjoy your meal."

"I'm sure it's going to taste as good as it smells. I think I'm in heaven already," she told him.

"Put it in writing that you were in heaven after eating the meal, and I'll frame it to hang on the wall with the testimonials of other celebrities who've eaten here. But none of them will be as famous as you."

Gentle laughter fell from her lips. "Except for the prince, who is in a category by himself."

"Agreed."

"What category is that?" Valentino asked after Matteo had left them alone.

"Isn't it obvious?" She started eating, then drank some wine.

He picked at his food, which wasn't at all like him. "For one night can't you forget who I am?" Suddenly his mood had turned darker and she felt his tension.

Over the glass, she said, "No more than you can. We all have a destiny. I saw you in action today and am so impressed with your knowledge and caring, I can't put it into words. All I know is that you should be the one featured on the video, not me.

"There's an intelligence in you that would convince anyone of anything. First thing tomorrow, I'm flying back to Arancia while you get this video done on your own. Then your mother will have no more reason to be worried."

His brows furrowed in displeasure. "Much as she would like you to be gone, you can't do that."

"Why not?"

"Because you're under contract to Vincenzo and me." As if she could forget. "The economic future of our two countries is resting on our new plan of which you are now an integral part."

She fought for breath. "But once I've finished the other video session in Arancia, then my work will be done. Just so you understand, I'm leaving Gemelli tomorrow after the filming and won't be seeing you again."

"Which presents a problem for me since I never want you out of my sight. Not *ever*," he added in a husky whisper.

She couldn't stop her trembling. "Please don't say things like that to me. A relationship outside a royal engagement or marriage could only be a tawdry, scandalous affair, so why are you talking like this?"

"Because I'm obsessed with you," he claimed with primitive force. "If it's not love, then it's better than love. I've never been in love, but whatever this feeling is, it's not going away. In fact, it's getting worse, much worse. I'm already a changed man. Believe me, this is an entirely new experience for me."

Incredulous, she shook her head. "We hardly know each other."

"How long did it take you to fall in love with your fiancé?"

She let out a small cry. "How did you find out I had a fiancé?"

"Who else but Abby."

"I wish she hadn't said anything."

"You still haven't answered my question."

"Berto and I were friends on neighboring farms before we fell in love. It's not the same thing at all."

"Obviously not. At the swimming pool last week you and I experienced a phenomenon as strong as a pyroclastic eruption. It not only shook the ground beneath us *before* we were up on the volcano, it shook my entire world so much I don't know myself anymore."

"Please don't say that!" She half moaned the words in panic.

"Because you know it's true?" he retorted. "Even if you weren't the perfect person to do this video for us, I would have found another means to be with you. I've given you all the honesty in me. Now I want all your honesty back. Did you agree to do this video because you wanted to help and felt it was your duty because of your friendship with Abby? Or are you here because you couldn't stay away from me?"

She buried her face in her hands. "Don't ask me that."

"I have to. You and I met. It's a fact of life. Your answer is of vital importance to me because I don't want to make a mistake."

"What mistake? What on earth do you mean?"

"We'll discuss it on the way back to the palace. Would you care for dessert?"

"I—I couldn't." Her voice faltered.

"That makes two of us."

When Matteo appeared, they both thanked him for the delicious food. He followed them out to the limo where they said their goodbyes.

Once inside, Valentino sat across from her as they left the restaurant and headed back to the city. He leaned forward. "Tell me about your fiancé. How did he die?"

She swallowed hard. "I'd rather not get into it."

"We're going to have to." He wasn't about to let this go until he had answers.

"Th-there was an accident."

"Were you with him when it happened?"

Tears scalded her eyelids. "Yes."

"Is it still so painful you can't talk about it?"

"Yes."

"Because you made it happen."

"Yes," she whispered.

"In what way?"

Just remembering that awful day caused her lungs to freeze. "I was helping him with his farm chores and told him I would drive the almond harvester while he sat up by the yellow contraption. You know, the kind that opens into a big upside-down umbrella to catch all the almonds at once?"

"I do. More almonds can be harvested with fewer helpers."

She nodded. "He said for me to stay back at the house, but I insisted on driving because I wanted to help him. I'd driven our family's tractor and knew what to do. We'd get the work done a lot faster. Berto finally agreed. As we were crossing over a narrow bridge, I got too close to the wall and the tractor tipped. Though I jumped out in time, he was thrown into the stream below.

"The umbrella was so heavy, it trapped his face in six inches of water. He couldn't breathe—I couldn't get to him or move it and had to run for help. By the time his family came, it was too late. He'd...drowned."

In the next second Valentino joined her on the seat and pulled her into his arms.

"I'm so sorry, Carolena."

"It was my fault, Val. I killed him." She couldn't stop sobbing.

He rocked her for a long time. "Of course you didn't. It was an accident."

"But I shouldn't have insisted on driving him."

"Couldn't he have told you no?"

She finally lifted her head. Only then did he realize she'd soaked his polo shirt. "I made it too difficult for him. My grandmother told me I could be an impossible child at times."

Valentino chuckled and hugged her against his side. "It was a tragic accident, but never forget he wanted you with him because he loved you. Do you truly believe he would have expected you to go on suffering over it for years and years?"

"No," she whispered, "not when you put it that way."

"It's the only way to put it." His arms tightened around her. "Abby told me he was the great love of your life."

No. Abby was wrong. Berto had been her *first* love. Until his death she'd thought he'd be her only love. But the *great* love of her life, the one man forbidden to her, was holding her right now. She needed to keep that truth from him.

"As I told you before, I'll always love Berto. Forgive me for having broken down like that."

CHAPTER FIVE

VALENTINO KISSED HER hair. "I'm glad you did. Now there are no more secrets between us." Before Carolena could stop him, he rained kisses all the way to her mouth, dying for his first taste of her. She turned her head away, but he chased her around until he found the voluptuous mouth he'd been aching for.

At first she resisted, but he increased the pressure until her lips opened, as if she couldn't help herself. He felt the ground shake beneath him as she began to respond with a growing passion he'd known was there once she allowed herself to let go.

Because they were outside the entrance and would need to go in shortly, he couldn't do more than feast on her luscious mouth. His lips roved over each feature, her eyelids, the satin skin of her throat, then came back to that mouth, giving him a kind of pleasure he'd never known before.

They kept finding new ways to satisfy their burning longing for each other until he didn't know if it was his moan or hers resounding in the limo. *"Carolena—"* he cried in a husky voice. "I want you so badly I'm in pain."

"So am I." She pulled as far away from him as she could. "But this can't go on. It should never have happened. Have you told Vincenzo about me?"

"No."

"I'm thankful for that. After being on the yacht with you, I suppose this was inevitable. Maybe it's just as well we've gotten this out of our system now."

He buried his face in her neck. "I have news for you, *bellissima*. You don't get this kind of fire out of your system. It burns hotter and hotter without cessation. Now that I know how you feel about me, we need to have a serious talk about whether I get married or not."

Her body started to tremble. *"What did you say?"*

"You heard me. I made a vow to myself and my mother there'd be no more women, and I meant it. So what just happened between us means an earthshaking development has taken place we have to dea—"

"Your Highness?" a voice spoke over the mic, interrupting him. "We've arrived."

Carolena let out a gasp. "I can't get out yet. I can't let the staff see me like this—"

He smiled. "There's no way to hide the fact that you've been thoroughly kissed. How can I help?"

"Hand me my bag so I can at least put on some lipstick."

"You have a becoming rash, all my fault."

She groaned. "I can feel it. I'll have to put on some powder."

"Your bag and your hat, *signorina*. Anything else?"

"Don't come near me again."

"I'm accompanying you to your apartment. Are you ready?"

"No." She sounded frantic. "You get out first. I'll follow in a minute."

"Take your time. We're not in a hurry." He pressed another hot kiss to her swollen lips before exiting the limo a man reborn. This had to be the way the captive slave felt emerging from his prison as Michelangelo chipped away the marble to free him.

In a minute she emerged and hurried inside the palace. Valentino trailed in her wake. He followed her into her apartment and shut the door. But he rested against it and folded his arms.

"Now we can talk about us in total privacy."

She whirled around to face him. "There *is* no us, Val. If you were a mere man engaged to a woman you didn't love, you could always break your engagement in order to be with a person you truly care about. In fact, it would be the moral thing to do for both your sakes."

"I hear a but," he interjected. "You were about to say that since I'm a prince, I can't break an engagement because it would be immoral. Is that what you're saying?"

A gasp escaped her lips. "A royal engagement following a royal betrothal between two families who've been involved for years is hardly the same thing."

"Royal or not, an engagement is an engagement. It's a time to make certain that the impending marriage will bring fulfillment. My sister hoped with all her heart the marriage to Vincenzo would bring about that magic because she loved him, but he wasn't in love with her and it never happened."

"I know. We've been over this before," Carolena said in a quiet voice. "But you made a vow to yourself and your family after your uncle Stefano's death. I agreed to come to Gemelli in order to help you and Vincenzo. I—I rationalized to myself that our intense attraction couldn't go anywhere. Not with your wedding dawning.

"But now for you to be willing to break your engagement to be with me is absolutely terrifying. You've helped me to get over my guilt for Berto's death, but I refuse to be responsible for your breakup with Princess Alexandra. You made a promise—"

"That's true. I promised to fulfill my royal duty. But that doesn't mean I have to marry Alexandra. After what you and I shared a few minutes ago, I need more time. Day after tomorrow parliament convenes. You and I have forty-eight hours before my wedding is officially announced to the media. *Or not.*"

If he was saying what she thought he was saying...

"You're scaring me, Val!"

"That's good. On the yacht you had the power to keep me from your bed, which you ultimately did. Your decision stopped us from taking the next step. But tonight everything changed.

"Whatever your answer is now, it will have eternal consequences for both of us because you know we're on fire for each other in every sense of the word. Otherwise you would never have met with me and Vincenzo to discuss our project in the first place. Admit it."

She couldn't take any more. "You're putting an enormous burden on me—"

"Now you know how *I* feel."

"I can't give you an answer. You're going to be king in seven weeks!"

"That's the whole point of this conversation. There'll be no coronation without a marriage. I'll need your answer by tomorrow night after the taping here is finished. Once parliament opens its session the next morning and the date for my wedding is announced, it will be too late for us."

Carolena was in agony. "That's not fair!"

His features hardened. "Since when was love ever fair? I thought you found that out when your fiancé died. I learned it when my sister died before she could hold her own baby."

Tears ran down her cheeks once more. "I can't think right now."

"By tomorrow evening you're going to have to! Until then we'll set this aside and concentrate on our mission to put Gemelli and Arancia on the world map agriculturally."

"How can we possibly do that? You've done a lot more than proposition me. I can hardly take it in."

"That's why I'm giving you all night to think about it. I want a relationship with you, Carolena. I'm willing to break my long-standing engagement to Princess Alexandra in order to be with you. In the end she'll thank me for it. Gemelli doesn't need a king yet."

"You can't mean it!"

"Had I not told you of my engagement, we would have spent that night on the yacht together. But the fact that I *did* tell you proved how important you were to me. I realized I wanted much more from you than one night of passion beneath the stars. Sleeping together to slake our desire could never be the same thing as having a full relationship."

His logic made so much sense she was in utter turmoil.

"However, there is one thing I need to know up front. If your love for Berto is too all consuming and he's the one standing in the way of letting me into your life, just tell me the truth right now. If the answer is yes, then I swear that once this video is made, I'll see you off on the jet tomorrow night and our paths will never cross again."

She knew Valentino meant what he said with every fiber of his being. He'd been so honest with her, it hurt. If she told him anything less she'd be a hypocrite.

"I would never have wanted to sleep with you if I hadn't already put Berto away in my heart."

"That's what I thought," he murmured in satisfaction.

"But when you speak of a relationship, we're talking long-distance. With you up on the volcano while I'm in court in a different country… How long could it last before you're forced to give me up and find a royal bride in order to be king? Your mother would despise me. Abby would never approve, nor would Vincenzo. The pressure would build until I couldn't stand the shame of it."

His eyes became slits. "Do you love me? That's all I want to know."

Carolena loved him, all right. But when he ended it—and he'd be the one to do it—she'd want to die. "Love isn't everything, Val."

"That's not what I wanted to hear, Carolena."

"I thought you gave me until tomorrow evening for my answer."

"I made you a promise and I'll keep it. Now it's getting late. I'll say good-night here and see you at eight in the morning in this very spot. *Buona notte,* Carolena."

Valentino was headed for his suite in the palace when his brother came out of the shadows at the top of the stairs wearing jeans and a sport shirt instead of his uniform. "Vito? What are you doing here? I didn't know you were coming!"

They gave each other a hug. "I've been waiting for you."

Together they entered his apartment. "I take it you've been with mother."

"*Sí.* She phoned me last week and asked me to come ASAP." Valentino had a strong hunch why she'd sent for her second son. "I arranged for my furlough early and got here this afternoon."

"It's good to see you." They sat down in the chairs placed around the coffee table. "How long will you be here?"

"Long enough for me to find out why our mother is so worried about you. Why don't you tell me about the woman you took up on the volcano last week before you spent part of the night dancing with her on the yacht. And all this happening *after* you'd set the date for your marriage to Alexandra."

Valentino couldn't stay seated and got out of the chair. "Do you want a beer?"

"Sure."

He went in the kitchen and pulled two bottles out of the fridge. After they'd both taken a few swallows, Vito said, "I'm waiting."

"I'm aware of that. My problem is finding a way to tell you something that's going to shock the daylights out of you."

With a teasing smile, Vito sat back in the chair and put his feet up on the coffee table. "You mean that at the midnight hour, you suddenly came upon the woman of your dreams."

Valentino couldn't laugh about this. "It was evening, actually. I'd just come from the helicopter. Carolena was in the swimming pool ready to take a dive."

"Aphrodite in the flesh."

"Better. Much better." The vision of her in that bathing suit never left him. He finished off the rest of his beer and put the empty bottle on the table.

"Abby's best friend, I understand. Did I hear mother right? She's helping you and Vincenzo with a marketing video?"

He took a deep breath. "Correct." Valentino explained the project to his brother.

"I'm impressed with your idea, but you still haven't answered my question." Vito sat forward. "What is this woman to you? If word gets back to Alexandra about your dining and dancing with her on the yacht, you could hurt her a great deal."

Valentino stared hard at his brother, surprised at the extent of the caring he heard in his voice. "For the first time in my life I'm in love, Vito."

"You?"

He nodded solemnly. "I mean irrevocably in love."

The news robbed his brother of speech.

"I can't marry Alexandra. There'll be no wedding or coronation in August, no announcement to Parliament."

Color left Vito's face before he put his bottle down and got to his feet. He was visibly shaken by the news.

"Until I met Carolena, I deluded myself into thinking Alexandra and I could make our marriage work by having children. Now I realize our wedding will only doom us both to a life of sheer unhappiness. I don't love her and she doesn't love me the way Michelina loved Vincenzo.

"Despite what our parents wanted and planned for, *I* don't want that kind of marriage for either of us. Tomorrow evening I'm planning to fly to Cyprus and break our engagement. The news will set her free. Hopefully she'll find a man she can really love, even if it causes a convulsion within our families."

Somehow he expected to see and hear outrage from his brother, but Vito did neither. He simply eyed him with an enigmatic expression. "You won't have to fly there. Mother has invited her here for dinner tomorrow evening."

His brows lifted. "That doesn't surprise me. Under the circumstances, I'm glad she'll be here. After I see Carolena off on her flight back to Arancia, I'll be able to concentrate on Alexandra."

"What are you planning to do with Carolena? You can't marry her, and Mother doesn't want to rule any longer."

Valentino cocked his head. "I'm not the only son.

You're second in line. All you'd have to do is resign your commission in the military and get married to Princess Regina. Mother would step down so you could rule. As long as one of us is willing, she'll be happy."

"Be serious," he snapped. "I'm not in love with Regina."

His quick-fire response led Valentino to believe his brother was in love with someone else. "Who is she, Vito?"

"What do you mean?"

"The woman you *do* love." His brother averted his eyes, telling Valentino he'd been right about him.

"Falling in love has totally changed you, Val."

"It has awakened me to what's really important. Carolena makes me feel truly alive for the first time in my life!"

Vito shook his head in disbelief. "When am I going to meet her?"

"The next time I can arrange it."

"When will you tell Mother you're breaking your engagement?"

"After I've talked to Alexandra and we've spoken to her parents. Will you meet the princes at the plane for me? Carolena and I will be finishing up the filming about that time. You'd be doing me a huge favor."

His brother blinked like someone in a state of shock. "If that's what you want." When he reached the door to leave, he glanced around. "Val? Once you've broken with Alexandra, you can't go back."

"I never wanted the marriage and have been putting it off for years. She hasn't pushed for it, either. We're both aware it was the dream of both sets of parents. I've always liked her. She's a lovely, charming woman who deserves to be loved by the right man. But I'm not that man."

After a silence, "I believe you," he said with puzzling soberness.

"A domani, Vito."

The film crew followed behind the limo as they came to the last orange grove. Carolena looked at the script one more time as the car pulled to a stop, but the words swam before her eyes. The hourglass was emptying. Once this segment of the taping was over, Valentino expected an answer from her.

Though he hadn't spoken of it all day, the tension had been building until she felt at the breaking point. She couldn't blame the hot sun for her body temperature. Since last night she'd been feverish and it was growing worse.

After reaching for her grandmother's sun hat, she got out of the limo and started walking down a row of orange trees where the photographer had set up this scene with the owner of the farm and his wife.

Her braid swung with every step in her walking boots. She felt Valentino's eyes following her. He watched as one of the crew touched up her makeup one more time before putting the hat on her head at just the right angle. She'd worn jeans and a khaki blouse with pockets. Casual yet professional.

Once ready, the filming began. Toward the end of the final segment, she held up a fresh orange to the camera. "Eating or drinking, the blood orange with the AG stamp brings the world its benefits from nature's hallowed spot found nowhere else on earth." She let go with a full-bodied smile. "*Salute* from divine Gemelli."

Valentino's intense gaze locked onto hers. *"Salute,"* he murmured after the tape stopped rolling and they started walking toward the limo. "The part you added at the end wasn't in the script."

Her heart thudded unmercifully. "Do you want to redo it?"

"Anything but. I've always considered Gemelli to be 'nature's hallowed spot.' You could have been reading my mind."

"It's hard not to. As I've told you before, you show a rare reverence for the island and its people."

As he opened the limo door for her, the rays of the late-afternoon sun glinted in his dark blond hair. "Your performance today was even more superb than I had hoped for. If this video doesn't put our message across, then nothing else possibly could. I'm indebted to you, Carolena. When Vincenzo sees the tape, he'll be elated and anxious for the filming to start in the lemon groves of Arancia."

"Thank you." She looked away from him and got in the limo, taking pains not to brush against him. Once he climbed inside and sat down opposite her, she said, "If we're through here, I need to get back to the palace."

"All in good time. We need dinner first. Matteo has not only lent us his boat, he has prepared a picnic for us to eat on board. We'll talk and eat while I drive us back." Despite having dinner plans that night, Val decided spending time with Carolena on her last night was too important to miss. He would make arrangements to see Princess Alexandra at the palace afterward.

Carolena had this fluttery feeling in her chest all the way to the shore, where they got out and walked along the dock to a small cruiser tied up outside the restaurant. There would be no crew spying on them here. His security people would be watching them from other boats so they could be strictly alone.

Throughout the night Carolena had gone back and forth fighting the battle waging inside her. By morning she knew what her answer would be. But right now she was scared to death because he had a power over her that made her mindless and witless.

While Valentino helped her on board and handed her a life jacket to put on, Matteo appeared and greeted them. The two men chatted for a minute before Val's friend untied the ropes and gave them a push off. Carolena sat on a bench while Valentino stood at the wheel in cargo pants and a pale green sport shirt.

After they idled out beyond the buoys, he headed into open calm water. Having grown up on an island, he handled the boat with the same expertise he exhibited in anything he did.

She saw a dozen sailboats and a ferry in the far distance. High summer in the Mediterranean brought the tourists in droves. Closer to them she glimpsed a few small fishing boats. Most likely they were manned by Valentino's security people.

When they'd traveled a few miles, he turned to her.

"If you'll open that cooler, I'll stop the engine while we eat."

Carolena did his bidding. "Your friend has made us a fabulous meal!" Sandwiches, salad, fruit and drinks. Everything they needed had been provided. Because of nerves, she hadn't been hungrier earlier, but now she was starving. By the way his food disappeared, Valentino was famished, too.

When they couldn't eat another bite, she cleaned things up and closed the lid. "Please tell Matteo the food was wonderful!" She planned to send him a letter and thank him.

Valentino took his seat at the wheel, but he didn't start the engine or acknowledge what she'd said. "Before we get back, I want an answer. Do I call off the engagement so you and I can be together without hurting anyone else? I haven't touched you on purpose because once I do, I won't be able to stop."

The blood pounded in her ears. She jumped to her feet and clung to the side of the boat. The sun had dropped below the horizon, yet it was still light enough to see the smoke from Etna. Everywhere she looked, the very air she breathed reminded her of Valentino. He'd changed her life and she would never be the same again.

But her fear of being responsible for someone else wasn't the only thing preventing her being able to answer him the way he wanted. Already she recognized that if she got too close to him, the loss she would feel when she had to give him up would be unbearable. To be intimate with him would mean letting him into her heart. She couldn't risk that kind of pain when their affair ended. An affair was all there could ever be for them.

If she left Gemelli first thing in the morning and never saw him again, she'd never forget him, but she'd convinced herself that by not making love with him, she could go on living.

"It's apparent the answer is no."

His voice sounded wooden, devoid of life. It cut her to the quick because she knew that by her silence she'd just written her own death sentence.

Slowly she turned around to face him. His features looked chiseled in the semidarkness. "I saw the light in every farmer's eyes when they talked with you. They were seeing their future king. Putting off your wedding and coronation to be with me won't change your ultimate destiny.

"But you were right about us. What we felt at the pool was like a pyroclastic eruption. They don't come along very often. I read that there are about five hundred active volcanoes on earth, and fifteen hundred over the last ten thousand years. That's not very many when you consider the span of time and the size of our planet. You and I experienced a rare phenomenon and it was wonderful while it lasted, but thank heaven it blew itself out before we were consumed by its fire. No one has been hurt."

"No one?" The grating question fell from the white line of his lips. She watched his chest rise and fall visibly before he made a move to start the engine.

In agony, Carolena turned and clung to the side of

the boat until he pulled into a dock on palatial property some time later.

A few of his staff were there to tie it up. After she removed her life jacket, Valentino helped her off the boat and walked her across the grounds to her apartment. By the time they reached her door, her heart was stuck in her throat, making her feel faint.

"I'm indebted to you for your service, Carolena. Tomorrow my assistant will accompany you to the helicopter at seven-thirty. He'll bring your grandmother's hat with him. Your jet will leave at eight-fifteen from the airport."

Talk about pain…

"Thank you for everything." She could hardly get the words out.

His hooded blue eyes traveled over her, but he didn't touch her. *"Buon viaggio, bellissima."*

When he strode away on those long, powerful legs, she wanted to run after him and tell him she'd do anything to be with him for as long as time allowed them. But it was already too late. He'd disappeared around a corner and could be anywhere in the palace by now.

You had your chance, Carolena. Now it's gone forever.

CHAPTER SIX

"Abby?"

"Carolena—thank heaven you called! Where are you?"

"I'm back at the office."

"You're kidding—"

"No." Carolena frowned in puzzlement.

"I thought you'd be in Gemelli longer."

"There was no need. I finished up the video taping last evening. I'm pleased to say it went very well. This morning I left the country at eight-fifteen. When the jet landed in Arancia, I took a taxi to my apartment and changed clothes before coming to the firm. It's amazing how much work can pile up in a—"

"Carolena—" Abby interrupted her, which wasn't like her.

She blinked. "What's wrong?"

"You don't know?" Her friend sounded anxious.

"Know what?" She got a strange feeling in the pit of her stomach.

"Vincenzo's source from Gemelli told him that the queen opened parliament this morning without Valentino being there and no announcement was made about his forthcoming marriage. Parliament only convenes four times a year for a week, so the opportunity has been missed."

Carolena came close to dropping her cell phone.

"When you were with him, did he tell you anything? Do you have any idea what has happened?"

"None at all." It was the truth. Carolena could say that with a clear conscience. "When the taping was over last evening, we returned to the palace with the camera crew and I went straight to bed once I got back to my apartment."

She had no clue where Valentino had gone or what he'd done after he'd disappeared down the hall. But if he had been in as much turmoil as Carolena... She started to feel sick inside. "This morning I had breakfast in my room, then his assistant took me to the helicopter at seven-thirty and wished me a good flight. I know nothing."

"It's so strange. Vincenzo has tried to get through to him on his cell phone, but he's not taking calls. Something is wrong."

"Maybe he decided to announce it at the closing."

"I said the same thing to my husband, but he explained it didn't work that way. Any important news affecting the country is fed to the media early on the first day for dissemination."

"Maybe Valentino and the princess decided to postpone their wedding for reasons no one knows about. From what I've seen of him, he's a very private person."

"You're right, but over the last year he and Vincenzo

have grown close. My husband is worried about him. Frankly, so am I."

That made three of them.

Carolena gripped the phone tighter. She'd told Valentino a relationship with him wouldn't work, so if he'd decided to call off the wedding, then he did it for reasons that had nothing to do with her. She refused to feel guilty about it, but she'd grown weak as a kitten and was glad she was sitting down.

"I'm sure he'll get back to Vincenzo as soon as he can. Do you think it's possible there was some kind of emergency that required his presence at the volcanology lab in Catania?"

"I hadn't even thought of that. I'll ask Vincenzo what he thinks."

For all Carolena knew, Val had returned the boat to Matteo where he could confide in his friend in private before parliament opened. But like Vincenzo, she was getting more anxious by the minute.

"Did I tell you Valentino had a copy made of the video? His assistant brought it to me. I've got it right here and will courier it to the palace so you and Vincenzo can see what you think."

"I have a better idea. Come to the palace when you're through with work. We'll have a light supper and watch it. Maybe by then Vincenzo will have heard from him. I take it you haven't seen the video yet."

"No, and I have to tell you I'm nervous."

"Nonsense. I'll send the limo for you at five o'clock. Max will be excited to see you."

"That little darling. I can't wait to hold him." The

baby would be the distraction she needed. But until quitting time, she had a stack of files to work through.

"*Ciao,* Abby."

Three hours later Abby greeted her at the door of their living room, carrying Max in her arms. His blue sunsuit with a dolphin on the front looked adorable on him. "If you'll take the video, I'll tend him for a while." Then, to the little boy, "You remember me, don't you?"

She kissed one cheek then the other, back and forth until he was laughing without taking a breath. "Oh, you precious little thing. I can tell you're all better."

In a few minutes Vincenzo joined them. The second Max saw him, he lunged for his daddy. Their son was hilarious as he tried to climb on everything and clutched at anything he could get his hands on.

After they ate dinner in the dining room, Abby put the baby to bed and then they went back to the living room to watch the video. The whole time her hosts praised the film, Carolena's thoughts were on Valentino, who'd been standing next to the cameraman watching her.

Where was he right now? Enough time had gone by for her anxiety level to be off the charts.

When the film was over, Vincenzo got to his feet and smiled at her. "It's outstanding from every aspect, but *you* made it come alive, Carolena."

"It's true!" Abby chimed in.

"Thank you. I enjoyed doing it. The farmers were so thrilled to meet Valentino in person and listen to his ideas, it was really something to watch."

"Tomorrow we'll drive to the lemon groves to set up appointments."

Abby hugged her. "You were fabulous, Carolena! That hat of your grandmother's was perfect on you. I'm sorry she's not alive to see you wearing it."

Carolena would have responded, but Vincenzo's cell phone rang, putting a stop to their conversation. He checked the caller ID, then glanced at them. "It's Valentino. I'll take it in the bedroom." With those words Carolena's heart fluttered like a hummingbird's wings.

Abby let out a relieved sigh. "Finally we'll learn what's going on. If he hadn't called, I was afraid my husband would end up pacing the floor all night. He worries about Queen Bianca, who's had her heart set on this marriage. She really likes Alexandra."

Every time Abby said something, it was like another painful jab of a needle, reminding Carolena of the grave mistake she could have made if she'd said yes to Valentino. Last night had been excruciating. Several times she'd let down her resolve and had been tempted to reach for the phone. The palace operator would put her call through to Valentino. And then what? She shivered. Beg him to come to her room so they could talk?

When she thought she couldn't stand the suspense a second longer, Vincenzo walked into the living room. For want of a better word, he looked stunned. Abby jumped up from the couch and ran over to him. "What's happened, darling?"

He put his arm around her shoulders. "He and Alexandra have called off their marriage."

Valentino had actually done it?

"Oh, no—" Abby cried softly.

"Valentino has spoken with the queen and Alexandra's parents. It's final. He told me he doesn't want to be married unless it's to a woman he's in love with." Carolena felt Vincenzo's searching gaze on her, causing her knees to go weak. Had Valentino confided in him about her?

"Michelina always worried about him," Abby whispered.

Vincenzo looked at his wife. "Evidently, Alexandra feels the same way, so in that regard they're both in better shape than their parents, who've wanted this match for years. He says that after sixteen years of being betrothed, he feels like he's been let out of prison. I'm one person who can relate to everything he said."

Abby hugged him tightly.

"But there's a big problem. Bianca doesn't want to continue ruling, so it will be up to parliament if they'll allow Valentino to become king without a wife. It's never been done, so I doubt it will happen."

"Where's Valentino now?"

"Since Vito is home on leave from the military and wants to spend time with their mother, Valentino is planning to fly here in the morning and finish up our project with Carolena."

The news was too much. Carolena sank into the nearest chair while she tried to take it all in.

"I told him we watched the video and have a few ideas. Apparently he's seen it several times, too, and has some suggestions of his own. We'll ask the nurse to tend Max so the four of us can make a day of it."

By now Carolena's stomach was in such upheaval, she was afraid she was going to be sick. "In that case, I need to leave and study the script we wrote for the filming here before I go to bed. Thanks for dinner. I'll see you tomorrow."

Abby walked her to the door. "I'll phone you in the morning to let you know what time the limo will come for you. It all depends on Valentino." She stared at Carolena. "He's fortunate that Alexandra wasn't in love with him. If Michelina hadn't loved Vincenzo so much, he—"

"I know," Carolena broke in. "But their two situations weren't the same and your husband is an honorable man." What had happened to Valentino's promise to not fail his parents like his uncle Stefano had done?

Abby's eyes misted over. "So is Valentino. Rather than put himself and Alexandra through purgatory, he had the courage to go with his heart. I admire him for that. The volcanologist in him must be responsible for going where others fear to tread. With that quality he'll make an extraordinary king one day when the time is right."

But he wouldn't, not if he followed in his uncle's footsteps.

With those words, Carolena felt her grandmother's warning settle on her like the ash from Mount Etna.

"See you tomorrow, Abby." They hugged.

"There's a limo waiting for you at the front entrance, but before you go, I have to tell you I've never seen you looking more beautiful than you did in that video. There was an aura about you the camera captured, as if you were filled with happiness. Do you know you literally glowed? The sadness you've carried for years seems to have vanished."

It was truth time. "If you're talking about Berto, then you're right. The trip to Gemelli has helped me put the past into perspective. I thank you for that. *Buona notte, dear friend.*"

Valentino's jet landed at the Arancia airport the next morning at 7:00 a.m. He told the limo driver waiting for him to drive straight to Carolena's condo building.

At quarter to eight they pulled around the back. He'd arrived here fifteen minutes early on purpose and would get inside through the freight entrance. Abby had told her they'd come for her at 8:00 a.m., but Valentino told Abby he'd pick up Carolena on the way from the airport to save time. They could all meet at the first lemon grove on the outskirts of Arancia at nine.

One of his security people went ahead to show him the way. Though she planned to be outside waiting, he wanted the element of surprise on his side by showing up at her door ahead of time.

The knowledge that he was free to be with her set off an adrenaline rush like nothing he'd ever known. He rounded the corner on the second floor and rapped on the door. A few seconds later he heard her voice. "Who's there?"

Valentino sucked in his breath. "Open the door and find out."

After a silence, *"Your Highness?"* It came out more like a squeak.

"No. My name is Val."

Another silence. "It *is* you."

The shock in her voice made him smile. "I'm glad you remembered."

"Of course I remembered!" she snapped. That sounded like the woman he'd first met. "You shouldn't have come to my condo."

"Why not? Circumstances have changed."

"They haven't where I'm concerned." Her voice shook.

"That's too bad because the pyroclastic eruption you thought had blown itself out was merely a hiccup compared to what's happening now."

"I can't do this."

"Neither of us has a choice."

"Don't say that—"

"Are you going to let me in, or do I have to beg?"

"I—I'm not ready yet," she stammered.

"I've seen you in a bathrobe before." The sight of her had taken his breath.

"Not this time!"

The door opened, revealing a fully dressed woman in a peasant-style white blouse and jeans. Her long sable hair, freshly shampooed, framed a beautiful face filled with color. With those green eyes, she was a glorious sight anytime. "Please come in. I need to braid my hair, but it will only take me a minute." She darted away.

He shut the door. "I'd rather you left it long for me," he called after her before moving through the small entrance hall to her living room. It had a cozy, comfortable feel with furnishings that must have belonged to her family. Lots of color in the fabric. Through the French doors he glimpsed a book-lined study with a desk and computer.

"I'm afraid it will get too messy."

Valentino had expected that response and wandered around the room. There was a statue on an end table that caught his eye. On close examination it turned out to be a reproduction of Rodin's *The Secret*. The sculpture of two white marble hands embracing could have described both the evocative and emotive nature of his experience with Carolena.

He found it fascinating she would have chosen this particular piece. There was an intimacy about it that spoke to the male in him. She was a woman of fire. He'd sensed it from the beginning and wanted to feel it surround him.

Next, he saw some photographs of her with a man in his early twenties, their arms around each other. This had to be Berto. They looked happy. The loss would have been horrendous in the beginning.

On one of the walls was a large framed photograph of a farmhouse. No doubt it was the one she wanted to buy back one day. His gaze dropped to the table below it, where he was able to look at her pictures comprising several generations.

"I'm ready."

He picked up one of them. "Your parents?" He showed the photo to her.

"Yes."

"There's a strong resemblance to your mother. She was beautiful."

"I agree," she said in a thick-toned voice.

"What happened to them?"

Her eyes filmed over. "Mother could never have another child after me and died of cervical cancer. A few years later my father got an infection that turned septic and he passed away, so my grandparents took over raising me. Later on, my grandfather died of pneumonia. He worked so hard, he just wore out. Then it was just my grandmother and me."

He put the picture down and slid his hands to her shoulders. "You've had too much tragedy in your young life."

Her eyes, a solemn green, lifted to his. "So have you. Grandparents, an uncle, a sister and a father gone, plus a kingdom that needs you and will drain everything out of you…"

Valentino kissed her moist eyelids. "You're a survivor, Carolena, with many gifts. I can't tell you how much I admire you."

"Thank you. The feeling is mutual, but you already know that." She'd confined her hair in a braid, which brought out the classic mold of her features.

"I came early so we could talk before we meet Vincenzo and Abby."

He could feel her tension as she shook her head and eased away from him. "Even though you've broken your engagement to Princess Alexandra, which is a good thing considering you don't love her, what you've done changes nothing for me. I don't want an affair with you,

Val. That's all it would be until you have to marry. After your uncle's death, you made that promise to yourself and your parents, remember?"

"Of course." He put his hands on his hips. "But I want to know about you. What do *you* want?"

The grandfather clock chimed on the quarter past. "It's getting late." She walked to the entrance hall.

Valentino followed her. "I asked you a question."

She reached for her straw bag on the credenza. "I want to finish this taping and get back to my law practice."

He planted himself in front of the door so she couldn't open it. "Forget I'm a prince."

Her jaw hardened. "That's the third time you've said that to me."

"What would you want if I weren't a prince? Humor me, Carolena."

He heard her take a struggling breath. "The guarantee of joy in an everlasting marriage with no losses, no pain."

That was her past grief talking. "As your life has already proved to you, there is no such guarantee."

Her eyes narrowed on him. "You *did* ask."

"Then let me add that you have to grab at happiness where you find it and pray to hold on to it for as long as possible."

"We can't. You're a prince, which excludes us from taking what we want. Even if you weren't a prince, I wouldn't grab at it."

His face looked like thunder. "Why not?"

"It—it's not important."

"The hell it isn't."

"Val—we need to get going or Abby and Vincenzo will start to worry."

"The limo is out in the back, but this conversation isn't over yet." He turned and opened the door. After their stops at the various farms, they would have all night tonight and tomorrow night to be together, not to mention the rest of their lives. "I brought your hat with me, by the way."

"Thank you. I would hate to have lost it."

He escorted her out to the limo. With the picture of the marble statue still fresh in his mind, he reached for her hand when they climbed into the car. He held on to it even though he sat across from her. The pulse at her wrist was throbbing.

"Was the Rodin statue a gift from Berto?"

"No. I found it in a little shop near the Chapelle Matisse in Vence, France, with my grandmother. I was just a teenager and we'd gone to France for the weekend. She didn't care for the sculpture, but I loved it and bought it with my spending money. I don't quite know why I was so taken with it."

"I found it extraordinary myself. It reminded me of us. Two would-be lovers with a secret. With only their hands, Rodin's genius brought out their passion." He pressed a kiss to the palm of hers before letting it go.

"I don't like secrets."

"Nor I, but you're being secretive right now."

"Now isn't the time for serious conversation."

"There'll be time later. Vincenzo has planned our itinerary. The farmer at the first grove speaks Mentonasc, so Abby is going to be our translator. She won't want to be in the video, but when we start taping tomorrow, Vincenzo and I are depending on you to get her in it. A blonde and a brunette, both beauties, will provide invaluable appeal."

"You're terrible," she said, but he heard her chuckle. Some genuine emotion at last.

"Matteo told me about the special bottle of Limoncello you express mailed to him from Arancia to thank him for the picnic. The man was very touched, especially by your signature on the label with the five stars next to it."

"You have a wonderful friend in him."

"He has put it up on the shelf behind the counter where all the customers will see it. When your video is famous, he will brag about it. Before we got off the phone he asked me to thank you."

"That was very nice of him." Before long they arrived at the first lemon grove. "It looks like we've arrived."

"Saved by the bell," he murmured.

Praying the others wouldn't look too closely at her, Carolena got out of the limo. It was a good thing the filming wouldn't be until tomorrow. If she'd had to deal with the crew's makeup man, he would know she felt ill after making her exit speech to Valentino.

To her relief, Abby was already talking to the farmer and his two sons. Being fluent in four languages made her a tremendous asset anytime, but Carolena could tell this farming family was impressed that Prince Vincenzo's wife could speak Mentonasc.

He introduced everyone. She could tell the family was almost overcome in the presence of two princes, but Abby had a way of making them feel comfortable while she put her points across. Before long, the four of them left to move on to the next grove. Carolena would have stayed with Abby, but Valentino cupped her elbow and guided her to their limo.

"We all need our privacy," he murmured against her ear after they got back in the car. He acted as though they'd never had that earlier conversation. Even though he sat across from her, being this close to him caused her to be a nervous wreck. His half smile made him so appealing, it was sinful.

"It's a good thing I'll be along tomorrow, too. The younger men couldn't take their eyes off of you. I'm going to have to guard you like a hawk."

In spite of how difficult it was to be alone with him, she said, "You're very good on a woman's ego."

"Then you can imagine the condition my ego is in to be the man in your life. In feudal times they'd have fought me for you, but they'd have ended up dying at the end of a sword."

"Stop—"

He leaned forward, mesmerizing her with those dark blue eyes. "I *am* the man in your life. The only man."

A shudder passed through her body. "I won't let you be in my life, and I can't be the woman in yours. When the taping is over, we won't be seeing each other again."

"Then you haven't read your contract carefully."

Her pulse raced in alarm. "I didn't sign a contract."

"You did better than that. You gave me and Vincenzo

your word. That's as good as an oath. Implicit in the contract is your agreement to deliver the videos and flyers with the AG logo to the fruit distributors around the country. We'll go together. It'll take at least a week. Fortunately my brother will be around to help my mother."

Aghast, she cried, "I can't be gone from the firm that long."

"Vincenzo already cleared it with Signor Faustino. Day after tomorrow we'll fly back to Gemelli to begin our tour. By then the tapes and flyers will be ready. I haven't had a vacation in two years and am looking forward to it."

She could see there was no stopping Valentino. Fear and exhilaration swept over her in alternating waves. "What about your work at the geophysics center?"

"I'm long overdue the time off. You're stuck with me. For security's sake, we'll sleep on the yacht at night and ferry across to the island by helicopter during the day. Don't worry. I won't come near you, not after you made your thoughts clear to me."

"You promise?"

He sat back. "I promise not to do anything you don't want me to do. It'll be all business until this is over."

"Thank you." She knew he would keep his promise. The only problem was keeping the promise to herself to keep distance between them.

"Our last stop tomorrow will be the Baretti farm. Judging from the photograph in your living room, the house has a lot of character."

"I loved it, but I don't want us to bother the new owners."

"We won't. You let us know when to stop and the cameraman will take some long shots while you talk about life on the farm growing up. When the film is spliced, we'll start the video with your visit. Will it be hard to see it again?"

Her heartbeat sped up. "I don't know."

"We don't have to do that segment if you decide against it."

"No. I'd like to do it as a tribute to my family." Emotion had clogged her throat.

"I'm glad you said that because I long to see the place where you grew up. I want to learn all about you. The first tree you fell out of, your first bee sting."

Valentino was so wonderful she could feel herself falling deeper and deeper under his spell. "I know about the putti but have yet to learn which staircase at the palace was your first slide. No doubt you spent hours in the Hall of Arms. A boy's paradise."

"Vito and I had our favorite suits of armor, but we put so many dents in them, they're hardly recognizable."

"I can't imagine anything so fun. My friends and I fought our wars in the tops of the trees throwing fruit at each other. The trouble we got into would fill a book. My grandmother would tell you I was the ringleader. And you were right. I did fall out of a tree several times."

His low chuckle warmed her all the way through and set the tone for the day. She had to admit it was heaven to be with him like this. Carolena needed to cherish every moment because the time they spent together would be coming to an end too soon.

Eight hours later when she was alone back at her condo, she called Abby's cell phone, desperate to talk about what was happening to her.

"Carolena?"

"Sorry to bother you." She took a deep breath. "Are you free?"

"Yes. The baby's asleep and I'm in the bedroom getting ready for bed. Vincenzo and Valentino are in the study talking business. Everything went so well today, they're both elated and will probably be up for another couple of hours. What's wrong?"

She bit her lip. "I'm in trouble."

"I *knew* it."

"What do you mean?"

"You and Valentino. Vincenzo and I watched you two that first night while we were having dinner when he couldn't take his eyes off you. You're in love."

No—

"My husband was certain of it when Valentino took you up on Mount Etna. You're the reason he called off his wedding."

"Don't say that, Abby! We haven't fallen in love. He's just infatuated. You know… forbidden fruit. It'll pass."

"He's enjoyed a lot of forbidden fruit over the years, but he never ended it with Alexandra until he met you."

"That's because he was with me the night his mother insisted on setting the wedding date. When confronted with the reality, it made him realize he can't marry a woman he doesn't love. *That* I understand. But it wasn't because of me. All I did was serve as the catalyst."

"Are you only infatuated, too?"

"What woman wouldn't be?" she cried in self-defense. "Unfortunately he's the first man since Berto to attract me, but I'll get over it."

After a pause. "Have you—"

"No!" she defended.

"Carolena, I was only going to ask if you two had talked over your feelings in any depth."

"Sorry I snapped. We've talked a little, but I'm afraid of getting too familiar with him." She'd come so close to making love with him.

"I've been there and know what you're going through. Let's face it. No woman could resist Valentino except a strong woman like you. He's temptation itself. So was Vincenzo. You'll never know how hard it was to stay away from him."

"Yes, I do. I lived through that entire experience with you. But my case is different. Please try to understand what I'm saying. Everything came together to lay the groundwork for the perfect storm because that's all it is. A perfect storm."

"Then what's the problem?"

"He wants me to fly down to Gemelli the day after tomorrow and spend a week distributing all the marketing materials with him. I—I can't do it, Abby."

"If you're not in love with him, then why can't you go? He has employed you to do a job for him."

"How can you of all people ask me that? Don't you remember after the baby was born? Your father hid you and was ready to fly you back to the States to get you away permanently from Vincenzo so there'd be no hint of scandal."

"But Vincenzo found me and proposed."

"Exactly. Your situation was unique from day one. Vincenzo was married to a princess before he married you. You carried his baby and the king made an exception in your case because he could see his son was in love with you. It's not the same thing at all with Valentino and me. He only *thinks* he's in love."

"So he's already gone so far as to tell you how he feels?"

She swallowed hard. "Like I said, I'm a new face, but certainly not the last one. Be honest, Abby. Though he never loved Alexandra, he'll have to find another royal to marry. In the meantime, if people see me with him, they'll link me with his broken betrothal and there really will be a scandal. I don't want to be known as the secret girlfriend who caused all the trouble."

Her statue of *The Secret* had taken on a whole new meaning since morning. She'd never look at it again without remembering the way he'd kissed her in the limo.

"What trouble? No one knows about you."

"No one except the entire palace staff, his best friend on the island, his colleagues at the volcanology institute in Catania *and* his mother. By the time we've traveled all around the island, the whole country will have seen us together. The queen doesn't want me back in Gemelli."

"Valentino loves her, but he makes his own decisions. If he wants you there, she can't stop him except to bring pressure to bear on you."

"What should I do?"

"I'm the last person to ask for advice."

"Do it anyway. I trust your judgment."

"Well, if I were in your shoes, I believe I'd give myself the week to honor my commitment to him. In that amount of time you'll either lose interest in each other or not. No one can predict the future, but while you're still under contract, do your part. Maybe it will help if you treat him like the brother you and I always wished we'd had."

A brother…

CHAPTER SEVEN

"VAL? SINCE WE'RE already on the eastern side of the island, why don't we stop for dinner at Matteo's restaurant before we fly back to the yacht." She wanted people around them and thought the suggestion pleased him.

"I'll call ahead and see what can be arranged."

Matteo looked happy to see them, but the place was busy and they could only chat for a moment with him. After another delicious dinner, she hurried out to the limo with Valentino, anxious to leave. They headed for the heliport on the eastern end of the island. Within a few minutes they were flying back to the yacht.

In three days they'd covered a lot of territory. He'd stuck to business while they'd dispensed the videos and flyers. When they were in the limo, he sat across from her and there was no touching beyond his helping her in and out of the car.

Each night she'd pleaded fatigue to keep her distance from him. To her surprise, he'd told her he, too, was tired and didn't try to detain her before she went to her cabin. Instead, he'd thanked her for a wonderful job and wished her a good night's sleep. She was a fool to wish that he wasn't quite so happy to see her go to bed.

The queen's spies would find no fault in him. His behavior abated Carolena's fears that the time they were forced to spend together on this project would make her too uncomfortable. In truth, she discovered she was having fun doing business with him. He knew so much about the economics that ran his country, she marveled. With others or alone, they had fascinating conversations that covered everything including the political climate.

Valentino remained silent until they'd climbed out of the helicopter. "We need to talk. Let's do it in the lounge before you go to bed."

She walked across the deck with him. When they entered it, she sat down on one of the leather chairs surrounding a small table.

"Would you like a drink?"

"Nothing for me, thank you."

He stood near her, eyeing her with a sober expression. "What were you and Matteo talking about while I took that phone call from Vito?"

Carolena had known he'd ask that question. "He... wanted to know if you'd broken your engagement. I told him yes."

"What else did he say?"

She couldn't handle this inquisition any longer. "Nothing for you to worry about. He's not only a good friend to you, he's incredibly discreet." She looked away to avoid his piercing gaze. "He reminds me of Abby in the sense that I'd trust her with my life."

Valentino studied her until she felt like squirming.

"Do you feel the same about me? Would you trust me with your life?"

The question threw her. She got up from the chair. "I'm surprised you would ask that when you consider I went up on the volcano with you. I'll say good-night now." It was time to go to bed.

"I'd still like a more in-depth answer." The retort came back with enviable calm. "Tell me what you meant earlier when you said you wouldn't grab at happiness even if I weren't a prince?"

"Do I really have to spell it out for you?"

"I'm afraid you do." His voice grated.

She eyed him soberly. "I don't want to be in love again and then lose that person. I've been through it once and can't bear the thought of it. Call me a coward, but it's the way I'm made.

"Whatever you do with the rest of your life, I don't want to be a part of it. As I told you on the yacht the night I thought I would be sleeping with you, I'll never forget how you made me feel, but that's a happy memory I can live with and pull out on a rainy day.

"To have an affair now is something else again. I couldn't do it with you or any man because it would mean giving up part of myself. And when the affair was over, I wouldn't be able to stand the pain of loss because I know myself too well."

He rubbed the back of his neck. "Thank you for your answer. It's all making sense now. Just so you know, I'll be flying to the palace early in the morning."

She was afraid to ask him why, in case he felt she was prying.

"You can sleep in, though I don't know another female who needed her beauty sleep less than you. The steward will serve you breakfast whenever you want it."

"Thank you."

"After I return at ten, we'll do our tour of the south end of the island."

His comment relieved her of the worry that he wouldn't be gone long. Already she missed him, which was perfectly ridiculous.

"After work we'll take the cruiser to a nearby deserted island where we'll swim and watch the wildlife. It's a place where we ought to be able to see some nesting turtles. If it were fall we'd see the flamingos that migrate there on their way to and from Africa. You should see it before you fly back to Arancia."

"I can't wait."

"Neither can I. You'll love it. *A domani.*"

Valentino knocked on Vito's bedroom door early the next morning. His brother was quick to open it wearing a robe. He needed a shave and looked as if he hadn't had any sleep. "What was so urgent I needed to fly here this early?"

Dark shadows below Vito's eyes testified that his younger brother was in pain. "Thanks for getting here so fast. Come on in."

He'd never seen Vito this torn up, not even after Michelina's death. "I take it this isn't about Mother. What's wrong?" He moved inside and followed him into the living room.

Vito spun around, his face full of too many lines for

a thirty-year-old. "I have a confession to make. After you hear me out, I'll understand if you tell me to get the hell out of your life."

Valentino's brows furrowed. "I'd never do that."

"Oh, yes, you would. You will." He laughed angrily. "But I can't keep this to myself any longer." His dark brown eyes filled with tears. "Do you want to know the real reason I went into the military five years ago?"

"I thought it was because you wanted to, and because our father said you were free to do what you wanted."

He shook his dark head. Vito resembled their mother. "What I wanted was Alexandra."

A gasp came out of Valentino. Those words shook him to the foundations.

"I fell in love with her. I don't know how it happened. It just did."

Valentino knew exactly how it happened. He knew it line and verse.

"All the years you were betrothed, you were hardly ever around, and when you were, it was only for a day. Whereas I spent a lot of time with her. One night things got out of control and I told her how I felt about her. We went riding and she told me she was in love with me, too. We ended up spending the weekend together knowing we could never be together again."

"Vito—"

"You were betrothed to her, and the parents had another woman picked out for me, so I left to join the military with the intention of making it my career for as long as possible. I was a coward and couldn't face you, but I should have."

Pure unadulterated joy seized Valentino. He didn't need to hear another word. It suddenly made sense when he remembered his brother occasionally telling him things about Alexandra that surprised Valentino. It explained the huge relief he saw in Alexandra's eyes when he'd called off the marriage. But what he'd thought was relief was joy.

In the next breath he gave his brother the biggest bear hug of his life, lifting him off the ground. "You're more in love with her than ever, right?"

Vito staggered backward with a look of disbelief in his eyes. "Yes, but how come you're acting like this? You have every right to despise me."

He shook his head. "Nothing could be further from the truth. If anything, I've been the despicable one for not ending it with Alexandra years ago. I knew something earthshaking had happened to make you go away. I was afraid I'd offended you in some way. Now that you've told me, I'm so incredibly happy for you and Alexandra, you could have no idea.

"Don't waste another moment, Vito. All this time you two have been in pain… Give up your commission and marry her. Grab at your happiness! Mother loves her, and her parents want to join our two families together. When they find out you're going to be king instead of me, they'll be overjoyed."

"I don't want to be king."

"Yes, you do. You told me years ago. The point is, *I* don't. I never wanted it."

"But—"

"But nothing," Valentino silenced him. "Mother is

perfectly healthy. Maybe she's going to have to rule for a lot longer than she'd planned."

His brother rubbed the back of his neck in confusion. "What's going on with you? Do I even know you?"

He grinned. "We're brothers, and I've got my own confession to make, but you'll have to hear it later. In the meantime, don't worry about me. And don't tell Mother I've been to the palace this morning. I'll be back in a few days." He headed for the door and turned to him. "When I see you again, I'd better hear that you and Alexandra have made your wedding plans or there *will* be hell to pay."

Valentino flew out the door and raced across the grounds to the helicopter. The knowledge that Vito and Alexandra had been lovers had transformed him, removing every trace of pain and guilt.

"Carolena?"

She peered around the deck chair where she'd been reading a magazine in her sunglasses. "Hi!"

This morning she'd put her vibrant hair back in a chignon and was wearing pleated beige pants with a peach-colored top her figure did wonders for. Between her sensational looks and brilliant mind, she was his total fantasy come to life.

"If you're ready, we'll get business out of the way, then come back and take off for the island." He'd told one of the crew to pack the cruiser with everything they'd need if they wanted to spend the night there.

Throughout the rest of the day they'd gotten things down to a routine and touched base with the many heads of fruit consortiums in the district. The plan to market the island's blood oranges under the AG logo had already reached the ears of many of them with rave results.

Valentino had demands for more of the videos made in Gemelli than he'd anticipated. He gave orders to step up production of the flyers, too. Two more days and he and Carolena would have covered the whole country. By this time next year he'd know if their efforts had helped increase their exports around the world and produced financial gains.

As he'd told Carolena, there were no guarantees in life. This plan of his and Vincenzo's to help their countries' economies was only one of many. It was far too early to predict the outcome, but since she'd come into his life, he had this feeling something remarkable was going to happen.

With their marketing work done, Valentino drove the cruiser under a late-afternoon sun along a string of tiny deserted islands with rocky coastlines.

Carolena had been waiting for this all day. "What's that wonderful smell in the breeze?"

"Rosemary and thyme. It grows wild here among the sand dunes and beaches. Vito and I spent a lot of our teenage years exploring this area. In the fall this place is covered with pink flamingos, herons and storks. We used to camp out here to watch them and take movies."

"I envy you having a brother to go on adventures with. No one's childhood is idyllic, but I think yours must have come close."

"We tried to forget that we were princes put into

a special kind of gilded cage. However, I would have liked your freedom."

"But it wouldn't have exposed you to the world you're going to rule one day. Someone has to do it."

He lifted one eyebrow. "That's one way of looking at it. Ten years ago we worked on our father to get legislation passed in parliament to declare this a natural preserve so the tourists wouldn't ruin it. Since that time, our Gemellian bird-watching society has seen continual growth of the different species, and I've had this place virtually to myself."

She laughed. "Seriously, that has to be very gratifying to you." His dedication to the country's welfare continued to astound Carolena. "This is paradise, Val. The sand is so white!"

He nodded. "It feels like the most refined granulated sugar under your feet. We'll pull in to that lagoon, one of my favorite spots."

The water was as blue as the sky. They were alone. It was as if they were the only people left on earth. After he cut the engine, she darted below to put on her flowered one-piece swimsuit. It was backless, but the front fastened up around the neck like a choker, providing the modesty she needed to be around Val.

When she came back up on deck, she discovered he'd already changed into black trunks. The hard-muscled physique of his bronzed body took her breath. His gaze scrutinized her so thoroughly, he ignited a new fire that traveled through hers.

"Not that the suit you're wearing isn't delectable, but what happened to that gorgeous purple concoction you were wearing when we first met? I've been living to see you in it again."

A gentle laugh broke from her. "You mean that piece of nothing?" she teased. "I've never owned anything indecent before. When I saw it in the shop before I flew down here with Abby, I decided to be daring and buy it. I was a fool to think I'd be alone."

"The sight of you almost in it put an exclamation point on the end of my grueling workday."

She blushed. "*Almost* being the operative word. You're a terrible man to remind me."

"You're a terrible woman to deprive me of seeing you in it again."

Carolena had been trying to treat him like a brother, but that was a joke with the heat building between them. She needed to cool off and there was only one way to do it. She walked to the end of the cruiser and without hesitation jumped into the water.

"Oh—" she cried when she emerged. "This feels like a bathtub! Heaven!"

"Isn't it?"

She squealed again because he'd come right up next to her. They swam around the boat, diving and bobbing like porpoises for at least half an hour. "I've never had so much fun in my life!"

He smiled at her with a pirate's grin that sent a thrill through her. "I'll race you to shore, but I'll give you a head start."

"You're on!" She struck out for the beach, putting everything into it. But when she would have been able to stand, he grabbed hold of her ankles and she landed in the sand. Laughter burst out of her. "That wasn't fair!"

He'd come up beside her and turned her over. "I know," he whispered against her lips. "But as you've found out, I play by a different set of rules. Right now I'm going to kiss the daylights out of you."

"No, Val—" she cried, but the second she felt his hungry mouth cover hers, she couldn't hold off any longer. This time they weren't in the back of the limo while the driver was waiting for them to get out.

There was nothing to impede their full pleasure as they wrapped their arms around each other. Slowly they began giving and taking one kiss after another, relishing the taste and feel of each other. While their legs entwined, the warm water lapped around them in a silky wet blanket.

"You're so beautiful I could eat you alive. I'm in love with you, *adorata*. I've never said it to another woman in my life, so don't tell me it isn't love."

She looked into his eyes blazing with blue fire. "I wasn't going to," she cried in a tremulous whisper before their mouths met in another explosion of desire. Carried away by her feelings, she quit fighting her reservations for the moment and gave in to her longings. She embraced him with almost primitive need, unaware of twilight turning into night.

"I'm in love with you, too, Val," she confessed when he allowed her to draw breath. "I've been denying it to myself, but it's no use. Like I told you on the yacht that first night, you make me feel immortal. Only a man who had hold of my heart could make me thankful I've been born a woman."

He buried his face in her throat. "You bring out feelings in me I didn't know were there. I need you with me, Carolena. Not just for an hour or a day." He kissed her again, long and deep, while they moved and breathed as one flesh.

"I feel the same way," she whispered at last, kissing his jaw where she could feel the beginnings of a beard. No man had ever been as gorgeous.

"Another time we'll come out here in the middle of the night to watch the turtle fledglings hatch and make their trek to the water. Tonight I want to spend all the time we have on the cruiser with you. It's getting cooler. Come on before you catch a chill."

He got up first and pulled her against him. Dizzy from the sensations he'd aroused, she clung to him, not wanting to be separated from him for an instant, but they had to swim back to the boat. Valentino grasped her hand and drew her into the water. "Ready?"

"Yes."

Together they swam side by side until they reached the back of the cruiser. He levered himself in first so he could help her aboard. "You take a shower while I get the cruiser ready for bed. We'll eat in the galley. But I need this first." He planted another passionate kiss on her mouth, exploring her back with his hands before she hurried across the deck and down the steps.

She'd packed a bag with the essentials she'd need. After carrying it into the shower, she turned on the water and undid her hair. It felt marvelous to wash out the sand and have a good scrub. Aware Valentino would want a shower, too, she didn't linger.

Once she'd wrapped her hair in a towel and had dried herself, she pulled out her toweling robe. But when she started to put it on, it was like déjà vu and stopped her cold. What was she doing?

Yes she'd broken down and admitted that she loved him, but nothing else had changed. Though he'd spoken of his love and need to be with her all the time, he was still a prince with responsibilities and commitments she could never be a part of.

Abby had suggested she treat Valentino like a brother in order to make it through the rest of the week, but that tactic had been a total and utter failure. Carolena was painfully, desperately in love with him.

If they made love tonight, her entire world would change. She'd be a slave to her need for him and act like all the poor lovesick wretches throughout time who'd made themselves available to the king when he called for them.

It was sick and wrong! No matter how much she loved Valentino, she couldn't do that to herself. Carolena couldn't imagine anything worse than living each minute of her life waiting for him to reach out to her when he had the time. Once he married and had children, that really would be the end for her.

If she couldn't have him all to herself, she didn't want any part of him. There was no way to make it work. None. She'd rather be single for the rest of her life.

On the yacht that first night she'd told him he'd passed his test and could leave her cabin with a clear conscience. Now it was time for her to pass her test and go away forever.

She quickly put on clean underwear and a new pair of lightweight sweats with short sleeves. The robe she buried in the bottom of the bag. After removing the towel, she brushed her hair back and fastened it at the nape with an elastic.

After putting her bag outside the door, she headed straight into the galley and opened the fridge to get the food set out for them. When she'd put everything on the table, she called to him. A minute later he showed up in a striped robe. He'd just come out of the shower and his dark blond hair was still damp. Talk about looking good enough to eat!

She flashed him a smile. "Is everything fine topside?"

"We're set for the night." His eyes took in her sweats. Carolena knew her friendly air didn't fool him, but he went along with her. "I like your sleepwear. Reminds me of Vito's military fatigues."

"This is as close as I ever hope to get to war," she quipped. "Why don't you sit down and eat this delicious food someone has prepared for us." He did her bidding. She poured coffee for them. "How is your brother, by the way? Will he be in Gemelli long before he has to go back on duty?"

"I don't know." His vague answer wasn't very reassuring. "He wants to meet you when we get back to the palace."

She bit into a plum. "I'm afraid that won't be possible."

Lines marred his handsome features. "Why would you say something like that? He's my only sibling still alive. Naturally I want him to meet you and get to know you."

"Under normal circumstances there's nothing I'd like more, but nothing about you and me is normal."

His head reared back. "What are you trying to tell me now?"

Carolena eyed him with a frank gaze. "I've already admitted that I'm in love with you, but I've come to my senses since we came back on board and I don't intend to sleep with you tonight or any other night. I want a clean break from you after I've finished out my contract, so there's no need to be involved with any members of your family."

He got that authoritative look. It was something that came over him even if he wasn't aware of it. "There isn't going to be a break."

"So speaks the prince. But this commoner has another destiny. Don't ask me again to forget that you're royalty. It would be pointless. Do you honestly believe I could stand to be your lover in your secret life and watch you play out your public life with a royal wife and children? Other foolish women have done it for centuries, but not me."

Valentino tucked into his pasta salad, seemingly not in the least bothered by anything she'd said.

"Did you hear me?"

"Loud and clear." He kept on eating.

Her anger was kindled. "Stop acting like a husband who's tired of listening to his nag of a wife. Have you ever considered why she nags him?"

"The usual reasons. I had parents, too, remember."

"You're impossible!"

Quiet reigned until he'd finished his coffee. After he put down the mug, he looked at her with those intelligent dark blue eyes. "How would *you* like to be my wife? I already know you have a temper, so I'm not shaking in my boots."

Her lungs froze. "That was a cruel thing to say to me."

His sinuous smile stung her. "Cruel? I just proposed marriage to you and that's the answer you give me?"

Carolena shook her head. "Stop teasing me, Val. Why are you being like this? I thought I knew you, but it's obvious I don't. The only time I see you serious is when you're wearing your princely mantle."

He sat back in the chair. "For the first time in my life, I've taken it off."

She started to get nervous. "Just because you broke your engagement, it doesn't mean you've changed into someone else."

"Oh, but I have!"

"Now you're scaring me again."

"Good. I like it when you're thrown off base. First, let me tell you about my talk with Vito this morning."

Carolena blinked. "That's where you were?"

"He sent me an urgent message telling me he needed to see me as soon as possible. Otherwise I would never have left you."

This had to do with their mother. Guilt attacked her. "Is your mother ill?" she asked.

"No. Last week I told Vito I was breaking my engagement to Alexandra. Since I had business with you,

I asked him to meet the princess's plane when she flew in to Gemelli."

"She came to the palace?"

"That's right. What I didn't know until this morning was that Vito and Alexandra were lovers before he went into the military."

The blood hammered in her ears.

"He signed up intending to make a career of it in order to stay away from her permanently. Neither my parents nor I knew why."

"Those poor things," she whispered.

Valentino nodded. "But after hearing that I'd broken our engagement, he found the courage to face me this morning. To my surprise, I learned she was on the verge of breaking it off with me, but Vito wanted to be the one to tell me. That was why she was so happy that I got there first."

Carolena could hardly take it in. "You mean, they've been in love all these years?"

"Yes. It's the forever kind."

She was dumbstruck.

"When I left Vito, I told him there'd better be a marriage between the two of them soon or he'd have to answer to me. Mother will have no choice but to see him crowned king. The promise that one of her sons will reign makes everything all right. He'll rule instead of me. No one will have to be disappointed, after all."

By now Carolena's whole body was shaking. "Are you saying you'd give up your dream in order to marry me?"

"It was never my dream. My parents thrust the idea upon me as soon as I was old enough to understand."

Dying inside, she got to her feet. "Does your mother know any of this?"

"Maybe by now, which brings me to what I have to say to you. I meant what I said earlier tonight. I want you with me all the time, day and night. Forever." He cocked his head. "Did you mean what you said the other day at your condo when I asked you what *you* wanted?"

Hot tears stung her eyelids. "Yes. But we both concluded it wasn't possible."

"Not both—" He leaned forward and grasped her hand. "I told you that true love had to be grabbed and enjoyed for the time given every mortal. When I asked you to fly up on Etna with me even though you knew there was a risk, you went with me because you couldn't bear to miss the experience."

"That was a helicopter ride. Not a marriage. There can't be one between you and me. You're supposed to be the King!"

"Am I not supposed to have any say in the matter, *bellissima?*"

"Val… You're not thinking clearly."

"I'm a free man, Carolena, and have never known my path better than I do now. When Michelina passed away, Vincenzo was free to marry Abby and he did so in the face of every argument. Lo and behold he's still the prince.

"Whether the government makes him king after his father dies, no one can say. As for me, I'll still be a prince when I marry you. The only difference is, I'll work for Vito after he's crowned."

"You mean *if* he's crowned. Your mother will forbid it."

"You don't know Vito. He wanted Alexandra enough to go after her. It looks like he's got the stuff to make a remarkable king. Once Mother realizes their marriage will save her relationship with Alexandra's parents, she'll come around."

"Does Vito want to be king?"

"I don't think he's given it much thought since everyone thought I'd be the one to assume the throne. But when we were younger and I told him I wanted to be a full-time volcanologist, he said it was too bad I hadn't been born the second son so I could do exactly what I wanted.

"When I asked him what he wanted, he said it might be fun to be king and bring our country into the age of enlightenment. Then he laughed, but I knew he wasn't kidding."

"Oh, Val…"

"Interesting, isn't it? At times, Michelina made the odd remark that he should have been born first. She and I were close and she worried for me always having to do my duty. I worried about her, too. She was too much under the thumb of our parents who wanted her marriage to Vincenzo no matter what."

"If people could hear you talk, they'd never want to trade places with you." She had a tragic look on her beautiful face. "As for your poor mother…"

"She's had to endure a lot of sorrow and disappointment and I'm sorry for that. Naturally I love her very much, but she doesn't rule my life even if she is the queen. I'm not a martyr, Carolena. It turns out Vito isn't, either. To have to marry another royal is archaic to both of us, but in his case he happened to fall in love with one."

"Your mother will think you've both lost your minds."

"At first, maybe. But just because she was pressured into marriage with my father doesn't mean Vito or I have to follow suit. The times have changed and she's being forced to accept the modern age whether she likes it or not. Michelina went through a surrogate to have a baby with Vincenzo. That prepared the ground and has made her less rigid because she loves her grandson."

"But you're her firstborn. She's pinned her hopes on you."

"Haven't I gotten through to you yet? Her hopes aren't mine. When I decided to get my geology degree, she knew I was going to go my own way even if I ended up ruling. After she finds out that Vito wanted to be betrothed to Alexandra years ago instead of me, she's going to see that you can't orchestrate your children's lives without serious repercussions."

"I'm too bewildered by all this. I—I don't know what to say."

"I want you for my wife. All you have to say is yes."

She sank back down in her chair. "No, that isn't all."

"Then talk to me. We've got the whole night. Ask me anything you want."

"Val—it isn't that simple."

"Why not?"

"I—I don't know if I want to be married."

"Because there are no guarantees? We've already had this conversation."

"But that was when we were talking hypothetically."

"Whereas now this is for real?"

She lowered her head. "Yes. For one thing, I don't think I'd make a good wife."

"I've never been a husband. We'll learn together."

"Where would we live?"

"Shall we buy your family's farm and live there?"

Carolena's head flew back. "I would never expect you to move to a different country and do that—your work for the institute is far too important!"

Valentino was trying to read between the lines, but she made it difficult. "I can tell the thought of living at the palace holds little appeal. We'll get our own place."

Her body moved restlessly. "You'd hate it. After a while you'd want to move back."

"There's nothing I'd love more after a hard day's work than to come home to my own house and my own bride. Would you like us to buy a farm here? Or would you prefer working for a law firm in Gemelli?"

She looked tortured. "I don't know." She got up from the chair again. "I can't answer those questions. You haven't even talked to your mother yet. It would be pointless to discuss all this when she doesn't know anything that's gone on with you."

"When we get back to the palace day after tomorrow, we'll go to her and tell her our plans."

"But we don't have any plans!"

He got to his feet. "We love each other and don't want to be separated. That forms the foundation of our plans. Come to bed with me and we'll work out the logistics of when and where we want to be married, how many children we want to have. Do we want a dog?"

"I'm not going to sleep with you."

"Yes, you are. There's only one bed on the cruiser, but if you ask me not to make love to you, I won't."

After a minute, she said, "You go on ahead. I'll be there once I've cleaned up the kitchen."

"I'll help. This will get me into practice for when we're married."

They made short work of it.

"I'll just get ready for bed," Carolena said.

"You do that while I turn out the lights."

She hurried out of the galley. He could tell she was frightened. Valentino was, too, but his fears were different. If he couldn't get her to marry him, then his life really wouldn't have any meaning.

Once he'd locked the door at the bottom of the stairs, he made a trip to the bathroom to brush his teeth. The cabin was cloaked in darkness when he joined her in bed still wearing his robe. She'd turned on her side away from his part of the bed. He got in and stretched out on his back.

"Val?"

"Yes?"

"Berto and I never spent a night together alone."

His thoughts reeled. "Not even after you were engaged?"

"No. Our families were old-fashioned."

He sat up in bed. "Are you telling me you two never made love?"

"It was because we didn't want to lie to the priest who'd asked us to wait."

"So you've never been intimate with a man."

"No. After he was killed, I kept asking myself what we'd been waiting for. I know now that a lot of my grief had to do with my sense of feeling cheated. I was so sure another man would never come along and I'd never know fulfillment. It made me angry. I was angry for a long time."

He squeezed her shoulder. "Carolena…"

"Once I started dating, I went through guy after guy the way the tabloids say you've gone through women. But after knowing you for the last week, it all had to have been made up because you don't have that kind of time."

A smile broke the corners of his mouth.

"The fact is, I don't have your experience, but that part doesn't bother me. I just wanted you to know the truth about me. I have no idea if I'd be a satisfying lover or not."

She was so sweet, it touched his heart. "That could work both ways."

"No, it couldn't. When you were kissing me out in the lagoon, I thought I might die on the spot from too much ecstasy." That made two of them. "I'm frightened by your power over me."

His brows knit together. "Why frightened?"

"Because I'm afraid it's all going to be taken away from me."

She'd had too many losses.

"Don't you know I have the same fear? I lost hope

of ever finding a woman I could love body and soul.
Yet the moment I was resigned to my fate, I discovered
this exquisite creature standing on the diving board of
my swimming pool. You've changed my life, Carolena
Baretti."

He rolled her into his arms and held her against his
body. "I want to be your husband."

She sobbed quietly against his shoulder. "I need more
time before I can tell you yes or no. I have too many issues welling up inside of me.

"When I get back to Arancia, I'm going to make an
appointment with a professional. I hope someone can
help me sort all this out. I should have gone to counseling after Berto died, but I was too wild with pain to
even think about it. Instead, I started law school and
poured all my energy into my studies."

"How did you end up becoming an attorney?"

"My grandmother insisted I go to college. She said
I needed to do something else besides farming in case
I had to take care of myself one day. For an old-fash-
ioned woman, she was actually very forward thinking.

"While I was at school studying business, we met
with some professors for career day. One of them encouraged me to try for the law entrance exam. I thought
why not. When I succeeded in making a high score, the
rest was history. Eventually I met Abby and for some
reason we just clicked. The poor thing had to listen
while I poured out my heart about Berto, but school
did help me."

He had to clear the lump in his throat. "Work's a
great panacea."

"Yes, but in my case it made me put off dealing with the things that were really wrong with me. Meeting you has brought it all to the surface. I don't want to burden you with my problems, Val. I can't be with you right now. You have to understand that if I can't come to you having worked things out, then it's no good talking about marriage. Please tell me you understand that."

She was breaking his heart. Abby had told him she'd been in a depression for a long time. Carolena reminded him of Matteo, who had certain issues that wouldn't allow him to marry yet.

He clutched her tighter, terrified he was going to lose her. "I do," he whispered into her hair. *I do.* "Go to sleep now and don't worry about anything."

"Please don't say anything to your mother about me. Please," she begged.

"I promise I won't."

"You always keep your promises. I love you, Val. You have no idea how much. But I can't promise you how long it's going to take me before I can give you an answer."

CHAPTER EIGHT

FOUR DAYS LATER the receptionist at the hospital showed Carolena into the doctor's office in Arancia for her appointment.

"*Buongiorno,* Signorina Baretti." The silver-haired psychologist got to his feet and shook her hand before asking her to sit down.

"Thank you for letting me in to see you on such short notice, Dr. Greco. Abby has spoken so highly of you, I was hoping you could fit me in."

"I'm happy to do it. Why don't you tell me what's on your mind."

"I should have come to someone like you years ago."

"Let's not worry about that. You're here now. Give me a little background."

He made a few notes as she started to speak. Pretty soon it all came gushing out and tears rolled down her cheeks. "I'm sorry."

"It's all right. Take your time."

He handed her some tissues, which she used. Finally she got hold of herself. "I don't know what more to tell you."

"I don't need to hear any more. What I've gleaned from everything you've told me is that you have two problems. The biggest one is an overriding expectation of the prince. Because he isn't meeting that expectation, it's preventing you from taking the next step in your life with him."

"Expectation?" That surprised her. She thought she was going to hear that she was losing her mind.

"I find you've dealt amazingly well with everything that's gone on in your past life. But you've got a big problem to overcome, and unless you face it head-on, you'll remain conflicted and depressed."

It was hard to swallow. "What is it?"

"You've just found out the prince wants to marry you. But it means that for your sake he plans to give up his right to sit on the throne one day as king and you don't like that because you've never imagined he could do such a thing. It hasn't been your perception. To some degree it has shocked and maybe even disappointed you, like glitter that comes off a shiny pair of shoes."

Whoa.

"When you were telling me about all the farmers you met who held him in such high esteem, your eyes shone with a bright light. I watched your eyes light up again when you told me how he's preparing the country in case of an eruption on Mount Etna. Your admiration for him has taken a hit to learn he's willing to be an ordinary man in order to be your husband."

"But his whole life has been a preparation for being king."

"Let me put this another way. Think of a knight

going into battle. In his armor astride his horse, he looks splendid and triumphant. But when he takes it off, you see a mere man.

"Your prince is a man first. What you need to do is focus on that."

She kneaded her hands. "Valentino's always telling me to forget he's a prince."

"That's right. The man has to be true to himself. If he had nothing to bring you but himself, would you take him?"

"Yes—" she cried. "He's so wonderful you can't imagine. But what if he marries me and then wishes he hadn't and wants to be king?"

"How old did you say he was?"

"Thirty-two."

"And he called off his wedding to a princess he doesn't love?"

"Yes."

"Then I'd say the man is more than old enough to know his own mind."

"It's just that he already makes a marvelous ruler."

"I thought you said his mother is the ruler."

"Well, she is."

"And he's not the king, so what you're telling me is that he's still marvelous just being a man, right?"

His logic was beginning to make all kinds of sense. "Yes."

"Your other problem is guilt that could be solved by a simple conversation with the queen."

Carolena gulped. "I don't think I could."

"You're going to have to because you're afraid she'll

never forgive you if you marry her son, thus depriving him of his birthright."

Dr. Greco figured all that out in one session? "What if she won't?"

"She might not, but you're not marrying her, and the prince isn't letting her feelings stand in the way of what he wants. It would be nice to have her approval, of course, but not necessary. There's no harm in approaching her and baring your soul to her. She'll either say yes or no, but by confronting her, you'll get rid of that guilt weighing you down."

Valentino had promised he wouldn't talk to his mother about her yet...

"My advice to you is to go home and let this percolate. When you've worked it all out, let me know."

It was scary how fast he'd untangled her fears so she could understand herself. The doctor was brilliant. She jumped to her feet, knowing what she had to do. "I will, Doctor. Thank you. Thank you so very much."

Valentino hunkered down next to Razzi. Both wore gas masks. "Those strombolian explosions are building in intensity."

"You're not kidding. Something big is going on."

He and Razzi had been camped up there for three days taking readings, getting any activity on film. His work kept him from losing his mind. He had no idea how long it would be before he heard from Carolena.

Valentino wasn't surprised to see that a new lava flow had started from the saddle area between the two Southeast Crater cones.

"Look, Razzi. More vents have opened up on the northeast side of the cone."

"There's the lava fountain. It's getting ready to blow."

He gazed in wonder as a tall ash plume shot skyward. Though it was morning, it felt like midnight. Suddenly there were powerful, continuous explosions. The loud detonations that had continued throughout the night and morning sent tremors through the earth.

"We're too close!" The ground was getting too unstable to stand up. "More lava fountains have started. This is it. Come on, Razzi. We need to move back to the other camp farther down."

They recognized the danger and worked as a team as they gathered their equipment and started their retreat. He'd witnessed nature at work many times, but never from this close a vantage point.

The continual shaking made it more difficult to move as fast as they needed to. Halfway to the other camp a deafening explosion reached his ears before he was thrust against the ground so hard the impact knocked off his gas mask.

Everything had gone dark. He struggled to find it and put it back on. In frustration he cried to Razzi, but the poisonous fumes filled his lungs. For the first time since coming up on Etna, Valentino had the presentiment that he might not make it off the volcano alive.

His last thought was for Carolena, whose fear of another loss might have come to pass.

Once Carolena had taken a taxi back to her condo, she made a reservation to fly to Gemelli later in the day.

This was one time she didn't want to burden Abby with her problems.

Officially, Carolena was still out of the office for another week, so she didn't need to make a stop there to talk to Signor Faustino. All she needed to do was pack another bag and take care of some bills before she called for a taxi to drive her to the airport.

The necessity of making all her own arrangements caused her to see how spoiled she'd become after having the royal jets at her disposal. It seemed strange to be taking a commercial jet and traveling in a taxi rather than a limo. Everything took longer. She was tired when she arrived in Gemelli at five-thirty that evening and checked herself into a hotel.

Because she hadn't seen or heard from Valentino for the past four days, she was practically jumping out of her skin with excitement at the thought of being with him again. Her first order of business was to phone the palace. She wanted to surprise him.

After introducing herself to the operator, she asked to speak to Valentino, but was told he was unavailable. The news crushed her. Attempting to recover, she asked if she could speak to Vito Cavelli. Through his brother she could learn Valentino's whereabouts, and possibly he would help her to meet with the queen.

Before long she heard a male voice come on the line. "Signorina Baretti? It's really you?"

"Yes, Your Highness."

"Please call me Vito. You're the famous video star."

"I don't know about famous."

"You are to me. Mother and I have seen the video. It's superb."

"Thank you. I was just going to say that if anyone is renowned, it's you for drawing all those interesting mustaches on the putti around the outside of the palace."

He broke into rich laughter that reminded her so much of Val, she joined in. "Are you calling from Arancia?"

She gripped her phone tighter. "No. I just flew in to Gemelli and am staying at the Regency Hotel."

"*Grazie a Dio* you're here," he said under his breath. His sudden change of mood alarmed her.

"What's wrong?"

"I was hoping you could tell me. Four days ago Valentino left for Catania, but I haven't talked to him since. I've left message after message."

That meant he was working on Etna.

"*Signorina?* Does my brother know you're here?"

"Not yet. I wanted to come to the palace and surprise him."

"Do you have his private cell phone number?"

"Yes. As soon as we hang up, I'll call him."

"Once you've reached him, will you ask him to return my call? I have something important to tell him."

Her brows furrowed. It wasn't like Valentino to remain out of reach. He was too responsible a person to do that. "Vito?"

"*Sì?*"

"There's a favor I'd like to ask of you."

"Name it."

"Would it be possible for me to talk to your mother

either tonight or in the morning? It's of extreme importance to me."

"I'm afraid she's not in the country, but she should be back tomorrow afternoon and then we'll arrange for you to meet with her."

More disappointment. "Thank you. Is she by any chance in Arancia?" Maybe she was visiting Vincenzo and Abby. Carolena should have called her friend, after all.

"No. She flew to Cyprus and left me in charge. I guess Valentino told you about me and Alexandra. The families are together now, discussing our plans to marry. We're thinking in four weeks."

It really was going to happen. "I'm very happy for you, Vito. I mean that sincerely."

"Thank you. I wish I could say the same for my brother."

"What do you mean?"

"It's my impression you're the only person who knows what's going on with him. He's not answering anyone's calls. This is a first for him. Our mother is worried sick about him."

Her eyes closed tightly. Carolena was the one responsible for him shutting down. She took a fortifying breath. "Now that I'm back, I'll try to reach him. Once I've contacted him, I'll tell him to get in touch with you immediately."

"I'd appreciate that. Good luck."

Fear clutched at her heart. Vito knew his brother better than anyone. To wish her luck meant she was going to need it. What if Valentino couldn't call anyone? What if he was in trouble? Her body broke out in a cold sweat.

"Good night, Vito."

"Buona notte, signorina."

As soon as she hung up, she phoned Valentino's number. Forget surprising him, all she got was to leave a message. In a shaky voice she told him she was back in Gemelli, that she loved him and that she was dying to see him. Please call her back.

Crushed because she couldn't talk to him, she got information for Tancredi's Restaurant so she could talk to Matteo. Maybe he'd spoken with Valentino. To her chagrin she learned it was his night off. If she'd like to leave a message… Carolena said no and hung up. The only thing to do was go looking for Valentino.

Again she rang for information and called the airport to schedule a commuter flight for seven in the morning to Catania airport. From there she'd take a taxi to the center where she'd been before. Someone would know how to reach Valentino if he still hadn't returned her call.

She went to bed and set her alarm, but she slept poorly. Valentino still hadn't called her back. At five in the morning she awakened and dressed in jeans and a T-shirt. After putting on her boots, she fastened her hair back in a chignon and left to get some food in the restaurant. Before taking a taxi to the airport, she knew she'd better eat first.

Everywhere she went was crowded with tourists. The commuter flight was packed and she had a long wait at the Catania airport before she could get a taxi to drive her to the institute.

Once she arrived, she hurried inside and approached the mid-twenties-looking man at the reception desk.

He eyed her with male appreciation. "May I help you, *signorina?*"

"I need to get in touch with Valentino Cellini."

The man smiled. "And you are…?"

"Carolena Baretti. I'm an attorney from Arancia who's been working with His Highness on a special project. I have to see him right away."

"I'm afraid that's not possible."

She refused to be put off. "Why not?"

"He's out in the field."

"Then can you get a message to him?"

"You can leave one here. When it's possible for him, he'll retrieve it."

This was getting her nowhere. "Would it be possible to speak to one of the pilots for the center? His name is Dante Serrano. He was the one who recently flew me up on Etna with the prince."

The fact she knew that much seemed to capture his attention. "I'll see if I can locate him." He made a call. After a minute he hung up. "Signor Serrano will be coming on duty within a few minutes."

"In that case, I'll wait for him in the lounge. Will you page me when he gets here?"

"Of course."

"Thank you."

Carolena hadn't been seated long when the attractive pilot walked over to her. She jumped up to greet him, but his expression was so solemn she knew something was wrong.

"Good morning, Dante. I was hoping to talk to you. I haven't been able to reach Valentino."

"No one's been able to reach him or his partner, Razzi. They were camped near a new eruption. The base camp received word that they were on their way back to it, but they lost contact."

"You mean th—"

"I mean, no one has been able to reach them yet."

"Then it must be bad," she cried in agony and grabbed his arms. "I can't lose him, Dante. I can't!"

"Let's not talk about that right now," he tried to placate her. "Half a dozen choppers have already taken off to search for them. This is my day off, but I was called in to help. Valentino's the best of the best, you know."

"I *do* know!" Carolena cried. "My life won't be worth living without him! I'm going with you!"

"No, no. It's too dangerous."

"I *have* to go with you. It's a matter of life and death to me. I love him. We're going to be married."

His eyes rounded before he exhaled a labored breath. "All right. You can come, but you'll do everything I say."

"I promise."

She followed him through the center and out the rear doors to the helipad. They ran to the helicopter. Once she'd climbed inside and strapped herself in the back, he found a gas mask for her. "When I tell you to do it, I want you to put this on."

"I will."

Another pilot joined them. Dante made a quick introduction, then started the engine. The rotors whined. Within seconds they lifted off.

At first, the smoking top of Etna didn't look any different to her. But before long the air was filled with ash. Afraid to disturb Dante's concentration, she didn't dare ask him questions. After ten minutes, the sky grew darker.

As the helicopter dipped, she saw the giant spectacular ash plume coming from a crater filling up with lava. She gasped in terror to think Valentino was down there somewhere.

"Put on your gas mask, *signorina*. We're going to land at the base camp."

She was all thumbs, but finally managed to do it after following his instructions. When they touched ground, Carolena thought there might be thirty geologists in the area wearing gas masks, but visibility was difficult.

"I want you to stay in the chopper until I tell you otherwise." By now he and the copilot had put on their masks.

"I will, but please find him."

"Say a prayer," he murmured. She bowed her head and did exactly that. To lose him now would kill her.

The two men disappeared. In a minute she heard the whine of rotors from another chopper. It set down farther away. People ran to it. She watched in agony as she saw a body being unloaded from it. Valentino's?

Forgetting Dante's advice, she climbed out of the chopper and started running. The victim was being transported on a stretcher to one of several tents that had been set up. She followed and worked her way inside the entrance, but there were too many people around to see anything.

The copilot who'd been on the chopper stood nearby. She grabbed at his arm.

He looked at her. "You weren't supposed to leave the chopper."

"I don't care. Is it Valentino?"

"I don't know yet, but I'll find out."

She held her breath until he came back. "It's Valentino's partner, Razzi."

"Is he…"

"Alive," he answered. "Just dazed from a fall."

"Where's Valentino?"

"The other chopper is bringing him in."

"So they found him!"

"Yes."

Her heart started to beat again. "Thank you for telling me that much." She hurried outside, praying for the other chopper to come.

The next minute felt like an eternity until she heard the sound of another helicopter coming in to land. She hurried over to the area, getting as close as she was allowed until it touched ground.

Carolena watched the door open, but there was no sign of Valentino. She was close to fainting, when Dante pulled her aside. Through his mask he said, "Valentino's head struck some volcanic rock. When they transported him out, he was unconscious but alive."

"Thank heaven." She sobbed quietly against him as they walked toward Dante's chopper.

"You can say that again. He's already been flown to the hospital. I'll fly you there now. Before long you'll be able to visit him."

"Thank you for bringing me up here. I'm indebted to you."

"He's lucky you love him enough to face danger yourself. Not every woman or man has that kind of courage."

She didn't know she had any until she'd been put to the test. It was only because of Valentino. He was her life!

"Razzi said they were eyewitnesses to an explosion that could have gotten them killed. I've heard that the footage they captured on film is the best that's ever been recorded at the institute. The guys are heroes."

They were. "So are you, Dante."

"Yeah?" He smiled.

"Yeah."

Carolena's thoughts drifted back to her conversation with Dr. Greco. He'd said it best. *And he's not the king, so what you're telling me is that he's still marvelous just being a man, right?*

"Your Highness?"

Valentino was lying in bed with his head raised watching television when a nurse came in. He'd been told he had a concussion and would have to stay in the hospital overnight for observation. Much as he wanted to get out of there, every time he tried to sit up, his head swam.

"Yes?"

"Do you feel up to a visitor?"

There was only one person he wanted to see. If she ever came to a decision and it was the wrong one, he wished his body had been left on the side of the volcano.

"Who is it?"

"This person wanted it to be a surprise."

It was probably Vito, who would have been contacted hours ago. He'd want to see Valentino for himself before he told their mother her firstborn was alive and well. But in case it wasn't his brother, Valentino's mind ran through a possible list of friends and colleagues. If it were Vincenzo, he would have just walked in.

"Shall I tell this person you're still indisposed?"

While he was trying to make up his mind, he heard a noise in the doorway and looked up to see Carolena come rushing in the room. "Val, darling—" she blurted in tears and flew toward him.

At the sight of her in a T-shirt and jeans she filled out to perfection, an attack of adrenaline had him trying to get out of bed. But she reached him before he could untangle his legs from the sheet and try to sit up. She pressed against him, wetting his hideous hospital gown with her tears.

"Thank heaven you're alive! If I'd lost you, I would have wanted to die."

He wrapped his arms around her, pulling her up on the bed halfway on top of him. "I'm tougher than that. How did you know I was in here?"

Moisture spilled from her fabulous green eyes. "I flew down to Gemelli last evening. When you didn't answer my call and Vito couldn't get through to you, either. I flew to Catania this morning and took a taxi to the institute."

Valentino was in shock. "You were there this morning?"

"Yes! I had to see you, but then Dante told me you were up on the volcano and there'd been no contact from you since the latest eruption, so I flew up there with him to the base camp."

His blood ran cold. "He took you up there?"

"He wouldn't have, but when I told him you and I were getting married and I couldn't live without you, he took pity on me and let me go with him to look for you."

It was too much to digest. His heart started to act up. "You're going to marry me?"

"As soon as we can." She lifted her hand to tenderly touch his head. "You're my man and I want everyone to know it." In the next breath she covered his mouth with her own. The energy she put into her kiss was a revelation.

"Adorata—" He could believe he'd died on Etna and had just awakened in heaven.

She pressed him back against the pillow and sobbed quietly until the tears subsided. His Carolena was back where she belonged.

"Did you know your mother is in Cyprus seeing about the plans for Vito's wedding to Alexandra? While they have their big day after all they've been through, wouldn't it be thrilling if we had our own private wedding with Vincenzo and Abby for witnesses as soon as possible? I'd love it if we could say our vows in the chapel at the palace.

"And while we're gone on a honeymoon, Vincenzo and Abby could stay at the palace with your mother so she could spend time with Michelina's little boy. I want everyone to be happy. The two of us most of all. What do you think?"

Tears smarted his eyes. She really understood what Valentino was all about. He shaped her face with his hands. "First, I think I want to know what has caused this dramatic change in you."

"A very wise doctor helped me get to the core of what was ailing me. He said I had a fixation on your royal person, which was true. He told me I was disappointed you were willing to forgo being king in order to marry me.

"But my disappointment really covered my guilt over your decision and it made me afraid. Then he asked me if I couldn't love the ordinary man instead of the prince. He said something about looking at you without your crown and battle armor. That question straightened me out in a big hurry and I couldn't get back down here fast enough to tell you."

"Battle armor?" Would wonders never cease? He kissed her lips once more. "Remind me to send the doctor a big bonus check for services rendered."

"I already wrote him one." She ran kisses along his jawline. "You've got a beard, but I like to see you scruffy."

"Maybe I'll let it grow out."

"Whatever you want. Oh—there's just one more thing. The doctor says my guilt will be cured after I've talked to your mother. Even though she'll never forgive me for ruining her dreams for you, I have to confront her."

"We'll do it together tonight."

"But you'll still be in here. The doctor won't release you until tomorrow. We'll talk to her then."

"In that case, come closer and give me your mouth again."

She looked toward the door. "Isn't this illegal? What if someone catches us?"

"Do we care? This is my private room."

"Darling," she whispered, hugging him to her. He was all she ever wanted. "What happened on the volcano? I have to know."

He let out a sigh and rehearsed what went on after the first lava fountain appeared. "When I saw that plume shoot into the atmosphere, I knew we needed to run for our lives."

She gripped him harder. "Were you terrified?"

"Not then. The sight was glorious."

"I saw it from a distance. I don't think there's anything in nature to compare to it."

"There isn't." He rubbed his hands over her back. "Do you remember when you were up there with me the first time and the ground shook?"

Carolena shivered. "I'll never forget."

"Well, try to imagine it so strong, neither Razzi nor I could stand up. That's when it started getting exciting. But the moment came when the force threw me forward. I hit the ground and lost hold of the things I was carrying. Then my gas mask came off."

"Val—"

"That's when I got scared because I couldn't find it in the darkness."

At this point she wrapped her arms around his neck and wept against his chest. "Dante says you're a hero for getting close enough to record the data. I adore you."

His breath caught. "You mean, you're not going to tell me I have to give up my profession?"

She lifted her head. "Are you kidding? Nothing could be more exciting than what you do. I plan to go up with you a lot. When we have children, you can introduce them to the mountain. We'll get the whole family in on the act."

A week later, Carolena sat in front of the same mirror in the same cabin on the yacht brushing her hair. She'd just showered and put on the white toweling robe hanging on the hook in the bathroom.

But there were differences from the first time she'd come down to this room. The first time she'd been on board, the yacht was stationary. Now it was moving. But the gentle waters of the Ionian carried it along like so much fluff. Their destination was the Adriatic. Valentino had mentioned Montenegro as one of their stops. To Carolena, it was all like part of a dream.

Only two hours ago the priest had performed the marriage ceremony in the chapel in front of loved ones and Valentino's best friend, Matteo. On her ring finger flashed an emerald set in white gold. She was now Signora Valentino Agostino Cellini, and she was nervous.

How strange for her to have been so fearless before marriage when she'd thought they were going to make love the first time. Now she really was a bride and her heart thudded with sickening intensity at the thought of it.

A rap on the door caused her to get up jerkily from the dressing table chair. When she turned, she saw that Valentino had slipped into the room wearing a navy robe. He moved toward her, so sinfully handsome her mouth went dry.

"I can tell something's wrong, *bellissima*. I know you missed your parents and grandparents at our wedding. I'd like to think they were looking on and happy. Let me be your family from now on."

It was a touching thing for him to say. She sucked in her breath. "You are. You're my whole life."

His eyes caressed her. "I thought you'd enjoy re-creating our first night on board, but maybe you would have preferred someplace else."

"Never. This is the perfect place."

"As long as you mean it."

"Of course I do."

She didn't know what his intentions were until he picked her up in his arms. "Then welcome to my life, *sposa mia*."

He lowered his mouth to hers and drank deeply as he carried her through the hall to the master suite. After he followed her down on the bed, he rolled her on top of him. "Never was there a more beautiful bride. I realize we've only known each other a short time, yet it seems like I've been waiting for you a lifetime. Love me, Carolena. I need you," he cried with such yearning, she was shaken by a vulnerability he rarely showed.

No longer nervous, her instincts took over and she began loving him. The rapture he created took her to a place she'd never been before. Throughout the night they gave each other pleasure she didn't know was possible.

"Don't ever stop loving me," she begged when morning came around. If they slept at all, she didn't remember. "I didn't know it could be like this, that I could feel like this." She laid against him, studying the curve of his mouth, the lines of his strong features. "I love you, Val. I love you till it hurts. But it's a wonderful kind of hurt."

"I know." He ran his hands through her hair. "Pleasure-pain is ecstasy. We have the rest of our lives to indulge in it to our heart's content." He gave her an almost savage kiss. "To think what we might have missed—"

"I don't want to think about it. Not ever. You set me on fire the first time you looked at me. Not everyone loves the way we do. It's overpowering."

"That's the way it should be when it's right."

She kissed his jaw. "Do you know who looked happy last night?"

"My mother."

Carolena raised up on her elbow. "You saw it, too?"

"She'd never admit it, but deep down she's glad her sons have found true love, something that was denied her."

Her eyes teared up. "After meeting you, I knew she'd always been a great mother, but the accepting way she has handled our news has made me admire her more than you could ever know. I'm growing to love her, Val.

I want to get close to her. She's missing her daughter and I'm missing my grandmother."

He hugged her tighter. "Do you have any idea how much it means for me to hear you say that?"

"It's so wonderful belonging to a family again. To belong to you."

"*You're* so wonderful I can't keep the secret Vincenzo wanted to tell you himself. When he springs it on you, promise me you'll pretend you knew nothing about it."

"They're going to have a baby."

His dark blue eyes danced. "If they are, I don't know about it yet. This particular secret concerns you."

"What do you mean?"

"Instead of handing you a check for invaluable services rendered to both our countries, he approached the latest owner of your grandparents' farm. After some investigation, he learned they're willing to sell it to you, but there's no hurry."

"*Val*— Are you serious?"

He rolled her over on her back and smiled down at her. "I thought that would make you happy. We'll use it as our second home when we fly to Arancia for visits."

"Our children will play in the lemon grove with Abby and Vincenzo's children."

"Yes. And when we get back from our honeymoon, we'll decide where we want to live."

She cradled his handsome face in her hands, loving him to distraction. "It's already been decided by Vito, but it's his secret. You have to promise not to tell him I told you."

His brows quirked. "My brother?"

"Yes. He said he's willing to be king so long as you're close by to help him. To quote him, 'The two Vs stick together.' He's already started a renovation of the unoccupied north wing of the palace where he says you two used to play pirates.

"I found out it has a lookout where you can see Etna clearly. It's the perfect spot for all your scientific equipment. He said the wing will be permanently closed off from the rest of the palace so it will be our own house with our own private entrance."

Her husband looked stunned. "You're okay with that?"

"I love the idea of being close to family. Think how much fun it would be for his children and ours, and they'll have a grandmother close by who will dote on them."

The most beautiful smile imaginable broke out on his face. "Are you trying to tell me you want a baby?"

"Don't you? After last night, maybe we're already pregnant."

"To make certain, I think we'll stay on a permanent honeymoon."

She kissed him until they were breathless. "You were right about the fire, darling. It keeps burning hotter and hotter. Love me again and never stop."

"As if I could…"

* * * * *

TO DANCE
WITH A PRINCE

CARA COLTER

To Rose and Bill Pastorek
with heartfelt thanks for creating such
an incredible garden, a 'mini-vacation'
for everyone who experiences it.

Cara Colter shares her life in beautiful British Columbia, Canada, with her husband, nine horses and one small Pomeranian with a large attitude. She loves to hear from readers, and you can learn more about her and contact her through Facebook.

CHAPTER ONE

THE HOWL OF PURE PAIN sent icicles down Prince Kiernan of Chatam's spine. He shot through the door of the palace infirmary, and came to a halt when he saw his cousin, Prince Adrian, lying on a cot, holding his knee and squirming in obvious agony.

"I told you that horse was too much for you!" Kiernan growled.

"Nice to see you, too," Adrian gasped. "Naturally, the moment you told me the horse was too much for me, my fate was sealed."

Kiernan shook his head, knowing it was all too true. His cousin, seven years his junior, was twenty-one, reckless, but usually easily able to deflect the consequences of his recklessness with his abundance of charm.

A fact Adrian proved by smiling bravely at a young nurse. Satisfied that the girl was close to swooning, he turned his attention back to Kiernan.

"Look, if you could spare me the lecture," Adrian said, "I am in desperate need of a favor. I'm supposed to be somewhere."

First of all, his cousin was never desperate. Secondly, Adrian rarely worried about where he was supposed to be.

"DH—that's short for Dragon-heart—is going to kill

me if I'm not there. Honestly, Kiernan, I've met the most fearsome woman who ever walked."

And thirdly, as far as Kiernan knew his cousin had never met a woman, fearsome or not, he could not slay with his devil-may-care grin.

"Do you think you could stand in for me?" Adrian pleaded. "Just this once?" The nurse probed his alarmingly swollen knee, and Adrian howled again.

What Kiernan was having trouble fathoming was how Adrian, who would be the first to admit he was entirely self-focused, was managing to think about *anything* at this particular moment besides his injury.

"Just cancel," Kiernan suggested.

"She'll think I did it on purpose," Adrian said through clenched teeth.

"Nobody would think you had an accident on purpose to inconvenience them."

"*She* would. DH, aka Meredith Whitmore. She snorts fire." An almost dreamy look pierced Adrian's pain. "Though her breath is actually more like mint."

Kiernan was beginning to wonder what his cousin had been given for pain.

"The fact is," Adrian said sadly, " DH eats adorable little princes like me for her lunch. Barbecued. She must have the mint after."

"What on earth are you talking about?"

"You remember Sergeant Major Henderson?"

"Hard to forget," Kiernan said dryly of the man in charge of taking youthful princes and turning them into disciplined, rock-hard warriors, capable of taking commands as well as giving them.

"Meredith Whitmore is him. The Sergeant Major. Times ten," Adrian said, and then whimpered when his knee was probed again.

"You're exaggerating. You must be."

"Would you just stand in for me? Please?"

"What would make me agree to stand in for you with a woman who likes her princes barbecued and who makes Sergeant Major Henderson look like a Girl Scout leader? I don't even know what I'm standing in *for*."

"It was a mistake," Adrian admitted sadly. "I thought it was going to be a lark. It sounded like so much more fun than some of the other official *lesser prince* options for Chatam Blossom Week."

Blossom Week was the Isle of Chatam's annual celebration of spring. Dating back to medieval times, it was a week-long festival that started with a fund-raising gala and ended with a royal ball. Opening night was a little over a week away.

Adrian continued, "I could have given out awards to the preschool percussion band, given the Blossom Week rah-rah speech *or* done a little dance. Which would you have picked?"

"Probably the speech," Kiernan said. "Have you given him something?"

"Not yet," the nurse said pleasantly, "but I'm about to."

"Lucky you," Adrian said, batting his eyes at her, "because I have the cutest little royal backside—ouch! Was that unnecessarily rough?"

"Don't be a baby, Your Highness."

Adrian watched her walk away. "Anyway, I said I'd learn a dance. I was going to perform with an up-and-coming troupe at the fund-raising evening. It's a talent show this year. My suggestion to call the fund-raiser *Raise a Little Hell* was vetoed. Naturally. It's going to be called *An Evening to Remember*, which I think is *totally* forgettable."

"I'm not taking your place for a dance number! We both know I can't dance. Prince of Heartaches causes Foot Aches, Too." It was a direct quote from a newspaper headline, with a very unflattering picture of Kiernan crushing some poor girl's foot at her debutante ball.

"Ah, the press is hard on you, Kiernan. They never nickname me. But in the past ten years you've been the Playboy Prince—"

That had been when Kiernan was eighteen, fresh out of an all-boys private school, one summer of freedom before his military training. He had been, unfortunately, like a kid let out in a candy shop!

"Then, the Prince of Heartaches."

At the age of twenty-three, Prince Kiernan had become engaged to one of his oldest and dearest friends, Francine Lacourte. Not even Adrian knew the full truth behind their split and her total disappearance from public life. But, given a history that the press was eager not to let him shake, it was assumed Prince Kiernan was to blame.

"Now," Adrian continued, "since Tiff, you've graduated to Prince Heartbreaker. Tut-tut. It would all lead one to believe you are so much more exciting than you are."

Kiernan scowled warningly at his cousin.

"Don't give me that look," Adrian said, whatever the nurse had given him relaxing the grimace on his face to a decidedly goofy grin. "Your tiff with Tiff."

While the press *loved* the high-spirited high jinks of Adrian, Kiernan was seen as too stern, and too serious. Particularly since two broken engagements to two very popular women he was seen as coldly remote.

He knew the title Prince Heartbreaker was probably going to be his mantle to bear forever, even if he lived out the rest of his days as a monk, which, after what he'd been through, didn't seem entirely unappealing!

After all, the future of his island nation rested solidly and solely on Kiernan's shoulders, as he was the immediate successor to his mother, Queen Aleda's, throne. That kind of responsibility was enough for one man to bear without throwing in the caprice of romance.

Adrian was fourth in line, a position he found deliciously relaxing.

"You should have thrown that Tiffany Wells under a bus," Adrian said with a sigh. "She deserved it. Imagine tricking you into thinking she was pregnant. And then do you let the world know the true reason for the broken engagement? Oh, no, a man of honor—"

"We're not talking about this," Kiernan said fiercely. Then, hoping to get back on one topic and off the other, "Look, Adrian, about the dancing thing, I don't see how I could help—"

"I don't ask much of you, Kiern."

That was true. The whole world came to Kiernan, asking, begging, requesting, pleading causes. Adrian never did.

"Do this, okay?" Adrian said, his words beginning to slur around the edges. "It'll be good for you. Even if you make a fool of yourself, it'll make you seem human."

"I don't seem human?" He pretended to be affronted.

His cousin ignored him. "A little soft shoe, charm the crowd, get a little good press for a change. It bugs the hell out of me that you're constantly portrayed as a coldhearted snob."

"Coldhearted? A snob?" He pretended to be wounded.

Again, he was ignored. "That's if you can survive the fire-breather. Who, by the way, doesn't like tardiness.

And you..." his unfocused eyes shifted to the clock, and he squinted thoughtfully at it "...are twenty-two minutes late. She's waiting in the Ballroom."

The smart thing to do, Kiernan knew, as he left his cousin, would be to send someone to tell the fire-breather Adrian was hurt.

But the truth was he had yet to see a woman who had managed to intimidate Adrian. Because if Kiernan was legendary for his remoteness, his cousin was just as legendary for his charm.

The press loved Prince Adrian. He played Prince Charming to his darker cousin's Prince Heartbreaker. And, oh, how women loved Prince Adrian.

Kiernan just had to see the one who did not.

Kiernan decided to go have a look at Adrian's nemesis before giving Adrian's excuses and dismissing her. In his most warmhearted and non-snobby fashion.

Meredith glared at the clock.

"He's late," she muttered to herself. The truth? She couldn't believe it! It was the second time Prince Adrian had been tardy!

She'd been intimidated by the young prince and his status for all of about ten seconds at their first meeting at her upscale downtown Chatam dance and fitness studio.

And then she'd seen he was like a puppy—using the fact he was totally adorable to have his way! Including being late. Meredith was so beyond being charmed by a man, even one as cute as him.

So, she'd laid down the law with him. And she'd been certain he wouldn't dare be late again, especially since she had conceded to changing their meeting place to the Chatam Palace Great Ballroom as a convenience to him.

Which just showed how wrong she could be when it came to men, even while she thought she was totally immune to sexy good looks and impossible charm!

Meredith glanced around the grandeur of the room and tried not to be overly awed at finding herself here.

She breathed in the familiar scents of her childhood. Her mother, a single woman, had been a cleaning lady. Meredith recognized the aromas of freshly shined floors, furniture wax, glass cleaners, silver polish.

Her mother would have been as awed by this room as Meredith was. Her mother had dreamed such big dreams for her daughter.

Ballet will open doors to worlds we can hardly imagine, Merry.

Worlds just like this one, Meredith thought gazing around the room. Wouldn't her mother be thrilled to know she was here?

Because every door that ballet could have opened for Meredith—and her mother—had slammed shut when Meredith had found herself pregnant at sixteen.

Morning sunshine streamed in the twelve floor-to-ceiling arched windows that were so clean they looked like they contained no glass. The light glinted across the Italian marble of the floors, and sparked in the thousands of Swarovski crystals of the three huge chandeliers that dangled from the frescoed ceiling.

Meredith glanced again at the clock.

Prince Adrian was half an hour late. He wasn't coming. Meredith had had her doubts about this whole scheme, but been persuaded by the wild enthusiasm of the girls.

Crazy to let the teenage girls, the ones she mentored

and loved and taught to dance, younger versions of herself, believe in fairy-tale dreams.

She, of all people, should know better.

Still, looking around this room, something stirred in her. She was going to dance here, prince or no prince.

In fact, that would be very in keeping with the charity she had founded, that gave her reason to go on, when all of her life had crashed down around her.

Meredith taught upbeat modern dancing as part of the program No Princes, which targeted the needs of underprivileged inner city female adolescents.

"You don't need a prince to dance," Meredith said firmly. In fact, that would make a good motto for the group. Perhaps she should consider adding it to their letterhead.

She closed her eyes. In her imagination, she could hear music begin to play. She had broken with ballet years ago, not just because her scholarship had been canceled. When she finally returned to dance, the only place that could ease the hurt of a heart snapped in two, she had found she could not handle the rigidity of ballet. She needed a place where her emotion could come out.

But even so, Meredith found herself doing the famous entrée of Princess Aurora in the Petipa/Tchaikovsky ballet, *The Sleeping Beauty*.

But then, she let the music take her, and she seamlessly joined the *allegro* movements of ballet with the modern dance that had become her specialty. She melded different styles of dance together, creating something brand new, feeling herself being taken to the only place where she was not haunted by memories.

Meredith covered the floor on increasingly light feet,

twirling, twisting, leaping, part controlled, part wild, wholly uninhibited.

She became aware that dancing in this great room felt like a final gift to the mother she had managed to disappoint so terribly.

The music that played in her head stopped and she became still, but for a moment she did not open her eyes, just savored the feeling of having been with her mother for a moment, embraced by her, all that had gone sour between them made right.

And then Meredith could have sworn she heard a baby laugh.

She spun around just as the complete silence of the room was broken by a single pair of hands clapping.

"How dare you?" she said, feeling as if Prince Adrian had spied on her in a very private moment.

And then Meredith realized it was the wrong prince!

It was not Adrian, eager and clumsily enthusiastic, like a playful St. Bernard, but the man who would be king.

Prince Heartbreaker.

Prince Kiernan of Chatam had slipped inside the door, and stood with his back braced lazily against the richness of the walnut. The crinkle of amusement around the deep azure of his eyes disappeared at her reprimand.

"How dare I? Excuse me. I thought I was in my own home." He looked astonished, rather than annoyed, by her reprimand.

"I'm sorry, Your Highness," she stammered. "I was taken off guard. That dance was never intended for anyone to see."

"More's the pity," he said mildly.

Meredith saw, instantly, that the many pictures of him printed by papers and tabloids did not begin to do him justice. And she saw why he was called Prince Heartbreaker.

Such astonishing good looks should be illegal. Paired with his station in life, it seemed quite possible he could break hearts with a glance!

Prince Kiernan was more than gorgeous, he was stunning. Tall and exquisitely fit, his perfectly groomed hair was crisp and dark, his face chiseled masculine perfection, from the cut of high cheekbones to the jut of a perfectly clefted chin.

Though he was dressed casually—it looked like he had been riding, the tan-colored jodhpurs hugging the cut of the muscle of his thigh—nothing could hide the supreme confidence of his bearing.

He was a man who had been born to great wealth and privilege and it showed in every single thing about him. But an underlying strength—around the stern line of his mouth, the way he held his broad shoulders—also showed.

And Meredith Whitmore was, suddenly, not an accomplished dancer and a successful businesswoman, but the cleaning lady's daughter, who had been trained to be invisible in front of her "betters," who had stupidly thrown her life away on a dream that had ended more badly than she ever could have imagined.

She thought of the unleashed sensuousness of that dance, and felt a fire burn up her cheeks. She prayed—desperately—for the floor to open up and swallow her.

But she, of all people, should know by now that the desperation of a prayer in no way led to its answer.

"Your Royal Highness," she said, and all her grace fled her as she did a clumsy curtsy.

"You can't be Meredith Whitmore," the prince said, clearly astounded.

"I can't?"

Even his voice—cultured, deep, melodic, masculine—was unfairly attractive, as sensual as a touch.

It was no wonder she was questioning her own identity!

Meredith *begged* the confident, career-oriented woman she had become to push the embarrassed servant's daughter off center stage. She begged the vulnerability that the memory of Carly's laugh had brought to the surface to go away.

"Why can't I be Meredith Whitmore?" Despite her effort to speak with careless confidence, she thought she sounded like a rejected actress who had been refused a coveted role.

"From what Adrian said, I was expecting, um, a female version of Attila the Hun."

"Flattering."

A hint of a smile raced across the firm line of those stern lips and then was gone.

It was definitely a smile that could break hearts. Meredith reminded herself, firmly, she hadn't one to break!

"You did give me a hard time for standing inside my own door," he said thoughtfully. "Adrian said, er, that you were something of a taskmaster."

The hesitation said it all. Meredith guessed that Prince Adrian had not worded it that politely. The fact that the two princes had discussed her—in unflattering terms—made her wish for the floor to open up redouble.

"I was actually about to leave," she said with the

haughtiness of a woman who was not the least vulnerable to him, and whose time was extremely valuable—which it was! "He's very late."

"I'm afraid he's not coming. He sent me with the message."

Meredith felt a shiver of apprehension. "Is it just for today? That Prince Adrian isn't coming?"

But somehow she already knew the answer. And it was her fault. She had driven him too hard. She had overstepped herself. He didn't want to do it anymore. She had obviously been too bossy, too intense, too driven to perfection.

A female version of Attila the Hun.

"I'm sorry. He's been injured in an accident."

"Badly?" Meredith asked. The prince, puppylike in his eagerness to please, had been hurt, and all she was thinking about was that she was being inconvenienced by his tardiness?

"He's been in a riding accident. When I left him his knee was the approximate size and shape of a basketball."

Meredith marshaled herself, not wanting him to see her flinch from the blow to her plans, to her girls.

"Well, as terrible as that is," she said with all the composure she could muster, "the show must go on. I'm sure with a little resourcefulness we can rewrite the part. We aren't called No Princes for nothing."

"No Princes? Is that the name of your dance troupe, then?"

"It is actually more than a dance troupe."

"All right," he conceded. "I'm intrigued. Tell me more."

To her surprise, the prince looked authentically interested. Despite not wanting to be vulnerable to him in any way, Meredith took a deep breath, knowing she could not pass up this opportunity to tell someone so influential about her group.

"No Princes is an organization that targets girls from the tough neighborhoods of the inner city of Chatam. At fifteen and sixteen and seventeen a frightening number of these girls, still children really, are much too eager to leave school, and have babies, instead of getting their education."

Her story, *exactly*, but there was no reason to tell him that part.

"We try to give them a desire to learn, marketable skills, and a strong sense of self-reliance and self-sufficiency. We hope to influence them so they do not feel they need rescuing from their circumstances by the first boy they perceive as a prince!"

Michael Morgan had been that prince for her. He had been new to the neighborhood, drifted in from somewhere with a sexy Australian accent. She was fatherless, craving male attention, susceptible.

And thanks to him, she would never be that vulnerable again. Though the man who stood before her would certainly be a test of any woman's resolve to not believe in fairy tales.

"And where do you fit into that vision, my gypsy ballerina?"

So, the prince *had* seen something. *His* gypsy ballerina? Some terrible awareness of him tingled along her spine, but she kept her tone entirely professional when she answered him. She, of all people, knew that tingle to be a warning sign.

"I'm afraid all work and no play is a poor equation for anyone, never mind these girls. As well as looking after a lot of paperwork for No Princes, I get to do the *fun* part. I teach the girls how to dance."

"Prince Adrian didn't seem to think it was fun," he said dryly.

"I may have pushed him a little hard," she admitted.

Prince Kiernan actually laughed, and it changed everything. Did the papers deliberately capture him looking grim and humorless?

Because in that spontaneous shout of laughter Meredith had an unfortunate glimpse of the kind of man every woman hoped would ride in on his white charger to rescue her from her life.

Even a woman such as herself, soured on romance, could feel the pull of his smile. She steeled herself against that traitorous flutter in her breast and reminded herself a man did not get the name Prince Heartbreaker because he was in the market for a princess!

In fact, before he'd been called Prince Heartbreaker, hadn't he been called the Playboy Prince? And something else? Oh, yes, the Prince of Heartaches. He was a dangerous, dangerous man.

"Kudos to you if you *could* push him hard," Prince Kiernan said wryly. "How did Adrian come to be a part of all this?"

It was a relief to hide behind words! They provided the veneer of rational, civilized thought, when something rebellious in her was reacting to him in a very upsettingly primal way!

"One of our girls, Erin Fisher, wrote a dance number that really tells the whole story of what No Princes does. It's quite a remarkable piece. It takes girls from hanging out on street corners flirting with boys, going nowhere, to a place of remarkable strength and admirable ambition. The piece has a dream sequence in it that shows a girl dancing with a prince.

"Unbeknownst to any of us, Erin sent it to the palace, along with a video of the girls dancing, as a performance suggestion for *An Evening to Remember*, the fund-raiser that will open Blossom Week. She very boldly suggested Prince Adrian for the part in the dream sequence. The girls have been delirious since he accepted."

Meredith was shocked by the sudden emotion that clawed at her throat. She shouldn't have a favorite, but of all the girls, Erin was so much like her, so bright, so full of potential. And so sensitive. So easily hurt and discouraged.

"I'm sorry for their disappointment," Prince Kiernan said, making Meredith realize, uneasily, he was reading her own disappointment with way too much accuracy.

Prince Kiernan was larger than life. He was *better* than the pictures. His voice was as sexy as a piece of raw silk scraped along the nape of a neck. He was a *real* prince.

But still, she represented No Princes. She *taught* young women not to get swept away, not to believe in fairy tales. She rescued the vulnerable from throwing their lives away on fantasies, as she had, no matter how appealing the illusion.

The abundance of tabloid pictures of actress Tiffany Wells' tearstained face since her broken engagement with this man underscored Meredith's determination not to be vulnerable in any way, to any man, ever again.

Her days of vulnerability were over.

"A little disappointment does nothing but build character," she said crisply.

He regarded her thoughtfully. She thrust her chin up and folded her arms over her chest.

"Again, I'm sorry."

"It's quite all right," she said, forcing her voice to be firm. "Things happen that are out of our control."

She would have snatched those words back without speaking them if she knew that they would swing the door of memory wide open on the event in her life that had been most out of her control.

Meredith slammed the door shut again, blinking hard and swallowing.

The prince was looking at her way too closely, again, as if he could see things she would not have him see. That she would not have anyone see.

"Goodbye," Meredith managed to squeak out. "Thank you for coming personally, Your Highness. I'll let the girls know. We'll figure something out. It's not a big deal."

She was babbling, trying to outrun the quiver in her voice and failing. She kept talking.

"The girls will get over it. In fact, they're used to it. They're used to disappointment. As I said, we can rewrite the part Prince Adrian was going to play. Anybody can play a prince."

Though she might have believed that much more strongly before standing in the damnably charismatic presence of a real one!

"Goodbye," she said, more strongly, a hint for him to go. The quiver was out of her voice, but she had not slammed the door on her worst memory as completely as she had hoped. She could feel tears sparking behind her eyes.

But Prince Kiernan wasn't moving. It was probably somewhere in that stuffy royal protocol book she'd been given that she wasn't supposed to turn her back on him first, that she wasn't to dismiss *him*, but she had to. She had to escape him gazing at her so piercingly, as if her whole life story was playing in her eyes and he could see it. It would only be worse if she cried.

She turned swiftly and began pack up the music equipment she had brought in preparation for her session with Adrian.

She waited for the sound of footfalls, the whisper of the door opening and shutting.

But it didn't come.

CHAPTER TWO

MEREDITH DREW TWO OR THREE steadying breaths. Only when she was sure no tears would fall did she turn back. Prince Kiernan still stood there.

She almost yearned for a lecture about protocol, but there was no recrimination in his eyes.

"It meant a lot to them, didn't it?" he asked quietly, his voice rich with sympathy, "And especially to you."

She had to steel herself against how accurately he had read her emotion, but at least he didn't have a clue as to why she was really feeling so deeply.

It felt like her survival depended on not letting on that it was a personal pain that had touched her off emotionally. So, again, she tried to hide behind words. Meredith launched into a speech she had given a thousand times to raise funds for No Princes.

"You have to understand how marginalized these girls feel. Invisible. Lacking in value. Most of them are from single-parent families, and that parent is a mother. It's part of what makes them so vulnerable when the first boy winks at them and tells them they're beautiful.

"So when a prince, when a real live prince, one of the biggest celebrities on our island recognized what they were doing as having worth, it was incredible. I think it made them have hope that their dreams really could come true. That's a hard sell in Wentworth. Hope is a dangerous thing in that world."

Kiernan's face registered Wentworth. He *knew* the name of the worst neighborhood on his island. She had successfully diverted him from her own moment of intense vulnerability.

But before she could finish congratulating herself, Prince Kiernan took a deep breath, ran a hand through the crisp silk of his dark hair.

"Hope shouldn't be a dangerous thing," he said softly, finally looking back at her. "Not in anyone's world."

Honestly, the man could make you melt if you weren't on guard. Thankfully, Meredith's life had made her stronger than that! She had seen lives—including her own—ruined by weakness, by that single moment of giving in to temptation.

And this man was a temptation!

Well, not really. Not realistically. He was a prince, and she was a servant's daughter. Some things did not mix, even in this liberated age. Her roots were in the poorest part of his kingdom. She was not an unsullied virgin. She had known tragedy beyond her years. It had taken away her ability to dream, to believe.

The only thing she believed in was her girls at No Princes. The only thing that gave her reprieve from her pain was dancing.

No, there were no fairy tales for her.

She did not rely on anyone but herself, and certainly not a man, not even a prince. That was why she had been so immune to Prince Adrian's charms.

Merry, Merry, Merry, she could almost hear her mother's weary, bitter voice, *when in all your life has a man ever done the right thing?*

Her mother had been so right.

So Prince Kiernan shocked Meredith now. By being the one man willing to do the right thing.

"I'll do it," he said with a certain grim resolve, like a man volunteering to face the firing squad. "I'll take Prince Adrian's place."

Meredith felt her mouth open, and then snapped shut again. There was no joy in the prince's offer, only a sense of obligation.

Naturally I'll marry you, Michael had lied to her when Meredith had told him about the coming baby.

Oh, darlin', pigs will fly before that man's going to marry you. You're dreaming, girl.

Meredith had a feeling the prince would *never* run out on his obligations. Still, she had to discourage him.

Teaching Prince Adrian the steps to the dream sequence dance had been one thing. Despite his royal status, working with the young prince had been something like dealing with a slightly unruly younger brother.

This man was not like that.

There were things a whole lot more dangerous than hope.

And Prince Kiernan of Chatam, the Playboy Prince, the Prince of Heartaches, Prince Heartbreaker, was one of them.

"It's not a good idea," Meredith said. "Thank you, anyway, but no."

The prince looked shocked that anyone could turn down such a generous offer. And then downright annoyed.

"You just have no idea how much work is involved," Meredith said, a last ditch effort to somehow save herself. "Prince Adrian had committed to several hours a day. We have just over a week left until *An Evening to Remember.* I don't see how we could get you caught up. Really." He didn't seem to be hearing her, so she repeated, "Thanks, but no."

Prince Kiernan crossed the room to her. Closer, she could see his great height. The man towered over her. His scent was drugging.

But not as much as the light in those amazing blue eyes. Still cool, there was something powerful there. His gaze locked on her face and held her fast in a spell.

"Do I look like a man who is afraid of work?" he asked, softly, challengingly.

The truth? He didn't have a clue what work was. He wouldn't know it probably took a team of people hours on their hands and knees to polish these floors, to clean the windows, to make the crystals on the chandeliers sparkle like diamonds.

But she didn't say that because when she looked into his face she saw raw strength beneath the sophisticated surface. She saw resolve.

And Meredith saw exactly what he was offering. He was *saving* the dreams of all the girls. As much as she did not want to be exposed to all this raw masculine energy every single day for the next week, was this really her choice to make?

Ever since Prince Adrian had agreed to dance in *her* production, Erin had dreamed bigger. Her marks at school had become astonishing. She had mentioned, shyly, to Meredith, she might think of becoming a doctor.

Meredith couldn't throw away the astonishing gift Prince Kiernan was offering her girls because she felt threatened, vulnerable.

Still, her eyes fastened on the sensuous curve of his full lower lip.

God? Don't do this to me.

But she already knew she was not on the list of those who had their prayers answered.

The prince surprised her by smiling, though it only intensified her thought, of *don't do this to me*.

"I'm afraid," he said, "it's probably you who doesn't know how much work will be involved. I have been called the Prince of Foot Aches. And you have only a short time to turn that around? Poor girl."

His smile heightened her sense of danger, of something spinning out of her control. Meredith wanted, with a kind of desperation, to tell him this could not possibly work.

Dance with him every day? Touch him, and look at him, and somehow not be sucked into all the romantic longings a close association to such a dynamic and handsome man was bound to stir up?

But she had all her pain to keep her strong, a fortress of grief whose walls she could hide behind.

And she thought of Erin Fisher, and the girl she herself used to be. Meredith thought about hopes and dreams, and the excited delirium of the dance troupe.

"Thank you, Your Highness," she said formally. "When would you be able to begin?"

Prince Kiernan had jumped out of airplanes, participated in live-round military exercises, flown a helicopter.

He had ridden highly strung ponies on polo fields and jumped horses over the big timbers of steeplechases.

He had sailed solo in rough water, ocean kayaked and done deep-sea dives. The truth was he did not lead a life devoid of excitement and, in fact, had confronted fear often.

What came as a rather unpleasant surprise to him

was the amount of trepidation he felt about *dancing*, of all things.

He knew at least part of that trepidation was due to the fact he had made the offer to help the No Princes dance troupe on an impulse. His plan, he recalled, had been to see the Dragon-heart with his own eyes, make Prince Adrian's excuses, and then dismiss the dance instructor.

One thing Prince Kiernan of Chatam was not, was impulsive. He did not often veer from the plan. It was the one luxury he could not afford.

That eighteenth summer, his year of restless energy, heady lack of restraint, and impulsive self-indulgence had taught him that for him, spontaneity was always going to have a price.

The military had given him an outlet for all that pent-up energy and replaced impulsiveness with discipline.

Those years after his eighteenth birthday had reinforced his knowledge that his life did not really belong to him. Every decision was weighed and measured cautiously in terms, not of his well-being, but the well-being of his small island nation. There was little room for spontaneity in a world that was highly structured and carefully planned. His schedule of appointments and royal obligations sometimes stretched years in advance.

Aware he was *always* watched and judged, Kiernan had become a man who was calm and cool, absolutely controlled in every situation. His life was public, his demeanor was always circumspect. Unlike his cousin, he did not have the luxury of emotional outbursts when things did not go his way. Unlike his cousin, he could not pull pranks, be late, forget appointments.

He was rigidly *correct*, and if his training and inborn sense of propriety did not exactly inspire warm fuzziness, it did inspire confidence. People knew they could trust him and trust his leadership. Even after Francine, the whispers of what had happened to her, people seemed to give him the benefit of the doubt and trust him, still.

But then his relationship with Tiffany Wells, an exception to the amount of control he exerted over his life, seemed to have damaged that trust. His reputation had escalated from that of a man who was coolly remote to a man who was a heartless love-rat.

There would be no more losses of control.

And while it was not high on his list of priorities to be popular, he did see performing the dance as an opportunity to repair a battered image. His and Tiffany's breakup was a year ago. It was time for people to see him as capable of having a bit of fun, relaxing, being human.

Was that why he'd said yes? A public relations move? An opportunity to polish a tarnished image, as Adrian had suggested?

No.

Was it because of the girls, then? He had been moved by Miss Whitmore's description of the goals of No Princes. Kiernan had felt a very real surge of compassion for underprivileged young women who wanted someone they perceived as important to value them, to recognize what they were doing as having merit.

But had that been the reason he had said yes? The reason he had been swayed to this unlikely cause that was certainly going to require more of him than signing a cheque, or giving a speech or just showing up and shaking a few hands? Was that the reason he'd said yes to a cause that had his staff running in circles trying to rearrange his appointments around his new schedule? Again, *no*.

So, was it her, then? Was Meredith Whitmore the reason he had said *yes* to something so far out of his comfort zone?

Kiernan let his mind go to her. She had astounding hazel eyes, that hinted at fire, unconsciously pouty lips, a smattering of light freckles and a wild tangle of auburn locks, the exact kind of hair that made a man's hands itch to touch.

Add to that the lithe dancer's body dressed in a leotard that clung to long, lean legs, and a too-large T-shirt that hinted at, rather than revealed, luscious curves. There was simply no denying she was attractive, but not in the way one might expect of a dancer. She was at odds with the dance he had witnessed, because she seemed more uptight than Bohemian, more Sergeant Major than free-spirited gypsy.

Beautiful? Undoubtedly. But the truth was he was wary of beauty, rather than enchanted by it, particularly after Tiffany. The face of an angel had hidden a twisted heart, capable of deception that had rattled his world.

Meredith Whitmore did not look capable of deception, but there was something about her he didn't get. She was young, and yet her eyes were shadowed, cool, measuring.

Not exactly cold, but Kiernan could understand why Adrian had called her Dragon-heart, like something fierce burned at her core that you would get close to at your own peril.

So, he had said yes, not because it would be a good public relations move, which it would be, not wholly on the grounds of compassion, though it was that, and not because of Meredith's beauty or mystery. It was not even her very obvious emotional reaction to her disappointment and her valiant effort to hide that from him.

No, he thought frowning, the answer to his agreeing to this was somewhere in those first moments when she had been dancing, unaware of his presence. But what *exactly* it was that had been so compelling as to overcome his characteristic aversion to spontaneity eluded him.

So, the astounding fact was that Prince Kiernan, the most precise of men, could not pinpoint precisely what had made him agree to do this. And the fact that he could not decipher his own motivations was deeply disturbing to him.

Now, he paused at the doorway of the ballroom, took a deep breath, put back his shoulders, and strode in.

He hoped to find her dancing, knowing the answer was in that, but she was not to be caught off guard twice.

Meredith was fiddling with electronic equipment in one corner of the huge ballroom, her tongue caught between her teeth, her brow drawn down in a scowl. She looked up and saw him, straightened.

"Miss Whitmore," he said.

She was wearing purple tights today, rumpled leg warmers, and a hairband of an equally hideous shade of purple held auburn curls off her face. She didn't have on a speck of makeup. She did have on an oversized lime green T-shirt that said, *Don't kiss any frogs.*

He was used to people trying to impress him, at least a little bit, but she was obviously dressed only for comfort and for the work ahead. He wasn't quite sure if he was charmed or annoyed by her lack of effort to look appealing.

And he wasn't quite sure if he felt charmed or annoyed that she looked appealing anyway!

"Prince Kiernan," she said, a certain coolness in her tone, which was mirrored in the amazing green gold of those eyes, "thank you for rearranging your schedule for this."

"I did as much as I could. I may have to take the occasional official phone call."

"Understandable. Thank you for being on time."

"I'm always on time." He could see why she intimidated Adrian. No greeting, no polite *how are you today?* There was a no-nonsense tone to her voice that reminded him of a palace tutor. He could certainly hear a hint of Dragon-heart in there!

"Brilliant," she said, and then stood back, folded her arms over her chest, and inspected him. Now he could also see a hint of Sergeant Henderson as her brows lowered in disapproval! He felt like he had showed up for a military exercise in full dress uniform when the dress of the day was combat attire.

"Do those slacks have some give to them? I brought some dance pants, just in case."

Dance pants? He disliked that uncharacteristic moment of spontaneity that had made him say yes to this whole idea more by the second. He wasn't going to ask her what dance pants were, exactly. He was fairly certain he could guess.

"I'm sure these will be fine," he said stiffly, in a voice that let her know a prince did not discuss his *pants* with a maiden, no matter how fair.

She looked doubtful, but shrugged and turned to the electronics. "I have this video I want you to watch, if you don't mind, Your Highness."

As he came and stood beside her, the scent of lemons

tickled his nostrils. She flicked a switch on a bright pink laptop. The light from the chandeliers danced in her hair, making the red threads in it spark like fire.

"This has had twelve million hits," she said, accessing a video-sharing website.

He focused on a somewhat grainy video of a wedding celebration. A large room had a crowd standing around the edges of it, a space cleared in the center of it for a youthful-looking bride and groom.

"And now for the first dance," a voice announced.

The groom took one of his bride's hands, placed his other with a certain likeable awkwardness on her silk-clad waist.

"This is the bridal waltz," Meredith told him, "and it's a very traditional three-step waltz."

The young groom began to shuffle around the dance floor.

Kiernan felt relieved. The groom danced just like him. "Nothing to learn," he pronounced, "I can already do that." He looked at his watch. "Maybe I can squeeze in a ride before lunch."

"I've already lost one prince to riding," she said without looking up from the screen. "No riding until we're done the performance."

Kiernan felt a shiver of pure astonishment, and looked at Meredith Whitmore again, harder. She didn't appear to notice.

She tacked on a *"Your Highness"* as if that made bossing him around perfectly acceptable. Well, it wasn't as if Adrian hadn't warned him.

"Excuse me, but I really didn't sign up to have you run my—"

Meredith shushed him as if he was a schoolboy. "This part's important."

He was so startled that he thought he might laugh out loud. No one, but no one, talked to him like that. He slid her a look as if he was seeing her for the first time. She *was* bossy. And what's worse, she was *cute* when she was bossy.

Not that he would let her know that. He reached by her, and clicked on the pause button on the screen.

It was her turn to be startled, but he had her full attention. And he was not falling under the spell of those haunting gold-green eyes.

"I am already giving you two hours a day of practice time that I can barely afford," he told her sternly. "You will not tell me what to do with the rest of my time. Are we clear?"

Rather than looking clear, she looked mutinous.

"I've set aside a certain amount of my time for you, not given you run of my life." There. That should remind her a little gratitude would not be out of order.

But she did not look grateful, or cowed, either. In fact, Meredith Whitmore looked downright peeved.

"I've set aside a certain amount of time for you, also," she announced haughtily. "I'm not investing more of my time to have you end up out of commission, too! We're on a very limited schedule because of Prince Adrian's horse mishap."

Prince Kiernan looked at Meredith closely. Right behind the annoyance in her gorgeous eyes was something else.

"You're deathly afraid of horses," he said softly.

Meredith stared up into the sapphire eyes of the prince. The truth was she was not deathly afraid of horses.

But she was deathly afraid of a world out of her control.

The fact that he had got the *deathly afraid* part of her with such accuracy made her feel off balance, as if she was a wide open book to him.

She felt like she needed to slam that book shut, and quickly, before he read too much of it. Let him think she was afraid of horses!

It wasn't without truth, and it would be so much better than the full truth. That Meredith Whitmore was afraid of the caprice of life.

"Of course I'm afraid of horses," she said. "They are an uncommon occurrence in the streets of Wentworth. My closest encounter was at a Blossom Festival parade, where a huge beast went out of control, plunged into the crowd and knocked over spectators."

"You're from Wentworth, then?" he asked, still watching her way too closely.

He seemed more interested in that than her horse encounter. Well, good. That alone should erect the walls between them. "Yes," she said, tilting her chin proudly, "I am."

But instead of feeling as if the barrier went up higher, their stations in life now clearly defined, when he nodded slowly, she felt as if she had revealed way too much of herself! She turned from the prince swiftly, and clicked on the Play button on the screen, anxious to outrun the intensity in his eyes.

She focused, furiously, on the video. As the groom looked at his new wife, something melted in that young man's face. It was like watching a boy transform into a man, his look became so electric, so filled with tenderness.

Too aware of the prince standing beside her, Meredith scrambled to find sanctuary in the familiar.

"If you listen," she said, all business, all dance

instructor, "the music is changing, so are the steps. The dance has a more *salsa* feel to it now. Salsa originated in Cuba, though if you watch you'll see the influences are quite a unique blend of European and African."

"This really is your world, isn't it?" Kiernan commented.

"It is," she said, and she prayed to find refuge in it as she always had. It was just way too easy to feel something, especially as the dance they watched became more sensual. It felt as if the heat was being turned up in this room. Prince Kiernan was standing so close to her, she could feel the warmth radiating off his shoulder.

On the video, the young groom's whole posture changed, became sure and sexy, his stance possessive, as he guided his new bride around the room to the quickening tempo of the music.

"Here's another transition," Meredith said, "He's moving into a toned down hip-hop now, what I'd call a new school or street version rather than the original urban break dancing version."

A man's voice, an exquisite tenor soared above the dancing couple. *I never had a clue, until I met you, all that I could be—*

And the man let go of his wife's hand and waist and began to dance by himself. He danced as if his new bride alone watched him. Gone was the uncertain shuffle, and in its place was a performance that was nothing short of sizzling, every move choreographed to show a love story unfolding: passion, strength, devotion, a man growing more sure of himself with each passing second.

"You'll see this is very sporty," Meredith said, "and these kind of moves require amazing upper body strength, as well as flexibility and good balance.

It's part music, part dance, but mostly guts and pure athleticism."

She cast him a look. The prince certainly would have the upper body strength. And she had not a doubt about his guts and athleticism.

What she was doubting was her ability to keep any form of detachment while she worked with him trying to perfect such an intimate performance.

The dancer on the computer screen catapulted up onto one hand, froze there for a moment, came back down, and then did the very same move on his other side. He came up to his feet, tossed off his jacket, and loosened his tie.

"If he takes anything else off I'm leaving," Kiernan said. "It's like a striptease."

She shot him a look. Now this was unexpected. Prince Kiernan a prude? Where was the man of *Playboy Prince* fame?

They watched together as the groom's feet and hips and arms all moved in an amazing show of coordinated sensuality. The bride moved back to the edges of the crowd, who had gone wild. They were clapping, and calling their approval.

As the final notes of the music died the young groom took a run back toward his bride, fell to his knees and his momentum carried him a good ten feet across the floor. He caught his wife around her waist and gazed up at her with a look on his face that made Meredith want to melt.

The young groom's face mirrored the final words of the song, *I have found every treasure I ever looked for.*

There was something so astoundingly intimate about the video that in the stillness that followed, Meredith found herself almost embarrassed to look at Kiernan, as if they had seen something meant to be private between a man and a woman.

She pulled herself together. It was dancing. It was theater. There was nothing personal about it.

"What did you think?"

"I thought watching that was very uncomfortable," Kiernan bit out.

So, he'd picked up on the intimacy, too.

"It was like watching a mating dance," he continued.

"I see we have a bit of prudishness to overcome," she said, as if the discomfort was his alone.

But when his eyes went to her lips, Meredith had the feeling that the prince had a way of persuading her he was anything but a prude.

Something sizzled in the air between them, but she refused to allow him to see she was intimidated by it. And a little thrilled by it, too!

Meredith put her hands on her hips and studied him as if he was an interesting specimen who had found his way under her microscope.

"You didn't see the romance in it?" she demanded. "The delight of entering a new life? The hope for the future? His love for her? His willingness to do anything for her?"

"Up to and including making a fool of himself in front of—how many did you say—twelve million people? Every male in the world whose bride-to-be has insisted they look at this video is throwing darts at a target with his face on it!"

"He didn't look foolish! He looked enraptured. Every woman dreams of seeing *that* look on their beloved's face."

"Do they?" He was watching her again, with that look in his eyes. Too stripping, too knowing. "Do you?"

Did she? Did some little scrap of weakness still exist in her that wanted desperately to believe? That did want to see a look like the one on that young groom's face directed at her?

"I'm all done with romantic nonsense," she said, not sure whom she was trying to convince. Prince Kiernan? Or herself?

"Are you?" he asked softly.

"Yes!" Before he asked *why*, before those sapphire eyes pierced the darkest secrets of a broken heart, she rushed on.

"Prince Kiernan, the truth is I am an exception to the rule. People generally *love* romantic nonsense. Romance is the ultimate in entertainment," Meredith continued. "It has that feel-good quality to it, it promises a happy ending."

"Which it doesn't always deliver," he said sourly.

The ugly parts of his life had been splashed all over the papers for everyone to read about. He was, after all, Prince Heartbreaker.

But Meredith was stunned that what she felt for him, in that moment, was sympathy. For a moment, there was an unguarded pain in his eyes that made him an open book to her.

Which was the last thing she needed.

"All I'm saying," Meredith said, a little more gently, "is that if you can do a dance somewhat similar to that, it will bring down the house. What do you think?"

"How about I'm not doing anything similar to that? Not even if the entertainment value is unquestionable."

"Well, of course not that dance precisely, but that

video captures the spirit of what we want to do with this portion of the dance piece."

"It's too personal," he said firmly.

"It's for a dream sequence, Your Highness. This kind of dancing is very much like acting."

"Could we *act* more reserved?"

"I suppose we could. But where's the fun in that? And the delicious surprise? You know, you do have a reputation of being somewhat, um, stodgy. This would turn that on its head."

"Stodgy?" he sputtered. "Stern, remote, unapproachable, even snobby I can handle. But stodgy? Isn't stodgy just another word for prudish?"

He looked at her lips again, and again his eyes were an open book to her.

Meredith had to keep herself from gasping at what she saw there, something primitive in its intensity, a desire to tangle his hands in her hair, yank her to him, and find out who was really the prude, who was really stodgy.

But he shoved his hands deep in his pockets, instead.

Was she relieved? Or disappointed by his control?

Relieved, she told herself, but it sounded like a lie even in her own mind.

"We'll modify the routine to your comfort level," she said. "Now, let's just see where you're at right now. We can try and tweak the routine after that."

She turned her back to him, gathering herself, trying to regain her sense of professionalism. She fiddled with her equipment and the "bridal waltz" came on again.

She turned back to him and held out her hand. "Your Highness?"

It was the moment of truth. She had a sudden sense,

almost of premonition. If he accepted the invitation of her hand *everything* was going to change.

He must have felt it, too, because he hesitated.

Meredith took a deep breath.

"Your Highness?"

He took her hand.

And Meredith felt the sizzle of it all the way to her elbow.

CHAPTER THREE

"THIS IS HOW WE WOULD open the number," Meredith said, "with a simple three-step waltz, just like the one in the video."

Prince Kiernan moved forward, trying not to think of how her hand fit so perfectly into his, or about the softness of her delicately curved waist.

He was also trying not to look at her lips! The temptation to show Miss Meredith Whitmore he was no prude, and not stodgy, either, was overwhelming. And since he didn't appear to be convincing her with his stellar dance moves, her lips were becoming more a temptation by the minute.

"Hmm," she said, "Not bad *exactly*. I mean obviously you know a simple three-step waltz. You just aren't, how can I say this? Fluid! Mind you, that might just work at the beginning of the number. It would be great to start off with a certain stand-offishness, an armor that protects you from your discomfort with closeness."

Was she talking about the theatrics of the damned dance or could she seriously read his personality that well from a few steps? The urge to either kiss her or bolt strengthened.

He couldn't kiss her. It would be entirely inappropriate, even if it was to make a point.

And he didn't have to bolt. He was the prince. He could just say he'd changed his mind, bow out of his participation in the dance.

"But right here," she said, cocking her head at the music, "listen for the transition, we could have you loosen up. Maybe we could try that now."

Instead of saying he'd changed his mind, he subtly rolled his shoulders and loosened his grip on her hand. He wasn't quite sure what to do with the hand on her waist, so he flexed his fingers slightly.

"Prince Kiernan, this isn't a military march."

Oh, there were definitely shades of Dragon-heart in that tone!

He tried again. He used the same method he would use before trying to take a difficult shot with the rifle. He took a deep breath, held it, let it out slowly.

"No, that's tighter. I can feel the tension in your hand. Think of something you enjoy doing that makes you feel relaxed. What would that be?"

"Reading a book?"

She sighed as if it was just beginning to occur to her he might, indeed, be her first hopeless case. "Maybe something a bit more physical that you feel relaxed doing."

He thought of nothing he could offer—everything he could think of that he did that was physical required control, a certain wide-awake awareness that was not exactly relaxing, though it was not unenjoyable.

"Riding a bicycle!" she suggested enthusiastically. "Yes, picture that, riding your bike down a quiet tree-lined country lane with thatched roofed cottages and black-and-white cows munching grass in fields, your picnic lunch in your basket."

He changed his grip on her hand. If he wasn't mistaken

his palm was beginning to sweat, he was trying so hard to relax.

She glanced up at him, reading his silence. "Picnic lunch in the basket of a bicycle is not part of your world, is it?"

"Not really. I'm relaxed on horseback. But then that's not part of your world."

"And," she reminded him, a touch crankily, "horses are the reason why you're in this position in the first place."

Again, he felt that odd little shiver about being spoken to like that. It could have been seen as insolent.

But it wasn't. Adrian had warned him, after all. But what he couldn't have warned him was that he would find it somewhat refreshing to have someone just state their opinion so honestly to him, to speak to him so directly.

"In the pictures of you in the paper," she went on, "your horses seem absolutely terrifying—wild-eyed and frothy-mouthed." She shuddered.

"Don't be fooled by the pictures you see in the papers," he said. "The press delights in catching me at the worst possible moments. It helps with the villain-of-the-week theme they have going."

"I think it's 'villain-of-the-month'," she said.

"Or the year."

And unexpectedly they enjoyed a little chuckle together.

"So, you've seriously never ridden a bike?"

"Oh, sure, I have, but it's not a favorite pastime. I was probably on my first pony about the same time most children are given their first bicycles. Am I missing something extraordinary?"

"Not extraordinary, but so *normal*. The wind in your

hair, the exhilaration of sweeping down a big hill, racing through puddles. I just can't imagine anyone not having those lovely garden variety experiences."

He was taken aback by the genuine sympathy in her tone. "You feel sorry for me because I've rarely ridden a bike down a country lane? And never with a picnic lunch in the basket?"

"I didn't say I felt sorry for you!"

"I can hear it in your voice."

"Okay," she admitted, "I feel sorry for you."

"Well, don't," he snapped. "Nobody ever has before, and I don't see that it should start now. I occupy a place of unusual privilege and power. I am not a man who inspires sympathy, nor one who wants it, either."

"There's no need to be so touchy. It just struck me as sad. And it occurred to me that if you've never done that, you've probably never played in a mud puddle and felt the exquisite pleasure of mud squishing between your toes. You've probably never had a few drinks and thrown some darts. You've probably never known the absolute anticipation of having to save your money for a Triple Widgie Hot Fudge Sundae from Lawrence's."

"I fail to see your point."

"It's no wonder you can't dance! You've missed almost everything that's important. But what's to feel sorry about?"

He was silent. Finally, he said, "I didn't know my life had been so bereft."

She shrugged. "Somebody had to tell you."

And then he chuckled. And so did she. He realized she had succeeded in making just a little of the tension leave him. But at the same time, they had just shared something that took a little brick out of the wall of both their defenses.

"Well," he said dryly. "Imagine doing a bike ride with an entourage of security people, and members of the press jumping out in front of you to get that perfect picture. Kind of takes the country lane serenity out of the picture, doesn't it?"

"The peaceful feeling is leaving me," she admitted. "Is it a hard way to live?"

"I don't have a hard life," he said. "The opposite is probably true. Everyone envies me. And this lifestyle."

"That's not what I asked," she said quietly. "I wondered about the price, of not knowing if people like you for you or your title, of having to be on guard against the wrong photo being taken, the wrong word being uttered."

For an astounding moment it felt as if she had invaded very private territory. It annoyed him that the one brick coming out of the wall seemed to be paving the way for its total collapse.

For a moment he glimpsed something about himself being reflected back in her eyes.

He was alone. And she knew it. She saw what others had not seen.

He reminded himself that he *liked* being alone.

He allowed the moment to pass and instead of telling her anything remotely personal, he said, "How about fly-fishing a quiet stream? For my relaxing thing that I think about?"

Ah, he was shoving bricks back in the wall. Thank goodness!

"Perfect," she said. The perfect picture. Impersonal. "That kind of fishing even has a rhythm, doesn't it? See? Hold that picture in your head, because the way you are moving right now is much better."

Of course the minute she said that, it wasn't!

"I've fished on occasion," she said. "Nothing as fancy as fly-fishing. A pole and a bobber on a placid pond on a hot day."

"Really? I've always found women make scenes when they catch fish."

She rapped him with sharp playfulness on his shoulder. He was so startled by the familiarity of the move he stumbled.

"What a terrible stereotype," she reprimanded him. "I can't stand that fragile, helpless, squeals-at-a-fish stereotype."

"So, you're not a squealer?" he said, something like a smile grazing his lips.

She blushed, and it was her turn to stumble. "Good God, I didn't mean it like that."

He studied her face, and his smile deepened with satisfaction. He drew her closer and whispered in her ear, "Now who's the prude?"

But he didn't quite pull it off. Because she was blushing. He was blushing. And suddenly a very different kind of tension hissed in the air between them. He narrowly missed her toe.

With a sigh, she let go of him, moved a few steps away, regarded him thoughtfully.

"Adrian, I mean Prince Adrian, did not have these kinds of inhibitions."

"Adrian could use a few inhibitions in my opinion."

She sighed again. She was exasperated already and they'd been at this for all of fifteen minutes. "Are you going to be difficult every step of the way, Your Highness?"

"I'm afraid so."

"I'm up for a challenge," she told him stubbornly.

"I'm afraid of that, too." He said it lightly, but he was aware he was not kidding. Not even a little bit.

Meredith marshaled herself.

"Okay, let's start again." She moved closer to him, held up her hand. He took it.

"Deep breath, slide your foot, forward, one, two, right, one, two...slide, Your Highness, not goose-step! Look right into my eyes, not at your feet. Ouch!"

"That won't happen if I look at my feet," he said darkly.

"It's an occupational hazard. Don't worry about my feet. Or yours. Look into my eyes. Not like that! I feel as if you're looking at something unpleasant that got stuck to your shoe."

He scowled.

"And now as if you are looking at a badly behaved hound."

He tried to neutralize his expression.

"Bored, reviewing the troops," she pronounced.

"I am not bored when I'm reviewing the troops!"

She sighed. "Your Highness?"

"Yes?"

"Pretend you love me."

"Oh, boy," he muttered under his breath.

"Ouch," she said as her foot crunched under his toe. Well, it wasn't really his fault. What a shocking thing to say to a prince.

Pretend you love me.

Oh, God, what had made her say that? As if the tension in the air between them wasn't palpable enough!

Thankfully, the prince had no gift for pretense. He was glaring at her with a kind of pained intensity, as if she was posed over him with a dentist's drill. It was making her want to laugh, but not a happy laugh.

The nervous laugh of one who might just have to admit defeat.

Meredith had never met anyone she couldn't teach to dance. But then, of course, anyone who showed up at her studio *wanted* to learn.

And the truth?

She'd never been quite so intimidated before.

And not solely by the fact that Kiernan was a prince, either.

It was that he was the most masculine of men. He oozed a certain potent male energy that made her feel exquisitely, helplessly feminine in his presence. Her skin was practically vibrating with awareness of him, and she was on guard trying to hide that. Twice she had caught him staring at her lips with enough heat to sizzle a steak!

Unfortunately her job was to unleash all that potent male energy, to harness the surprising but undeniable chemistry between them, so that it showed in dance form. If she could manage that, she knew her prediction—that he would bring down the house—was entirely correct.

But Kiernan seemed as invested in keeping control as she was in breaking through it to that indefinable something that lurked beneath the surface of control.

"Maybe that's enough for the first day," she conceded after another painful half hour of trying to get him to relax while waltzing.

He broke his death grip on her hand with relief that was all too obvious.

"Same time tomorrow," she said, packing her gear. "I think we'll forget the waltz, and work on the next section tomorrow. I think you may find you like it. Some of the moves are amazingly athletic."

He didn't look even remotely convinced.

And an hour into their session the next morning neither was she!

"Your Highness! You have to move your hips! Just a smidgen! Please!"

"My hips are moving!"

"In lock step!"

Prince Kiernan glared at her.

Meredith sighed. "You want them to move more like this." She demonstrated, exaggerating the movement she wanted, a touch of a Tahitian fire dance. She turned and looked back at him.

The smoldering look she had wanted to see in his eyes while they were dancing yesterday was in them now.

It fell solidly into *the be careful what you wish for* category.

"Your turn," she said briskly. "Try it. I want to practically hear those hips *swishing*."

"Enough," he said, folding his arms over the solidness of his chest. "I've had enough."

"But—"

"No. Not one more word from you, Miss Whitmore."

His expression was formidable. And his tone left absolutely no doubt who the prince was.

Prince Kiernan was a beautifully made man, perfectly proportioned, long legs, flat hips and stomach, enormously broad shoulders.

But the way he moved!

"I'm just trying to say that while your bearing is very proud and military, it's a terrible posture for dancing!"

"I said not one more word. What part of that don't you

understand?" His tone was warning. "I need a break. And so do you."

He turned his back on her, took a cell phone from his pocket and made a call.

She stared at his broad back, fuming, but the truth was she was intimidated enough not to interrupt him.

When he turned back from his call, his face was set in lines that reminded her he would command this entire nation one day. He already shouldered responsibility for much of it.

"Come with me," he said.

Don't go anywhere with him, a voice inside her protested. It told her to stand her ground. It told her she had only days left to teach him to dance! They had no time to waste. Not a single second.

But Prince Kiernan expected to be obeyed and there was something in his tone that did not brook argument.

Meredith was ridiculously relieved that he didn't seem to need a break from *her*, only from dancing. He had already turned and walked away from her, holding open the ballroom door.

And Meredith was shocked to find herself passing meekly through it, actually anticipating seeing some of his palace home. She had always entered the palace grounds, and the ballroom directly through service entrances.

He went down the hallway with every expectation that she would follow him.

She ordered herself to rebel. To say that one more word that he had ordered her not to say.

But for what purpose? Why not follow him? Things were going badly. They certainly couldn't get any worse.

They hadn't even shared a chuckle this morning. Everything was way too grim, and he was way too uptight. Except for the *warrior about to ravish maiden* look she'd received after demonstrating how hips were supposed to move, the prince's guard was way up!

As it turned out, all she saw of the interior was that hallway. Still, it was luxurious: Italian marble floors, vases spilling over with fresh flowers set in recessed alcoves, light flooding in from arched windows, a painting she recognized, awed, as an original Monet. She had a cheap reproduction of that same painting in her own humble apartment.

The prince led her out a double French-paned glass door to a courtyard, and despite the freshness of the insult of being ordered not to say another word, something in Meredith sighed with delight.

The courtyard was exquisite, a walled paradise of ancient stone walls, vines climbing them. A lion's head set deep in one wall burbled out a stream of clear water. Butterflies glided in and out of early spring blooms and the warm spring air was perfumed with lilacs.

A small wrought iron table set with fine white linen was ready for tea. It was laid out for two, with cut hydrangeas as a centerpiece. A side table held a crystal pitcher, beaded with condensation from the chilled lemonade inside it. A three-tiered platter, silver, held a treasure trove of delicate pastries.

"Did you order this?" she asked, astounded. She barely refrained from adding *for me?* She felt stunned by the loveliness of it, and aware she felt her guard was being stormed.

As an only child she had dreamed tea parties, acted them out with her broken crockery, castoffs from houses her mother had cleaned. Only her companion then had been a favorite teddy bear, Beardly, ink stained by some disdainful rich child who'd had so many teddy bears to choose from that this vandalized one had made its way to the cleaning lady's daughter.

This time her companion was not nearly so sympathetic or safe!

"Sit down," he told her. Not an invitation.

The delight of the garden, and the table set for tea, had stolen her ability to protest. She sat. So did he. He poured lemonade in crystal goblets.

She took a tentative sip, and bit back a comment that it was fresh, not powder. As if he would know that lemonade could be made from a pouch!

"Have a pastry," he said.

Pride wanted to make her refuse the delicacies presented to her, but the deprived child she'd been eyed the plate greedily, and coveted a taste of every single treat on it. In her childhood she had had to pretend soda crackers and margarine were tea pastries. She selected a cream puff that looked like a swan. She wanted to look at it longer, appreciate the effort and the art that went into it.

And at the same time she did not want to let on how overawed she was. She took a delicate bite.

She was pretty sure Prince Kiernan had deliberately waited until she was under its influence before he spoke.

"Now," he said sternly, "we will discuss *swishing*."

The cream puff completely undermined her defenses, because she said nothing at all. She made no defense for swishing. None. In fact, she licked a little dollop of pure white cream off the swan's icing-sugar-dusted feathers.

For a moment, he seemed distracted, then he blinked and looked away.

But there was less sternness in his tone when he spoke.

"I am not swishing my hips," he told her. "Not today, not tomorrow, not ever."

The sting was taken out of it completely by the fact he glanced back at her just as she was using her tongue to capture a stray piece of whipped cream from her lips and seemed to lose his train of thought entirely.

"I think," she said reverently, "that's about the best thing I've ever tasted. Sorry. What were you saying?"

He passed the tray to her again. "I don't remember."

She was sure a more sophisticated person would be content with the cream puff, but the little girl in her who had eaten soda crackers howled inwardly at her attempt to be disciplined.

She mollified her inner child by choosing a little confection of chocolate and flaky pastry. He was doing this on purpose. Using the exquisiteness of the treats to bribe her, to sway her into seeing things his way.

"It was something about swishing," she decided. The pastry was so fragile it threatened to disintegrate under her touch. She bit it in half, closed her eyes, and suppressed a moan.

"Was it?" he growled, the sound of a man tormented.

"I think it was." She opened her eyes, licked the edge of the pastry, and a place where chocolate had melted on her hand. "That was fantastic. You have to try that one."

He grabbed the chocolate confection in question and

chomped on it with much less finesse than she would have expected from a prince. He seemed rattled.

"Do these have drugs in them?" she asked.

"I was just about to ask myself the same thing. Because I can't seem to keep my mind on—"

"Swishing," she filled in for him, eyeing the tray. "Never mind. It's not as important as I thought. We'll figure out something you're comfortable with."

He smiled, at first she thought because he had been granted reprieve from swishing. Then she realized he was smiling at her. "You have a sweet tooth. One wouldn't know to look at you."

Between his smile and the confections, and the fact he *looked* at her, she didn't have a chance.

"Yes," Meredith conceded, "let's forget swishing. It would have been fun. There's no doubt about that. The audience would have gone wild, but it's not really *you* if you know what I mean."

"Why don't you try that one?"

He was rewarding her for the fact he had gotten his way. She could not allow herself to be bribed. "Which one?"

"The one you are staring at."

"I couldn't possibly," she said wistfully.

"I'd be disappointed if you didn't."

"In that case," she said blissfully and took the tiny chocolate-dipped cherry from the tray. "Do you eat like this every day?"

"No," he said a trifle hoarsely, "I must say I don't."

"A pity."

Outside the delightful cloister of the garden, she heard the distinctive clop of hooves on cobblestone.

"Ah," he said with a bit too much eagerness, getting

up. "There's my ride. Please feel free to stay and enjoy the garden as long as you like. Tomorrow, then."

Again, it was not a suggestion or a question. No, she had just been given a royal dictate. He was done dancing for the day, whether she was or not.

He strode away from her, opened an arched doorway of heavy wood embedded in the rock wall and went out it.

Do something, Meredith commanded herself. So she did. She took a butter tart and popped the entire thing in her mouth. Then, ashamed of her lack of spunk, she leapt from her chair and followed him out the gate. She had to let the prince know that time was of the essence now. If he rode today they would have to work harder tomorrow. She'd made one concession, but she couldn't allow him to think that made her a pushover, a weakling so bowled over by his smile and tea in the garden that he could get away with anything.

She burst out of the small courtyard and found herself in the front courtyard of the castle. She stood there for a moment, delighted and shocked by the opulence of the main entrance courtyard in front of the palace.

The fountain at its center shot geysers of water over the life-size bronze of Prince Kiernan's grandfather riding a rearing warhorse. The courtyard was fragrant, edged as it was with formal gardens that were bright with exotic flowering trees.

The palace sat on top of Chatam's most prominent hill, and overlooked the gently rolling countryside of the island. In the near distance were farms and red-roofed farmhouses, freshly sown fields and lush pastures being grazed by ewes and newborn lambs.

In the far distance was the gray silhouette of the city of Chatam, nestled in the curves of the valley. Beyond that was the endless expanse of the sea.

Ancient oaks dappled the long driveway that curved up the hill to the palace with shade. At the bottom of that drive was a closed wrought iron and stone gate that guarded the palace entrance. To the left side of the gate was a tasteful stone sign, with bronze cursive letters, *Chatam Palace*, on the right, an enormous bed of roses, not yet in bloom.

Finding herself here, on this side of the gates, with the massive stone walls and turrets of the castle rising up behind her, was like being in a dream but Meredith tried to remind herself of the task at hand. She had to make her expectations for the rest of this week's practice sessions crystal-clear.

In front of the fountain, a groomsman in a palace stable uniform held a horse. Prince Kiernan had his back to her, his hand stroking one of those powerful shoulders as he took the reins from the groomsman and lifted a foot to the stirrup.

Meredith was not sure she had ever seen a man more in his element. The prince radiated the power, confidence and grace she had yet to see from him on the dance floor.

He looked like a man who owned the earth, and who was sure of his place in it.

The horse was magnificent. It was not one of the frightening horses she had seen in pictures, of that she was almost positive. Though large, and as shiny black as Lucifer, the horse stood quietly, and when he sensed her come out the gate he turned a gentle eye to her.

Except for nearly being trampled by that runaway

at the Blossom Festival parade all those years ago, Meredith had never been this close to a horse.

Instead of her planned lecture, she heard an awed *ooh* escape her lips.

Prince Kiernan glanced over his shoulder when he heard the small sound behind him.

And she, the one he thought he had successfully escaped, the one who could make eating a pastry look like something out of an X-rated film, stood there with round eyes and her mouth forming a little O.

He could leap on the horse and gallop away in a flurry of masculine showmanship. But there was something about the look on her face that stopped him.

He remembered she was afraid of horses.

He slipped his foot back out of the stirrup, and regarded Meredith Whitmore thoughtfully.

"Come say hello to Ben," he suggested quietly, dismissing his groomsman with a nod.

The debate raged in her face. Well, who could blame her? They had already crossed some sort of invisible line by having tea together. She was obviously debating the etiquette of the situation, wanting to be strictly professional.

And after watching her eat, he could certainly see the wisdom in that!

But he was aware of finding her reaction to the impromptu tea in the garden refreshing.

And he was aware of not being quite ready to gallop away.

And so what was the harm in having her meet his horse? He could tell she didn't want to, and that at the same time it was proving as irresistible to her as the crumpets had been. She moved forward as if she was being pulled on an invisible string. He could see her pulse racing in the hollow of her throat.

"Don't be afraid," Kiernan said.

She stopped well short of the horse. "He's gigantic," she whispered.

Prince Kiernan reached out, took her hand and tugged her closer.

They had been touching while they danced, but this was different. Everything about her was going to seem different after the semi-erotic experience of watching her devour teatime treats.

Still, he did not let her go, but pulled her closer, and then guiding her, he held her hand out to the horse.

"He wants to get your scent," he told her quietly.

The horse leaned his head toward her, flared his nostrils as he drew a deep breath, then breathed a puff of warm, moist air onto her hand where it was cupped in Kiernan's.

"Oh," she breathed, her eyes round and wide, a delighted smile tickling her lips. "Oh!"

"Touch him," Kiernan suggested. "Right there, between his mouth and his nose."

Tentatively, she touched, then closed her eyes, much as she had done when she decapitated the pastry swan with her lovely white teeth.

"It's exquisite," she said, savoring. "Like velvet, only softer."

"See? There's nothing to be afraid of."

But there was. And they both knew it.

She drew her hand away quickly from the horse's nose, and then out of the protection of Kiernan's cupped palm.

"Thank you," she said, and then rapidly, "I have to go."

He knew that was true, but he heard, not the words, but the fear, and frowned at it. The place where her heartbeat pulsed in her throat had gone crazy.

"Not yet," he said.

There was something in him that would not be refused. It went deeper than the station he had been born to, it went deeper than the fact he spoke and people listened.

There was something in him—a man prepared to lay down his life to protect those physically weaker than him—that challenged him to conquer her fear.

"Touch him here," he suggested, and ran his hand over the powerful shoulder muscle under the fringe of Ben's silky black mane.

She glanced toward the gate, but then made a choice. Hesitantly Meredith laid her hand where Kiernan's had been.

"I can feel his strength," she whispered, "the pure power of him."

Kiernan looked at where her hand lay just below the horse's wither, and felt a shattering urge to move her hand to his own chest, to see if she would feel his power, too, his strength.

Insane thoughts, quickly crushed. How was he supposed to dance with her if he followed this train of thought? And yet still, he did not let her go.

"If you put your nose to that place you just touched, you will smell a scent so sweet you will wonder how you lived without knowing it."

"I hope I'm not allergic," she said, trying for a light note, he suspected, desperately trying to break out of the spell that was being cast around them. But it didn't work. Meredith moved close to the horse, stood on tiptoe and drew in a deep breath.

She turned back to the prince, and he smiled with satisfaction at the transparent look of joyous discovery on her face.

"I told you," he said. "Do you want to sit on him?"

"No!" But the fear was gone. He saw her refusal, not as fright, but as an effort to fight the magic that was deepening around them.

"It's not dangerous," Kiernan said persuasively. "I promise I'll look after you."

He didn't know what he had said that was so wrong, but she suddenly went very still. The color drained from her face.

"Maybe another time," she said.

"You're trembling," Prince Kiernan said. "There's no need. There's nothing to be afraid of."

Meredith knew a different truth. There was so much to be afraid of people couldn't even imagine it.

But when she looked into Prince Kiernan's eyes, soft with unexpected concern, it felt as if the fear was taken from her. Which was ridiculous. The fact that she was inclined to trust him should make her feel more afraid, not less!

"Here, I'll help you up. Put your foot here, and your other hand here."

And she did. Even though she should have turned and run, she didn't. The temptation was too great to refuse.

She was a poor girl from Wentworth. And even though she had overcome her humble beginnings, she was still only a working woman.

This opportunity would never, ever come again.

To sit on a horse in the early spring sunshine on

the unspeakably gorgeous grounds of the Palace of Chatam.

With Prince Kiernan promising to protect her and keep her safe.

I promise I'll look after you. Those words were fair warning. She had heard those words, exactly those words, before.

When she had told Michael Morgan she was going to have his baby. And he had told her not to worry. He'd look after her. They would get married.

She could see the girl she had been standing on the city hall steps, waiting, her baby just a tiny bulge under her sweater. Waiting for an hour and then two. Thinking something terrible must have happened. Michael must have been in an accident. He must be lying somewhere hurt. Dying.

Her mother, who had refused to attend the ceremony, had finally come when it was dark, when city hall was long closed, and collected Meredith, shivering, soaked from cold rain, from the steps.

That's where trust got you. It left you way too open to hurt.

But even knowing that, Meredith told herself it would be all right just to allow herself this moment.

She took Kiernan's instructions, put her foot in the stirrup and took the saddle with her other hand. Despite her dancer's litheness, Meredith felt as if she was scrambling to get on that horse's back. But then strong hands lifted her at the waist, gave her one final shove on her rump.

Despite how undignified that final shove was, she settled on the hard leather of the saddle with a sense of satisfaction.

For the first time—and probably the only time—in her life, Meredith was sitting on a horse.

"Should we go for a little stroll?"

She had come this far. To get off without really riding the horse seemed like it would be something of a shame. She nodded, grabbed the front of the saddle firmly.

With the reins in his hands, Kiernan moved to the front of the horse. Instead of taking her for a short loop around the fountain, or down the driveway to the closed main gate, he led the horse off the paved area and onto the grass that surrounded the palace.

The whole time, his voice soothing, he talked to her.

"That's it. Just relax. Think of yourself as a blanket floating over him." He glanced back at her. "That's good. You have really good balance, probably from the dancing. That's it exactly. Just relax and feel the rhythm of it. It goes side to side and then back and forth. Do you feel that?"

She nodded, delighting in the sensation, embracing the experience. She thought after a moment he would turn around and lead her back to the courtyard, but he didn't.

"You'll see the first of the three garden mazes on your left," he said. "I used to love trying to find my way out of it when I was a boy."

He amazed her by giving her a grand tour of parts of the palace grounds that were not open to the public. But even had they been, the public would never have known that was the place he rode his first pony, that was where he fell and broke his arm, that was the fountain he and Adrian had put dish detergent in.

With the sun streaming down around her, the scent of the horse tickling her nostrils, and Kiernan out in front of her, leading the horse with such easy confidence, glancing back at her to smile and encourage her, Meredith realized something.

Perhaps the scariest thing of all.

For the first time since the accident that had taken her baby six years ago, she felt the tiniest little niggle of something.

It was the most dangerous thing of all. It was happiness.

CHAPTER FOUR

WHEN KIERNAN GLANCED BACK at Meredith, he registered her delight. There was something about her that troubled him. She was too serious for one so young. Something he could not understand haunted the loveliness of the deep golds and greens of her eyes.

And yet looking at her now those ever-present shadows, the clouds, were completely gone from her eyes. It made her lovely in a way he could not have guessed. He turned away, focused on the path in front of him. Her radiance almost hurt.

"Oh," she said. "Kiernan! He's doing something!"

Kiernan turned to see the horse flicking his tail. He laughed at the expression on her face.

"Now, that's a *swish*," he said. "A bothersome fly, nothing more."

But some tension had come into her, and he was driven to get rid of it.

"On this whole matter of swishing," he said solemnly. "A hundred years ago I could have had you hauled off to the dungeon to straighten you out about who was the boss. Ten days of bread and water would have mended your ways."

He was rewarded with her laughter.

"And if it didn't, I could have added rats."

"Really, Kiernan," she laughed, "you've proven you can have your way for a pastry. Hold the rats."

Have his way? Having his way with her suddenly took on dangerous new meaning. He could practically feel her hair tangled in his hands, imagine what it would be to take the lushness of her lips with his own.

He risked a glance at her, and saw, guiltily, that her meaning had been innocent. He was entranced by her sunlit face, dancing with laughter.

Her laughter was a delicious sound, pure mountain water, gurgling over rock, everything he had hoped for when he had given in to a desire to chase the shadows from her eyes. More.

The laughter changed her. It *was* the sun coming out from behind clouds. Meredith went from being stern to playful, she went from being somewhat remote to eminently approachable, she went from being beautiful to being extraordinary.

He laughed, too, a reluctant chuckle at first, and then a real laugh. Their combined laughter rang off the ancient walls and suffused the day with a light it had not had before.

Kiernan knew it was the first time in a long, long time that he had laughed like this. It was as if his relationship with Tiffany had brought out something grim in him that he never quite put away.

But then the moment of exquisite lightness was over, and as he gazed up into the enjoyment on her face he realized that he was not fully prepared for what he saw there. Even though he had encouraged this moment, he did not feel ready for the bond of it. There was an utter openness between them that was astounding.

He felt like a man who had been set adrift on ice, who was nearly frozen, and who had suddenly glimpsed the promise of the warm golden light of a fire in the distance.

But his very longing made him feel weak. What had he been thinking? He needed to guard against moments like this, not encourage them.

Kiernan was not sure he had ever felt quite that vulnerable. Not riding a headstrong horse over slippery ground, not even when the press had decided to crucify him, first over Francine, ten times worse over the Tiffany affair.

He turned abruptly back toward the courtyard, but when they arrived, he stood gazing up at her, not wanting to help her off the horse.

To touch her now, with something in him so open, felt as if it guaranteed surrender. He was Adam leaning toward the apple; he was Sampson ignoring the scissors in Delilah's hand.

Hadn't Tiffany just taught him the treacherous unpredictability of human emotion?

Still, Meredith wasn't going to be able to get off that horse without his help.

"Bring that one leg over," he said gruffly, and then realized he hadn't been specific enough, because she brought her leg over but didn't twist and swing down into the stirrup, but sat on his horse, prettily side-saddle.

And then, without warning, she began to slide off.

And he had no choice but to reach out and catch her around her waist, and pull her to him to take the impact from her.

She stood there in the circle of his arms, her chin tilted back, looking into his face.

"Kiernan," she said softly, "I don't know how to thank you. That was a wonderful morning."

But that was the problem. The wonder of the morning

had encouraged this new form of familiarity. Barriers were down. She hadn't used his proper form of address.

She didn't even know she hadn't, she was so caught in the moment. And she never had to know how he had *liked* how his name had sounded coming off her lips.

But it was just one more barrier down, one more line of protection compromised. He should correct her. But he couldn't. He hated it that the moment seemed to be robbing him of his strength and his resolve, his sense of duty, his *knowing* what was right.

Aside from Adrian, who was this comfortable with him, there were few people in his world this able to be themselves around him, this able to bring out his sense of laughter.

Francine had. Tiffany never.

She did not back out of the circle of his arms, and he did not release her. The laughter was gone from her face. Completely. She swallowed hard.

The guard he had just put up felt as if it was going to crumple. *Completely.* And if it did, he would never, ever be able to build it back up as strong as it had been before, like a wall that had been weakened by a cannonball hit.

"Your Highness?"

Now, she remembered the correct form of address. Too late. Because now he longed to hear his name off her lips.

That's what he had to steel himself against.

"Yes?"

"Thank you for not letting me fall," she said.

But the truth? It felt as if they were falling, as if they were entering a land where neither of them had ever been, without knowing the language, without having a map.

"It's not if you fall that matters," he said quietly. "Everyone falls. It's how you get up that counts."

A part of him leaned toward her, wanting, almost desperately to explore what was happening between them. As if, in that new land he had glimpsed so briefly in her eyes, he would find not that he was lost.

But that he was found.

And that he was not alone on his journey.

Kiernan gave himself a mental shake. He couldn't allow himself to bask in that feeling that he had been *seen*, this morning, not as a prince, but for the man he really was. And he certainly couldn't allow her to see that her praise meant something to him.

Music suddenly spilled out an open window above them. She cocked her head toward it. "What on earth?' she asked. "What kind of magic is this?"

The whole morning had had that quality, of magic. Now, it seemed imperative that he deny the existence of such a thing.

"It's not magic!" he said, his tone suddenly curt. "The palace chamber quartet is practicing, that's all. It happens every Tuesday at precisely eleven o'clock."

He liked precise worlds. Predictable ones.

"Your Highness?"

He looked askance at her.

"Shall we?"

Of course he wasn't going to dance with her! He was too open to her, too aware of how the sun shone off her hair, of the light in her eyes, of the glossy puffiness of her lips. He had a horse that needed looking after. Her laughter and his had already made him feel quite vulnerable enough.

And yet this surprise invitation had that quality of delicious spontaneity to it that he found irresistible. Plus, to refuse might deepen her puzzlement, and if she studied the mystery long enough, would she figure it out?

That there was something about her he liked, and at the same time, he disliked liking it. Intensely.

But there was one other thing.

He had seen a light come on in her today. It still shone there, gently below the surface, chasing away a shadow he had realized had been ever-present until this morning.

He might want to protect himself.

But not enough to push her back into darkness.

And so he dropped the reins, uncharacteristically not caring if the horse bolted back to the stable. He felt like a warrior at war, not with her, but with himself. Wanting to see her light, but not at the expense of losing his power.

He felt as if he was walking straight toward his biggest foe. Because, of course, his biggest foe was the loss of control that she threatened in him.

Here was his chance to wrest it back, to take the challenge of her to the next level. He gazed down at her, and then took her hand, placed his other one on her waist.

There was something about the spontaneity of it, about the casualness of it, about the drift of the music over the spring garden, that did exactly what she had wanted all along.

Something in him *breathed*. He didn't feel rigid. Or stiff. He felt on fire. *A man who would prove he was in charge of himself.*

A man who could flirt with temptation and then just shrug it off and walk away.

A man who could see her light, and be pulled to it, and want it for her, but at the same time, not be a moth that would be pulled helplessly into the flame.

He danced her around the courtyard until she was breathless. Until she was his whole world. All he could see was the light in her. All he could feel was the sensuous touch of her fingertips resting ever so lightly on the place where his back met his hip. All that he could smell was her scent.

The last note of music spilled out the window, held, and then died. He became aware again of a world that was not Meredith. The horse stood, his head nodding, birds singing, sun shining, the scent of lilacs thick in the air.

Now, part two of the equation. He had danced with the temptation.

Walk away.

But she was finally looking at him with the approval a prince deserved. He steeled himself not to let it go straight to his head.

"That was fantastic," Meredith said softly.

"Thank you." With a certain chilly note, as if he didn't give a fig about her approval.

"I think you're ready to learn a few modern dance step moves tomorrow."

Tomorrow. He'd been so busy getting through the challenge of the moment that he'd managed to completely forget that.

There were more moments to this challenge. Many more.

Kiernan had known she would be that kind of girl.

The if you give an inch, she'll take a mile kind.

The kind where if you squeezed through one challenge she threw at you, by the skin of your teeth, only, another would be waiting. Harder.

And just to prove she had much harder challenges in

store for him, she stood on her tiptoes and brushed his cheek with her lips.

Then she stepped back from him, stunned.

But not as stunned as he was. That innocent touch of her lips on his cheek stirred a yearning in him that was devastating. Suddenly his whole life seemed to yawn ahead of him, filled to the brim with activities and obligations, but empty of the one thing that truly mattered.

It doesn't exist, he berated himself. He'd learned that, hadn't he?

For a moment, she looked so surprised at herself that he thought she might apologize. But then, she didn't. No, she crossed her arms over her chest, and met his gaze with challenge, daring him to say something, daring him to tell her how inappropriate it was to kiss a prince.

But he couldn't. And therein was the problem. She was challenging his ability to be in perfect control at all times, and he hated that.

Resisting an impulse to touch the place on his cheek that still tingled from the caress of her soft lips, Kiernan turned from her, and went to his horse. He put his leg in the stirrup and vaulted up onto Ben's back. Without looking back, he pressed the horse into a gallop, took a low stone wall, and raced away.

But even without looking, he knew she had watched him. And knew that he had wanted her to watch him and be impressed with his prowess.

Some kind of dance had begun between them. And it had nothing at all to do with the performance they would give at *An Evening to Remember.*

On the drive home from the palace, Meredith replayed her audacity. She'd kissed the prince!

"It wasn't really a kiss," she told herself firmly. "More like a buss. Yes, a buss."

Somehow she had needed to thank him for all the experiences he had given her that day.

"So," she asked herself, "what's wrong with thank you?"

Still, if she had it to do again? She would do the same thing. She could not regret touching her lips to the skin of his cheek, feeling the hint of rough stubble beneath the tenderness of her lips, standing back to see something flash through his eyes before it had been quickly veiled.

She parked her tiny car in the laneway behind her apartment, a walk-up located above her dance studio in Chatam. She owned the building as a result of an insurance settlement. The building, and No Princes, had been her only uses for the money.

Both things had given her a little bit of motivation to keep going on those dark days when it felt like she could live no more.

Tonight, when she opened the door to the apartment that had given her both solace and sanctuary, she was taken aback by how fresh her wounds suddenly felt.

It had been six years since it had happened.

A grandmother who had just picked up her granddaughter from day care walking a stroller across a street. Who could know why Meredith's mother, Millicent, had not heard the sirens? Tired from working so hard? Mulling over the dreams that had been shattered? A stolen vehicle the police were chasing went through the crosswalk. Meredith's mother, Millicent, had died at the scene, after valiantly throwing her body in front of the stroller. Carly had succumbed to her injuries a few days later, God deaf to the pleas and prayers of Meredith.

Now, the apartment seemed extra empty and quiet tonight, no doubt because today, for the first time in so long, Meredith had allowed herself to feel connected to another human being.

Meredith set her bag inside the door, and went straight to the bookshelf, where there were so many pictures of her baby, Carly. She chose her favorite, took it to the couch, and traced the lines of her daughter's chubby cheeks with her fingertips.

With tears sliding down her cheeks, she fell asleep.

When she awoke she was clutching the photo to her breast. But instead of feeling the sadness she always felt when she awoke with a photo of her daughter, she remembered the laughter, and the happiness she had felt today.

And felt oddly guilty. How could she? She was not ready to be happy again. Nor could she trust it. Happiness came, and then when it went, as it inevitably did, the emptiness was nearly unbearable.

Meredith considered herself strong. But not strong enough to hope. Certainly not strong enough to sustain more loss. She was not going to embrace the happiness she had felt today. No, not at all. In fact, she was going to steel herself against it.

But the next morning she was aware she was not the only one who had steeled herself against what had happened yesterday.

If Meredith thought they had made a breakthrough yesterday when she had ridden the horse and Kiernan had danced in the courtyard with her, she now saw she was sadly mistaken.

He had arrived this morning in armor. And he danced

like it, too! Was the kiss what had done it? Or the whole day they had experienced together? No matter, he was as stiffly formal as though he had never placed his hand on her rump to sling her into the saddle of his horse, as if he had never walked in front of her, chatting about his childhood on the palace grounds.

Meredith tried to shrug her sense of loss at his aloofness away and focus on the job at hand.

She had put together a modified version of the newlyweds' dance from the internet and Prince Kiernan had reluctantly approved the routine for *An Evening to Remember.* She had hoped to have some startling, almost gymnastic, moves in it, which would show off the prince's amazing athletic ability.

But the prince, though quite capable of the moves, was resistant.

"Does the word *sexy* mean anything to you?"

Something burned through his eyes, a fire, but it was quickly snuffed. "I'm doing my best," he told her with cool reserve, not rattled in the least.

But he wasn't. Because she had glimpsed his best. This did not even seem like the same man she had danced with yesterday in the courtyard, so take-charge, so breathtakingly masculine, so sure.

The stern line of his lip was taking on a faintly rebellious downward curve. Pretty soon, he would announce *enough* and another day of practice would be lost.

Not that yesterday had been lost.

She sighed. "You know the steps. You know the rudiments of each move. But you're like a schoolboy reciting math tables by rote. Something in you holds back."

"That's my nature," he said. "I'm reserved. Something in me always holds back." His eyes fastened on her lips, just for a split second, and she felt her stomach do a loop-the-loop worthy of an acrobatic airplane.

If he didn't hold back, would he kiss her? What would his lips taste like? Feel like? Given her resolve to back away from all those delicious things she had felt yesterday, Meredith was shocked by how badly she wanted to know. She was shocked by the sudden temptation to throw herself at him and take those lips, to shock the sensuality out of him.

But she also needed for both of them to hold back if she was going to keep her professional distance. And she needed just as desperately for him to let go if she was going to feel professional pride in teaching him!

It was a quandary.

"Is it your nature to be reserved," she questioned him, "or your role in life?"

"In my case, those are inextricably intertwined."

He said that without apology.

"I understand that, but in dancing there is no holding back. You have to put everything into it, all that you were, all that you have been, all that you hope to be someday."

The question was, if he gave her all that, how was she going to walk away undamaged?

"This is a ten-minute performance at a fund-raiser," he reminded her, "not the final exam for getting into heaven."

But that's what she wanted him to experience, *exactly*. She realized for her it had become about more than their performance.

There was a place when you danced well, where you became part of something larger. It was an incredible feeling. It was a place where you rose above problems.

And tragedies. A place where you were free of your past and your heartaches. Yes, just like touching heaven.

But somehow she could not tell him that. It was too ambitious. He was right. It was a ten-minute performance for the fund-raiser opening of Blossom Week. Meredith was here to teach him a few dance steps, nothing more.

When had it become her quest to unlock him? To show him something of himself that he had never seen before? To want him to experience *that* feeling. Of heaven.

And that she was dying to see?

It had all become too personal. And she knew that. She had to get her own agenda straight in her head.

Teach him to do the routine, perform it well, and be satisfied if the final result was passable if not spectacular. The prince putting in a surprising appearance, making a game effort at the steps would be enough. The people of Chatam would *love* his performance, a chance to see him let his hair down, even if he was somewhat wooden.

Though, for her, to only accomplish a passable result would feel like a failure of monumental proportions. Especially since she had glimpsed yesterday what he could be.

Her eyes suddenly fell on two jackets that hung on pegs inside the coat check at the far end of the ballroom. They were the white jackets of the palace housekeeping staff.

As soon as she saw them, she knew exactly what she had to do.

And as she contemplated the audacity of her plan, she could have sworn she heard a baby laugh, as if it was *so* right.

It was a memory of laughter, nothing more, but she could see the face of the beautiful child who had been taken from her as clearly as though she still had the photo on her chest.

She was aware again, of something changing in her. Sweetly. Subtly. It wasn't that she wasn't sad. It was that the sadness was mixed with something else.

A great sense of gratitude for having known love so deeply and so completely.

Meredith was suddenly aware that her experience with love had to make her a better person.

It had to.

Her daughter's legacy to her had to be a beautiful one. That was all she had left to honor her with.

And if that meant taking a prince to a place where he was not so lonely and not so alone, even briefly, then that was what she had to do.

It wasn't about the dance they were doing at all.

It was about the kind of person she was going to choose to be.

And yes, it was going to take all her courage to choose it.

She moved past the prince to the coat check, plucked the jackets off the wall, and then turned back and took a deep breath.

Yesterday, spontaneity had brought them so much closer to the place they needed to be than all her carefully rehearsed plans and carefully choreographed dance steps.

Today, she hoped for magic.

CHAPTER FIVE

THE PRINCE BADLY WANTED his life back. He wanted *An Evening to Remember* to be over. He wanted the temptation of Meredith over; watching her demonstrate hip moves, taking her hand in his, touching her, looking at her and pretending to love her.

It was easily the most exhausting and challenging work he had ever done, and the performance couldn't come quickly enough in his opinion.

Though, somewhere in his mind, he acknowledged over would be over. No more rehearsals. No more bossy Meredith Whitmore. Who didn't respect his station, and was impertinent. Who was digging at him, trying to find the place in him he least wanted her to see, refusing to take no for an answer.

Who could make eating pastries look like an exercise in eroticism one minute, and look at a horse with the wide-eyed wonder of a child the next. Whose lips had felt like butterfly wings against his cheek.

Stop, Kiernan ordered himself.

She was aggravating. She was annoying. She was damnably sexy. But she was also *refreshing* in a way that was brand new to him. She was not afraid to tell him exactly what she thought, she was not afraid to make demands, she was not afraid of him, not awed by his station, not intimidated by his power.

And that, he reluctantly admitted, was what he was going to miss when it was all over. In so much of his life he was the master. What he said went. No questions. No arguments. No suggestions. No discussion.

How was it that in a dance instructor from Wentworth, he felt he had met his equal?

There was no doubt going to be a huge space in his life once she was gone. It seemed impossible she could have that kind of impact after only a few days. But he didn't plan to dwell on it.

Prince Kiernan was good at filling spaces in his life. He had more obligations than he had time, anyway, and many of those were stacking up as he frittered away hours and hours learning the dance routine he was coming to hate.

"We're going to go somewhere else today," Meredith announced, marching back over from the coat room with something stuffed under her arm. "I think the ballroom itself may be lending to the, er, stuffiness, we're experiencing. It's too big, too formal."

But he knew it wasn't the room she found stuffy. It was him.

"First stodgy, now stuffy," he muttered.

"Don't act insulted. You said yourself the role you play has made you that way."

"No, you suggested it was the role I played. I said I was born this way. And I never used the word stuffy. I think I said reserved."

"Okay, whatever," she said cheerfully. "We're going to do a little experiment today. With your reserve."

Oh-oh, this did not bode well for him. He was already hanging onto his control by the merest thread.

"Here," she said pleasantly, "put this on."

She handed him one of the white jackets she had stuffed under her arm. The one she handed him had the name *Andy* embroidered over one pocket in blue thread. He hesitated. What was the little minx up to?

Mischief. He could see it in the twinkle in her eye.

He should stop her before she got started, and he knew that. But despite the fact he had told himself he wasn't going to dwell on it, soon their time together would be over. Why not see what mischief she had planned? That spark in her eye was irresistible anyway, always reminding him that there was a shadow in her.

Like the unexpected delight of taking her for tea and then on that ride, this was part of the unexpected reprieve he'd been given from the stuffy stodginess of his life. He was aware he *wanted* to see what she had up her sleeve today.

So he slipped the white jacket over his shirt and did up the buttons. It was too tight across the chest, but she inspected him, and frowned. She went back to the coat check and reappeared with a white ball cap.

"There," she said, handing it to him. "Pull it low over your eyes. Perfect. All ready to smuggle you out of the palace." She shrugged into a white jacket of her own. It said *Molly* on the pocket.

"We can't smuggle me out of the palace," he said, but he was aware it was a token protest. Something in him was already taking wing, flying over the walls.

"Why not?"

"There are security concerns. I have responsibilities and obligations you can't even dream of. I can't just waltz out of here without letting anyone know where I'm going and why."

"To improve your waltz, I think you should. See?

There's that reserve again. Your Highness—no, make that Andy—have you ever broken the rules?"

"I don't have the luxury," he told her tightly.

She smiled at him. "Prince Kiernan of Chatam doesn't. Andy does. Let's go. It's just for a little while. Maybe an hour. In some ways, you're a prisoner of your life. Let's break out. Just this once."

He stood there for a moment, frozen. Again, he had a sense of her saying what no one else said.

And seeing what no one else saw.

She didn't see the prince. Not entirely. If she did, she would not have dared to touch his cheek with her lips yesterday. She saw a man first. The trappings of his status underwhelmed her. She saw straight through to the price he paid to be the prince.

And she wanted to rescue him. There was a kind of crazy courage in that that was as irresistible as the mischief in her eyes.

Of course he couldn't just go. It would be the most irresponsible thing he had ever done.

On the other hand, why not? The Isle of Chatam was easily the safest place in the world. He was supposed to be at dance class. No one would even miss him for a few hours.

Suddenly what she was offering him seemed as impossible to resist as the mischief that made her eyes spark more green than brown.

Freedom. Complete freedom, the one thing he had never ever known.

"Coming, Andy?" she said.

He sighed. "Molly, I hope you know what you're doing."

"Trust me," she said.

And Kiernan realized he was starting to. The one

thing he wanted to do least was trust a woman! And yet somehow she was wiggling her way past his defenses and entering that elite circle of people that he truly trusted.

He followed her outside to the staff parking lot. She led him to the tiniest car he had ever seen, a candy-apple-red Mini.

She got in, and he opened the passenger door and slid in beside her. His knees were in approximately the vicinity of his chin.

"They've gotten used to me at the service entrance," she said. "I'll just give them a wave and we'll breeze on through."

And that's exactly what happened.

In moments they were chugging along a narrow country road, he holding on for dear life. Kiernan had never ridden in a vehicle that was so...insubstantial. He felt as if they were inches above the ground, and as if every stone and bump on the road was jarring his bones. He actually hit his head on the roof of the tiny vehicle.

"Where are we going?" he asked.

"Remember I asked you about squishing mud up through your toes?"

"Yes, I do."

"That's where we're going."

"I don't want to squish mud up between my toes," he said, though he recognized his protest, once again, as being token. The moment they had driven through that back service gate to the palace something in him had opened.

He had made a decision to embrace whatever the day held.

"It doesn't matter if you want to or not. Andy does."

"But why does he?" he asked.

"Because he likes having *fun*."

"Oh, I see. There's nothing stuffy or stodgy about our man, Andy."

"Exactly," she said, and beamed at him with the delight of a teacher who had just helped a child solve a difficult problem. "Andy, you and I are about to give new meaning to *Dancing with Heaven*."

"I don't know the old meaning, Molly."

"You've never seen *Dancing with Heaven*? It's a movie. A classic romantic finding-your-true-self movie that has dance at its heart. It starred Kevin McConnell."

He didn't care for the dreamy way she said that name.

"I'll have to put watching *Dancing with Heaven* on your homework list."

"Andy doesn't like homework."

"That's true."

"He likes playing hooky. But when he's at school?"

"Yes?"

"He winks at the teacher and makes her blush."

"Oh-oh," she said.

"He likes motorcycles, and black leather, driving too fast, and breaking rules."

"My, my."

"He likes loud music and smoky bars, and girls in too-short skirts and low-cut tops who wiggle their hips when they dance."

"Oh, dear."

"He thumbs his nose at convention. He's cooled off in the town fountain on the Summer Day celebrations, disobeyed the Keep Off signs at Landers Rock, kept his hat on while they sing the national anthem."

"That's Andy, all right."

"He likes swimming in the sea. Naked. In the moonlight."

Unless he was mistaken, Meredith gulped a little before she said, "I've created a monster."

"You should be more careful who you run away with, Molly."

"I know."

"But they say every woman loves a bad boy."

Something in her face closed. She frowned at the road. Kiernan realized how very little he knew about her, which was strange because he felt as if he knew her deeply.

"Do you have a boyfriend?" He hadn't thought to ask her that before. There were no rings on her fingers, so he had assumed she was single. Now he wondered why he had assumed that, and wondered at why he was holding his breath waiting for her answer.

"I'm single." Her hands tightened on the wheel.

"I'm surprised." But ridiculously *relieved*. What was that about, since if ever there was a man sworn off love it was him? Why would he care about her marital status?

Only because, he assured himself, he didn't even want to think about her with a bad boy.

She hesitated, looked straight ahead. "I became pregnant when I was sixteen. The father abandoned me. It has a way of souring a person on romance." He heard the hollowness in her voice, but he could hear something more.

Unbearable pain. And suddenly his concern for protecting his own damaged heart evaporated.

"And the baby?" he asked quietly. Somehow he knew this woman could never have an abortion. Never.

And that adoption seemed unlikely, too. There was something about the fierce passion of that first dance he had witnessed her performing that let him know that. She would hold on to what she loved, no matter what the cost to her.

He glanced at her face. She was struggling for control. There was something she didn't want to tell him, and suddenly, with an intuition that surprised him, he knew it was about the shadow that he so often saw marring the light in her eyes.

He held his breath, again, wanting, no, *needing* to know that somehow she had come to trust him as much as he had come to trust her, even if it was with the same reluctance.

"It was a little girl. I kept her," she whispered. "Maybe a foolish thing to do. My mom and I had to work night and day cleaning houses to make ends meet. But I don't regret one second of it. Not one. All I regret is that I couldn't be with her more. With both of them more."

He felt a shiver go up and down his spine.

"My mom picked her up from day care for me on a particularly hectic day. They were crossing a street when a stolen car being chased by the police hit them."

Her voice was ragged with pain.

"I'm so sorry," he said, aware of how words were just not enough. "You seem much too young to have survived such a tragedy."

In a broken whisper she went on, "She wasn't even a year old yet."

Her shoulders were trembling. She refused to look at him, her eyes glued to the road.

He wanted to scream at her to pull over, because he needed to gather her in his arms and comfort her. But from the look on her face there were some things there was no comforting for.

"I'm so sorry," he said again, feeling horrible and helpless. He reached out and patted her shoulder, but she shrugged out from under his hand, her shoulder stiff with pride.

"It's a long time ago," she said, with forced brightness. "Today, let's just be Molly and Andy, okay?"

It couldn't be *that* long ago. She wasn't old enough for it to have been that long ago.

But she had trusted him with this piece of herself.

And her trust felt both fragile and precious. If he said the wrong thing it felt like this precious thing she had offered him would shatter.

Still, he could not quite let it go. He had to listen to the voice inside him that said, *ask her*.

"Could you tell me their names? Your baby's and your mother's?" he asked, softly, ever so softly. "Please?"

She was silent for so long that he thought she would refuse this request. When she answered, he felt deeply moved, as if she had handed him her heart.

"Carly," she whispered. "My baby's name was Carly. My mother's was Millicent, but everyone called her Millie."

"Carly," he said softly, feeling it on his tongue. "Millie."

And then he nodded, knowing there was nothing else to say, but holding those names to him like the sacred trust that they were.

There was something about the way he said her daughter and mother's names, with genuine sadness, and a simple reverence, that gave Meredith an unexpected sense of being comforted. Over the past days she had come to know Prince Kiernan in a way that made it easy to forget he was still the most powerful man in the land.

Something about the way he uttered those names made her understand his power in ways she had not before. His speaking Carly's name was oddly like a blessing.

Meredith felt tears at his gentleness sting her eyes, but she did not let them flow. Kiernan reached out, and loosed her hand from the gearshift, and gave it a hard squeeze before letting it go.

Why had she told him about Carly? And her mother? She could have just as easily left it at she was single.

Was it because she was asking him to let his guard down? And that request required more of her, too? Was it because some part of her had trusted he would handle it in just the right way?

Whatever it was, she waited for a sense of vulnerability to come, a sense that she had revealed too much of herself.

But it did not. Instead, she felt an unexpected sense of a burden that she had carried alone being, not lifted, but shared.

A prince sharing your burden, she scoffed at herself, but her scorn did not change the way she felt, lighter, more open.

But for now, she reminded herself, a newfound sense of awe of Kiernan would not forward her goal. He needed to be taken off his pedestal if she ever hoped to get him to dance as if he meant it.

So for today, Kiernan was not a prince, not the most wealthy, most influential, most powerful man in Chatam. Today he would be just Andy. And she was not a woman with an unbearable sadness in her past, just *Molly*, two palace housekeeping workers playing hooky from work for the day.

They arrived at the small unmarked pullout, the trail-head for what Meredith considered one of the greatest treasures of the Isle of Chatam, Chatam Hot Springs.

Meredith opened the boot of her small car, and loaded "Andy" down with bags and baskets to carry up the steep trail that wound through the sweetly scented giant cedar woods. She was enjoying this charade already. She would have never asked a prince to carry her bags!

Meredith was relieved to see, as they came around the final twist in the trail, there was not a single soul at Chatam Hot Springs. The natural springs were a fa-vorite local haunt, but not this early in the day and not midweek. She had taken a chance that the hot springs would be empty, and they were.

Kiernan set down his cargo and gazed around. "What a remarkable place."

Puffs of mist rose above the turquoise waters that filled a pool edged by slabs of flat black slate rocks. Freshwater falls cascaded down a mossy outcropping at the far end of the pool. Lush ferns, and bunches of grass, sown with tiny purple and blue wildflowers, surrounded the rocks and the pool.

"You've never been here?"

"I've heard of it, and seen photographs of it many times. But to come here? When the royal entourage ar-rives, security would necessitate closing it to the people who enjoy it most. I have so many other pleasures at my disposal that it would seem unduly selfish to want this one, also."

She was already vulnerable to him because some-how the way he had reacted to her history had been so quietly *right*. Now she saw that despite the fact he lived in a position that could have easily bred arrogance, it had not. Kiernan clearly saw his position not as one of absolute power, but one of absolute service.

Still, the time for being too serious today was over.

"Oh, Andy," she chided him. "You're talking as if you think you're royalty!"

Still, she was delighted he had never been here before, pleased that she was the one who had brought him to something new, beautiful and unexpected.

"Oh, Molly," he said contritely. "You know me. Delusions of grandeur."

"I have a plan for bringing you down a few notches, Andy."

"I can barely wait."

And it actually sounded as if he meant that, as if he was embracing this experience with an unexpected eagerness.

"Well, then, kick off your shoes, and roll up your pants," Meredith suggested. "This is what I want to show you."

He didn't even argue with her.

Hidden in a tiny glade beside the hot springs, separated from the main pool by a dripping curtain of thick foliage, was a dip in the ground, approximately a quarter the size of the ballroom, that was filled with oozing, gray mud.

Meredith waded in. "Careful, it's—" just as she tried to warn him, one of her feet slipped. But before she even fully registered she was falling, Kiernan was beside her. He wrapped his arm around her waist, took her arm, and steadied her.

"Oh, Molly, you're a clumsy one. I'd give up those dreams of being a dancer if I were you."

She felt as if she could not get enough of the playful tone in his voice.

"I'll give up my dancer dreams if you'll give up yours of being a prince."

"Done," he said, with such genuine relief they both laughed.

"It's warm," he said, astounded, apparently unaware that even though he had let go of her waist, he still held her arm. "I've never felt anything quite like this."

And neither had she. Oh, the mud was exquisite; warm and thick, it oozed up through her toes, and then around her feet, and ankles, up her calves, but it was his hand, still steadying her arm, which she had never felt anything like.

They had been touching each other for days now.

But, except for that magical moment when the music had spilled over the courtyard, their dancing together had been basically all business. Their barriers had both been so firmly up. But that kiss she had planted on his cheek had taken the first chink out of those barriers, and now there were more chinks falling.

And so this outing and this experience wasn't all business even if she had cloaked her motivation in accomplishing a goal.

Meredith looked at Kiernan's face, dappled with sunshine coming through the feathery cedars that surrounded the pool, and something sighed within her. His face was exquisite, handsome and perfect, but she had never seen the expression she saw on it now.

Prince Kiernan's eyes were closed. He looked completely relaxed, and something like contentment had crept into the normally guarded lines of his face. He tilted his chin to the sun, and took a deep breath, sighed it out.

It was good.

But it wasn't enough.

She wanted, *needed* to see with a desperation not totally motivated by her end goal, the prince lose his inhibitions, that *restraint*, that was like an ever-present palace guard, surrounding him. Keeping others away from him. But also keeping him away from others.

She let go of his hand. She stooped, and buried her own hand in the mud, closed her fist around an oozing gob of goo. For a moment she hesitated.

It was true. Kiernan was just way too restrained. He could never reach his potential as a dancer while he carried that shield around him.

But this was probably still just about the worst idea she had ever had. She lived in a land still ruled by a very traditional monarchy. Schoolchildren and soldiers started their day by swearing their allegiance and obedience to this man's mother, Queen Aleda. But in time it would be him they stood and pledged their hearts to.

He had already shouldered much of the mantle of responsibility. Meredith knew, partly from the newspapers, and confirmed by the phone calls he sometimes had to take during dance practice, his interest in the economic health of the island was keen, that he had sharp business acumen, and that some of his initiatives had improved the standard of living for many people who lived here.

He promoted Chatam tirelessly abroad. He headed charities. He sat on hospital boards. He was the commander-in-chief of the military.

This man who stood with her, his pants rolled up to his knees, had influence over the lives of every single person in Chatam.

Really, it was no wonder he had trouble relaxing! So, this was probably one of the worst ideas Meredith had ever had. She *was* too cheeky. You did not, after all, in a land ruled by a monarchy, pick up a handful of oozing soft mud and hurl it at your liege!

But Meredith was committed to her course. Knowing somehow, in her heart, not her head, this was, absurdly, wonderfully, the *right* thing, she let fly with a handful of mud.

It caught him in the chest, and he staggered back a step, startled. He opened his eyes and stared down at the mud bullet that had exploded on his shirt.

His reaction would tell her a great deal about this man.

Furious anger?

Remote silence?

Complete retreat?

But, no, a smile tickled his lips, and when he looked up at her, she felt she might weep for what she had unmasked in his eyes.

"Disrespectful wench," he said. "I'd swear you are looking for a few nights in the dungeon."

There was a delightful playfulness in his tone.

"Andy! Are you in your prince delusion again? Dungeons, for pity sake! I suppose you'll be telling me about bread and water and rats next. Poor you. Tut-tut."

"Prince delusion? Oh, no, not at all. I'm in my warrior delusion, and you have just called me to battle. But I'm going to warn you, all prisoners go to the dungeon. If you please me, I might spare you the rats."

She giggled, a trifle nervously, because something

smoked in his eyes when he talked of making her his prisoner.

What had she started? And could she really handle it?

Kiernan stooped and came up with his big hand full of mud. He squinted at her thoughtfully, drew back his arm and took aim.

She began to run an awkward zigzag pattern through the sucking mud. The dark sludge he hurled whisked by her head.

"Ha-ha," she called over her shoulder. Meredith ducked, picked up her own mud ball and flung it back at him. But he'd had time to rearm, too.

Their mud balls crossed paths with each other, midair. His hit her solidly on the arm, with a warm, soft splat. It was like being hit with a dollop of just-out-of-the-oven pudding. Her missile wobbled through the air and went straight for his head.

Despite the fact he raised his arm in defense against the slow-flying projectile, it exploded against his raised bicep, and particles of it landed on his cheek, blossoming there like the petals of a mud flower. She drew her breath, shocked by her own unintentional audacity.

"I'm so sorry!" she called.

"Not nearly as sorry as you're going to be," he warned her.

He stopped, carefully wiped the muck off his cheekbone, and glared at her with mock fierceness. But Meredith saw there was nothing mock about the fact he did now look like a warrior! Of the barbaric variety that painted their faces before they went to battle.

He let out a cry worthy of that warrior and came after

her, stooping and hucking mud as fast as he could fill his hands with it.

In moments the glade rang with his shouts and her playful shrieking. They threw mud back and forth until they were both covered in dark blotches, until their hair was lost under ropy dreadlocks of sludge, their hands were like mud mitts at their sides, and their clothes had disappeared under layers of smelly black goo. Finally, only his teeth and the whites of his eyes still looked white. Andy's shirt was probably beyond repair.

The glade filled with the sounds of their laughter and playful insults, the sounds of them gasping for breath as they struggled to run through the sucking mud to escape each other's attacks.

"Take that, Molly!"

"You missed! Andy, you throw like a girl."

"*You* missed. *You* throw like a girl."

"But I am a girl!"

"A girl? A mud monster, risen from the deep! Take that!"

They were laughing so hard they were choking on it. It rang off the rocks around them, rode on the mist.

Despite the noise, the chaos, the hilarity, something quiet blossomed in Meredith. Something she had felt, ever so briefly on that horse yesterday, but other than that not for a long, long time.

Joy.

The quiet awareness of it knocked her off balance. With Kiernan hot on her heels, his raised hand full of mud rockets, she slipped. She went down in slow motion, somehow managing to twist so she wouldn't go into the muck face first. The mud cushioned her fall, and she fell on her back with a sucking *splat*.

She watched as Kiernan, too close, tried desperately

to stop, but his arms windmilled, and he fell right on top of her, saving her from the worst of his weight by bracing his arms around her.

She stared up into the face of her warrior prince. His eyes were alight with laughter, looking bluer than she had ever seen them look. His smile, against the backdrop of his muddy face, was brilliant, white as snow against a stone.

She had never felt anything quite so exquisite. She rested in a bed of warm mud, her skin slippery and sensuous with it. And Kiernan, equally as slippery, held himself off of her, but there were places their bodies met. His hard lines were pressed into the soft curves of her legs and her hips.

She touched him every day. But his guard had always been up.

Hers had been, too.

Only something, delicate and subtle, had shifted between them.

The laughter died in the air around them, and was replaced with a silence so profound that it vibrated with a growing tension, a deep awareness of each other.

He stared down at her, and some unguarded tenderness crept into his muddy, warrior's face.

Still holding most of his weight off her with one arm, he touched her lip with the hand he had just freed, scraped gently with his thumb.

Her joy escalated into exhilaration at the exquisite sense of being touched in such an intimate place, in such an intimate way.

"You have mud right here," he whispered, by way of excuse, but his voice hoarse.

For a splendid moment it felt as if every barrier was

down between them. Every one. As if her world was as wide open as it had ever been.

Everything became remarkable: the song of a bird nearby, the feel of the mud cushioning her, the smells that tickled her nostrils, the green of the fern plumes behind him.

Where his legs were sprawled across hers, the slide of their skin together where it made slight contact at their hips, the amazing light in his sapphire eyes, the scrape of his thumb against her lip, the slick muddiness of his hair, the sensual curve of his lips.

He was so close to her she could see the dark beginning of stubble on his cheeks, and his chin. He was so close to her his breath stirred across her cheek, feather-light, as intimate as his thumb which remained on her lips. He was so close to her she could smell the scent of him, wild and clean as the forest, over the scent of the minerals in the mud that covered them.

She closed her eyes against the delicious agony of wanting a moment to last forever.

To escalate.

"I warned you there would be consequences if I took you prisoner," he said, the words playful, while his tone was anything but.

Was he going to kiss her? Even as a rational part of her knew they could never pull back from that again, a less rational part of her wanted the taste of his lips on hers, wanted to feel them.

She took her hand, as if it didn't matter it was mud-covered, and traced a possessive line down the hard plane of his jaw. She touched it to the fullness of his lip.

As if it didn't matter to him that it was mud-covered, he teased her finger gently, nibbled it with his teeth.

She felt the featherlight touch of his lip against the skin of her finger. Was it possible to die of sensation?

If this—the merest touch of his lips to something as inconsequential as her finger—could cause this unbelievable rise of sensation within her, what would it be like if he took her lips with his own?

She felt as if it would be a death of sorts.

The death of all she had been before, the rising up of something new, the rising up within her of a spirit that was stronger and more resilient than she had ever imagined, similar to that spirit that rose in her when she danced.

A place that was without thought, and without history.

Heaven.

Brazen with wanting, she slipped her muddy hands around the column of his neck, and pulled him down to her.

His weight settled on her more fully, chest to the soft curve of breast, hard stomach to delicate swell, muscled legs to slender ones, fused.

A whisper of sanity called her back from the brink.

And then called louder, *stop.*

It reminded her of the price of such a heated moment, lives changed forever.

But in that moment, she didn't care if there was a price.

And apparently neither did he.

Because his lips touched hers. The fact they were both mud-slicked only increased the danger, the sensuality, the delicious sense of being swept away, of not caring about what happened next, of being pulled by forces greater than themselves.

His very essence was in the way he kissed her.

Kiernan tasted, not of mud, but of rain in a storm, pure, clean, elemental. His kiss was tender, welcoming, and yet the strength and leashed passion were sizzling just below the surface.

It had been so long since Meredith had allowed anything or anyone to touch her, emotionally or physically.

She had not even known the hunger grew in her, waiting for something, someone to touch it off, to show her she was ravenous.

She was ravenous, and Kiernan was a feast of sensation.

Everything about him swirled around her—the light in his sapphire eyes, the line of his hard body against hers, the taste of his lips, the hollow of his mouth—all those broken places within her were being touched by sensation that was fulfilling and healing and exhilarating.

It was madness. Exquisite, delicious, compelling madness.

And she had to stop it. She had to.

Except that she was powerless, in the grip of something so amazing and wondrous she could not have stopped it if her very life depended on it. She was just not that strong.

But he was.

He pulled back from her, she saw strength and temptation war in his eyes, and she was astounded—and saddened—when his strength won. He pulled himself away from her, hesitated, dropped back down and placed one more tiny kiss on the corner of her lip, and then pulled his weight completely off her and stood gazing down at her.

Meredith saw control replace the heat in his eyes.

She watched awareness dawn in his eyes, saw his reluctant acquiescence to the guard he always surrounded himself with.

She knew, with a desperate sadness, this moment was over.

CHAPTER SIX

KIERNAN COMPOSED HIMSELF, held his hand to her. She took it, and her body made an unattractive slurping sound as he tugged, and then yanked hard to free her from the mud.

If he said he was sorry, she felt she would die.

But he did not say that, and she felt a strange sense of relief that she could tell he was not sorry. Not even a little bit.

And neither was she, even though the consequences of what had just happened hung over her.

Neither of them spoke, looking at each other, aware with an awareness that could not be denied once it had been acknowledged.

He dropped her hand, but not her gaze.

"Thank you," he said softly.

She knew exactly what he meant. That moment of being so alive, so incredibly vibrantly alive had been a gift to both of them.

She had not even been aware how much she lived in a state of numbness until she had experienced this wonderful hour with him. It had been carefree, and laughter-filled, wondrous. Meredith felt as if she had been exquisitely and fully alive in a way she had not been for a long, long time.

If she ever had been that alive, that fully engaged, that spontaneous, that filled with wonder for the simple, unexpected miracle of life.

Still, leaving the utter and absolute magic of the moment, Meredith felt as if she was going to cry.

She covered the intensity of the moment by pasting a smile on her face. "You're welcome. People pay big money for the mud treatment at the spa."

"Yes," he said, watching her closely, as if he knew she was covering, as if he knew exactly how fake that smile was. "I know."

And of course he would know. Because that was his world. Spas and yachts and polo ponies.

His world. He had playfully said he would take her prisoner, but the truth was his world was a prison in many ways.

And he could not invite her into it.

She did not have the pedigree of a woman he would ever be allowed to love.

Love. How had that word, absolutely taboo in her relationship with him, slipped past all her guards and come into her mind?

But now that it had come, Meredith was so aware how this moment was going to have a tremendous cost to her. Because, she had ever so briefly glimpsed his heart. Because she had seen the coolness leave his eyes and be replaced with tenderness. Yes, this moment had come at a tremendous price to her. Because she had let her guard down, too.

For a moment she had wanted things she could not have. Ached for them.

Still, if she had this choice to make over, how would she do it? Would she play it safe and stay in the ballroom, tolerating his wooden performance, allowing his mask to remain impenetrable?

No, she would change nothing. She would forever be grateful she had risked so much to let him out of his world, and his prison. Even if it had only been a brief reprieve.

And in return, hadn't she been let out of hers?

He turned from her, but not before she caught the deeply thoughtful look on his face, as if every realization she was having was also occurring to him.

He walked back through the fern barrier, leapt into the hot springs completely clothed. She watched his easy strength, as he did a powerful crawl that carried him across the pool to the cascading water of the falls. She quelled the primitive awareness that tried to rise in her.

Instead, she dove into the pool, too. Her skin had never felt so open to sensation. He had climbed up on a ledge underneath the falls, and she saw the remnants of their day falling off of him as if it had never happened.

It was time to clean herself of the residue of the day, too. She swam across the pool and pulled herself up on the ledge beside him.

The fresh, cold water was shocking on her heated skin. It pummeled her, was nearly punishing in its intensity.

Though she and Kiernan stood side by side, Meredith was painfully aware some distance now separated them, keeping their worlds separate even in the glorious intimacy of the cascading water world that they shared.

She slid him a look and felt her breath catch in her throat.

His face was raised to the water, his eyes closed as

what was left of the mud melted out of his hair and dissolved off his face, revealing each perfect feature: the cut of high cheekbones, the straight line of his nose, the faint cleft of his chin.

The white of Andy's shirt had reemerged, but the shirt had turned transparent under the water, and clung to the hard lines of Kiernan's chest. She could see the dark pebble of his nipple, the slight indent of each rib, the hollow of a taut, hard belly. It made her mouth go dry with a powerful sense of craving.

To touch. To taste. To have. To hold.

Impossible thoughts. Ones that would only bring more grief to her if she allowed them any power at all. Hadn't her life held quite enough grief?

Was it the coldness of the water after all that heat, or her awareness of him that was making her quiver?

Meredith felt herself wanting to save this moment, to remember the absolute beauty of it—and of him—forever.

He finally turned and dove cleanly off the ledge, cutting the water with his body. With that same swift, sure stroke, Kiernan made his way back across the mineral pond to where he had set the baskets. How long ago? An hour? A little longer than an hour?

How could so much change in such a short amount of time?

She dove in, too, emerged from the pond, dripping, and flinging back the wetness of her hair. She saw, from the brief heat in his eyes before he turned away, that Molly's shirt must have become as transparent as Andy's.

She glanced down. And she had accused him of boring underwear? Her bra—a utilitarian sports model made for athletic support while dancing—showed clearly through the wet fabric. But from the look on his face you would have thought she was wearing a bra made out of silk and lace!

She shoved by him, and rummaged through the baskets, tucked a towel quickly around herself and then silently handed him a towel and a change of clothing.

Was there the faintest smirk on his face from how quickly she had wrapped herself up?

"You're prepared," he said.

Yes. And no. There were some things you could not prepare for. Like the fact you hoped a man would tease you about being a prude, like the fact it was so hard to let go of a perfect day.

But he didn't tease her, or linger. He ducked behind a rock on one side of the glade and she on the other. She did not want to think of him naked in a garden, but she knew the temptation of Eve in that moment, and fought it with her small amount of remaining strength.

The trip back was eerily silent, as if they were both contemplating what had happened and how to go forward—or back—from that place.

Meredith drove back through the same service entrance to Chatam Palace. On the way in she had to stop and show ID, and her palace pass. She did not miss the stunned look on the face of the guard as he recognized the prince squished in the seat beside her. He practically tossed her ID back through her window, drew himself to attention and saluted rigidly.

It could not have been a better reminder of who the man beside her *really* was.

And the look of shock on the guard's face to see the prince in such a humble vehicle with a member of the palace staff, could not have been a better reminder of who she really was, too.

He was not Andy. She was not Molly.

He was a prince, born to position, power and prestige. She was a servant's daughter, a woman who had given birth to an illegitimate child, a person with so much history and so much baggage.

She let the prince out, barely looking at him. He barely looked at her.

They did not say goodbye.

Meredith wondered if he would show up for their scheduled dance session tomorrow.

Would she?

The whole thing had become fraught with a danger that she did not know how to handle.

And yet, even that tingling sensation of danger as she drove away from the palace after dropping Kiernan off there, served as a reminder.

She was alive.

She was alive, and for the first time in a long, long time, she was aware of being deeply grateful that she was alive. The pain. The glory. The potential to be hurt. The potential to love. It was all part of the most incredible dance.

There was that word again.

Love.

"Forbidden to me," Meredith said. Because of who he was. Because of who she was, and especially because of where she had already been in the name of love.

But of course, what had more power than forbidden fruit?

When Prince Kiernan walked through the doors of the ballroom the next morning, Meredith did not know whether she was relieved he had come, or sorry that she had to be tested some more.

He was right on time as always.

They exchanged perfunctory greetings. She put on the music. He took her hand, placed his other with care on her waist.

The trip to the hot springs had obviously been an error in every way it was possible for something to be an error.

This was turning out to be just like the day she had ridden his horse and they had danced in the courtyard to the chamber music spilling out the palace windows.

Prince Kiernan's guard came down, but only temporarily!

And when it went back up, it went way up!

After half an hour of tolerating a wooden performance from him, Meredith was not tingling with awareness of being alive at all! She was tingling with frustration. Was he dancing this badly just to put her off? Maybe he was hoping she would cancel the whole thing. And maybe she should.

Except she couldn't. It was too late now to start over with someone else. The girls, rehearsing separately, at her studio, had practiced to perfection. They were there night and day, putting heart and soul into this.

She wasn't letting them down because Prince Kiernan was the most confoundedly stubborn man in the world.

But really, enough was enough!

"This is excruciating," she said, pulling away from him, folding her arms across her chest and glaring at him.

Somewhere under that cool, composed mask was the man who had chased her, laughter-filled, through the mud.

"I warned you I had no talent."

"Call somebody," she snapped at him. "It's like a

game show where you have a lifeline. Call somebody, and use your princely powers. Have them find us the movie *Dancing with Heaven*. And deliver it. Right here. Right now."

It was an impossible request. The movie was old. It would probably be extremely difficult if not impossible to find.

For a moment he looked like he might argue, but then he chose not to, probably because he wanted to do just about anything rather than dance.

With her.

With some new tension in the air between them. Harnessed, it would make for an absolutely electrical dance performance.

Resisted, it would make for a disastrous dance performance.

He took a cell phone out of his pocket, and placed a call.

"Tell them not to forget the popcorn," she said darkly. "And I'd like something to drink, too."

"You're being very bossy," he said. "As usual."

Within minutes his cell phone rang back. "It's set up in the theater room," he said.

"Can't we watch it here?"

"No, we can't. I'm not sitting on an icy cold floor to watch a movie. Not even for you."

Not even for you. She heard something there that she knew instantly he had not intended for her to hear. Something that implied he would do anything for her, up to and including going to the ends of the earth.

She deliberately quelled the beating of her heart and followed the prince to where he held open the ballroom doors for her.

It was the first time Meredith had been in the private

areas of the interior of the palace. The ballroom, along with the throne room, and a gallery of collected art was in the public wing of the palace, open to anyone who went there on a tour day.

Now, Prince Kiernan led her through an arched door flanked by two palace guards who saluted him smartly. The door led into the private family quarters of the palace.

They were in a grand entranceway, a formal living room on one side, a curving staircase on the other. The richness of it was startling: original old masters paintings, Persian rugs, priceless antiques, draperies and furniture upholstered in heavy brocaded silks. A chandelier that put the ones in the ballroom to shame spattered light over the staircase and entry.

Kiernan noticed none of it as he marched her up the wide stairs, under the portraits of his ancestors, many of whom looked just like him, and all of whom looked disapproving.

"What a happy looking lot," she muttered. "They have aloofness down to a fine art."

He glanced at the portraits. "Don't they?" With *approval*.

So *that's* where he got his rigidity!

"Maybe I'm wasting my time trying to break past something that has been bred into each Chatam for hundreds of years." And that they were proud of to *boot*.

"I've been trying to tell you."

And maybe if she hadn't been stupid enough to take him on that excursion yesterday, she would have believed him.

"This floor is where guests stay," he said, exiting the staircase that still spiraled magnificently upward. He led her down a wide corridor.

Bedroom doors were open along either side of the hallway and she peeked in without trying to appear too interested. The bedrooms, six in all, three on either side of the hallway were done in muted, tasteful colors. The décor had the flavor and feel of pictures Meredith had seen of very upscale boutique hotels.

It occurred to Meredith that princes and presidents, prime ministers, princesses and prima donnas had all walked down these corridors.

It reminded her who the man beside her *really* was, and she felt a whisper of awe. He opened the door to a room at the end of the long hallway.

Meredith tried not to gape. The "theater room" was really the most posh of private theaters. The walls were padded white leather panels with soft, muted light pouring out from behind them. The carpets were rich, dark gold with a raised crown pattern in yet darker gold. There were three tiers of theater style chairs in soft, buttery distressed leather. Each chair had a light underneath it that subtly illuminated the aisle. The chairs faced a screen as large as any Meredith had ever seen.

Two chairs were in front of all the others, and Kiernan gestured to one of them. Obviously she was sitting in a chair that would normally be slated for the most important of VIP's. She settled into the chair.

"Who's the last person who sat here?" She could not stop herself from asking.

If Kiernan thought the question odd he was polite enough not to let on. "I think it was the president of the United States. Nice man."

Never had she been more aware of who Kiernan really was.

And who she really was.

A man in a white jacket, very much like the one she

had borrowed from Andy, arrived with a steaming hot bowl of popcorn for each of them. He pushed a button on the side of her seat, and a tray emerged from the armrest.

"I was kidding about the popcorn," she hissed at Kiernan, but she took the bowl anyway.

"A drink, miss?"

Part of her was so intimidated by her surroundings, she wanted to just say no, to be that invisible girl who had accompanied her mother to work on occasion.

But another part of her thought she might never have on opportunity like this again, so, she was making the most of it. She decided to see how flummoxed the man would be if she ordered something completely exotic and off the wall—especially for ten o'clock in the morning. "Oh, sure. I'll have a virgin chi-chi."

The servant didn't even blink, just took the prince's order and glided away only to return a few minutes later.

"My apologies," he said quietly. "We didn't have the fresh coconut milk today."

She had to stifle a giggle. A desire to tease and say, *see that that doesn't happen again.* Instead, she met the man's eyes, and saw the warmth in them, and the lack of judgment.

"Can I get you anything else?"

"No, thank you for your kindness," she said. And she meant it.

She took a sip, and sighed. The drink, even without the fresh coconut milk was absolute ambrosia.

The movie came on. For the first few minutes Meredith was so self-conscious that Prince Kiernan was beside her. It felt as if she was on a first date, and they were afraid to hold hands.

Dancing with Heaven was dated and hokey, but the dance sequences were incredible, sizzling with tension and sensuality.

Though she had seen this movie a dozen times, Meredith was soon lost in the story of a spoiled self-centered young woman who walked by a dance studio called Heaven, peeked in the window, and was entranced by what she saw there. The dance instructor was a bitter older man whose career had been lost to an injury. He taught dance only for the money, because he had to.

Through what Meredith considered some the best dance sequences ever written, the young woman moved beyond her superficial and cynical attitude toward life and the instructor came to have hope again.

Wildly romantic, and sizzling with the sexual chemistry between the two, the instructor fought taking advantage of the young heiress's growing love for him, but in the end he succumbed to the love he had for her and the unlikely couple, united through dance, lived happily ever after.

What had made her insist the prince see this ridiculous and unrealistic piece of fluff?

When it was over, Meredith was aware of tears sliding down her face. She wiped at them quickly before the lights came up, set down her empty glass and her equally empty popcorn dish.

"Now you know what I expect of you. I'll see myself out. See you in the morning."

Kiernan saw that Meredith was not meeting his eyes. Something about the movie had upset her.

He ordered himself to let it go, especially after yesterday. Not that he wanted to think about yesterday.

He'd kissed her, and it hadn't been a little buss on

the cheek, either. No, it had been the kind of kiss that blew something wide open in a man, the kind of kiss that a man did not stop thinking about once it had happened.

It was the kind of kiss that made a man evaluate his own life and find it seemed empty, and without color.

The problem was they had been pretending to be ordinary.

And between an ordinary man and an ordinary woman maybe such things could happen without consequences.

But in his world? If he went where that kiss invited him to go, *begged* him to go, the world she knew would be over.

She had trusted him with her deepest secrets. How would she like those secrets to be exposed to the world? If he let his guard down again, if he allowed things to develop between them, Meredith would find her past at the center ring of a three-ring circus. Pictures of her baby would be dug up. Her mother's past would be investigated. Her ex would be found and asked for comments on her character.

So, even though the movie had upset her, it would be best to let her go.

And yet he couldn't.

He stepped in front of her.

"Are you upset?" he asked quietly.

She looked panicked. "No. I just need to go. I need to—"

"You're upset," he said. "Why? Did the movie upset you?"

"No, I—"

"Please don't lie to me," he said. "You've never done it before, and you have no talent for it."

She was silent.

He tipped her chin. "Did it remind you of your baby's father?" he asked softly. "Is that the way you felt about him?"

He remembered the sizzling sensuality between the on-screen couple, and he felt a little pang of, good grief, *envy*. But this wasn't about him. He could actually feel her trembling, trying to hold herself together.

"Talk to me, Meredith."

"It had a happy ending," she whispered. "I deplore happy endings! If it weren't for the dance sequences, I would have never asked you to watch such drivel!"

But he was stuck at the *I deplore happy endings* part. How could anyone so young and so vibrant have stopped believing in a happy ending for herself?

"My baby's father was older than me, twenty-two. He was new to the neighborhood, and all the girls were swooning over his curly hair and his suave way. I was thrilled that he singled me out for his attention. Thrilled."

Kiernan felt something like rage building in him at the man he had never met, the man who had used her so terribly, manipulated and fooled a young girl. But he said nothing, fearing that if he spoke, she would clam up.

And he sensed she needed to talk, she needed to say these things she had been holding inside. And he needed to be man enough to listen, without being distracted by her lips and the memory of their taste, without wanting *more* for himself. Without putting his needs ahead of her own.

"If I had married Michael, my baby's father, it would have been a disaster," she said. "I can see that now. As hard as it was for me and my mom to make ends meet, it would have only been harder with him. You want to know how bad my taste is in men? Do you want to know?"

He saw the regret in her eyes and the pain, and he wanted to know everything about her. Everything.

"He didn't even come to the funeral."

She began to sob.

And he did what he should have done yesterday in the car, what he had wanted to do.

He pulled her into his chest, and ran his hand up and down her back, soothing her, encouraging her. *Let it out.*

"I loved him, madly. I guess maybe I held on to this fantasy he was going to come to his senses, do the right thing, come back and rescue me. Prove to my mother she was wrong. Love us."

If he could have, he would have banished the shame from her face.

"Kiernan," she said softly, "he didn't care one fig about me. Not one. And I fooled myself into thinking he did. How can a person ever trust themselves after something like that? How?"

He loved that she had called him his name, no formal address. Wasn't that what was happening between them? And what he was fighting against?

Deepening trust. Friendship. Boundaries blurring. But as he let her cry against him, he knew it was more. Mere friendship was not something that would put his guard up so high. And mere friendship would never have him feeling a nameless fury at the man who had cruelly used her, walked away from his responsibilities, broken her heart as if it was nothing.

His fury at a man he had never met abated as he

became aware of Meredith pressed against him, felt the sacredness of her trust, and this moment.

He was not sure that he had ever felt as much a man as he did right now.

"You deserved so much better," he finally said.

"Did I?" She sounded skeptical.

He put her away from him, looked deep into the lovely green of her eyes. "Yes," he said furiously, "you did. As for trusting yourself? My God, cut yourself some slack. You were a child. Sixteen. Is that what you said?"

"Seventeen when Carly was born."

"A child," he repeated firmly. "Taken advantage of by an adult man. His behavior was despicable. To be honest? I'd like to track him down and give him a good thrashing!"

She actually giggled a little at that. "Maybe the dungeon?"

He felt relieved that she was coming around, that he saw a spark of light in her eyes. "Exactly! Extra rats!"

"Thank you," she said, quietly.

"I'm not finished. As for not trusting yourself? Meredith, you have taken these life experiences and made it your mission to change things for others. Do you remember what I said to you when you thanked me for not allowing you to fall off the horse?"

"Yes," she whispered, "You said it's not how you fall that matters. You said everyone falls. You said it was how you got up that counted."

He was intensely flattered that she had heard him so completely. He spoke quietly and firmly. "And how you are getting up counts, Meredith. Helping those Wentworth girls honors your baby. And your mother. And you."

She gave him a watery smile, pulled away from him,

not quite convinced. "Oh, God, look at me. A blithering idiot. In front of a prince, no less."

And she turned, he could tell she was going to flee, and so he caught her arm. "I'm not letting you go, not just yet. Let's have tea first."

Just in case he was beginning to think he was irresistible, she said, "Will it have the little cream puff swans?"

"Yes," he said. "It will."

He guided her out of the theater and to the elevator at the end of the hallway and took her to his private apartment.

"It's beautiful," she said, standing in the doorway, as if afraid to come in. And maybe he should have thought this out better.

Once she had been in here, would he ever be completely free of her? Or would he see her walking around, pausing in front of each painting like this, always?

"Is it you who loves Monet?" she asked.

He nodded.

"Me, too. I have several reproductions of his work."

"I understand," Kiernan said, "that he was nearsighted. That wonderful dreamy, hazy quality in his landscapes was not artistic license but how he actually saw the world. You know what I like about that?"

She looked at him.

"His handicap was his greatest gift. Your hardships, Meredith?"

She was looking at him as if he had a lifeline to throw her. And he hoped he did.

"Your hardships are what make you what you are. Amazingly strong, and yet good. Your goodness shines out of you like a light."

He turned away to look after tea. But not before he

saw that maybe he had said exactly the right thing after all, but maybe not enough of it. She did not look entirely convinced.

He had tea set up on the balcony that overlooked the palace grounds and the stunning views of Chatam.

"Instead of allowing your falls to break you," he insisted quietly, sitting her down, "you have found your strength."

"No, really I haven't."

Now he felt honor-bound not to let her go until she was convinced. Of her own goodness. Of her innate strength. Of the fact that she had to let go of all that shame. Of the fact she was earning her way, by the way she chose to live her life, to a new future.

"I want to know every single thing there is to know about you. I want to know how you've become the remarkable woman you are today." And he meant that.

She looked wildly toward the exit, but then she met his eyes. But just to keep him from feeling too powerful, then she looked at the tray of goodies a servant was bringing in.

"Oh," she said. "The cream puffs."

"I know how to get your secrets out of you, Meredith."

"There's nothing remarkable about me."

"Ah, well, let me decide."

She mulled that over, and then sighed. Almost surrender. He passed her the tray. She took a cream puff, and sighed again. When she bit into it and closed her eyes he knew her surrender was complete.

They talked for a long, long time. It was deep and it was true and it was real. He felt as if they could sit there and talk forever.

It was late in the afternoon before Meredith looked at her watch, gasped, and made her excuses. Within seconds she was gone. Kiernan was not sure he had ever felt he had connected with someone so deeply, had ever inspired trust such as he had just experienced from her.

Kiernan sat for a long time in a suite that felt suddenly cold and empty for all the priceless art and furniture that surrounded him. It felt as if the life had gone out of it when Meredith had.

Without her the room just seemed stuffy. And stodgy.

He'd liked having her here in his very private space. He'd liked watching the movie with her and how she had not tried to hide the fact she was awed that a president had sat in her chair. He liked how she had acknowledged Bernard who had brought their popcorn and drinks, not treated him as if he was invisible, the way Tiffany always had.

And damn it, he'd liked that movie.

Silly piece of fluff that it was, it was somehow about people finding the courage to be what they were meant to be, to bring themselves to the world, to overcome the strictures of their assigned roles and embrace what was real for them.

And, finally, he had loved how she had come into his space, and how between cream puffs and his genuine interest and concern for her she had become so open. And liked what the afternoon told him about her.

Above all things, Meredith was courageous.

A hardscrabble upbringing, too many losses for one so young, and yet he saw no self-pity in her. She was taking the challenges life had given her and turning them into her greatest assets. She had a quiet bravery to get on with her life.

That's what she was asking of him. To bring his

courage to the dance floor. To dance without barriers, without a mask, and without a safety net.

She was asking him to be who he had been, ever so briefly, when they had chased each other through the mud.

Wholly alive. Completely, unselfconsciously himself.

No guards. No barriers.

And she was asking him to be who he had been just now: deep and compassionate.

Really, what she was asking of him would require more courage than just about anything he had ever done. At the hot springs he had shown that unguarded self to her. And again today there had been something so open and unprotected about their interaction after the movie.

Prince Kiernan felt as if he stood on the very edge of a cliff. Did he take a leap of faith, trusting if he jumped something—or someone—would catch him? Or did he turn away?

"For her sake," he said to himself, "You turn away."

But he didn't know if he was powerful enough to do that. He knew he wanted these last days with her before it was over.

So he could have moments and memories, a secret, something sacredly private in his life, to savor when she was gone.

CHAPTER SEVEN

"FROM THE TOP," Meredith said. Today's dancing session, she knew, was going no better than yesterday's. The movie had changed nothing.

No, that was not true.

It had changed everything.

It had changed her. Maybe not the movie, exactly, but what had happened after.

When Kiernan had held her in her arms, it had felt as if everything she had been fighting for since the death of her mother and baby—independence, strength, self-reliance—it had felt as if those things were melting.

As if some terrible truth had unfolded.

All those qualities that she had striven toward were just distractions from the real truth. And the truth was she was so terribly alone in this world.

And for a moment, for an exquisite, tender moment in the arms of her country's most powerful man, she had not felt that. Sitting beside him on the balcony of his exquisite apartment, surveying all his kingdom, pouring out her heart, telling her secrets, she had not felt that.

For the first time in forever, Meredith had not felt alone.

And it was the most addictive sensation she had ever

felt. She wanted to feel it again. She wanted to never let go of it.

Worse, she had a tormented sense that, though Kiernan walked with kings and presidents, she had seen what was most *real* about him. It was the laughter at the hot springs, it was his confidence in his horse, it was the tenderness in his eyes as he had listened to her yesterday.

And she had to guard against the feeling that he caused in her.

Because just like the wealthy heiress and the dance instructor in the movie, their worlds were so far apart. But unlike the movie, which was pure escapist fantasy after all, they could never be joined. And the sooner she accepted the absoluteness of that the better.

This morning she felt only embarrassed that she had revealed herself so totally to him. Talked, not just about Michael and Carly, which was bad enough, but about her childhood, growing up with a single mom in Wentworth, and then repeating her family's history by becoming one herself.

She'd told him about ballet, and her mother's hope and losing the scholarship when she became pregnant. She'd told him about those desperate days after Carly was born, her mother being there for her, despite her disappointments, Millie loving the baby, but never quite forgiving her daughter.

She told him about the insurance settlement after the tragedy that allowed her to own her own dance studio and form No Princes, and how guilty she felt that her dreams were coming true because the people she had loved the most had died.

Oh, yes, she had said way, way too much. And today, it was affecting *her* dancing.

She was the one with the guard up. She was the one who could not open herself completely. She was the one who could not be vulnerable on the dance floor. She was trying desperately to take back the ground she had lost yesterday.

And she was failing him. Because she could not let him in anymore. She could not be open.

She was as rigid and closed as the prince had been on that first day. It was the worst of ironies that now he seemed as open as she was closed!

"What's wrong?" he asked.

The tender concern in his eyes was what was wrong! The fact she was foolishly, unrealistically falling in love with him was what was wrong!

"You know what?" he said, snapping his fingers. "I know I have the power to fix whatever is wrong!"

Yes, he did. He could get down on one knee and say that though the time had been short he realized he was crazy about her. That he couldn't live without her.

All this work. All this time with No Princes and Meredith's weaknesses were unabated! She despised that about herself.

"One call," he said, and smiled at her and left the room.

When he returned he had a paper bag with him, and with the flourish of a magician about to produce a rabbit, he opened it and handed her a crumpled white piece of fabric.

"Ta-da," he said as she shook out the white smock.

"What is this?"

"I think I've figured it out," he said, pulling another smock from the bag and tugging it over his own shirt.

It had Andy embossed across the breast.

She stared down at the smock in her hand. Sure enough, he had unearthed Molly's smock.

"Remember when you told me this kind of dancing is like acting?"

Meredith nodded.

"Well, I'm going to be Andy for the rest of the rehearsals. And you're going to be Molly."

She stared at him stunned. She wanted to refuse. She wanted to get out of this with her heart in one piece.

But she could not resist the temptation of the absolute brilliance of it. If she could pretend to be someone else, if she could pretend he was someone else, there was a slim chance she could save this thing from catastrophe. And maybe, at the same time, she could save herself from the catastrophe of an unattainable love.

But it seemed the responsibility for saving things had been wrested from her. Kiernan took charge. He went and put on the music, turned and gazed at her, then held out his hands to her.

"Shall we dance, Molly?"

She could only nod. She went and took his hands, felt the way they fit together. Her resolve, which she could have sworn was made of stone, melted at his touch.

"Remember Andy?" he said, smiling down at her as they began the opening waltz.

She gave herself over to this chance to save the dance. "Isn't he that devilish boy who won't do his homework?"

"Except he did watch *Dancing with Heaven*."

"Used class time, though."

"That's true."

Kiernan had those opening steps down *perfect*. A little awkwardness, a faint stiffness, a resolve to keep his distance in his posture.

The transition was coming.

"Andy," she reminded him, getting into the spirit of this, embracing it, "winks at the teacher and makes her blush."

And Kiernan became that young fellow—on the verge of manhood, able to tie his teacher in knots with a blink of sapphire-colored eyes.

"I think he makes her drop things, too," Meredith conceded, and her blush was real. "And forget what she's teaching at all."

Kiernan smiled at her with Andy's wicked devil-may-care-delight. Through dance he became the young man who rode motorcycles, and wore black leather. He was the guy who drove too fast and broke rules.

Something about playing the role of the bad boy unleashed Kiernan. He was playful. He was commanding. He was mischievous. He was *bad*.

His hips moved!

They moved to the next transition, and Kiernan released her hand. He claimed the dance floor as his own.

He claimed it. Then he owned it.

Meredith's mouth dropped open as he tore off the smock that said Andy on it, and tossed it to the floor.

Before her eyes, Kiernan became the man who liked loud music and smoky bars, and girls in too-short skirts and low-cut tops who wiggle their hips when they dance. He became the guy who cooled off in the town fountain, claimed Landers Rock as his own, kept his hat on during the anthem.

He became a man so comfortable with himself that he would delight in swimming in the sea naked under the moonlight.

And then came the final transition.

And he was no longer an immature young man, chasing skirts and adrenaline rushes, breaking rules just for the thrill of having said he had done it.

Now he was a man, claiming the woman he wanted to spend the rest of his life with.

He crossed the floor to her, and they went seamlessly to the finale—dancing together as if nothing else in the world existed except each other, and the heat, the chemistry between them.

Meredith was not Meredith. She was Molly.

And something about being Molly unleashed her just as much as being Andy had unleashed him. She didn't have a history. She was just a girl from the kitchen who wanted something more out of life: not drudgery, but a hint of excitement wherever she could find it.

By playing Molly, Meredith came to understand her younger self.

And forgive her.

Finally, with both of them breathless, the music stopped. But Kiernan did not let her go. He stared at her silently, his eyes saying what his mouth did not.

She pulled away from him. Her smile was tremulous.

"It was perfect," she breathed.

"I know. I could feel it."

She had to get hold of herself; despite this breakthrough she had to find the line between professional and personal. She had to get over the feeling of wanting to take his lips and taste them, of wanting more than she could have, of wanting more than he could offer her.

"You know what would be brilliant?" Meredith said crisply. "We can alter the real performance dream sequence slightly so that it is Andy and Molly, and Andy transforms into a prince."

He was looking at her just as he had on the balcony of his private suite. With eyes that saw right through her professional blither-blather to the longing that was underneath.

She was only human.

And he was only human.

If she was going to keep this thing on the tracks until the performance at *An Evening to Remember* she had to make a drastic decision, and she had to make it right now.

"You know what this means, don't you?"

He shook his head.

"We're finished."

"Finished?"

"We're done, Prince Kiernan." It was self-preservation. She could not dance like that with him every day until the performance and keep her heart on ice, keep him from seeing what was blossoming inside her.

Like a flower that would be cut.

"We've got two practices left," he said, frowning at her.

"No," she said firmly, with false brightness, "there's nothing left to practice. Nothing. I don't think we should do it again. I don't want to lose the freshness of what we just did. We're done, Prince Kiernan. The next time we do that dance, it will be at *An Evening to Remember.*"

Instead of looking relieved that dance class was finally over, Kiernan looked stunned.

She felt stunned, too. She was ending it. The suddenness of it made her head spin. And she felt bereft. It was over. They would have one final dance together, but it was already over. She was ending this craziness right here and right now.

"So," she said with forced cheer, holding out her

hand to shake his, "good work, Your Highness. I'll see you opening night of Blossom Week, for *An Evening to Remember*. Gosh. Only a few nights away. How did that happen?"

But instead of shaking her hand, two business people who had done good work together, the prince took her hand, held it, looked with deep and stripping thoughtfulness into her eyes. Then he bowed over her hand, and placed his lips to it.

Meredith could feel that familiar devastating quiver begin in her toes.

"No," he said, straightening and gazing at her.

"No? No *what*?"

"No, it won't be opening night before we meet again."

"It won't?" It felt just like their first meeting, when he had told her she couldn't be Meredith Whitmore. He said things with the certainty of one who had the power to change reality, who *always* had his own way.

"You've shown me your world, Meredith," Kiernan said quietly. "You gave that to me freely, expecting nothing in return. You gave me a gift. But I would like to give you something in return, a gift of my own. Come experience an evening in my world."

Her mouth opened to say *no*. It wasn't possible. She was trying to protect herself. He was storming the walls.

"It's the least I can do for you. I'll send a car to pick you up tonight. We'll have a farewell dinner on the yacht."

Farewell. Did his voice have an odd catch in it when he said that?

Say *no*. Every single thing in her that wanted to survive screamed at her to say no.

But what woman, no matter how strong, no matter how independent, no matter how much or how desperately she wanted to protect her own heart could say no to an evening with a prince, a date out of a dream?

It wasn't as if she could get her hopes up. He'd been very clear. A farewell dinner. One last time to be alone together. The next time they saw each other would be very public, for their performance.

On pure impulse, Meredith decided she would give herself this. She would not or could not walk away from the incredible gift he was offering her.

She would take it, greedily. One night. One last thing to remember him by, to hold to her when these days of dancing with him, laughing with him, baring her soul to him, were but a distant memory.

"Yes," she whispered. "That would be lovely."

It wasn't a *date*, Meredith told herself as she obsessed about what to wear and how to do her hair and her makeup and her nails. It wasn't a date. He had not called it that. A gift, he had said, and even though she knew she should have tried harder to resist the temptation, now that she hadn't, she was giving herself over to the gift wholeheartedly.

She intended to not think about a future that did not include him. She was just going to take it moment by moment, and enjoy it without contemplating what that enjoyment might cost her later.

Hadn't she done that before? Exchanged heated looks and stolen kisses with no thought of the consequences?

No, it was different this time. She was a different person than she had been back then. Wasn't she?

And so, trying to keep her doubts on the back burner, with her makeup subtle and perfect, her nails varnished with clear lacquer, dressed in a simple black cocktail dress with a matching shawl, her hair upswept, the most expensive jewelry she could afford—tiny diamonds set in white gold—twinkling at her ears, she went down her stairs, escorted by a uniformed driver, to where the limousine awaited her. She thanked God that all the years of dancing made her able to handle the incredibly high heels—and the pre-performance jitters—with seeming aplomb.

Passersby and neighbors had stopped to gawk at the black limo, and the chauffeur holding it open for her.

It was not one of the official palace vehicles with the House of Chatam emblem on the door, but still she waved like a celebrity walking the red carpet, and slid inside the door.

The luxury of it was absolutely sumptuous. She was offered a glass of champagne, which she refused. The windows of the backseat were darkly tinted, so all the people staring at her as they passed could not see her staring back at them.

The car glided through the streets of Chatam into the harbor area, and finally arrived at a private dock. The yacht, called *Royal Blue*, bobbed gently on its moorings.

A carpet had been laid out to prevent her high heels from slipping through the wide-spaced wooden planks of the dock. Light spilled out every window of the yacht, danced down the dock and splashed out over inky dark waters.

The lights illuminated interior rooms. It wasn't a boat. It was a floating palace.

And against the midnight darkness of the sky, she could see Prince Kiernan. He was outside on an upper deck, silhouetted by the lights behind him, leaning on a railing, waiting.

For her.

She wanted to run to him, as if he was not a prince at all, but her safe place in this unfamiliar world of incredible wealth.

Instead, she walked up the carpet, and up the slightly swaying gangway with all the pose and grace years of dancing had given her. She knew his eyes were only for her, and she breathed it in, intending to enjoy every second of this gift.

The crew saluted her, and her prince waited at the top of the gangway.

Prince Kieran greeted her by meeting her eyes and holding her gaze for a long time, until her heart was beating crazily in her throat. Then he took her hand, much as he had in the ballroom, bowed low over it, and kissed it.

"Welcome," he said, and his eyes swept her.

Every moment she had taken with her hair and her makeup, her jewelry and her dress was rewarded with the light in his eyes. Except that he seemed to be memorizing her. He had said *welcome*, but really, hadn't he meant goodbye?

"You are so beautiful," he said, the faintest hoarseness in that cultured voice.

"Thank you," she stammered. She could have told him he looked beautiful, too, because he did, dressed in a dark suit with a crisp white shirt under it. At the moment, Kiernan was every girl's fairy-tale prince.

"Come," he said, and he slipped his hand in hers, and led her to a deeply padded white leather bench in the bow of the boat.

As the crew called muted orders to each other the

yacht floated out of its slip and they headed out of the mouth of the harbor.

"I just have to let you know in advance, that as hard as I tried to completely clear my calendar for this evening, I'm expecting an overseas call from the Minister of Business. I'll have to take it. I hope it will be brief, but possibly not. I hope you won't be bored."

Meredith was used to these kinds of interruptions from their dance classes.

"Bored? How could I be bored when I have this to experience?" She gestured over the view of dark sea, the island growing more distant. "It looks like a place out of a dream."

The lights of Chatam, reflected in the dark water, grew further away.

"It will be breezy now that we're underway. Do you want to go in?"

She shook her head, and he opened a storage unit under a leather bench, found a light blanket and settled it on her shoulders. Then Kiernan pressed against her to lend her his warmth.

As the boat cut quietly around the crags of the island, she found she and Kiernan talked easily of small things. The girls' excitement for the upcoming performance, Erin Fisher's remarkable talent and potential, Prince Adrian's recovery from his injury, the overseas call Kiernan was expecting about a business deal that could mean good things for the future of Chatam.

After half an hour of following the rugged coastline of Chatam, the yacht pulled into a small cove, the engines were cut, and the quiet encircled them as she heard the chain for the anchor drop.

"It's called Firefly Cove," he said. "Can you see why?"

"Oh," she breathed as thousands and thousands of small lights pricked the darkness, "it is so beautiful."

The breeze picked up, and he took the blanket and offered her his hand. They went inside.

It was as beautiful as outside.

There was really nothing to indicate they were on a boat, except for the huge windows and the slight bobbing motion.

Other than that the décor was fabulous—modern furniture covered in rich linens, paintings, rugs, an incredible chandelier hung over a dining table set for two with the most exquisite china.

All of it could have made her feel totally out of place and uncomfortable. But Kiernan was with her, teasing, laughing, putting her at ease.

Dinner came out, course after course of the most incredible food, priceless wines that an ordinary girl like her would never have tasted under other circumstances.

But rather than being intimidated Meredith delighted in the new experiences, made easy because of how her prince guided her through them.

They went back out on the deck for after-dinner coffee, he draped the blanket around her shoulders again, and tucked her into him. They sat amongst the fireflies and talked. At first of light things: the exquisiteness of the food they had just eaten, the rareness of the wines, the extraordinary beauty of the fireflies; the stars that filled the night sky.

But Meredith found herself yearning for his trust, the same trust that she had shown him the day they had watched the movie.

With a certain boldness, she took his hand, and said, "Tell me how you came to earn all those horrible nicknames. Playboy Prince. Prince of Heartaches. Prince Heartbreaker. I feel as if I've come to know you, and those names seem untrue and unfair."

But was it? Wasn't he setting her up for heartbreak right now? Without even knowing it? He'd been clear. Tonight was not hello. It was goodbye.

But she wasn't allowing herself to think of that.

No, she was staying in this moment: the gentle sway of the sea beneath her, his hand in hers, his shoulder touching hers.

She was staying in this moment, and moving it toward deeper intimacy even if that was crazy. She wanted him to know, even after they'd said goodbye, that she had known his heart.

"Thank you," he said with such sincerity, as if she had *seen* him that she quivered from it, and could not resist moving a little more closely into his warmth. "Though, of those titles, the Playboy Prince was probably neither untrue nor unfair."

He recounted his eighteenth summer. "I found myself free, in between getting out of private school and going into the military. Until I was eighteen, my mother had been very vigilant in restricting the press's access to me. And women hadn't been part of my all-male world, except as something desired from a distance, movie star posters on dorm room walls. So, I wasn't quite used to the onslaught of interest on both fronts.

"And like many young men of that age, I embraced all the perks of that freedom and none of the responsibility. Unfortunately, my forum was so public. There was a frenzy, like a new rock star had been unveiled to the world. I didn't see a dark side or a downside. I was flattered by the attention of the press and the young women. I dated every beautiful woman who showed the least interest in me."

"And that was many," Meredith said dryly.

Still, she could feel the openness of him, and something sighed within her. She had trusted him, and now he was trusting her.

"That's what I mean about the Playboy Prince title having truth to it," he said ruefully. "But after that summer of my whole life becoming so public, I became more discerning, and certainly more cynical. I started to understand that very few of those young women were really interested in *me*. It was all about the title, the lifestyle, and the fairy tale. I could be with the most beautiful woman in the world and feel so abjectly lonely.

"But for a short while, I searched, almost frantically for *the* one. I'm sure I broke hearts right and left because I could tell after the first or second date that it just wasn't going to work, and I extricated myself quickly. Somehow, though, I was always the one seen as responsible for the fact others pinned their unrealistic hopes and dreams on me."

Was that what she was doing? By sitting here, enjoying his world and his company, was she investing, again, in unrealistic hopes and dreams?

Just one night. She would give herself that. It wasn't really pinning hopes and dreams on him. It was about knowing him as completely as she could before she let him go back to his world, and she went back to hers.

"I'd known Francine Lacourte since I was a child," Kiernan continued. "We'd always been close, always the best of friends."

"The duchess." She felt the faintest pang of jealousy at the way he said that name. With a tender reverence.

"She was the funniest, smartest woman I ever met.

She was also the deepest. She had a quality about her, a glow that was so attractive. She shunned publicity, which I loved."

"You were engaged to her, weren't you?"

"Ever so briefly."

"And you broke it off, bringing us to nickname number two, the Prince of Heartaches. Because she never recovered, did she?"

Which, now that she thought about it, Meredith could see was a very real danger.

But Kiernan smiled absently. "The truth that no one knows? I didn't break it off. She did."

He was telling her a truth that no one else knew? That amount of trust felt exquisite.

"But that's not what the press said! In fact, they still say she is in mourning for you. She has become very reclusive. I don't think I've seen one photograph of her in the paper since you broke with her. And that's years ago. It really is like she has disappeared off the face of the earth."

"Our friends at the press take a fact—like Francine being reclusive—and then they build a story around it that suits their purposes. It has nothing to do with the truth. For a while there was even a rumor started by one of the most bottom feeding of all the publications that I had murdered her. How ridiculous is that?"

"That's terrible!"

"I am going to tell you a truth that very few people on this earth know. I know I don't have to tell you how deeply private this conversation is."

Again, Meredith relished this trust he had in her, even as she acknowledged it moved her dangerously closer to pinning unrealistic hopes and dreams on him!

"That depth and quality and glow in Francine that I

found so attractive? She had a deep spiritual longing. Francine joined a convent. She had wanted to do so for a long, long time. She loved me, I think. But not the way she loved God."

"She's a nun?" Meredith breathed, thinking of pictures of her that had been republished after his broken engagement to Tiffany Wells. Francine Lacourte was gorgeous, the last person one would think of as a nun!

He nodded. "She chose a cloister. Can you imagine the nightmare her new life would have been if the paparazzi got hold of that? Because I have a network around me that can protect me from the worst of their viciousness, I chose to let them create the story that titillated the world."

"You protected her," Meredith whispered.

"I don't really see it like that. She gave me incredible gifts in the times we spent together. I was able to return to her the privacy she so treasured."

"By taking the heat."

"Well, as I say, I have a well-oiled machine around me that protects me from the worst of it. The press can say whatever they want. I'm quite adept at dodging the arrows, not letting them affect me at all. So, if I could do that for Francine, why wouldn't I?"

Hadn't she known this for weeks? In her heart, with her sense of *knowing* him growing? That the prince was actually the opposite of how he was portrayed by the press?

"And then you graduated to being the Prince Heartbreaker," Meredith said.

"Tiffany came along later, and I was well aware it was *time*. Very subtle pressure was being brought on me to find a suitable partner. I had been deeply hurt by Francine's choice, even as I commended her for making it. At some level I think I was looking for a woman who was the antithesis of her, which Tiffany certainly was. Bubbly. Beautiful. Light. Lively. Tiffany Wells was certain of her womanly wiles in this seductive, confident way that initially I was bowled over by."

There were few men who wouldn't be, Meredith thought, with just a touch of envy.

"I was a mature man. She was a mature woman. Eventually, we did what mature adults do," he admitted. "I'm ashamed to say for the longest time I mistook the sexual sizzle between us as love. Still, we were extremely responsible. Double protected.

"But as that sexual sizzle had cooled to an occasional hiss, I realized it was really the only thing we had in common."

"She bored you!" Meredith deduced.

He looked pained. "Her constant chatter about *nothing* made my head hurt. I was feeling increasingly disillusioned and she, unfortunately, seemed increasingly enamored.

"I told her it was over. She told me she was pregnant."

Meredith gasped, but he held her hand tighter, looked at her deeply. "No, Meredith, it is not your story. I did not abandon a pregnant woman."

CHAPTER EIGHT

PRINCE KIERNAN TOLD Meredith the rest of the story haltingly. After overcoming the initial shock of Tiffany's announcement he had weighed his options with the sense of urgency that the situation demanded.

He had done what he felt was the honorable thing, a man prepared to accept full responsibility for his moment of indiscretion.

His engagement had been announced, and they had set a date for the very near future, so that Tiffany's pregnancy would not be showing at the wedding. The press had gone into a feeding frenzy. Tiffany had appeared to adore the attention as much as he was appalled by it. She was "caught" out shopping for her gown and flowers, having bachelorette celebrations with her friends, even looking at bassinettes.

"When we were together, we could not have one moment of privacy. The cameras were always there, we were chased, questions were shouted, the press always seemed to know where we were. Now, uncharitably, I wonder if she didn't tip them off. But regardless, our lives became helicopters flying over the palace, the yacht, the polo fields, men with cameras up trees and in shrubs.

"On this point, Meredith, you were absolutely correct

in what you said to me on the day we began dance practice. Romance is glorious entertainment. It sells newspapers and magazines and it ups ratings. Interest in us, as a couple, was nothing short of insatiable."

"How horrible!" Meredith said.

"You'd think," he said dryly. "Tiffany loved every moment of it. For me, it felt as if I was riding a runaway train that I couldn't stop and couldn't get off of."

"But you did stop it. But what of the baby? In all the publicity that followed, I never once heard she was pregnant."

"Because she wasn't."

"What?"

"Before that incident it had never occurred to me that a person—particularly one who claimed to love you—could be capable of a deception of such monstrous proportions as that. Luckily for me, the truth was revealed before we were married. Unluckily, it was the night before the wedding."

He went on to say a loyal servant, assigned to Tiffany, had come in obvious distress late on the eve of the wedding to tell him something that under normal circumstances he would have found embarrassing. But the fact that *pregnant* Tiffany was having her period had saved him. Despite the lateness of the hour, he had confronted Tiffany immediately, and the wedding had been cancelled.

But now the whole world saw him as the man who had coldheartedly broken a bride's heart on the eve of all her dreams coming true. The press seemed tickled by the new role they had assigned him, Prince Heartbreaker.

Tiffany, on the other hand, seemed to be enjoying the attention as much as ever, photographed often, sunglasses in place, shoulders slumped, enthusiastically playing the part of the party who was suffering the most and who had been grievously wronged.

"Why on earth wouldn't you let the world know what and who she really is?" Meredith demanded, shocked at how protective she felt of him. "Why are you taking the brunt of the whole world's disappointment that the fairy tale has fallen apart?"

"Now you sound like Adrian." He paused before he spoke. "I saw something in Tiffany's desperate attempt to capture me that was not evil. It was very sad and very sick. I glimpsed a frightening fragility behind her mask of supreme confidence.

"How fragile only a very few people know. Tiffany had attempted suicide after I uncovered her deception."

"It sounds like more manipulation to me," Meredith said angrily.

"Regardless, I was not blameless. I gave in to temptation, let go of control when I most needed to keep it. I put Tiffany in a position where she hoped for more than what I was prepared to offer, I put myself in a position of extreme vulnerability.

"I don't think Tiffany could have handled her deception being made public, the scorn that would have been heaped on her."

"She certainly seems to handle it being heaped on you rather well. Her total lack of culpability enrages me, Kiernan."

He shrugged. "I've been putting up with the attacks of the press since I was a young man. I'm basically indifferent to what they have to say."

"You protected her, too. Even though she is not the least deserving of your protection!"

He shrugged it off. "Don't read too much into it, Meredith. I'm no hero."

"Just a prince," she said and was rewarded with his laughter.

"Just a man," he said. "Underneath it all, just a man."

But a good one, she thought. A man with a sense of decency and honor. A man who had not abandoned the woman he thought carried his child.

The man of her dreams. So, so easy to fall in love with him.

A steward came and whispered in his ear.

"I'm so sorry. That's the call I have to take."

The truth? She was glad for a moment alone to sort through the new surge of emotion she felt at his innate decency, at his deeply ingrained sense of honor.

"Don't think anything of it," she assured him. She didn't mind. She wanted to sit here and savor his trust and the world he had opened to her. But she badly needed distance, too.

The steward brought her a refill for her coffee, the day's paper, and a selection of magazines.

After staring pensively at the sea for a long time, she needed any kind of distraction to stop the whirling of her thoughts. She picked up the paper.

In the entertainment section she stopped dead.

There was a picture of society beauty Brianna Morrison under the headline Prince Heartbreaker's New Victim?

But Miss Morrison looked like anything but a victim! She was hugging a gossamer green dress to her, her choice for the Blossom Week Ball, the event that would culminate the week's celebrations.

"I couldn't believe it when I was asked," she gushed to the interviewer. "It is like a dream come true."

It seemed something went very still in Meredith. She was sharing the prince's yacht tonight. But he had been very clear. This was farewell.

The prince giving the peasant girl a final gift of himself before moving back to his real life.

But he had asked another woman to the ball.

Well, of course he had. Meredith had always known she didn't belong in this world. Brianna Morrison's family was old money, the Morrisons owned factories and businesses, real estate, and shipping yards.

And tonight he had said pressure, subtle or not, was being brought on him to find a suitable partner. Brianna was beautiful and accomplished. Her family's interests and the interests of the Chatams had been linked for centuries.

And then there was Meredith Whitmore. A dance instructor, more devoted to her charity than her business, a woman with a hard past.

No, the prince had decided to give his dance instructor a lovely night out.

A small token of appreciation. He had never claimed it was anything more than a way of saying goodbye to her and the world they had shared for a few light-filled days.

She had been crazy to encourage his confidences, some part of her hoping and praying she was in some way suitable for his world and that he would see it.

She set down the paper and called the steward. "Could we go back to Chatam, please? I'm not feeling well."

In seconds, Kiernan was at her side.

"I hope you didn't end your phone call on my behalf," she said coolly, not wanting to see the concern on his face, deliberately looking to the sea that was beginning to chop under a strengthening wind.

"Of course I did! You're not feeling well? It's probably the roughening sea, but I can have my physician waiting at the dock."

"No, it's not that serious," she said, trying not to melt at his tender concern, trying to steel herself against it. "I'm sure it is the sea. I just need to go home."

"I'll give the order to get underway immediately." He rose, scanned her face, and frowned.

Then he saw the open newspaper.

She leaned forward to close it, but he stayed her hand, bent over and scanned the headline.

"You read this?" he asked her.

She said nothing, tilted her chin proudly, refused to look at him.

"Is this why you're suddenly not feeling well? It was arranged months ago," he said quietly.

"It's none of my business. I'm well aware I don't belong in your world, Prince Kiernan. That this has been a nice little treat for a peasant you've taken a liking to."

"It is not that I don't think you belong in my world," he said with a touch of heat. "That's not it at all! And I don't think of you as a peasant."

"Of course not," she said woodenly.

"Meredith, you don't understand the repercussions of being seen publicly with me."

"I might use the wrong fork?"

"Stop it."

"I thought this was such a nice outfit. You probably noticed it was off the rack."

"I noticed no such thing. It's a gorgeous outfit. You are gorgeous."

"Apparently. Gorgeous enough to see you privately."

"Meredith, you need to understand the moment you are seen with me, publicly, your life will never be the same again. Taking you to that ball would be like throwing you into a pail of piranhas. The press would have started to rip you apart. You've told me some shattering secrets about yourself. Do you want those secrets on all the front pages providing titillation for the mob? I won't do that to you."

"Of course," she said, "You're protecting me. That's what you do."

"I am trying to protect you," he said. "A little appreciation might be in order."

"Appreciation? You deluded fool."

He looked stunned by that and that made her happy in an angry sort of way so she kept going.

"You've chosen women in the past that build you up with their weakness, who need their big strong prince to protect them, but I'm not like that."

"I've chosen weak women?" he sputtered.

"It's obvious."

"I'm sorry I ever told you a personal thing about myself."

She was sorry he had, too. Because it had made her hope for things she couldn't have. She couldn't stop herself now if she wanted to.

"I'm a girl from Wentworth. Do you think there's anything in your world that could frighten me? I've walked in places where I've had a knife hidden under my coat. I've been hungry, for God's sake. And so exhausted from working and raising a baby I couldn't even hold my feet under me. I've buried my child. And my mother. Do you think anything in your cozy, pampered little world could frighten me? The press? I could handle the press with both my hands tied behind my back.

"Don't you dare pretend that's about protecting me. Your Royal Highness, you are protecting yourself. You don't want anyone to know about tonight. Or about me. I'm the sullied girl from the wrong side of the tracks. You're right. They would dig up my whole sordid past. What an embarrassment to you! To be romantically linked to the likes of me!"

"I told you everything there is to know about me," he said quietly, "and you would reach that conclusion?"

"That's right!" she snapped, her anger making her feel so much more powerful than her despair. "It's all about you!"

She banished everything in her that was weak. There would be plenty of time for crying when she got home.

After the trust they had shared, the intimacy of their dinner, the growing friendship of the last few days, this was *exactly* what was needed.

Distance.

Anger.

Distrust.

And finally, when she got home, then there would be time for the despair that could only be brought on from believing, even briefly, in unrealistic dreams.

But when she got home, she realized she had done it on purpose, created that terrible scene on purpose, driven a wedge between them on purpose.

Because she had done the dumbest thing of her whole life, even dumber than believing Michael Morgan was a prince.

She had come to love a real prince. And she did not think she could survive another love going wrong.

And the truth? How could it possibly go right?

"What is wrong with you?" Adrian asked Kiernan the next day.

"What do you mean by that?"

"Kiernan! You're not yourself. You're impatient. You're snapping at people. You're canceling engagements."

"What engagement?"

"You were supposed to bring Brianna Morrison to the ball. The worst thing you could have done is cancelled that. One more tearstained face attached to your name. She's been getting ready for months. Prince Heartbreaker rides again."

"Is that a direct quote from the tabs?"

"No. That is so much kinder than the tabs. They're having a heyday at your expense. This morning they showed Brianna Morrison throwing her ball dress off a bridge into Chatam River."

"Make sure she's charged with littering a public waterway."

"Kiernan! That's cold! You are just about the most hated man on the planet right now."

Yes. And by the only one that mattered, too.

Adrian was watching him closely. "And there's that look again."

"What look?"

"I don't know. Moody. *Desperate.*"

"Adrian, just leave it alone," he said wearily.

"If something is wrong, I want to help."

"You can't. Not unless you can learn to dance in—" he glanced at his watch "—about four hours."

Adrian's eyes widened. "I should have known."

"What?" Kiernan said. What had he inadvertently revealed?

"Dragon-heart. She's at the bottom of this."

Kiernan stepped in very close to his young cousin. "Don't you ever call her that again within my hearing. Do you understand me?"

"She did something to make you so mad," Adrian said. "I know it."

"No, she didn't," Kiernan said. "I did. I did something that made me so mad. I gave my trust to the wrong person."

Adrian was watching him, his brow drawn down in puzzlement. "I'll be damned," he said. "You aren't angry. You're in love."

Kiernan thought it would be an excellent time for a vehement denial. But when he opened his mouth, the denial didn't come out.

"With Dra— Meredith?"

"It doesn't matter. It's going nowhere. After I revealed my deepest truths to her do you know what she did? She called me a deluded fool!"

Adrian actually smiled.

"It's not funny."

"No, it's a cause for celebration. Finally, someone who will take you to task when you need it."

"Don't side with her. You don't even like her."

"Actually, I always did like her. Immensely. She wouldn't settle for anything less than my best. She was strong and sure of herself and intimidating as hell, but I liked her a great deal."

"Do you know what she said to me? She said I deliberately chose weak women. What do you think about that?"

"That she's unusually astute. Finally, someone who will tell you exactly what they think instead of filtering it through what they think you want to hear."

"You never told me you thought my women were weak," Kiernan said accusingly.

"Because they were heart-stoppingly beautiful. I thought that probably made up for it. I always knew you never dated anyone who would require you to be more than you were before. I thought it was your choice. That you had decided love would take a minor role in your life. Behind your duties."

"I think I had thought that. Until I fell in love. It doesn't accept minor roles."

"So, you do love her!" Adrian crowed.

"It doesn't matter. I had her to the yacht for dinner last night, and she opened the paper and saw I was escorting Brianna to the ball. She left in a temper."

"Uh, real world to Kiernan: any woman who is having dinner with a man will be upset to find he has plans with another woman for later in the week."

"I told her it had been planned for months."

"Instead of *I'll cancel immediately*?" Adrian shook his head and tut-tutted.

"I told her it was for her own good. She has some things in her past I don't want the press to get their hands on. I was protecting her!"

"I bet she loved that one."

"It's true!"

"She isn't the kind who would take kindly to you micromanaging her world."

"She's not. She doesn't trust me. I showed her everything I was, and she rejected it. She believed the worst of me, just like everyone else is so quick to do."

"Kiernan, you are making excuses."

"Why would I do that?"

"You are terrified of what that woman would require of you."

"I'm not."

"Don't you get it? This is your chance. You might only get one. Take it. Be happy. Do something for yourself for once. Go sweep old Dragon-heart right off her feet."

"Don't call her that."

"I can't believe I missed it!" His cousin became uncharacteristically serious. "She's worthy of you, Kiernan. She's strong. And spunky. She's probably the best thing that ever happened to you. Don't let it slip away."

And suddenly Kiernan thought of how awful she had looked when she had left the yacht. She was afraid. He'd taken that personally, as if it was about him. But of course she was afraid! She had lost everything to love once before. She was terrified to believe in him, to trust.

And Adrian was right. He was *not* doing the right thing. Sulking because she didn't trust him, not seeing what lay beneath that lack of trust. Why should she trust the world? Or him? Had the world brought her good things? No, it had taken them. Had love brought her good things? No, it had shattered her.

Instead of seeing that, he had insisted on making it about him.

He was going to have to be a better man than that to be worthy of her. He was going to have to go get her from that lonely world she had fled to in her fear and distrust.

Kiernan of Chatam was going to have to learn what it really meant to be a woman's prince.

Something sighed within him.

He was ready for the challenge. He was about to go rescue the maiden from the dragon of fear and loneliness she had allowed to take up residence in her heart.

"I don't know what to do," he admitted.

Adrian smiled. "Sure, you do. You have to woo the girl. Just the same as any old Joe out there on the street. She isn't going to just fall at your feet because you're a prince, you know. For God's sake, she runs an organization called No Princes. Playing hard to get is going to be a point of pride with her.

"And don't look so solemn. For once in your life, Kiernan, have some fun."

The show must go on, Meredith thought as she found herself, in a white smock in a crowded dressing room, waiting, her heart nearly pounding out of her chest. She had never been this nervous about a performance.

"Miss Whit," one of the girls said excitedly. "He's here. He's come. Ohmygod, he's the most glorious man I ever laid me eyes on."

"*My* eyes," Meredith corrected woodenly.

"The music's starting," Erin whispered. "Oh, I can't believe this is happening to me. My production is becoming a reality. I just looked out the curtain. Miss Whit, it's standing room only out there."

For them. She had to pull this off for them, her girls, all that she had left in her world.

"I'm on," Erin said. "I'm so scared."

Meredith shook herself out of her own fear, and went and gave her protégée a hard hug.

"Dazzle them!" she said firmly.

And then she stood in the wings. And despite her gloom, her heart began to swell with pride as she saw Erin's vision come to life. The girls in the opening number carried the buckets of cleaning ladies, or wore waitresses' uniforms. Some of them carried school bags. All had on too much makeup. They were hanging around a street lamp, targets for trouble.

And here came trouble. Boys in carpenter's aprons, and baker's hats, leather jackets with cigarettes dangling from their lips.

The girls and the guys were dancing together, shy, flirtatious, bold, by turns.

And then Erin, who had been given the starring role, was front and center in her white smock that said Molly over the pocket, and she was staring worshipfully at a boy in a white jacket that said Andy on the pocket.

The lights went off them, and the empty spot on the stage filled with mist.

It was time for the dream sequence.

The three-step bridal waltz began to play, and feeling as if she was made of wood, Meredith came on stage.

Kiernan was coming toward her.

How unfair that while she suffered, he looked better than ever! No doubt to make his costume more realistic, he had a few days growth of unshaven beard.

Meredith went to him, felt her hand settle into his, his hand on her waist.

Her eyes closed against the pain of it.

Last time.

Even as she thought it, she could hear a whisper ripple through the crowd. It became a rumble as the spotlight fell on them, and recognition of Kiernan grew.

"You look awful," he said in her ear.

"I've been working very hard with the girls," she whispered back haughtily. She stumbled slightly. He covered for her.

"Liar. Pining for me."

She tried to hide her shock. "Why would a girl like me pine for you?" she snapped at him. "We both know it's impossible."

He was looking at her way too hard.

"You're afraid," he said in an undertone. "It was never really horses you were afraid of. It was this."

The crowd was going crazy. Not only had they recognized their prince, but he was doing something completely unexpected. Kiernan and Meredith picked up the pace, and he found his feet. She tried not to look at the expression on his face.

"Don't be silly," she told him in an undertone. "I told you nothing about your world frightens me."

"You're afraid of loving me. You have been from the moment we met."

"Arrogant ass," she hissed.

"Stubborn lass," he shot back.

She could feel the fire between them coming out in the way they were dancing. It was unrehearsed, but the audience was reacting to the pure sizzling chemistry.

She couldn't look away from him. His look had become so fierce. So tender. So protective. So filled with longing.

He knew the truth, anyway, why try to hide it? Why not let it come out in this dance?

It occurred to her that even if he couldn't have her, even if she would never be suitable for his world, that he wanted her, and that he wished things were not the way they were.

One last time, she would give herself this gift.

She would be Molly and he would be Andy, just two crazy ordinary kids in love. Everything changed the moment she made that decision. She would say to him with this dance what she intended to never admit to him in person.

She found her feet. She found his rhythm.

And they danced. She let go of all her armor. She let go of all her past hurt. She let go of all her fear. She let go of that little worm of self-doubt that she was not good enough.

Meredith danced as she had never danced, every single secret thing she had ever felt right out there in the open for all the world to see.

At some point, she was not Molly. Not at all. She was completely herself, Meredith Whitmore.

For this one priceless moment, she didn't care who saw her truth. Though thousands watched, they were alone, dancing for each other.

And then he let her go, and the crowd became frenzied as he moved into his solo piece.

He tore off the white smock.

And suddenly she saw his truth. It was not dancing as Andy that allowed him to dance like this.

It was dancing as Kiernan.

Everything he truly was came out now: sensual, strong, commanding, tender. Everything.

By the time he came across the floor to her that one last time, the tears were streaming down her face for the gift he had given her.

He had given her his everything.

He had put every single thing he was into that dance. Not for the audience who was going wild with delight.

Not for the girls who cheered and screamed from the wings.

For her. He stared down at her.

It was not in any way a scripted part of the performance. He took her lips with exquisite tenderness.

She tasted him, savored, tried to memorize it.

With the cheering in the building so loud it sounded as if the rafters would collapse on them, she pulled away from the heaven of his lips, touched his cheek. Though the whole world watched it felt, still, as if they were alone.

Goodbye.

"Thank you," she whispered through her tears. "Thank you, Kiernan." And then she turned and fled.

CHAPTER NINE

IT WAS THE DAY AFTER *An Evening to Remember.*
Meredith's phone had been ringing off the hook, but
she wouldn't answer.

Still, people left messages. They wanted lessons from
her dance school. They wanted to donate money to No
Princes.

Erin Fisher's excited voice told her she had been offered a full scholarship to Chatam University.

The press wanted to know what it felt like to dance
with a prince. They wanted to know if she had been the
one to teach the prince with two left feet to dance like
that. They especially wanted to know if there was *something* going on, or if it had all been a performance.

After several hours of the phone ringing she went
and pulled the connection out of the wall.

She didn't want to talk to anybody.

Maybe not for a long, long time.

Just as she had suspected, the video had been posted
online within seconds of the performance finishing.

The website had collapsed this morning, for the first
time in its history, from too many hits on that video.

"Most of those hits from me," Meredith admitted
ruefully. She had watched their dance together at least
a dozen times before the site had crashed.

Seeing something in it, basking in it.

Was love too strong a word?

Probably. She used it anyway.

There was a knock on her door. She hoped the press had not discovered where she lived. She tried to ignore it, but it came again, more insistent than the last time. She pulled a pillow over her head. More rapping.

"Meredith, open the damn door before I kick it down!"

She pulled the pillow away from her face, sat up, stunned, hugging it to her.

"I mean it. I'm counting to three."

She went and peered out her security peephole.

"One."

Prince Kiernan of Chatam was out on her stoop, in an Andy jacket and dark glasses.

"Two."

She threw open the door, and then didn't know what to do. Throw herself at him? Play it cool? Weep? Laugh?

"Lo, Molly," he said casually.

Don't melt.

"Just wondered if you might like to come down to the pub with me. We'll have a pint and throw some darts."

"Once you lose the sunglasses everyone will know who you are." Plus, they'd probably all seen the Andy getup on the video. He'd be swamped.

"Let's live dangerously. I'll leave the glasses on. You can tell people I have a black eye from fighting for your honor."

"Kiernan—"

"Andy," he told her sternly.

"Okay, Andy." She folded her arms protectively over her chest. "Why are you doing this?"

He hesitated a heartbeat, lifted the glasses so she could look into his eyes. "I want us to get to know each other. Like this. As Andy and Molly. Without the pressure of the press following us and speculating. I want us to build a solid foundation before I introduce you to the world. I want you to know I have your back when they start coming at you."

"You're going to introduce me to the world?" she whispered. "You're going to have my back?"

"Meredith, I miss you. Not seeing you was like living in a world without the sun. It was dark and it was cold."

She could feel the utter truth of it to her toenails.

"I miss the freedom I felt with you," he went on quietly. "I miss the sense of being myself in a way I never was before. I miss being spontaneous. I miss having fun. Will you come out and play with me? Please?"

She nodded, not trusting herself to speak.

"Come on, then. Your chariot awaits."

She could not resist him. She had never been able to resist him.

"I'm in my pajamas."

"So you are. Ghastly things, too. I picture you in white lace."

She gulped from the heat in his eyes.

"Go change," he said, and there was no missing the fact she had just been issued a royal order.

"Royal pain in the butt," she muttered, but she stood back from the door, and let him in.

Surely once he saw how ordinary people lived—tiny quarters, hotplate, faded furniture—he would realize he was in the wrong world and turn tail and run.

But he didn't. True to Andy he went and flung himself on her worse-for-wear couch, picked up a book she hadn't looked at for weeks and raised wicked eyebrows at her.

"Did you dream of me when you read this?" he asked.

"No!" She went and slammed her bedroom door, made herself put on the outfit—faded jeans, a prim blouse—that was the least like the one she had worn the other night on the yacht. It was the casual outfit of an ordinary girl.

But when she reemerged from the bedroom, the look in his eyes made her feel like a queen.

Feeling as if she was in a dream, Meredith followed him down the steep stairs that led from her apartment to the alley. Leaning at the bottom of the stairs was the most horrible-looking bike she had ever seen.

Kiernan straddled it, lowered his sunglasses, patted the handlebars. "Get on."

"Are you kidding? You'll kill us both."

"Ah, but what a way to go."

"There is that," she said, with a sigh. She settled herself on the handlebars.

His bike riding was terrible. She suspected he could barely ride a bike solo, let alone riding double. He got off to a shaky start, nearly crashing three times before they got out of her laneway.

Once he got into the main street he was even more hazardous, weaving in and out of traffic, wobbling in front of a double-decker bus.

"Give 'em the bird, love," he called when someone honked angrily when he wobbled out in front of them.

She giggled and did just that.

At the pub, true to his word, he left the glasses on.

She thought people might recognize him, but perhaps because of the plain lucridness of the whole thought that a prince would be in the neighborhood pub, no one did.

They ordered fish and chips, had a pint of tap beer, they threw darts. Then they got back on the bike and he took the long way home, pedaling along the river. She wasn't sure if her heart was beating that fast because of all the times he nearly dumped them both in the inky water of the Chatam Channel, or because she was so exhilarated by this experience.

"Where is this going?" Meredith asked sternly when he dropped her at her doorstep with a light kiss on the nose.

"My whole life," he said solemnly, "I've known where everything was going. I've always had an agenda, a protocol, a map, a plan. The very first time I saw you dance, I knew you had something I needed.

"I didn't know what it was, but whatever it was, it was what made me say yes to learning the number for *An Evening to Remember.*"

"And do you know what it was now?" she asked, curious, intrigued despite herself.

"Passion," he said. "My whole life has been about order and control. And when I saw you dance that day I caught a glimpse of what I had missed. The thing is, I felt bereft that I had missed it.

"Meredith, you take me to places I have never been before. And I don't mean a hot spring or a pub. Places inside myself that I have never been before. Now that I've been there, I can't live with the thought of not going there anymore."

He kissed her on the nose again. "I'll see you tomorrow."

"Look," she said, trying to gain some control back, "I just can't put my whole life on hold because you want me to take you places!"

He laughed, and leaned close to her. "But I've been saving my money so I can get us a Triple Widgie Hot Fudge Sundae from Lawrence's. To share."

"That's incredibly hard to resist," she admitted.

"The sundae or me?"

"The sharing."

"Ah." He looked at her long and hard. "Embrace it, Molly. Just embrace it."

"All right." She surrendered.

And that's what she did. She put her whole life on hold.

But not really.

She just embraced a different life.

Carefree and full of adventure.

Over the next few weeks, as Andy and Molly, they biked every inch of that island. They discovered hidden beaches. They ate ice cream at roadside stands. They laughed until their sides hurt. They went to movies. They roller-skated.

And just when she was getting used to it all, that familiar knock came on the door, but it was not Andy who stood there. Not this time.

This time it was Prince Kiernan of Chatam, in dark suit trousers and a jacket, a crisp white shirt, a dark silk tie.

He bowed low over her hand, kissed it.

"Aren't we going bike riding?" she asked.

"I love your world, Meredith, but now it's time for you to come into mine."

"I—I— I'll have to change," she said, casting a

disparaging look down at her faded T-shirt, her pedal pushers, and old sneakers.

"Only your clothes," he said quietly. "Nothing else. Don't change one other thing about you. Promise me."

"I promise," she said, and scooted back into her bedroom to find something suitable to wear for an outing with a prince. A few minutes later, in a pencil skirt of white linen and a blue silk top, she joined him.

"Are you ready for this?" he asked, holding out his hand to her.

"Ready for what, exactly?" She took his hand, gazed up at him, still unable to quite grasp that a prince was wooing an ordinary girl like her.

"My mother wants to meet you."

"She does?" Meredith gulped. "Why?"

"Because I told her I've met the woman I intend to spend the rest of my life with."

Meredith took a step back from him, not sure she had heard him correctly, her heart beating an ecstatic tattoo within her chest. "But you haven't told me that yet!"

He cocked his head at her, and grinned. "I guess I just did."

She flew into his arms, and it felt like going home. It felt exactly the way she had wanted to feel her whole life.

"You know how I feel right now?" she whispered into his chest. "I feel safe. And protected. I feel cared about. I feel cherished."

"You make me feel those things, too," he whispered back.

"And I feel absolutely terrified. Your mother? That makes everything seem rather official."

"You see, that's the thing. After you've met my

mother, it's going to be official. You're going to be my girl. And then my fiancée. And then my wife."

"Huh. Is that your excuse for a proposal?"

He laughed. "No. Just forewarning you of what's to come." And then he frowned. "If you can handle the pressure. You won't believe the pressure, Meredith. I'm afraid your life will never be the same. Be sure you know what you want before you walk out that door with me."

But she had been sure a long time ago. She knew exactly what she wanted. She placed her hand back in his, and felt her whole world was complete.

Someone with a camera had already discovered the limousine parked at her curb, because this time the royal emblem shone gold on the door. The camera was raised and their picture was taken getting into the car together.

He sighed.

But she squeezed his hand and laughed.

"I may be terrified of your mother," she said, as he settled in the deep leather of the seat beside her, "but I'm not afraid of anything else about being with you. Nothing." She laid her head on his shoulder and soaked in the strength and solidness of him, soaked in how very right it felt to be at his side.

For a moment there was the most comfortable of silences between them.

"Did you hear that?" he asked, as the car pulled away.

"I'm sorry, did I hear what?"

He looked out the window, twisted over his shoulder to look behind them, settled back with a puzzled look on his face.

"Meredith, I could have sworn I heard a baby laugh."

She smiled, and the feeling of everything in the world being absolutely right deepened around her.

"No," she said softly, "I didn't hear it. But I felt it. I felt it all the way to my soul."

Kiernan raised his hand to knock on the door of his mother's quarters. He'd been annoyed that upon delivering Meredith his mother had dismissed him with an instruction to come back in an hour. She had drawn Meredith in and closed the door firmly behind them.

He knew his mother! The inquisition had probably started. Especially after Tiffany, whom his mother had not liked from the beginning, Queen Aleda would feel justified in asking aggressive questions, making quick judgments. Meredith was probably backed into a corner, quivering and in tears.

But as he stood at the door, he was astounded to hear laughter coming through the closed door. He knocked and opened it.

Both women looked up. Meredith was seated, his mother looking over her shoulder. He saw he had underestimated Meredith again. He was going to have to stop doing that.

He noticed his mother had one hand resting companionably on Meredith's shoulder. His mother did not touch people!

Both women were focused on something on the table, and he recognized what it was.

"Photo albums?" he sputtered. "You've just met!"

"Never too soon to look at pictures of you as a baby," Meredith said. "That one of you in the tub? Adorable."

"The tub picture?" He glared at his mother, out-raged.

"What could I do?" Queen Aleda said with a smile. "Meredith asked me what my greatest treasure was."

And then the two women exchanged a glance, and he was silent, in awe of the fact their mutual love of him could make such a strong and instant bond between these two amazing women.

In the days and weeks that followed, Kiernan's amazement at Meredith grew and grew and grew.

The day after their first official public outing, when he had taken her to watch a royal horse run in the Chatam Cup, speculation began to run high. Some version of the picture of Meredith leaning over the royal box to kiss the nose of the horse had made every front page of every major paper around the world.

His press corps was instantly swamped with enquiries. When had he begun dating his dance instructor? Who was she? And especially, what was her background?

"This is the beginning," he'd told her. "How do you want to handle it?" Meredith called her own press conference.

Yes, she was dating the prince. Yes, they had met while she taught him the dance number for *An Evening to Remember*. No, she was not worried about his history, because she had a history of her own.

And in a strong, steady voice, without any apology Meredith had laid herself bare. All of it. Wentworth. The too-young pregnancy. Her abandonment by the father of her child. The baby. The lost dance dreams. The grind-ing poverty. The tragedy that took her mother and her child. The insurance money that had allowed her to start No Princes.

She had left the press without a single thing to dig

for. And instead of devouring her, the press had *adored* her honesty, and the fact she was just one of the people. Unlike so many celebrities that the press waited breathlessly to turn on, their love affair with Meredith was like his own.

And like that of all the people of Chatam.

The more they knew her, the more they loved her.

And she loved them right back. She became the star of every event they attended, the new and quickly beloved celebrity. From film festivals at Cannes to her first ski trip to catch the last spring snow in Colorado, she bewitched everyone who met her.

She was astonishingly at home, no matter where he took her.

But the part he loved the most was that none of it went to her head. She was still the girl he had first met. Maybe even more that girl as she came into herself, as love gave her a confidence and a glow that never turned off.

Meredith could be on the red carpet at a film premiere one day, and the next day she was just as at home on her bicycle, visiting a Chatam farmer's market. She delighted in surprising brides and grooms in Chatam on their wedding days by dropping by the reception to offer her good wishes.

When he begged her to allow him to offer her security, she just laughed at him. "I've already been through the worst life can give out, Kiernan. I'm not afraid."

And she really wasn't. Meredith was born to love. It seemed her capacity to give and receive love was endless.

And since he was the major benefactor of all that love, who was he to stop her?

Besides, he knew something he had not known a few

months ago, and probably would not have believed if someone had tried to tell him.

There were angels. And Meredith had two who protected and guided her. What other explanation for the series of coincidences that had brought them together? How had she landed right on his doorstep? How had Adrian come to be injured so that the right prince could meet her? How was it that Kiernan had gone against his own nature, and agreed to learn to dance? How was it he had seen something in her from the very beginning, that he could not resist?

From that first moment, watching her dance, Kiernan had known she held a secret that could change his life. Known it with his heart and not his head.

And only angels could have made him listen to his heart instead of his head.

But angels aside, there was no ignoring the very human side of what was happening to them.

He *wanted* her. He wanted her in every way that a man could want a woman. Their kisses were becoming more fevered. The times when they were alone were becoming a kind of torture of *wanting*.

The thing was, he would never take her without honor.

Never. What that other man had done to her was unconscionable. He would never be like him, never, ever remind Meredith of him. He would not use her obvious passion for him, or her willingness to have his way with her. He always backed away at the last possible moment.

There were honorable steps a man had to take to be with his woman. He had to earn his way there. It did not matter that it was his intention to marry her, and it was, even though he knew they had only known each other a short while, only months.

But he knew his own heart, too.

And he knew it was time.

CHAPTER TEN

MEREDITH WOKE UP to a sound at her window. Something was hitting against it. She groaned and pulled the pillow over her head.

Kiernan was probably right. She was going to have to move to a building with security. That was probably some fledging reporter out there hoping to get the shot that would make his career.

Despite her attempts to ignore it, the sound came again, louder. A scattering of pebbles across her pane.

And then louder yet!

She got up, annoyed. They were going to break the window! But when she shoved it up, and leaned out, ready to give someone a piece of her mind, it was Kiernan who stood below her.

"What are you doing?" Her annoyance now was completely faked. Sometimes she could still not believe this man, a prince outside, and a prince inside, too, was looking at her like that. With such open adoration in his eyes.

Of course the feeling was completely mutual!

"I have a surprise for you."

"What time is it?" she asked with completely faked grumpiness.

"Going on midnight."

"Kiernan, go home and go to bed."

"Quit pretending you can resist me. Get dressed and come down here."

She stuck out her tongue at him and slammed the window shut, but she quickly changed out of her pajamas, yanking on an old dance sweatsuit.

"I see you are working hard at impressing me," he said, kissing her on the nose as she reached the bottom of her stairs.

"As you are me," she teased back. "Waking me at midnight. I have work tomorrow. We don't all have lives of leisure."

This was said completely jokingly. She seemed, more than anyone else, to respect how hard he worked, and how many different directions he was pulled in a day. He was still savoring the newness of having someone at his side who was willing to back him up, to do whatever she needed to do to ease his burdens, to make his life simpler.

He held open the door of an unmarked car for her. Tonight as no other he did not want the press trailing them.

She snuggled under his arm. "What are you up to?"

But he wouldn't tell her.

They sailed through the roadblock he'd had put up to close the popular road, just for this one night. Meredith peeked out the car window with curiosity, and then recognition. "Are we going where I think we are going?"

The car stopped at the pull-out for Chatam Hot Springs. He held out his hand to her and drew her out of the car, led her up the path, lit by torches tonight, that led the way to the springs.

When they got there, he savored the look on her face. No detail had been overlooked.

There were torches flaming around the pool, but the bubbling waters of the springs were mostly illuminated by thousands upon thousands of candles that glowed from every rock and every surface.

"I didn't bring a suit," she whispered, looking around with that look he had come to live for.

A kind of *pinch me I must be dreaming* look.

"There's a change tent for you over there," he said. "You'll find a number of bathing suits to choose from."

She emerged from the tent a few minutes later, and he, already changed, was waiting on the edge of a rock with his feet dangling in the water. He smiled at her choice. Though there was staff here, they were invisible at the moment.

"The black one," he said with a shake of his head. "I was hoping for something skimpier. The red one, with the polka dots."

"How did you know about the red one with the polka dots?" she demanded.

"Because I picked each one myself, Meredith."

"That must have been very embarrassing for you," she said. "Careful, the press will dub you the pervert prince."

He leered at her playfully. "And let's hope it's deserved."

This is how it was with them. Endlessly playful. Teasing. Comfortable. Fun. And yet the respect between them also grew.

As did the heat.

As she crossed the slippery rock to him he could easily see that the black tank-style suit was so much more sexy than the polka dot bikini! Instead of sitting demurely beside him, Meredith pretended to touch his shoulders lovingly and then shoved with all her might.

And then turned and ran.

He caught up with her at the mud pool.

And they played in the mud, and swam and played some more until they were both exhausted with joy.

And then he sent her back to the change tent.

Where he knew all the rejected bathing suits had been whisked away, and in their place were designer gowns like the ones she had refused to let him buy for her for all the public outings they had attended.

While she changed, a table was set up for them and waiters appeared, along with a chef fussing about the primitive conditions he'd had to prepare his food in.

When she'd emerged from the change tent this time, Kiernan's mouth fell open. Meredith had stunned him with her beauty even in the off-the-rack dresses she insisted on wearing.

But now she had chosen the most racy of the gowns that he had picked out for her. It was red and low-cut.

She had even put on some of the jewelry he had put out for her, and a diamond necklace blazed at her neck and diamond droplets fell from her ears.

"I am looking at a princess," he said, bowing low over her hand and kissing it.

"I've told you *no* to this extravagance, Kiernan."

And yet, despite her protest, he could not help but notice that she was glowing with a certain feminine delight. She knew she looked incredible.

He led her to the table, laid out with fine linen and the best of china, and the waiters served a sumptuous feast.

She knew most of the palace staff by name, and addressed each of them.

When they had finished eating, she smiled at him. "Okay. I give it to you, you can't ever top this."

"But I will."

"You can't."

He called one of the waiters and a cooler was brought to their table. Inside it was one Triple Widgie Hot Fudge Sundae and two spoons.

In that perfect environment, their worlds combined effortlessly.

"I love it all," she said. "But you shouldn't have bought all the dresses, Kiernan. I can't accept them, and you probably can't return them."

"I'm afraid as my wife you'll be expected to keep a certain standard," he said. "And as your husband I will be proud to provide it for you."

He dropped down on his knee in front of her, slid a box from his pocket and opened it.

Inside was a diamond of elegant simplicity. He knew her. He knew she would never want the flashy ring, the large karat, the showpiece.

And he knew her answer.

He saw it in her eyes, in the tears that streamed down her face, in the smile that would not stop, despite the tears.

"Will you marry me?" he asked. "Will you make my world complete, Meredith?"

"Yes," she whispered. "Of course yes, a thousand times yes."

He rose to his feet, gathered her in his arms and held her. And his world finally was complete.

* * *

Meredith stared at herself in the mirror. She was in her slip at the dressing table, the bridal gown hung behind her. For a moment her eyes caught on it, and she felt a delicious quiver of disbelief.

Could this really be her life? A wedding gown out of a dream, yards and yards of ivory silk and seed pearls. Could this really be her life? Crowds had begun to form early this morning, lining the streets of Chatam from downtown all the way to Chatam Cathedral.

"You look so beautiful," Erin murmured.

Meredith gazed at the girl behind her.

Despite the pressure to have a huge wedding party, Meredith had chosen to have one attendant, Erin Fisher.

"So do you," she said.

"It's your day," Erin said, nonetheless pleased, "just focus on yourself for once, Miss Whit."

"All right."

"Now don't you look beautiful?"

She *did* look beautiful. More beautiful than she could have ever imagined she was going to look.

And it wasn't just the wedding gown, the hair, the makeup.

No, a radiance was pouring out of her, too big to contain within her skin.

"Are you crying?" Erin asked in horror. "Don't! We just did the makeup."

Meredith had been offered a room at the palace to get ready, and ladies in waiting to help her. She had said no to both. She wanted to be in this little apartment over her studio one last time. She wanted *her* girls to be around her.

Erin handed her a tissue and scolded. "I hope those are happy tears."

Meredith thought about it for a moment. "Not really, no."

"You are about to marry the most glorious man who ever walked and those aren't happy tears? Honestly, Miss Whit, I'm going to pinch you!"

"Don't pinch me. I might wake up."

"Tell me why they aren't happy tears."

"I was crying for the girl I used to be, the one who expected so little of life, who had such small dreams for herself. I was thinking of the girl who stood on those city hall steps, in a cheap dress, holding a tiny posy of flowers. I was thinking of the girl who felt so broken, as if it was her fault, some defect in her that caused him not to come, not to want to share the dream with her.

"If she could have seen the future she would have been dancing on those steps instead of crying. The truth? A different life awaited her. One that was beyond the smallness of her dreams."

"My dreams were so small, too," Erin whispered. "What would have become of me, if all that stuff hadn't happened to you? There would have been no Fairytale Ending group for me."

By vote, just last week, the girls, with Meredith's blessing, had changed the name of No Princes.

Because sometimes there just were princes.

And because, even when there weren't, everyone could make their own fairy-tale ending, no matter what.

"I think the universe has dreams for all of us that are bigger than what we would ever dare dream for ourselves," Meredith said quietly. "I even have to trust that losing my baby was part of a bigger plan that I will never totally understand. Maybe it made me stronger, deeper, more able to love. Worthy of that incredible man who loves me."

"Okay, stop!" Erin insisted, dabbing at her eyes. "My makeup is already done, too. Promise me, Miss Whit, that this day will be just about you and him. Not one more unhappy thought."

"All right," Meredith agreed, more to mollify the girl than anything else.

"We can't be walking down the cathedral aisle looking like a pair of raccoons," Erin said.

"Maybe you should have invested in waterproof makeup," a voice behind them said.

Erin whirled. "Prince Kiernan! Get out!" She tried to shield Meredith with her body. "You can't see her right now. It's bad luck."

"Luckily, I'm not superstitious. Could you give us a moment?"

For all the confidence she was developing, Erin wasn't about to make a stand with the prince of her country. She whirled and left the room.

Kiernan came up behind Meredith, rested his hand on her nearly naked shoulder. "This is pretty," he said touching her hair.

See? That was the problem with the promise she had made to Erin. This day could not be exclusively about the two of them.

"I thought it might be a little, er, too much," Meredith said, "but Denise is in hairdressing school. It was her gift to me. How can you refuse something like that?"

"You can't," he agreed. "Besides, it truly is beautiful."

"You really shouldn't be here," she chided him gently,

but the fact that he was here was so much better than a pinch.

This man was her life, her reason, her love, her reality.

"I had to see you," he said softly, "I have a gift for you and suddenly I realized that you needed to have it now, that I wanted you to have it close to your heart today."

All the gifts he had brought her over the course of their courtship could fill a small cottage. After they had become engaged, Meredith had quit asking him to stop. It filled him with such transparent joy to give her, a girl who had spent so much of her life with nothing, lovely things. She had learned to accept each gift graciously, because by doing so, she would receive the *real* gift.

His smile. A moment together in a busy, busy world. His touch on her arm. His eyes looking into her eyes with such wonder.

Now, Kiernan produced a small silver necklace, a cameo.

He pressed it into her hand, and she hesitated. When she touched a concealed button on the bottom of the locket it sprang open, revealing two tiny photos.

One was a picture of Carly, her head thrown back in laughter. And the other was a picture of her mother, looking young and strangely joyous.

"Where did you get this? My mother hated having her picture taken. And she so rarely looked like this, Kiernan. She looks so happy here."

"Ah, princedom has its privileges. I had the whole island scoured until I found just the right photos of both of them. Do you know when that was taken, Meredith? The picture of your mother?"

"No."

He named the date.

The tears spilled. The picture had been taken on the day of Meredith's birth.

"I wanted them to be with us," he said gently, "as close to your heart as I could get them."

"There goes the makeup," she accused him, and there went her idea that the day belonged to him and her, exclusively. What a selfish thought to entertain! This day belonged to Carly and her mother, too.

"You look better without it. The makeup."

"I know, but Rachel is in cosmetology."

"Let me guess. A gift?"

"Yes."

"And by accepting it, you *give* the gift just like the day you agreed to marry me."

The door to the room whispered open again.

"Kiernan! Out!"

There was no question of talking his way out of it this time, because it was his mother who had entered the room.

"Queen Aleda," Meredith said, truly surprised. "What are you doing here?" She had never been embarrassed about her tiny apartment, but she had certainly never expected to entertain a queen here, either.

"There are days when a girl needs her mother," the queen said. "Since your own cannot be here, I was hoping you would do me the grave honor of allowing me to take her place."

"Oh, Aleda," Meredith whispered. Of all the surprises of becoming Kiernan's love, wasn't his mother one of the best of them?

She was seen as reserved and cool, much as her son was. The truth about these two people? They guarded what was theirs, and chose very carefully who to give it to. And when they did give it?

It was with their entire hearts and whole souls.

Kiernan kissed her on her cheek, and bussed his mother, too, before quickly taking his leave. He left whistling *Get Me to the Church on Time*.

Queen Aleda quickly did what she did best—she took charge.

And Meredith realized, warmly, that this day belonged to Queen Aleda, too.

"None of that," Meredith was chastened for the new tears, "It will spoil your makeup."

Queen Aleda gathered the dress, hugged it to her briefly, looked at her soon-to-be daughter-in-law tenderly.

"Come," she said, "I'll help you get into it. The carriage will be here shortly."

Meredith was delivered to the cathedral in a white carriage, drawn by six white horses.

The people of Chatam, who seemed to have embraced her *more* for her past than less, lined the cobblestone streets, and threw rose petals in front of the carriage. The petals floated through the air and were stirred up by the horses' feet. It was as if it was snowing rose petals.

So, this day also belonged to them, to those people who had patiently lined the street for hours, waiting for this moment, a glimpse of the woman they considered to be *their* princess. They called her the people's favorite princess, and every day she tried to live up to what they needed from her. It had been a thought of pure selfishness to think this day was only about her and Kiernan.

The cathedral was packed. A choir sang.

And he waited.

At the end of that long, stone aisle, Kiernan waited

for her, strong, sure, ready. Her prince in a world she had once believed did not have princes, her very own fairy-tale ending.

Meredith moved toward him with the certainty, with the inevitability of a wave moving to shore.

And realized this day, and her whole life to follow, didn't really belong to her. And not to him, either.

It belonged to the force that had served them so well, the force that they would now use the days of their life serving.

It belonged to Love.

EPILOGUE

HE WENT HERE SOMETIMES, by himself, usually when he had a special occasion to celebrate. A birthday. An anniversary. They were part of it, and he could not leave them out.

It was not the nicest of graveyards, just row after row of simple crosses, no shrubs, or green spaces, no elaborate headstones, few flower arrangements.

The world would have been shocked, probably, to see Prince Kiernan of Chatam in this place, a grim, gray yard in the middle of Wentworth.

But he was always extra careful that he was not followed here, that no one hid with their cameras to capture this most private image of him.

It had become a most special place to him. He always brought flowers, two bouquets. He paused now in front of the heartbreakingly small grave, next to a larger one, brushed some dust from the plain stones set in the ground and read out loud.

"Carly, beloved." He set the tiny pink roses on her stone.

"Millicent Whitmore, beloved." He set the white roses there.

He did not know how the world worked. He felt a

tingle as he read that word. *Beloved*. How had a child long dead, whom he had never even met, become so beloved to him?

How could he feel as if he *knew* Millicent Whitmore, Millie as he called her affectionately, when he had never met her either?

Kiernan understood now, as he had not before marrying Meredith, that there was a larger picture, and despite his power and prestige he was just a tiny part of that.

He understood, as he had not before marrying Meredith, that sometimes great things could transpire out of great tragedies.

The death of a child, and her grandmother, had set a whole series of events in motion that not one single person could have ever foreseen or predicted.

Still, this is what love did: if he could give Meredith back her baby, even if it meant he would never meet her, and never have the life he had now, he would do it in a breath, in a heartbeat.

"I want you to know, Carly," he said softly, "that the new baby in no way replaces you. You are a sacred member of our family. Always and forever."

He felt her then, as he sometimes did, a breath on his cheek, a softness on his shoulder, a faint smell in the air that was so good.

"I brought you a picture of her. We've named her Amalee." He laid the picture, framed in silver, of his new baby and her mother between the two graves.

The picture he laid down was a private portrait, one that had never been released to the press. The baby had a wrinkled face, piercing gray eyes, and a tangle of the most shockingly red hair.

And Meredith in that picture looked like what she was: a mother who had already lost a child and would guard this one with a fierceness that was both awe-inspiring and a little frightening.

She looked like what she was: a woman certain in her own power, a woman who knew she was loved above all things.

Meredith was a woman who knew that if her husband ever had the choice to make: Chatam, his kingdom, or her, he would not even hesitate.

She was his kingdom.

He stepped back then, and sighed, asked silently for a blessing on the christening that would happen today, his baby's first public appearance. Already the people of Chatam lined the streets, waiting to welcome this new love to their lives.

He was left feeling humbled by the goodness of it all.

Each day his and Meredith's relationship became closer, deeper, stronger. The new baby, Amalee, felt as if she was part of a tapestry that wove his heart ever more intricately into its pattern.

Kiernan now knew, absolutely, what he had been so drawn to that first day that he had seen Meredith dance when she thought she was alone.

He had witnessed the dance of life.

And known, at a level that went so deep, that by-passed his mind and went straight to his heart, she was the one who could teach him the steps.

He learned a new one every day.

Love was a dance that you never knew completely,

that taught you new steps, that made you reach deeper and try harder.

Love was the dance that brought you right to heaven's door.

"Thank you," he whispered. And then louder. "Thank you."